The Trouble with Tigers

Roxane Dhand was born in Kent and entertained her sisters with imaginative stories from a young age. She studied English and French at London University and in 1978 moved to Switzerland where she began her professional career in public relations. Back in England and many years later on, she taught French in both the maintained and private sectors. Now retired, she is finally able to indulge her passion for storytelling. This is her third novel, after *The Pearler's Wife* and *The Orphan of Good Hope*.

THE TROUBLE
WITH TIGERS

Roxane Dhand

This edition published in Great Britain in 2022
by Orion Dash, an imprint of The Orion Publishing Group Ltd,
Carmelite House, 50 Victoria Embankment
London EC4Y 0DZ

An Hachette UK company

1   3   5   7   9   10   8   6   4   2

A CIP catalogue record for this book
is available from the British Library.

ISBN (Paperback) 978 1 3987 1066 5
ISBN (eBook) 978 1 3987 1003 0

Printed and bound in Great Britain by

www.orionbooks.co.uk

To Harry

Chapter 1

Cawnpore, India
April 1902

The town of Cawnpore stretched out on a plain alongside the River Ganges. Like most of the European community, Royce and Lilly Myerson lived to the south-east, where homes were scattered along wide, maintained roads with leafy walks between.

Their spacious green bungalow had at one time belonged to an army officer. Surrounded by a high mud wall, it stood in the middle of well-planted gardens, in a cantonment away from what the whites called the native city. A hive of human endeavour, thousands lived off its one main avenue, Chandni Chowk, amongst a network of crooked alleys, and scraped a meagre living from whatever they could sell.

That afternoon, wearing a silk-satin tea dress and her grandmother's pearls, Lilly reflected that it was too hot and the light too harsh to be out at this time of day. The Ganges was so low that in a curve of the river, a buffalo stood ankle-deep in the water too sluggish to move in the heat. Madness, she thought. No Englishman would venture out in such a temperature, not even to walk his dog.

Shielding her face with a lace-edged parasol, she turned down a palm-fringed lane where thick clouds of dust plumed high in the air.

Soldiers raising puffs of sand as they exercised their horses along the broad, worn road were common enough, but that mid-April afternoon, there was a great deal more traffic than usual. Crowds poured down the streets – there were no footpaths in town – in a succession of disorderly rickshaws, men in flannels and white brogues strode out as if late for tennis and whole families seemed on the move.

Teddy shielded his eyes with the flat of his hand. 'Why's it so dusty, Mama?'

Lilly looked down at her young son and smoothed the hair back from his forehead. He'd recently had his hair cut, but the fringe was still too long and fell into his eyes. The barber Royce favoured encouraged one style for all, copied from a newspaper picture affixed to his wall.

'I think there must be something going on, Teddy.'

'What something?' He put a finger to his brow.

'I don't know, but we have our own special outing, don't we? Just you and me. It doesn't matter what anyone else is doing.'

She held out her hand. 'Come on. We're nearly at the park. You can play on the swings and then on the way home, we might find an ice cream. So, young man – let's hop to it and get ourselves to the park!'

For a few paces Teddy did, literally, hop from one foot to the other but then seemed to lose heart.

It's always the same, Lilly thought. Swings, something sticky to eat and then home. She could hardly call it exciting but at least he was out of the house, away from his lessons and getting some air in his lungs.

Less than five minutes later found them in front of a pair of high, wide gates. Beyond lay cool, palm-shaded gardens. With gravelled walkways bordered by fragrant brushes and tall, sturdy trees, the park was a luxuriant oasis of cool, soothing greenery.

Attached to the intricate wrought iron, a coloured poster displayed a circus tent and a lion tamer with an oily moustache and whip. Lilly took a step closer and raised her parasol to read the print.

Teddy squinted up at her, shielding his eyes from the sun. 'What does it say, Mama?'

'There's a circus this afternoon, near to the railway station. I imagine that's where all those people are going.'

Teddy's reaction was instant. He jumped up and down, almost performing a jig. 'Can we go too?'

It was on her lips to say no, that the park was outing enough, but the words that came out were at odds. 'It will have to be our secret if we go. If you can promise not to tell Papa, or Granny or *Ayah*, then I don't see why not.'

He pulled his hand from hers and mimed an elaborate cross on his chest. 'Cross my heart and hope to die. If I am asked, I'll tell a lie.'

His face was such a study in earnest resolve, she couldn't hold back her laughter. 'Very well then, young man. You're not to be untruthful but remember not a word of our secret to Papa.'

Lilly held on tight to Teddy's hand as he dragged her along the short distance from the ticket wagon to the circus tent across the trampled, yellowing grass.

A red-nosed clown stood sentry by the flap to the tent. He leaned down to Teddy and held out a programme. His face was covered in white greasepaint, triangular black eyebrows arched up to his hairline and he'd painted an oversized smile round his mouth.

She patted her son on the bottom. 'Say thank you to the nice clown.'

Teddy took a step backwards and clutched at her dress. 'I don't like his face.'

Lilly thought he had a point. At this close distance, the clown seemed more frightening than funny, his expression stiff and cold. She accepted the programme and smiled. 'I'm so sorry. This is my son's first time at the circus, and I think he's a touch overwhelmed.'

The clown shrugged off her explanation with a hitch of one harlequined shoulder, then turned his attention elsewhere.

Lilly placed the flat of her hand at Teddy's back. 'Come on. Let's find somewhere to sit.' She steered him towards the far side of the ring, where she found a couple of vacant seats at the end of a ringside row. Teddy clambered onto the bench and she squeezed in beside him.

On the opposite side of the ring, officers from the military station had grouped together, turned out in their scarlet jackets with ropes of gold braid at the shoulder. She gave a faint sigh of relief. There would be no one there that she knew.

Further around, European businessmen in bow ties and morning coats had come along with their wives, familiar even from a distance in straw hats and pale dresses, their children shoehorned between them; she knew that they all would know her.

Instinctively, Lilly pulled down the brim of her bonnet and swivelled in her seat towards the section where the native ladies sat on circular wooden steps. Decked out in their most beautiful garments, they clustered in a confusion of coloured tiers like birds, stacked high in a tree.

She glanced at her son, who seemed happy enough, then turned her gaze back to the ring, wishing she'd thought this trip through. She was mulling over how they could get out of the tent without being seen when something made her look up. A thin lady with glasses and a polka-dotted dress had raised her hand in recognition, the hand saying what the mouth from that distance could not.

Mrs McPherson from the Army and Navy Stores.

A sickening wave of nerves flickered through her, but Lilly smiled, nodded and waggled her fingers. News would get straight back to Royce; imagining the worst, she swallowed, her throat dry as dust.

Teddy fidgeted by her side. His chubby little hands were ink-stained and she silently berated herself for the yellow smudge on his white cotton shirt – turmeric from his lunchtime dhal. She would be disciplined for that if Royce noticed it.

She lifted him onto her lap and rocked him back and forth. 'We shouldn't have come,' she whispered. What Royce would say if he found out was beyond thinking. She turned her head towards her little boy and told herself it didn't matter a bit. Despite the anxiety in the pit of her stomach, the look in his eyes was worth all the censure she might face later on.

She forced a cheerful tone. 'This is so exciting, isn't it?'

Teddy swung his legs from side to side. 'When's it going to start?'

'Hop down so I can have a look.' Lilly lifted the matinee programme off her lap and held it out before her. 'At three o'clock. That's what it says right here.'

'When's that?'

She checked her watch. 'In about five minutes, when everybody is sitting down.'

'Why's it smelly?' He pinched his nose between his thumb and forefinger.

The odour beneath the canvas was pungent; the faint reek of animal manure, a strong waft of horse and caramelised sugar, she thought, and a cocktail of scents she could only guess at.

Lilly paused for a moment. 'That's the smell of the sawdust they put in the ring so the animals you're going to see don't hurt their feet.' She looked up from the printed sheet.

'Dogs?' His eyes lit up.

'There are going to be horses and geese. And it says here that a man has some lions that do all sorts of tricks.'

'Won't there be any dogs?' His eyes searched her face.

Before she could reply, the brass section in the band struck up a fanfare and the ringmaster, a burly dark-haired man in a black, calf-length jacket and top hat, ran into the ring blowing short blasts on his whistle. A hush fell over the stands.

'Lay-dees and gen-tel-men!' he boomed into his megaphone, his voice deep and rich. 'Boys and girls! Welcome to Warren's Circus. We hope this magical occasion will cast its spell and entertain you this afternoon. If you believe in enchantment, this is where you will find it, in the superb strength and skill and speed of our spectacular scenes. In the tradition of circus in India, we proudly present many novelties and a plethora of artists. We have a magnificent stable of Arabian horses, four cages of wild performing animals, three great Burma elephants, aerialists, clowns and so very much more.'

From deep within the tent, the crowd began to cheer but Teddy tugged at her sleeve.

Lilly bent down to hear him above the racket and felt the touch of his breath on her cheek.

'I don't understand what the man said.'

'He's trying to be clever with words. It's what grown-ups do sometimes to make themselves sound important.'

'Does Papa?'

She played with the gold band on her finger. 'Not ever.' She didn't say that the words Royce used were so perfectly clear in their meaning that even a five-year-old would understand them.

'Do you?'

She shook her head. 'I never try to look important.'

With a wave to quiet the crowd, the ringmaster called out, 'And now, ladies and gentlemen, from Warren's Circus, please welcome Miss Moscovitch into the ring.'

On his cue, the band struck up a galop in a lively tempo and Lilly felt the music resound in the depths of her chest.

Sunlight poured down from the open top of the tent and in a swirl of grey dust, two broad-backed, white horses hurtled into the ring. Costumed in ruched tutu and stockings, a young girl of not more than thirteen or fourteen stood astride them, a silver-slippered foot straddling each rump. Two shimmering gauze wings seemed to sprout from her shoulders and as she cantered past, the bright green of her eyes shone like two circles of glass.

Round and around she rode, while in oversized shoes, a clown shuffled behind, his arms stretched out to catch her.

'Hurry up!' Teddy cried, his cheeks blotched pink with excitement. 'Go faster!'

Lilly too found herself caught up, clapping to urge the clown on, who then stopped and swivelled round as the horses galloped towards him. A second clown, wearing an orange wig and red trousers that reached to his chest, burst through the curtains where the performers came in. Waving a large, paper-covered hoop, he threw it to the first clown, who held it into the ring, high above his shoulder.

As the horses thundered towards it, the girl leaped forward, somersaulted through the hoop, bursting through the tissue paper, and landed back safe on her mounts.

Teddy had moved to the edge of his seat, his eyes round with awe. 'A fairy, Mama.'

Already the circus had wrapped its magic around him and held him fast, dazzling and bewitching as it wove its irresistible spell.

And yet.

She glanced again at her watch and felt a prickling of panic. We'll never get home in time, she said to herself, again and again and again.

As the final strains of the music played, Miss Moscovitch slowed her charges to deafening applause from her fans.

'Let me see, Mama,' Teddy cried, his hand tapping at her elbow.

Lilly scooped him up so that he could watch, cradling him against her until the band fell silent, and Miss Moscovitch trotted her horses away.

Without a moment's pause, a roll on the drums cued the ringmaster and the show sped on in a madcap assortment of acts.

Men on stilts, clowns who handed out sweets to the children from inside their hats, a lady who trained chickens that did tricks for the crowd. Monkeys rode round on the back of ponies, jugglers hurtled their clubs high into the air and silver-clad acrobats tumbled and jumped.

Teddy shrieked with delight when the elephants lumbered into the ring, gently swinging their trunks. They wore giant harnesses on their heads, their foreheads painted in bright colours, their eyes circled in red.

At the end of the performance, after the audience sang God Save the King and clapped till their fingers were sore, Lilly held back in the tent while the crowd moved slowly away.

Outside, on their way to the gate, they stopped by a makeshift pen where the performing animals were corralled.

An elephant twirled its trunk in Teddy's direction, then dropped it into a bucket of water.

'Can we stroke the elephants?' Teddy stared as it drained the water into its trunk.

Lilly thrust out her arm to stop him rushing forward. All around the enclosure there were signs in bright red letters: DANGER – KEEP OUT. DO NOT TOUCH THE ANIMALS.

'What's it doing now?' Teddy fumbled in his pocket for a sweet and stretched out his arm, close to the fence.

She snatched at his wrist. 'Don't, Teddy. It says that we are not allowed to.'

He pushed out his bottom lip. 'Why?'

'They are wild animals and dangerous, not like cats and dogs. It's not safe to put your hand inside the fence and feed them.'

'I want to touch the elephant's trunk and find out where the water went.'

'It's still there until he puts his trunk in his mouth and swallows it down.'

'How does he smell things?'

Lilly did her best imitation of a trunk, wiggling her fingers and stretching out her arm to tickle him in the ribs. 'Elephants have a special nose in the end of their trunk, which can sniff out a little boy who is ready for his tea.'

Teddy squealed with laughter. 'What am I having today?'

'I don't know what Cook is making but we'll find out as soon as we're home.'

As they continued towards the way out, Lilly caught sight of Mrs McPherson loading her children into a rickshaw.

The constant buzz of gossip amongst the European community was too rife to ignore and she knew she would have been seen.

Lilly squeezed her hand around the handle of her parasol until her fingers ached. Poking the beast in his den during trading hours was nothing short of madness, but it would be better if Royce heard about the circus from her and not from a notorious purveyor of gossip.

Fighting the apprehension in her chest, she bent down to her son. 'Do you know what? I think after all we will tell Papa about our adventure. Let's see if we can find a rickshaw, then we'll go straight round to his shop.'

Chapter 2

It was almost six o'clock by the time they reached the Emporium, but the sun was still high, trapping the heat beneath the Burma teak rafters.

Inside the building, in a vast heap of cotton dhoti, Paramjit, Royce's partner – a Khatik Hindi of regal proportions – sat on a stool in the corner and was policing the entrance through half-shut brown eyes.

When he saw her hesitate by the door, Paramjit placed his palms together in an obsequious namaskar. '*Memsahib*, how nice you are coming but with the entrance you are interfering. I must be asking you to hurry in.'

Lilly heard the hint of criticism in his tone and shooed Teddy towards the display of toys Royce kept at the back of his store.

Royce was behind a square-topped desk counting out the day's takings, snapping a rubber band around each packet of notes as he sorted them into denominations. He liked Queen Victoria's portrait facing upwards, staring her grim-faced approval before he shoved the money into the safe and ostentatiously spun the dial.

As she approached, he caught at her arm and yanked her towards him. 'What are you doing here, Lilly? And why is Teddy not with his tutor?'

A hard knot constricted her throat. 'I took Teddy to the circus,' she began to stammer. 'I came straight here to tell you myself.' She glanced across at their son, but he was engrossed with something he'd pulled out from a box.

Royce sharpened his pencil with a penknife and made an entry in his ledger. 'I don't recall discussing an outing today, wherever it was you took the boy.'

'I decided on a whim. It's the last day the circus is in Cawnpore and I wanted to give him a treat. It was put on especially for the children. Please don't be angry about it.' Lilly's hands felt clammy as she anticipated the explosion.

Royce's voice was harsh, laced with annoyance. 'It's a bit late for that, wouldn't you say?'

Lilly clamped her chin to her chest and studied the spots on the floorboards, knowing not to meet his gaze even though she could feel him studying her as keenly as he might inspect a bale of suspect cloth. She was used to doing as she was told, pleasing and obeying, fading into the shadows where she would provoke least offence. Their appearance in his domain had not gone down well and she knew that later, there would be consequences. She smoothed her damp hands over her skirt.

Paramjit scratched his crotch then snapped his fingers together. 'Someone outside looking, Sahib.'

Through the open door, Lilly saw a broad-shouldered man eyeing up the entrance and for a moment it seemed he'd come in. Out in the fierce sunlight, she knew the man would not be able to see Royce within the shade of the shop, but after a few more moments, her husband removed his steel-rimmed spectacles, got up from his stool, straightened his frock coat and moved to the door. He watched the man looking at a neighbouring shop sign.

Royce leaned his weight on the door frame and called across the veranda. 'Is there anything I can do for you?'

The man wandered back to the front door and came into the store. He was not as old as she first supposed, most likely in his early twenties, quite good-looking in a flashy, sun-bronzed way. 'I was wondering about nailing up one of our advertisements.'

Lilly glanced at Royce's averted head and noticed that the barber had shaved him badly that morning and left scabby nicks under his chin. He looked the man up and down. She watched her husband take in the cheap cream suit that was poorly stitched and too short in the leg and the wrinkled white, high-collared shirt.

Royce himself took great care with his clothes: the knee-length frock coat he wore over his waistcoat, a pristine white shirt with detachable collar and trousers with grey and black stripes.

Lilly saw the sneer on his face and when he spoke his voice held no warmth. 'You're not pasting anything to my woodwork.'

The man took a deep breath. 'Tiffert's Circus is coming to Cawnpore, to set the scene for King Edward's corona-tion in June. I'm the advance publicity man.' He held out his hand. 'Duffy B. Puttnam at your service.'

Royce's frown was so forbidding, the young man didn't go on. He dropped his outstretched hand and stood frozen to the spot.

Teddy abandoned his inspection of the toy display and scampered towards his father. 'Papa! Papa! Can I go to another circus?' He wrapped his arms around Royce's knees. 'We went today, Mama and me. I saw elephants and a fairy on a horse and monkeys and geese but I promised Mama I wouldn't tell.'

Royce looked down at his son, his arms stiff by his sides. 'Go back and play with the toys. You can tell me about it at home when I get back from work.'

'All right,' Teddy said carefully and scampered away.

Royce shifted his gaze back to the door. 'Is there to be a street parade, Duffy B. Puttnam, Advance Publicity Man for Tiffert's Circus?'

Lilly knew what he was doing. He repeated words out loud to fix them in his mind. He had the man's name, the job he held and the circus for which he did it.

'Of course.'

'Permits all in order?'

Duffy Puttnam nodded but a hint of doubt flickered across his face. 'The publicity department will have seen to that, make no mistake. How else are we to whet the public's appetite if we don't show them what's on offer?'

Royce thrust his hand into his pocket and stirred up his small change. 'I doubt you'll attract much of an audience. There's already been a circus in town and they're upping sticks tomorrow. No one's going to have spare rupees to fork out on more tickets.'

'It's a shame you might think that. In our experience India loves a circus. Tiffert's Circus has been touring India for twenty-odd years. Warren's might have just been here, but we are much better. People are guaranteed to come.'

'Scant interest to me, old chap.' Her husband paused and walked over the floorboards to Lilly's side and rested a damp, heavy hand on her shoulder in much the same way as a policeman might caution a criminal. 'We prefer the theatre, don't we, Plumpty? Far more civilised.' His fingers tightened against her neck, dampening the fabric of her dress.

Lilly removed his hand and kissed it, clasping it between her fingers. It was not so much a gesture of affection as a means of keeping his hand from touching her. 'When is your circus coming to town, Mr Puttnam?'

'A few weeks yet and the posters are temporary – we use special glue that is easy to remove and leaves no residue.'

'But the monkeys might tear them down and eat the paper and ingest the glue you have used to post them up.'

'I could tack them up if you feel that would be more in the interests of animal welfare.' He pulled a circle of leather from his pocket that was studded with tacks and shot her a wink. 'Do you want to take a look?' He held the poster towards her.

Even though Royce's hand tightened its grip on hers, Lilly felt the surge of excitement in her stomach. 'I love the circus. I took my little boy to Warren's this afternoon.'

She pulled her hand away, deliberately evading Royce's eye. She was already in trouble and it would be worse later on, but just at that moment she didn't want to see the displeasure on his face. She turned so that the light from the open doorway shone on the flyer and read the headline out loud. '"*The MASTODON of modern entertainment enterprise*". That's quite a declaration.'

Mr Puttnam looked at her, his eyes imploring. 'Would you not help a man do his job?'

Of course, she wanted to answer, but instead she said, 'Do you have an act as well as being the advance publicity man?'

'Wild animal trainer. I work with tigers, with nothing more to protect me than a whip and agile feet.'

'Goodness. That must surely be a sight worth seeing.'

'The animal acts are the most popular in the circus, but to attract an audience, we must advertise that we are coming. So, all right to use tacks?'

Lilly nodded. 'That would be for the best, I think. And good luck with your mastodon.'

★

Royce came home just before dark.

He intercepted her on her way back from reading Teddy his bedtime story. Smiling to herself at the antics of naughty Peter in Mr McGregor's garden, at the sound of Royce's step, she faltered.

'Good luck with your mastodon,' Royce jeered. He slid his arm round her waist and hauled her along the veranda towards her dressing room. 'You don't even know the meaning of the word. You haven't a brain in your head. Frankly, you're an embarrassment – fit for nothing but sitting about all day on your arse.'

Lilly stared at the picture of her son on the dressing table and retreated behind the imaginary wall she used to block her husband out. A mastodon was a long-extinct relative of the modern elephant, but she knew better than to educate him on that.

He pointed the forefinger of his right hand and jabbed it against her chest. Jab-jab-jab like a man prodding an unresponsive switch. 'I want an explanation for the circus.'

'I just didn't think it through!' she burst out. 'I didn't know myself that I was going to take Teddy until the moment I decided I would.'

'I decided I would.' He mimicked her voice, high-pitched like a boy soprano. 'Where did you get the money?'

'I still have my last month's allowance.'

He couldn't argue with that. He knew she had not left the house in weeks. He held out his hand. 'Give it to me.'

Lilly crossed to the chest of drawers below the window and took out a dark, enamelled box. She put it down on the divan, next to where he was standing. 'It's all there except for the rickshaw fare and the twenty annas I spent on the tickets.'

Reflected in the mirror, she saw him reach back with his hand. His anger always came at full tilt and was as unpredictable as the weather in England. Before she could twist out of reach, he lowered his arm, then began the slow polishing of his spectacles as he made her wait. 'Please do not shout. I don't want the whole household privy to your histrionics, and I confess myself bewildered as to why you never learn. Talking to a stranger and pretending to have an opinion that anyone would take an interest in is ridiculous; that Duffy B. Puttnam should nail his posters to the trees and spare the monkeys their indigestion. Surely you must understand that your behaviour in the Emporium was unacceptable.'

She lowered her chin to mask how scared she was feeling. 'I'm very sorry, Royce.'

'You're always sorry. What does sorry actually mean to you, Plumpty? I don't want you to be *sorry*. I want you to be *better* and that circus man looked at you in a way I did not care for. You behaved like a tart.' Royce stretched down his brown, nicotine-stained fingers from a tightly squeezed fist. 'You haven't explained why you defied me today and encouraged my son to tells lies.'

'It was an error of judgement,' she heard herself say. 'I know I should have asked you first if we both might go but try not to be too cross.'

He thrust his face at hers. 'How are we going to make you learn from all these mistakes of yours?'

Lilly steeled herself. The anticipation of the punishment set her heart thudding in her chest. It was difficult to breathe, as if she'd run up a steep hill. 'Please don't . . .'

He spread his arms wide in a gesture of incomprehension. 'Excuse me?' His tone was flat, unmodulated. It was the voice he used to correct.

'I accept that I have done wrong and that my punishment is for my own good so that I learn from my mistakes and don't make them again. But this afternoon, I gave our son such a treat. You should have seen how excited he was at the circus. He was so happy, Royce. He thought it was a fairy tale come true.'

He picked up the whalebone from the top of her dresser and bounced it repeatedly on the flat of his palm. With every flick of the rod, she could see him tallying up her failings. 'Because of *you* I'm late back from the store. Because of *you* my son has developed the taste for a lie. Because of *you* dinner will be late and my mother will have to wait for her food.

'Three times today, that I know about for certain, you have defied me.' He pointed out the spot where he wanted her to lie. 'Without doubt there will have been more.'

They stood face to face and yet, for once, he appeared unsettled. His grey silk tie was askew, his collar stud exposed, and a muscle jumped to the side of his eye.

'I don't have time to deal with you now, but this is not the end of this conversation by any means. I will see you after supper and decide how you will be punished. Now . . .' he smiled, his mood turned on a sixpence. He walked to the wardrobe and rooted through her evening clothes. Pulling out a hanger, he dropped the dinner gown on a chair. It was a black and white silk, tight-bodiced creation with a scooped neck lined in scratchy white lace and a bustle and long train behind. To get it on would necessitate her most rib-squeezing stays and he knew she particularly disliked it. 'Whisk yourself into this, darling. You smell like you've spent a day on the farm.'

Lilly raised her arm and sniffed at her sleeve and for once, she had to agree. The circus had invaded her clothes.

★

It was a beautiful moonlit evening out on the veranda, the sky speckled with stars.

Royce settled her in the most comfortable chair, fluffing up cushions at her back, pouring out her coffee, checking she was comfortable in a voice that was almost gentle.

Drawing up his own chair until he was sitting close, Royce brought up the letter that had come sometime that day. Lilly had seen it on the hall table as she'd returned from the Emporium but knew better than to touch it. Even though it had her name on the envelope, Royce did not permit her to receive private correspondence unless he'd opened and read through it first.

He sat down and pulled his trouser creases up over his knees. 'You've had a letter from your mother.'

She took his hand and kissed it. 'Have I?'

He pulled the envelope from inside his velvet jacket. 'She says she's in Nainital.'

Lilly tried to be interested but wasn't really. Her mother wafted in and out of her life but never endured. 'Is she on holiday?' She'd vaguely heard of the place as somewhere the British went for the hot weather.

He threw the envelope into her lap. 'Read it for yourself.'

Lilly glanced at him, trying to judge his mood. She would double-check first, just to make sure and held it up, to see if he would snatch it back. 'Would that be all right?'

'Here.' He tore the letter from the envelope and flapped it under her nose.

She took it from him, her hands shaking a little, still not quite sure if he would really allow her to read it.

Behind them in the sitting room, the grandfather clock on the long windowless side of the room bonged the hour. The nine stern chimes echoed throughout the bungalow, reminding her of the world she had not wanted, yet which now subsumed her.

'Would you mind if I go inside? There's not enough light out here to read.'

He took a cigarette from a sandalwood box on the table. Three times, he bounced it on the arm of the chair to compact the tobacco, then he lit up, watching her closely as he exhaled the smoke and shook out the match. 'Be my guest.' He took her hand and half pulled her to her feet. 'Take your time. No need to rush back.'

'Thank you, Royce,' she murmured mechanically, feeling the wobble in her legs as she turned towards the lamplight indoors.

She took a stuffed leather seat adjacent to the lamp and angled the letter to the light. Lilly was disappointed her mother's letter was short, but she could hear the breezy tone of her voice as she read. She had taken rooms in Nainital – well, actually her husband Frederick had taken rooms – but she was divorcing him. He'd become dull, she wrote, like Keymer before him.

Lilly rested her head against the back of the chair. There'd be more to it than that, but her mother hardly ever told the truth. The letter gabbled on. She'd met someone else – a District Commissioner with the ICS – but they were not due to marry until later in the year.

She lowered the page to her lap. The prestigious Indian Civil Service. No merchant trader for her mother, then, on the outer edge of social acceptability. She would never marry someone outside the service of British India and thus deemed no gentleman, however much money he had.

Lilly picked up the letter and continued to read. In the meantime, her mother went on, it was a pity to spend hours and hours in the delicious cool weather all by herself in the hills when there were spare rooms in the guesthouse.

To sum up, would Lilly come and keep her company?

Lilly felt a flutter of excitement. Time away in the hills with her son was almost too good to be true.

The letter ended with an exhortation to write back immediately because it would be a nuisance not to know if she was coming or not.

And then.

Under her signature she had scrawled that she was awfully sorry but the two old girls who ran the place didn't accept children.

Lilly sagged in her chair and covered her face with her hands. For a few precious seconds she had dared to hope. She would never leave her son behind, even in the unlikely event that Royce would allow her to go. He had her chained to the path he directed her to follow and rarely let her out of his sight. Going to the hills with her mother was nothing more than a dream.

With an effort, Lilly went back to the veranda and meticulously placed the letter by his ashtray before regaining her seat. He lounged in his seat tapping at the air with his foot. 'Well?'

'Her invitation was very generous, but I wouldn't be able to take Teddy so I'll write and say no.'

He laid his hands along the edge of the table, side by side, fingers aligned. 'I have decided you'll go.'

If he had struck her, she couldn't have been more stunned. 'But I can't go without Teddy. The ladies who run the guesthouse don't allow children.'

He paused for barely a second. 'The boy is too attached to you. Very few children stay in India beyond the age of six or seven so you might as well get used to what that's going to feel like. Consider it a warm-up from someone who knows better than you.' His face was set like a rock.

'I'm sending Teddy to England to one of the top schools – that's the purpose of all these tutors who are costing me an arm and leg. He's going to be a doctor and for that, academically he must work extra hard as one of his parents is as thick as pig shit.'

Lilly kept her eyes on his face and watched his brow as it furrowed into a mass of deep creases. She crossed her legs and pushed back in her chair, trying to create some distance between them.

'You interrupting his lessons is not part of my plan.' He jammed a thumbnail between his teeth.

Beyond the veranda, insects chirped in the grass. She shook her head to clear it. I have to pay attention, she told herself. I mustn't let myself become distracted. 'I made a mistake, and I am very sorry.' She gripped the arms of her chair, her throat tightening around the words. 'Tell me what I must do to make up for it but please do not part me from Teddy.'

She saw the storm brewing inside him. Sweat glistened on his forehead, his breath came faster and faster, his lips drawn back to a snarl. 'I dare say you *are* sorry – you say it often enough – but the fact remains you chose to take Teddy to the circus without seeking my permission.' He twisted round and swung at her with the back of his hand.

Her palm flew to the cheek where his blow had landed but she didn't cry out.

'I told you there would be a consequence for sneaking out behind my back this afternoon so sending you to Nainital for three months should give you ample time to reflect on your disobedience.' He picked up the letter and stowed it in his pocket. 'I will arrange it with your mother. You'll leave at the beginning of May.'

Panic spread from the pit of her stomach to the muscles of her face. His black eyes were on her, judging her behind his wire-rimmed spectacles, and she knew she mustn't react. Three months enforced separation from her son was worse than any beating he could have inflicted. It was the ultimate in cruelty and as Royce got up from his chair, she saw the blaze of triumph in his eyes.

Chapter 3

For the next two weeks, Royce was pitiless. Over and over, at each meal, during every conversation, Lilly was held to account for taking their son to the circus.

At breakfast, the day before she was due to leave for the hills, the prospect of leaving Teddy almost undid her.

She was on the point of begging Royce to reconsider when her mother-in-law twisted round to the servant who stood guard behind her chair and slapped at his arm with her napkin. The skin on her arms was squeezed tight under her peach-coloured blouse, and coloured jewels flashed on her fingers and wrists.

'Tell Cook to make more fritters for Mr Royce. He is going to Darjeeling with Teddy and needs to eat up.'

Lilly stowed her hands beneath the table and dug her nails into her palms. 'I didn't realise that you both were going on your own trip away, Royce. Is it for pleasure or business?'

In front of his mother, he played the perfect gentleman. 'Darling! You must have forgotten. I told you a while back that Teddy is being interviewed for a place at St Joseph's School. It's a wonderful pat on the back to you, given our little fellow is so young.'

Lilly kept her expression blank. 'Isn't that a residential school?'

Royce put his arm round her shoulders and dampened a corner of his napkin in his water glass. He dabbed at her mouth. 'You've left a little egg there on your top lip. Must be clean and tidy at all times. Standards, Plumpty. Standards.'

She leaned limply against him whilst inside she screamed. 'Is Teddy to be sent away to school right now? I thought he was going to England later on for his education.'

'He'll be better prepared when I send him there.'

She hesitated for a moment, like a reluctant swimmer contemplating an icy sea. Eventually she said, her voice perilously close to cracking, 'Should I not cancel my trip with Binnie and come with you? Schools are rowdy places and Teddy isn't used to crowds.'

Her husband pulled a silver pocket watch from his jacket and stared at its glass face. He frowned slightly and stood up, snapping the locks on his briefcase, which lay on the chair beside him. 'I would never deny you time away with your own mama and in any case, *Ayah* is coming with us.'

Lilly thought she might be having a heart attack, so sharp was the pain beneath her ribs. Royce could take Teddy anywhere and she would never know where they had gone. 'If you wouldn't mind, I would prefer to come with you than go to the hills. Binnie is perfectly able to take care of herself, but Teddy still needs his mama.'

She silently appealed to her mother-in-law, but Maduran was nodding, her face set in its habitual line of reproof. 'You're far too soft with him. It will do him the power of good to be with boys his own age. It will be the very making of him.'

He's five years old, Lilly thought, but said nothing. He'd had his say. She'd had her say. They sang from the same hymn sheet. There was no point in producing a counter-argument. Any criticism of the perfect selves would provoke silence or a violent outburst of anger. There was no point to her existence in Royce's eyes.

She glanced across at the silver-framed wedding photograph that hung on the wall and thought back to the early days of their marriage, looking for the time when things had been different. Royce still looked the same. He was always perfectly groomed, with his oiled hair slicked back off his face and a walrus moustache he waxed into shape. But six years on, he was not the same man. She had made excuses for him at first. The stresses of running a business. The responsibility of a second child on the way. But after Caroline died and she'd tried to stand up for herself, she'd had the words beaten out of her mouth with his fist.

Lilly looked away and gazed out at the garden. Enclosed by trellised walls, it was soaked with blazing colour; orange-red flowers, crimson petals, the scents strong and sickly. Nothing would grow here without water drawn by human hand, labouring under the relentless sun. It was a world away from the gentle colours and subtle perfume of the plants in her grandparents' house. She closed her eyes and envisioned the immaculate, rolling lawns, Grandpa's herbaceous borders stuffed with cottage garden flowers – carnations and pinks that were subtle, not harsh. Outhouses where fruit was stowed after harvesting, a wild garden that was never mowed, a walled kitchen garden at the end of which was a huge, near-derelict barn with its hay-scented air. She longed passionately for the soft landscape of home, the gentle rain and the fragrance of honeysuckle on a warm summer's evening; everything was still so real to her, many thousands of miles away.

Safe in her private world, she continued to reminisce until Royce's harsh cough drew her back to reality.

She looked back at her husband. 'Do you ever think of us going back as a family to England with Teddy?'

Frozen-faced, Royce picked up his briefcase, but just as he was about to leave, she heard herself sniff. With deliberate slowness, he lowered the leather bag to the chair on which he had been sitting. 'I thought we had decided against tears.' He put his hand on her shoulder, but she felt the press of his fingers as he dropped a kiss on the top of her head and tossed a cologne-scented handkerchief into her lap.

Lilly stared at the linen square and dashed a hand at her eye before a stray tear could leak out and betray her. She dredged up a smile that she knew was too bright, too artificial, not her. 'I am not going to cry, Royce. You don't have to worry on that score.'

The fingers tightened a fraction. 'There's a good girl. Can't have you blubbing when there's nothing to blub about, can we?'

His mother raised her eyebrows very slightly as if she couldn't quite make sense of their exchange. She scraped the seeds from a slice of papaya and turned to Royce. 'You had better be off to your work or the morning will run away with the girl if she's not careful. She'll have a lot to do if she's to be ready to travel tomorrow.'

Lilly sat with her hands in her lap while Royce re-engaged with his briefcase and crossed the dining room floor, whistling an indistinguishable tune through his teeth. When he reached the door, he opened it and turned, his hand resting on the handle. His eyes never left Lilly's face as he said, 'As it is your last day with Teddy for a few months, I thought you could take him to the park.'

'That was nice of him,' his mother remarked to his retreating back.

'Yes, it was,' she said, pouring herself some tea.

Yet what she'd said was not what she thought. Royce's offer was no spur of the moment act of charity, and he didn't mean one word of it. It was a public performance for his mother's benefit. He knew Lilly would give her eye teeth for time alone with Teddy, but if she took him to the park, he would punish her and if she didn't, she would despise herself for letting him win. She felt the familiar dull ache in the pit of her stomach.

'Royce is always caring for your needs.' The pendulous cheeks wobbled as she spoke.

Lilly tightened her grip on her teacup and knew that Maduran had seen.

Her mother-in-law's eyes held a steely glint. 'He's a good provider for you and the boy. You should have another child. It will stop you wallowing. No man cares for a wife with a miserable face.'

Lilly wondered if she knew how rarely he came near her these days but there was nothing to be gained in confiding how she felt. No one listened anyway. So, for the sake of her son, while Teddy sang his favourite song at the top of his voice, she hummed and clapped along.

Later that afternoon, Lilly found Teddy playing in his bedroom. He was astride his rocking horse and as he swung forwards and back, his black hair fell in a straight fringe over his eyes.

Royce had imported the toy from Germany, and it was a handsome beast with glass eyes, a mane and tail made with real hair, and a painted red saddle and bridle fashioned from scraps of leather and metal. After his teddy bear, it was his favourite toy.

Teddy twisted to look at her. 'Is it time for my bath?'

'Not quite, but there's something I want to tell you. I'm going away for a little while with Grandma Binnie.'

'Why?'

'We are going to the hills while the weather is too hot in Cawnpore.'

'Why?'

'Grandma has taken some rooms in a boarding house and she has asked me to go with her.'

Teddy crinkled his forehead. 'What did *Baap* say?'

'Call him Papa.'

'Are we going too? What about my lessons and *Dadi?*'

'Grandmother Maduran will stay here, and you are going to visit a boarding school with Papa.'

'What is it?'

'It's a place where little boys can learn their lessons together and you will make lots of new friends. Your father says that a good education is the most important thing for you and he's going to take you to have a look and you will see for yourself.'

'I like my tutor here and what will *Ayah* do if she does not have me to look after?'

She swallowed hard, hearing the panic in his voice, and forced herself to say, 'There's absolutely nothing to worry about, poppet. *Ayah* is going with you on your big adventure to see the school. In any case, it isn't decided for certain that you are going to go there. You're going to have a look to see if you like it, that's all.'

'But you're not coming?'

Lilly almost gave in to tears. 'Not this time.'

She set her back to her son and crossed to the soiled clothing basket. She lifted the lid and pulled out a crumpled white vest. Quickly balling it up in her fist, she tucked it in the waist of her skirt.

When she turned round, she felt a tiny bit better.

Teddy yawned prodigiously, forgetting to put up his hand.

'Time you were getting ready for bed, young man!' Lilly clung to the practicality of routine. She opened the top drawer of the dressing table and pulled out a nightshirt.

She held it up. 'How about the blue one tonight?'

'I'm not wearing that. *Ayah* already has the one I'm going to put on when I've had my bath. She said *Baap* wanted her to put me to bed, not you.'

He hopped off his horse and padded across the floorboards towards her, his leather *chappals* slapping on the oiled wood. Her little son patted a spot on the bed where he wanted her to sit and she knew exactly where Teddy had copied that from.

'Is your noggin all clogged with cobwebs, Plumpty?' He spoke in an intimation of his father's voice and even mimicked the thumbnail between his teeth. 'And Papa's trying to brush them out. Is that why he makes you stand in the garden? So the wind will blow them away?'

Lilly refused to react even though a knife of certainty pierced her heart – Royce was teaching Teddy to despise her.

'Whatever Papa has said, I'm going to read you your bedtime story. What shall it be tonight?'

'Peter Rabbit!' he cried, throwing himself on the bed. 'The bit where Mr McGregor chases him, and he hides in the watering can.'

Chapter 4

The morning sky was intensely blue, the sun fierce and the glare intolerable.

The previous day had been a frenzy of packing and sorting out of essentials for three months in the hills. The luggage had gone ahead but Royce insisted on seeing her off and drove to the station in his horseless carriage. In the car, Teddy sat on the front seat next to his father and Lilly was forced to sit behind the driver on the box-like boot; the insignificant attendant behind the king and his heir.

Teddy was chatting animatedly, excited about the outing, oblivious to what was really going on.

'I've a little surprise for you, Lilly,' Royce called over his shoulder. 'Your mother is meeting us at the station. I got you adjacent seats on the train and decided it would be a nice treat for you to travel up together.'

She says she's in Nainital. That's what he'd told her, but it was clear to Lilly that Royce had co-opted her mother into escorting her to the hills. He would never trust her to make the journey by herself. 'I thought she was already there.'

'Why would you think so? She said she had taken rooms, not that she was already ensconced. But she's on the train, very happy for me to pay her fare.'

Lilly remembered the exact moment he had told her that her mother was in Nainital, but she said only, 'When did you arrange that?'

'The details are unimportant. Now, hold onto your hat while I put my foot down. We wouldn't want you to be late for the train.'

The Ramgotty Steam Locomotive was waiting on the northbound platform.

The white-washed station was unbearably bright; Lilly stood amidst a pile of dress baskets, bedding and hatboxes. Suffocating in her travelling clothes, she gazed miserably at a file of women with baskets on their heads who wound down the scorching platform like a brilliant snake.

Royce planted his feet and wagged a nicotine-stained finger. 'A letter every day, Plumpty. Even when you stop tonight. I don't want to have to down tools and come to Nainital to check you are where you are supposed to be, do I now?'

Lilly's hand was trembling as she pulled a fan out of her bag and flapped at her face. 'I'm not going to the ends of the earth, Royce. It was your decision to send me away to Nainital and you are coming to fetch me in three months' time. Where else am I likely to get to with my mother's close eye on me?'

The muscle in Royce's jaw clenched and unclenched. 'Don't answer back. You will write the minute you get there.' Royce squeezed Lilly's arm to press home his point.

And you can check the date and postmark on the letters to make sure I don't run away. 'I'll write every day, Royce. You don't have to worry, but please will you send me news of Teddy from time to time?'

He eyed her with a sort of pity then turned his face away so she couldn't read his thoughts.

The train drew in and baked in the sun. Lilly held out her arms and hugged her son to her chest. 'I love you for ever and ever,' she said. 'I'll be home before you know it, my treasure.'

'Don't worry, Mama. *Ayah* will look after me.'

Royce looked pointedly at the station clock. 'Let the boy go and get on the train.' He gave her a shove.

She automatically dropped her hands, reeling that her last contact with Teddy had been so brutally cut off. A number of porters had taken the luggage to the ladies' compartment and stowed it in the overhead racks. Blindly, she followed behind.

As a bell rang, she sank onto her seat.

Wearing cool, pastel muslin and a shady hat, her mother sat opposite in the stifling carriage, a little dog snuffling by her side. It looked like a terrier of some sort, not that Lilly was any expert.

Lilly couldn't remember the last time they'd spoken – a few years at least – and for a second she was wordless, nerves stirring her stomach. 'Hello, Binnie,' she said at last, her voice tight. 'It's been quite a while.'

Lilly's mother would not hear of being called anything other than her first name. Looking more like thirty-five than her forty-five years, she was blonde-haired, impeccably dressed, expensive. With a full generous mouth and folds of glossy hair swept up over her ears, her dark eyebrows and deep brown eyes contrasted curiously. Binnie bent forward and kissed the air, somewhere close to her cheek.

'Goodness, whatever have you got on? Your outfit is quite three seasons out of date and no one is wearing that ghastly colour. No wonder Royce has sent you away.'

Lilly glanced down at her clothes and had to agree. Royce dressed her in clothes more suited to someone her grandmother's age but she didn't have any say in the matter.

Gripping one of the horizontal bars that dissected the window-frame, Lilly stared out as the train began to move.

Teddy stood on the platform, his right hand in his father's, and waved with his left, alternatively blowing kisses and smiling.

I can't leave him, Lilly thought. I have to get off right now. She almost reached to pull the alarm chain.

'I can't leave him,' she murmured. Never for a moment had she imagined that she could ever be this unhappy. Beginning to sob, she opened her bag in search of a hanky. Right at the top, folded in two was a piece of paper. She pulled it out to look. One of Teddy's drawings: a picture of them both in front of a circus tent that he had labelled, *Mama and Me.*

Lilly folded her hands between her knees and bit back her tears.

Binnie got up from her seat and sat down beside her. With a gloved hand, she took hold of Lilly's arm, but her grip was firm and brooked no argument.

'Listen to me. Your grief is raw and you think just now that you can't bear the separation, but you'll find that you can. Teddy will be all the better for it and eventually he will be sent away for his education. Children are very adaptable and there's nothing worse than a clingy mother. So buck up and make the most of the time away from Royce.' Binnie's voice held an edge.

'I will never forgive Royce for this pain I feel here.' Lilly placed a hand against her heart. 'I will never, ever forgive him.'

Binnie's dog started barking when the train picked up speed. He charged around the carriage, jumping up and down until he was almost bouncing off the walls.

Lilly leaned forward and tapped her mother's knee. 'Can't you do something about your dog? Why is he on the verge of a volcanic explosion?'

Binnie had the look of a gaoler chained to a lunatic. 'Poochie's curious nature means one has to put up with the odd manic fit.'

'Have you tried to train him?' Almost before the question was out, Lilly regretted it. Binnie was too wrapped up in the drama of her own life to expend any effort where she felt it unnecessary; training her pet would be prioritised down the line, like passing the care of her daughter to her in-laws in Gloucestershire.

But still, this trip, she supposed, was something to thank her for.

As the locomotive ate up the miles, Lilly realised the longer she sat in her seat, the further she was travelling away from *him*. In her high-necked collar and nipped in brown skirt, she barely registered her discomfort. The following evening – or even the day after that – she would be two hundred and sixty miles away in Nainital and for three months, would not have to see him or endure the tyranny of obedience with which he bound her to him. It was as if the shackles had been removed from her wrists and she was no longer fettered to the man who was – quite literally – her keeper. Time with her mother might even be preferable.

She stared out of the window as the train rattled along, chugging through rural India past parched little villages with myriad fields divided by low mounds of soil. The train stopped at small, whitewashed stations with unpronounce-able names until they arrived at Haldwani. There, they transferred to a *doolie dak* and made the five-mile journey to Kathgodam in the large boxlike conveyance that was suspended on the long sides from poles. Carried on the shoulders of eight bearers, it was an agonisingly slow and uncomfortable way to travel.

Changing to a *dak-gharry*, a further horse-drawn twenty miles in the rickety postal vehicle saw them at Kaladhungi, where they spent the night in the Murray Hotel. The place was run-down, the garden overgrown and the grass unkempt. It was a sordid, second-rate lodging house whose ancient rooms had stains on the walls and cracks in the mortar and reeked of incense and unwashed sheets. Lacy cobwebs dangled from the lampshades in greyish clumps and a thin mist seemed to hang in the air. *Is your noggin all clogged with cobwebs, Plumpty?* She stopped herself dead, afraid of losing control.

I won't think about him now or I really might go mad.

Next day, before the morning sun had a chance to lighten the landscape, the blowing of a trumpet pulled Binnie from her sleep. The trumpet belonged to the *doolie dak* that was to take them from Kaladhungi to Nainital. Lilly had barely slept, torn by conflicting emotions. Whilst relieved to be on her own for the first time in years, she imagined Teddy alone in his bedroom, sleep dust still in his eyes, and dressed in the clothes *Ayah* put on him. Had she remembered to put him to bed with his favourite toy bear? Had she read him a story to settle him to sleep? Stop it, Lilly, she chided herself; *Ayah* has looked after him since the day he was born. She can cope with his peculiarities probably better than you.

As they rose in the dark and scrambled into their clothes by the light of a single candle, her thoughts, for the moment, stopped whirling. Binnie declared it was too early for breakfast, but before climbing back into the *doolie*, they drank tea from a stand on the opposite side of the street.

Binnie blew on her drink. 'Did you write to Royce?'

'No, I didn't and even if I had, where would I post a letter from here?' It was a tiny act of rebellion.

Binnie nodded, Poochie barked and Lilly thought they both looked pleased.

Preceded by a line of bearers wearing brightly coloured loin cloths, their luggage balanced on cloth-covered heads, they rode along the route from Kaladhungi, which wound in sweeps and curves up the mountainside for twenty-two miles through a dense, dank jungle of Himalayan cedar and patches of tangled wild rose. On a path barely wider than a railway track in places, the *doolie* snaked its way upwards, turning sharply every few yards while dew dripped like thin rain from the overhanging branches.

Hours later, they tumbled out of their wooden conveyance at Nainital, six thousand feet above sea level. Stiff limbed and awkward from every jerk and rut, light-headed from the thin mountain air, Lilly fumbled for the handle of her travelling case.

After the red, parched plains of pre-monsoon Cawnpore, Lilly was entranced by the luxurious foliage and the myriad variations of green. Almost immediately their luggage was on the ground, they were surrounded by hopeful porters who squabbled amongst themselves as to who would assist the *memsahibs*.

Lilly left Binnie to negotiate with the porters and walked beyond them to the edge of the dark green lake. Staring at the water, which lapped gently against the slime-covered steps, at the far end she saw a row of sailboats that bobbed up and down on the surface and experienced a calm she couldn't explain. She started to count the tethered boats but felt a tear well at the corner of her eye. Teddy was learning to add up, and had he been with her, she might almost have found herself happy.

As they climbed the steep twisting path to the boarding house, Binnie stopped on a bend and put her hand on Lilly's arm. 'I was wondering while we are here at Nainital, if you would mind awfully not letting on that I am your mother.'

Lilly had almost predicted the request. She looked up to see a kite, wheeling and swooping in the chilly air, and let out a sigh. 'All right, but I do not want to become involved in conversations with you that would be acceptable between close friends but not between mother and daughter. If you understand what I mean.'

Binnie let out her high, forced laugh, then placed a finger against her lips. 'All secrets will lie safe in here. We will share nothing that could cause embarrassment or talk of anything that might reach your husband's ears.'

'Did he offer you cash to spy on me?'

'Do you really think I'd be that base?'

Giddy for lack of air and with a sick sense of foreboding deep in her heart, Lilly knew that she would and banged on the solid front door.

Rohilla Lodge did not have much to offer and its owners had made little effort to smarten it up for the summer visitors but within days, Binnie declared she had never been in better health or spirits.

Fleeing from the hot weather, she threw herself into social life within Nainital's intimate community with all the enthusiasm of a debutante at the start of her season. Wearing her smart frocks, she dined out four or five times a week and left her cards throughout the town. She attended teas, picnics, balls, fetes and polo matches, and each morning exchanged hill station gossip as she strolled along Upper

Mall Road. The preserve of the whites, it connected the two ends of the lake and only a handful of well-to-do Indians were allowed to share it. The vast majority used the lower mal. This was the cold or *thandi* side of the lake – so called as it was never warmed by the sun.

One Sunday morning, Binnie pointed a teaspoon at her. 'You should accept everything on offer, Lilly. Once you have made the effort to participate a little, more invitations will come your way and once you have been out and about, believe me, you will feel so much better when you go home. If you want to be accepted, you have to join in, or people will think you dull and not worth the bother.'

Lilly dunked a buttermilk biscuit in her tea and bit into the soggy crust. Before she could finish it off, Poochie jumped up and whipped the remainder from her hand. 'I'm not.'

'I really can't imagine where you get this dreadful low self-esteem. Must be your father's side. There are literally dozens of bachelors up here on leave and there's certain to be one who'll catch your eye.'

Poochie jumped up and began to bark at the ceiling. Lilly had no idea what was going on in his head. 'Shall I take the dog out for a walk, Mother?'

Binnie waggled the spoon. 'I asked you not to refer to me in that appalling way, even in private. People might hear and think I'm ancient.'

'I can't be bothered with the meaningless small talk. No one has anything interesting to discuss other than the last gymkhana they attended or the shortcomings of their latest *ayah*. Everyone attends the same events so there is nothing fresh to talk about. The same people, their same stories. I'd rather lose myself in a book.'

'But gossip is so delicious.'

Lilly stared at her mother's lips, even at this early hour coloured by an unnatural shade. 'It will get you into hot water if you don't take a tighter rein on your tongue.'

Binnie gave a small smile that barely reached her eyes. 'Your grandmother once said that about you.'

'Well then, learn from my mistake.' Hoping to distract the dog, Lilly poured the dregs of her tea into a saucer and stirred in a teaspoon of sugar. She put it on the floor and chimed it with her nail. 'After church this morning, what are your plans for the day?'

'I'm not that certain. But I'm going to the Club this afternoon for tea and a rubber of bridge, then we'll see how the land lies. There's talk of putting on a play for King Edward's coronation so I'm going to sign up for that. There's always a ridiculous rivalry for the chief parts, but as I both sing *and* act as well, I feel certain to land one of the best. You could volunteer to play the piano. Granny Wilkins said you were quite a talent.'

'I've rather let it slip, I'm afraid, since the piano at home is not fit to practise on.'

'You should pal up with Conti Moore. The whole family's musical and she's gifted in her own right.'

Poochie placed his paw on the saucer and upended it, splattering the tea onto the tiled floor.

'I haven't written to Royce so I must do that. I'm surprised he didn't fetch me home after I failed to write the first night at the hotel.'

Binnie got up from her chair and scooped up her pet. 'Fight fire with fire. Why don't you think back to what you did last week and write seven letters? Post one a day, then you won't have to think about him for an entire week.' She set off towards the door and threw over her shoulder, 'Could you mop up Poochie's tea, dahling? Haven't got the time myself.'

★

Sunday morning was the chief weekly reunion of the European community. After the service, outside on the veranda of the church, the congregation gathered to drink tea, discuss the sermon and catch up on gossip.

'I say, I don't think we've met.'

Lilly turned to face a slim young lady in her early twenties wearing a flowered blue cotton dress. Underneath her Sunday hat that had artificial flowers over the brim, she wore her thick blonde hair swept up in a chignon and there was no trace of powder to hide the freckles across her nose. She wore gloves and carried a furled parasol by its tip.

Lilly held out her own gloved fingers. 'I'm Lilly Myerson and I'm staying at Rohilla Lodge for a few months.'

'Oh, we know who you are! I'm Conti Moore and that is my brother Noel.' She pointed the handle of her parasol at a tall, lean man with thinning, sandy hair. Unlike the majority of men present who were uniformed in morning coats and grey trousers, he wore a flannel shirt and a shapeless pair of old corduroys that had clearly seen better days.

Conti twirled her parasol the right way up. 'We wondered if you are not doing anything right now if you would like to join us at the high-altitude zoo?'

Lilly looked at her watch but had nowhere in particular to be. 'I didn't know there was a zoo in Nainital.'

'That's part of the joke of the name because there's not a zoo there at all, just a collection of cages and some stabling. It is further up the hill from where you are staying, which is why we thought of it.' Conti's brother stood beside her, his eyes twinkling in amusement. He, too, held out his hand and as his hand closed on hers, she saw that the

41

fingers were long, nails clipped and clean and there were fine golden hairs on the back of his knuckles. 'Noel Moore. Occasional tiger-hunter, Beethoven aficionado and older brother to Conti.'

He looked to be mid-thirties, possibly a little younger, but the thinning hair was muddling. 'We have a chap from the circus staying with us up at the house for a few weeks so we thought we'd whizz up and have a shufty at what he's been doing day after day.'

Lilly felt a flicker of excitement. 'Is the circus here?'

He shook his head. 'No. Just a couple of the artists.'

'What's your fellow's act?'

Conti flung an arm around her brother's waist. 'He has a tiger – Mister Stripes – who he says is the only performing tiger in captivity and he has trained it to sit on a stool and do all sorts of clever things inside a cage. We're going to go and watch him work but we're going to keep out of sight so we don't put him off.'

Lilly's pulse quickened. 'That sounds dangerous.'

Conti dropped her arm and gave a shaky little laugh. 'Isn't that why people go to the circus – to be scared witless? You always remember the wild animal acts or the high wire, not the clowns or the performing geese.'

Lilly nodded. 'I went to the circus a few weeks ago with my son. He loved all the animals but, you're right, it was the high-risk acts that stuck in my mind.'

One by one, carriages drew up under the church porch. The ladies made their elaborate farewells, stuffed children onto seats while the gentlemen finished their conversations and then climbed aboard.

Noel began to pace, long strides, backwards and forwards across the veranda as if to mimic an animal in its cage. 'So, are you going to come with us?'

She watched him carefully for any sign that he might not mean what he said. It had been a long while since anyone had asked her to anything, and she wasn't certain the invitation was sincere. 'I'd love to come if you're sure you want me along.'

He wiped his forehead with a square of blue cloth and looked directly at her. He was obviously taken aback by her remark but recovered quickly. 'I can't think of a better way to spend an afternoon than with a gorgeous girl on each arm. Let's trot along to the tonga terminus and see if we can persuade—'

'Noel.' Conti drew in her lip and put a restraining hand on his arm. 'We said we were going to walk everywhere today. Remember we're supposed to be watching the pennies.'

'Sorry. Clean forgot.'

'I can pay,' Lilly blurted out, frightened that somehow the outing might be cancelled. More than that, though, she wanted to stay in their company.

What would make a man risk his life inside a cage with a wild animal? An animal that could kill its trainer with one swipe of a front-leg claw?

They found a patch of shade and dropped down on the grass and Lilly sat between them to watch the trainer work.

The tiger was huge, far bigger than Lilly had imagined; its head reached almost to the trainer's waist and its striped fur was glossy with health. It padded around the perimeter of the cage and then sat down, licked at its paw and began to wash behind an ear.

For several minutes they stared at the inside of the cage. The trainer began by making the tiger lie until it was told to sit, then roll over and move to its stool. It sniffed around the base, as if checking that it was safe, then leaped up and sat on its rump.

Lilly leaned towards Noel and whispered. 'What's the trainer's name?'

'Duffy Puttnam. He's with an outfit called Tiffert's.'

'I'm sure I've met him. He came to Cawnpore to publicise their circus and my husband gave him short shrift.'

'Mister Stripes reminds me of a domestic cat,' Conti said.

Noel turned his head, his grey eyes smiling from between pale lashes. 'That's what you are supposed to think. Duffy doesn't use the whip to aggravate the tiger, so it appears docile and obedient. He says it reassures the audience.'

Lilly thought the trainer also seemed at ease. Arms by his sides, he stood in the middle of the cage and as the animal walked past, he trailed his nails through its fur.

Noel lightly touched her elbow. 'Duffy says he's trained Stripes to jump over his head and is now working on getting the tiger to lie across his shoulders.'

'Why on earth would anyone want to do that?' Lilly asked.

Noel stood up and offered her a hand to her feet. 'Because he can, I suppose, although I'd never be that mad.'

It was almost a week before Lilly saw the Moores again.

An hour after lunch the following Saturday, while Binnie was dressing for her afternoon at the Yacht Club, Lilly sat at the writing table in her little sitting room, frowning at the sheet of paper. Her teeth clamped round the end of her fountain pen, she paused, wondering how to continue the long fiction she was writing. She didn't mention that she'd made some new friends, that she'd seen a circus performer working with his tiger. Instead, she stuck to topics she knew would be safe: what she was reading, Binnie's dog, the weather.

In addition to his insistence that she write to him each day, Royce wanted a daily account of how she was spending his money.

Even after seven years in India, she still struggled with the currency.

Shortly after they were married, Royce had stood over her, flexing his whalebone. 'I cannot understand why you cannot get it into your head. It's exactly like pounds, shillings and pence but in India we call the denominations rupees, annas and pice. Head up your columns R.A.P., R.A.P., R.A.P.,' he yelled as he smacked the side of the table.

'That's the ticket,' he said when she'd got her columns down on paper. 'Four pice make an anna, and sixteen annas in a rupee. How many pice in a rupee?'

'I don't know, Royce. At home, I never really had to deal with money.'

'Then I shall have to drill you, Lilly. We can't have an ignoramus in the family, can we, old thing?'

It took her no time at all to tot up the columns in the account book he'd thrust at her chest before she left the house in Cawnpore; arithmetic had never been the problem.

She got up from the table and wandered over to the upright piano and lifted the lid. It was dusty with misuse, so she ran her sleeve across the length of the keyboard. Flexing her fingers, she placed her right hand on the yellowing keys and picked out a tune she'd learned as a child. Soon she found it impossible not to let her left hand join in and sat down on the stool to play.

Lilly felt the draft on the back of her neck as the door opened and displaced the air. She swivelled on the piano stool and let the smile spread on her face. 'Noel! What a lovely surprise.'

'I didn't know you could tickle the ivories.'

'Rusty, I'm afraid, but I confess to enjoy bashing away. I'm sure you know the piece.'

He nodded. 'I do. It's Beethoven's *Für Elise.*'

Lilly laughed. 'I've always called it *Furry Leaves* and no one's ever corrected me. What brings you here this afternoon?'

'I pootled along on the off chance of catching you alone as I haven't seen you since the high-altitude enclosure last Sunday. Conti and I were hoping we might have run into you at the Club.' Noel stood on the hearth rug and lit a cigarette, his elbow resting on the mantelpiece. 'You weren't at the polo match either on Thursday.'

She felt strangely touched that he'd noted her absence. 'I don't go out and about very often. My husband doesn't approve, and I don't play bridge. I'm more of a Happy Families card player.'

His eyes had wandered to the writing table where a photograph of Teddy stood by a bowl of white roses. 'Is that your son?'

She felt the pain of the boy's absence in every nerve of her body. Fighting the quiver in her lips, she said, 'Yes. He's five years old.' Pre-empting the inevitable question, she continued, 'He stayed in Cawnpore with his father.'

He glanced at her and his expression suggested he had taken in the 'surgery' she had performed to cut Royce from the frame. 'No picture of your husband?'

'No.'

His eyes lingered on her face. 'Did you make a mistake?'

Lilly did not want to be drawn in that direction. 'Not with Teddy. Would you like some tea?'

'No, thanks. Can't abide the stuff. But let me tell you why I popped in. After drinks tonight at the Club when the band have finished playing, my sister is hosting a séance, if you felt like stretching your legs. She's a terrible gatherer, my sister, always hunting up new people and as you're about the same age, she's rather hoping you'll become friends. Conti's also become pally with one of the circus folk who does card readings and scary stuff with something she calls her ouija board.'

As he had done outside the church, Noel began to pace.

Royce did that, pacing up and down as a prelude to hitting out with his hand. 'Will you please stand still? It's unsettling to talk to a pendulum.'

'Sorry. Bad habit of mine. What did you think of the tiger trainer?'

Truthfully, she hadn't spared him a thought and wondered why he asked. 'I was surprised he was training his animal on a Sunday, which is supposed to be a day of rest.'

'He can't afford to take any time off. He's working the tiger every day so that it learns a new routine for next season. He's come to me particularly because he wants a second tiger to join his act and Stripes must show him the ropes. Against my better judgement, and only because of the money he's offering, I've said I will try to hunt one down for him.'

Lilly understood all too well the feeling of being stalked and subsequently trapped. She hated the idea of animals confined to a life in a cage and performing tricks to entertain the public. 'Is that so?' she asked, not quite managing to keep the judgement out of her voice.

A look she couldn't interpret flickered across his suntanned face. 'If I catch him a wild cat, he says he can

47

bill it as such and increase the gate sales. Conti's rather spoony on him and I think that's why they're doing the séance thing – to see if she has any chance with him at all.'

'I thought a séance was to do with contacting dead spirits.'

'Madame Margot's tricks are quite ingenious.'

Lilly let out a snort. 'Tell me you made up that name.'

He placed a hand against his heart. 'Word of honour. That is her name. But I do most sincerely believe that she is a gifted con artist and hoodwinks the susceptible. At the very least, she is very charming and rather beautiful and will put on a good show of some sort.'

'Like the famous American Fox sisters, who made a fortune out of a bogus story about contacting the spirit of a murdered peddler.'

'I'm impressed.'

'My English grandmother loves a good ghost story.'

'Were you brought up in England?'

'Yes, and I wish I was still there.'

'India not to your liking?' He spoke softly, drawing her in.

'It's a bitter disappointment.'

He looked again at the photograph on the table. 'How long have you been out here?'

'It's been nearly eight years since I arrived in Bombay. I'd go back tomorrow if I could.'

'If you keep yourself homesick it will be your undoing.'

'What do you mean?'

He rubbed a finger along the side of his nose. 'Nothing is more annoying to someone who has never lived anywhere else than to listen to people lamenting their fate in living here. Don't lay the blame on India for everything that's askew in your life.'

Lilly widened her eyes. 'Are you telling me off?'

'Just don't shut your eyes to India's blessings.'

'Give India a chance?'

The question raised his eyebrows. 'Precisely, given it must have been your choice to come?'

Lilly lowered the lid on the piano and turned towards the window. 'I can appreciate why you might say I regret the decision if the original choice had been mine.'

'Wasn't it?' he asked. A small crease appeared between his brows.

'I'm afraid not.' She gave a small shake of her head. 'I was only sixteen and imposed choice will torment one for ever.'

He pushed his spectacles up to the bridge of his nose with a forefinger. 'Well, Conti and I would be pleased to see you at the séance tonight, if you'd like to come.'

Lilly was on the point of inventing a headache but instead dropped down on the button-backed sofa and drew up her legs beneath her. 'Where is Madame Margot performing her grand deception?'

'At my place.'

Her heart sank. Noel's bungalow, Lake View, was perched at the top of a near-vertical slope at the far end of The Flats, an area of flattened ground at the other end of the lake, so called after the devastating landslide of 1880. She couldn't bear the thought of the climb. 'Couldn't they hold it in the committee room at the Yacht Club?'

Instinctively he seemed to recognise her difficulty. 'It's a bit of a pull up from the Mall, I know, but I could send a conveyance for you.'

'Aren't the palanquin-bearers playing up?'

The bearers had a poor reputation for reliability and frequently held their passengers to hostage, dropping the palanquin in the middle of the road and walking off, stranding their 'fare' until more money exchanged hands.

Noel had a knack of putting her at ease. 'I wasn't proposing that you should run the gauntlet with those chaps. I have my own *jampan wallahs*. I'll send them down for you.'

This was possibly worse. A papoose-like conveyance, the *jampan* consisted of a strong khaki-colour cotton cloth slung like a hammock from a bamboo staff and carried by four or more men. The passenger could either sit sidewise holding onto the pole or lie flat on his back helpless as a baby in a papoose.

The alternative was far more attractive.

'Maybe I'll just stay here at Rohilla Lodge tonight, and turn in after supper. I have to finish writing to my husband as well, or I'll be well and truly in the doghouse.'

'Or I could trot down and walk up with you. We could take it in stages. You'll be fine till we cross The Flats and then, as the road rises, we'll stop on each corner to give you a chance to regain your puff. It'll do you good to exercise your lungs. It's the best way to acclimatise to the thinner air.' There was a warmth in his tone that hinted at more than courtesy; it made Lilly feel suddenly shy.

She picked up a half anna stamp from the writing table and stared at the likeness of Queen Victoria. 'I'll tell you what. If I'm going to come, I'll see you there. I don't want to put you out.'

Shortly after six o'clock, Lilly took a rickshaw along Mall Road.

The rickshaw *wallah*, wearing a *lungi* – a strip of checked cloth wrapped around his body and tied at the waist – and a filthy singlet, puffed and sweated, his arm muscles bulging with effort as he pulled her to the far end of The Flats.

He drew up in front of a woman with hennaed hands who was selling jewellery, her wares set out on a cloth before her. 'You want buy something, Mem?'

Lilly shook her head and spoke to the rickshaw puller's back. 'Can't you go any further?'

He turned, wiping at his dripping face with a rag. 'Too steep. Can't pull you up. You should be walking.'

Marooned by the side of the road, wearing a bronze-coloured evening frock, a rope of glass beads at her neck – Royce had not let her take her decent jewellery away – and silly nubuck shoes, Lilly was filled with dismay at the sight of the craggy winding path that snaked up the hillside.

If you're going to the séance, you'll have to walk the rest of the way by yourself. So just do it, Lilly. Take off your shoes if you have to.

In the course of the long climb up, she often had to stop to find the breath to go on. She passed a ramshackle dwelling whose tin roof was weighted down with stones; a woman in a pink sari was washing a brass dish over the shallow drain that ran past her door. On another corner, a dark figure in a loin cloth squatted on his haunches roasting corn cobs on an open fire, a monkey tethered to a chain by his side.

Eventually she came to Lake View, a sprawling bungalow that sat above a tiered garden, flanked by giant oaks and a lone deodar tree stood sentinel at the side entrance. Like most Nainital houses, it had a rambling honeysuckle trained under the eaves and alongside it, climbing roses were in bloom.

Legs aching from fatigue and blisters burning her heels, she limped up the four steps to the wide veranda, which looked out towards the snow-capped mountains. Focused on the effort required, at the front she almost tripped over a man in crumpled shirt sleeves and shorts that were none too clean, his knees bare and socks rolled to his ankles. He was sitting in a tatty basket weave chair and looked hot, his lean boyish face now burned brown by the sun. He was smoking a cigarette, a glass of whisky in his hand.

She squared her shoulders and introduced herself. She decided she wouldn't mention that she had watched him train his tiger, as she felt Noel would not want her to. 'Hello. I'm Lilly Myerson. We met before at my husband's shop in Cawnpore.'

'Did we?' He pointed to a small side table. 'Help yourself to a drink.'

There was no reason that he should have remembered so brief an encounter but his words still stung all the same. 'Do you have any water? It's been a bit of a climb.'

'Keep off the H2O. It's lake water, you know, and as polluted as anything you'll put in your mouth in India. Totally toxic unless you were brought up here and have drunk it all your life or can say for certain it's been boiled.' He smiled and, in the space where his lips opened up, smoke rolled out like London smog.

Lilly flinched, her hand flying to her stomach.

He flicked a finger and thumb towards her middle. 'Not expecting, are you?'

'No. Just thinking of the gallons I've consumed since I arrived here.'

'Trots?'

Lilly shook her head and poured herself a slug of whisky. She heard her mother's laugh from somewhere inside. 'Have they started the séance?'

'Not yet, but there's a frightful woman inside already, holding forth about something or other. Her voice was getting on my nerves, so I came out to give my sensitive

52

South African ears a rest from the Britishers inside.' He watched her lift the glass. 'Drink up – that's the ticket. The grog will help to purge any lingering bugs.'

Lilly could not detect an accent. 'I'm afraid Binnie only has two topics of conversation.'

In the glance he gave her, she saw he had her mother pegged. 'Men and money.'

Lilly leaned against the edge of the table and watched him over the rim of her glass. 'You've discovered that already?'

'It's a small community. People talk if you've a mind to listen.' He leaned back in his chair, a hand behind his head. 'What's your story, Mrs Myerson?'

Lilly felt a start of surprise and barely knew what to say. People hardly ever asked her a personal question. 'I don't have a story.'

'Ah! Not prepared to say. I shall have to make one up in that case.' He pretended to think. 'You've run away – but what from?'

She put her head on one side, waiting for him to go on. 'Disenchantment.'

Lilly nodded her head. 'That's not bad.'

'Are you on the lookout for an adventure? Married woman seeking footloose bachelor in a small hillside station?'

'Not with someone who has yet to introduce himself.'

'Spoken for?'

'No one speaks for me, Mr Footloose, but I'm married and have a son.' The words shot out before she had time to think. *Keep a fetter on your tongue, Lilly.*

'Where is his father?'

'He's in Cawnpore where he lives with his mother.' She glanced at her watch. 'Just about now, they'll be sitting down together eating their evening roti.'

He shot a look at a bearer. 'A local chap?'

Lilly followed his gaze. 'You mean a native.'

'So?'

'He's English. His mother's native.'

He lowered his free hand towards the floorboards. 'And you are way down there. Keeping your place with no voice to speak.'

She took a large sip of her drink but failed to swallow it all. A tickle lodged in her throat and made her cough. 'How could you possibly know that?'

'I've seen it before.'

Her eyes watered as she fought off another cough. 'Do you have family?'

His mouth curved but the smile was non-committal. 'Work and whisky are enough for me. But are you all right? Not swallowed a fly, I hope.'

'I'm fine. Whisky and I are not intimately acquainted, that's all.'

He threw away his cigarette and spoke as if his interest had burned up in the last puff of smoke. 'You do seem vaguely familiar, I'll give you that.'

She didn't want him to know that she remembered him so clearly in his creased linen suit and had recently watched him work. 'As I said, we met before in Cawnpore, but I hadn't realised you were the circus lodger Noel told me about.'

'What makes you say that?'

Flustered for a few seconds, she jerked her chin at the criss-crossing of white scars on his legs. 'Not so much the person but the marks of your trade.'

'Indeed.'

'But not on your arms though.'

'A tiger will leap on your shoulders. I always wear a padded leather jacket – so no obvious marks on my arms. Frightens the ladies and couldn't be doing with that.'

'A ladies' man then.'

'I am not insensitive to a pretty girl.' He sprang up from his chair. 'We should go in,' he said and turned to the door. 'Duffy B. Puttnam, by the way, as you've clearly forgotten.'

Once inside, Lilly was less than thrilled to see that her mother was already seated at the far end of the table next to Delphine Harmond – the wife of a high-court judge in Calcutta – and was leaning in towards her, whispering behind her hand. Mrs Harmond was tainted with scandal and would be encouraged to give up her secrets on the promise that they would go no further than the strong box that her mother claimed held her word.

The story went that Mrs Harmond had not been properly severed from her previous marriage and had borne her judge husband three or four children, none of whom was legitimate. More telling, however, was that her complexion and stunning beauty was clearly the result of a liaison between a European and an Indian. Snubs against her were widespread in the invitations that had not come her way and so her presence at the séance was nothing short of intriguing.

Binnie let out an excited high-pitched peal of laughter and fluttered at the air with her ostrich feather fan. 'Really? My parents also had a Sloane Square address,' she said in her very loud, very best Belgravia voice. 'They might easily have been neighbours. How potty a thought is that?'

Lilly feared for the indiscretions an unsuspecting Mrs Harmond would give up.

Looking around the teak table, which sat on an animal skin in the middle of the room, she saw that there were eight of them, including the Moores and their guests. For a second, Lilly let herself imagine that she was back in her grandmother's drawing room. If she shut her eyes she could travel back across the miles and see it in all its detail.

Here too there were English curtains, standard lamps and a vase of flowers on the mantelpiece, and a Schiedmayer piano that she supposed belonged to Conti, the talented pianist. The walls were hung with hunting trophies and a charcoal drawing of the Tower of London. It was signed N Moore. She thought it strange that everyone seemed to carry a little bit of England with them, even though Noel said he had never actually been.

Noel smiled and waved his hand. 'I'm so pleased you came!' he said.

Self-consciously, she fingered the beads at her neck and felt the tingling in her cheeks as delight registered on his face. Binnie was wrapped up in her conversation, flushed from her cocktail and still had not drawn breath. Lilly doubted she'd even seen her come in.

The grandfather clock in the hall struck eight. Its solemn chimes echoed through the room and brought the conversation to a halt.

Dressed in a close-fitting dress of heliotrope silk, Madame Margot – her eyebrows knit tight in concentration – sat at the head of the table. Somehow Lilly had imagined a kohl-eyed fortune reader with rings on her fingers and hoops through her ears. In her exquisite, sleeveless evening gown, she seemed vastly overdressed for what had been advertised as a 'casual affair'. But every male eye in the room was trained upon Mrs Harmond; her beauty had them all mesmerised. They look like starving dogs, Lilly thought. Waiting to be tossed a scrap.

Madame Margot cleared her throat and spread her hands palms down on the wooden surface. 'I believe it's time to begin if I might claim your attention and could someone dim the lamps? We don't require a total blackout, just enough light to see by, and will someone close the door and pull the curtains? I don't want anyone thinking that I have an accomplice who sneaks in when the room is dark. There will be no physical manifestations, rapping or knocking, as is the practice of some sham mediums I could mention.'

Duffy spoke behind his hand. 'Do you believe in spiritualism?'

Lilly shook her head. 'I'm not sure what it is.'

'The idea that ghosts exist and that we can communicate with them. It has a huge following in the United States of America.'

Lilly studied the flat wooden board on the table in front of them. The letters of the alphabet were painted on it in two semi-circles above a straight line of numbers from nought to nine. The words 'yes' and 'no' were in each of the uppermost corners and 'goodbye' was written at the bottom. It seemed a most unlikely contrivance to communicate with the departed, but if people's spirits did go on after death, she might be able to talk to her little girl.

'Keep your eyes closed, everyone, and place your forefinger lightly on the ouija. There must be no question that anyone present has manipulated the board.' Madame Margot had a cultured, hypnotic voice. 'I will ask the spirit world if there is anyone who wants to pass a message through me. I am a facilitator, if you will, and through me, the spirits will talk to you. The planchette will spell out the message by pointing to the letters one by one.'

Lilly leaned in towards Duffy. 'Are you a convert?'

He seemed to feel her scepticism. 'Everyone wants to believe in something mystical or magical. Once an idea has been planted, it's what gives us hope.'

'Something to hang onto in our less happy moments.'

'Exactly.'

'How are we to see the message if our eyes are closed?'

Madame Margot had overheard their whisperings. 'You may open them when the planchette begins to move and call out the letters as they are spelled out. I will write them down on here.' She tapped a sheaf of writing paper with her nails. 'If you will permit me to begin, we shall see what we shall see.' Margot tipped back her head and began to breathe in and out through her nose. Pure theatre, Lilly thought.

'Here we go,' Duffy whispered.

'Have you done this before?'

'Oh yes. Many times. She's absolutely marvellous.'

Lilly heard the admiration in his voice, but it was the shine in his eyes that gave him away; the shock gave her a peculiar sensation as if someone had punched her in the chest. 'Is it a hoax?'

'You'll have to make your own mind up about that, but for now stop talking and concentrate. The trance can take a while.'

Lilly almost put her palms together in mock submission but fell quiet, closed her eyes and gave in to the silence. In the distance she heard the clanging of the prayer bell from the Hindu Temple on the lake, the over-loud ticking of the clock on the wall, dogs howling, a window banging in the wind somewhere.

Lilly thought she was about to begin, but instead Madame Margot again cleared her throat. 'The seating around the table is wrong. I'm trying to summon up the spirits but there are disbelievers keeping them away. If you are here because you are hoping to see a spectacle, I must ask you to leave.'

Lilly's fingers flew to her face to cover the scorch of

the reprimand she felt in her cheeks then she dropped them to her lap.

Madame Margot pointed at the man in a jacket bound with gold braid. 'Commodore Brownlee, change places with Noel, and Duffy will change with Mrs Harmond. I'm also going to swap from the ouija board to the planchette.'

'What's that?' Commodore Brownlee pushed himself up from his seat and adjusted the thick monocle wedged in his right eye.

Margot scooped up the ouija board and leant it against one side of her chair. From the other side, she took hold of a teardrop-shaped board and placed it on the table. 'It's a spirit writing device. See the two casters underneath and the hole at the tip? I'm going to insert a pencil into the hole and place my two hands on the board. And on this sheet' – she pulled the sheaf of paper towards her – 'which will sit beneath the board, I will write the message the spirit is wanting to communicate to any one of you around the table.'

She waited until the revised seating arrangement had been effected. 'Place your hands on your knees and close your eyes and we will try again. I am the only person in contact with the planchette and any communication will pass through me. The pencil will do as it wishes but I warn you, it may yield nothing.'

Lilly stole a peek and saw that Margot had tilted back her head, both hands side by side on the planchette.

'Is there a spirit present who wishes to pass a message?'

Lilly snapped her eyes shut as she heard the board begin to move.

A minute or two went by.

'Is that the message?' Margot's hands were still. 'Open your eyes and we will see if this means anything to anyone here.'

She lifted the board off the paper, and they all saw that she had spelled out the word IMPOSTER on the blank sheet.

'Well now,' she said as seven pairs of eyes traded glances back and forth. 'I don't suppose anyone will admit ownership of *that* message.'

At ten thirty, Lilly was searching out a plausible excuse to leave. Binnie was hard at work, speaking in the voice she had perfected for extracting gossip from the unwary and was manipulating Commodore Brownlee as if he were a piece on a chessboard, each move carefully thought out to ambush and checkmate her quarry. She was living up to her mantra: take your fun where you find it.

Poor man, Lilly thought. He doesn't stand a chance.

By midnight, the party had drifted out onto the veranda. A half-moon peered through the clouds lending a brightness to the sky, and the air crackled with insects.

Lilly sat on the top step, her hands clasped around her knees. Wearing a white shirt that smelled freshly washed, Noel sat beside her on the rough stone, his dog, Goose – a young collie with intelligent eyes and a talent for snoring – lay with his nose and a possessive paw across his foot. She could not help but make a comparison with her mother's manic pet.

'Have you ever sat up all night and watched the stars?' she said.

'Many, many times.'

'Are you troubled by portents?'

He shot up an eyebrow. 'I haven't ever given them much thought. Are you thinking who the message might have been intended for?'

'Yes, I suppose I am.'

'Everyone in their own way is an imposter.'

Lilly was surprised to hear him say that. 'Are you?'

He fondled the dog's silky head. 'When I was young, my mother had a house at the bottom of the valley and all my chums were local boys. Natives. When we moved up to Naini for the summer, I dropped them all and only had Britishers as friends. Concealing the fact that I knew them makes me shudder now, but no one admitted to fraternising with the Indians.'

Lilly voiced what had been long on her mind. 'The British have their own caste system in India and I doubt there are many who can say they have lived a life free from pretence.'

Noel swivelled to face her. 'India is a two-faced nation. Take Naini, for example. In the off season, we all go about our business with no one to impress. We let the monkeys invade our houses and do their damage, and we turn a blind eye. We eat with our hands like the natives and decry the British. But when it is the summer season – when the Britishers come up from the plains – we present another face to the world. We clean up our act and sit at a table and eat with knives and forks. We discuss the weather and cricket and call the race that rule us *jolly fine fellows*.'

She stared at him in surprise, never having heard a white European openly admit to such a thing. 'Exactly,' she said, nodding. 'It infuriates me, playing the game of being more British than British. The things that we're expected to turn a blind eye to in the name of our devotion to Home. I am sure, too, that your errands of mercy in killing the man-eating tigers will be seen in this light. A service rendered to the King and his Empire. Jolly well done, old chap.'

Noel forked his fingers through his hair. 'But it doesn't make me feel less ashamed and I'm trying to do something about it.'

Lilly suspected he'd have his work cut out. 'A bit of an

uphill struggle, I'd have thought.'

'I have a patch of land in Choti Haldwani that I'm ploughing money into when funds permit. I'm setting it up as a model farm.'

Even in the lamplight, she could not fail to see the candour in his eyes. She tilted her head to one side. 'I'd love to hear your plans.'

'A few years back, I bought forty acres of land and have divided it into holdings that are leased to my native tenants. They've dug irrigation channels, planted seeds and grown vegetables but it is not fenced in and therefore vulnerable to wild animals. We've started to build a wall around the farm to protect the crops but it is grindingly slow. That's why I'm taking any work that comes my way, even if it is not to my taste.'

Lilly felt he was about to say more but his gaze strayed to the other end of the veranda where a window stood open. To the accompaniment of a fine piano, her mother was singing with great spirit and energy. It was a song that everyone seemed to know as they joined in lustily with the chorus.

'How does Binnie sit in the east–west divide?'

'She's the most awful snob and has very strong prejudices.'

'And you're her daughter although you both pretend you're not.'

'How on earth do you know? She'd be horrified if you even thought she was old enough to have a daughter my age.' She said it in an undertone.

'Secrets will out in a small community.'

'Duffy said something similar before the séance. What's the story with him and Margot?'

'Is there one?' He seemed a little put out.

'He's besotted with her.'

'In what way?'

Lilly felt embarrassed that she didn't have the words to explain. 'He seems to like looking at her.'

He settled his spectacles on the bridge of his nose. 'Anyone that beautiful will command attention. But delightful as she is, Duffy has no business to be looking at all.'

'Is that you as a protective brother speaking? You said Conti had set her cap at him.'

'I'm not Conti's parent. She can choose her own friends but if it were left up to me, I wouldn't have singled him out.'

'Why ever not?'

'Oh, I don't know. Just a feeling that once he has his tiger, he'll have got what he came for and won't hang around.'

He dropped his hand on her arm and again she felt he might say more but Duffy strolled up the veranda, a glass of grog in his hand. 'Binnie says it's time you were rolling home,' he said to Lilly. 'But she's not coming back to the boarding house herself just yet so could you let the dog out for five minutes if it's still in the sitting room.'

Noel got up at once. 'Let me send you home in the *jampan*. It's too dark to see properly and the *jampan wallahs* know the way blindfold.'

Lilly felt a surge of relief. 'That would be so kind. I'm not sure how I'd manage on my own.'

Noel turned to go about his task and Duffy offered her his hand to pull her to her feet. Together they went down the four stone steps to the garden and walked around a line of washing slung between two trees.

A cigarette dangling from the corner of his mouth, he leaned on a magnolia tree while she limped towards the gate, which was cut out of the high iron railings and secured the property from the road with a giant bolt.

The heady night smell of the jasmine blossom made her dizzy and she stumbled on an exposed root. 'Ow! I really didn't need to do that to my toes.'

A smile played about his mouth. 'Feet sore?'

'I'd give anything to take off these ridiculous shoes.'

'Why don't you?'

She caught the challenge in his eye. It was gone in a second and she found herself with no response to offer.

'Take them off in the jampan. Waggle your toes in the face of convention. No one's going to know.'

Lilly stepped through the wrought-iron gate and swung it closed. When she faced him through the bars their eyes were on a level. He was short for a man but with the chest and shoulders of a weightlifter. Now it is shut, she thought. The world is locked out. Just as my husband likes it.

'What are you thinking?' There was an odd glint in his eye.

'That I am watching you through a cage,' she said. 'Like the poor tiger you train.'

He pulled on his cigarette, one eye shut against a swirling curl of smoke. 'But tigers will escape and run for the hills, if the door is left ajar.'

Held aloft in Noel's conveyance, headfirst to save her from sliding out, Lilly lay back against the cushions and was borne down the long descent on the shoulders of four *jampanis*, confident and sure-footed as mountain goats. She looked up at the stars, feeling unsteady for more reasons than her current position.

The *jampan wallahs* set her down in front of the guesthouse.

Holding onto the rickety handrail with one hand, her

shoes in the other, she trod carefully as she mounted the wooden staircase to the red front door, mindful that the two elderly sisters whose guest she was would already have turned in for the night.

Thankfully, the demented dog was neither heard nor seen and she was able to continue up and up to her room in the roof.

She went to the window to draw the curtains. Lamplight flooded in from the street and backlit the window. A face stared back at her through the glass; it was old, pale, grown fat. It was not a face she recognised as her own.

Lilly turned away and took Teddy's vest from a drawer. She lay down on the ancient wooden bed, buried her face in the soft cotton and breathed in the scent of her child.

Chapter 5

The following morning, a painful throbbing in her heels woke Lilly early.

After breakfast in the dining room, her mother nowhere to be seen, she retired to her sitting room where she sat alone with her emotions, surrounded by an array of different-sized pans – all strategically placed to catch drips from the leaking roof. The room looked down onto the street and smelled of mildew and rain-swollen drains.

She got up and threw a log on the fire; staring into the flames, she allowed herself to float back to England, barely aware that the drawing room door had opened. England had its own fragrant scent – lush grass, wet leaves, a garden after a shower, the sharp tang of harvest dry wheat. It did not *smell*.

'A penny for them.'

Lilly swung round to face Miss Pearl, the younger of the two Miss Pinkneys. She was small and dainty like a piece of fragile china. With her sister, Miss Opal, they ran the boarding house where she and her mother were staying. 'Oh! Those thoughts are worth less than that.'

Miss Pearl sank down in an elderly armchair and picked up her needlework. She was chain stitching the words *Soiled Undergarments* onto a beige canvas bag. 'I'm all ears. I love a good chat.'

'It's hard enough to go there in my head, let alone say the words out loud. I was just thinking about England.'

Her eyes were bright with interest. 'Have you been?'

'I grew up there. It's rather a long story.'

Miss Pearl peered through a silver *pince-nez*. 'I'm in no rush.'

Lilly was tempted to say nothing, to keep the homesickness deep inside but there was a softness in the old lady's manner that encouraged her to speak. 'I spent my childhood in Cheltenham with my grandparents. One day, out of the blue when I was sixteen, Granny received a letter from my mother here in India saying that I was to travel from Tilbury Docks to Bombay, where she would reclaim me after all those years apart.'

'Was that expected?'

'No, I don't think it was. But I was sent off nonetheless. Granny was very upset to see me go.'

Pearl Pinkney stowed her needle in the canvas. 'So, when you arrived in India?'

Lilly leaned her back against the chimney breast. 'I vividly remember arriving in Bombay and staying at a hotel where I thought my mother would be waiting.'

Miss Pearl looked at her with her head on one side. 'But she wasn't?'

'No. My mother's disinterest in me is a long legacy. She'd gone off somewhere to escape the heat and I was sent to boarding school in Bandra. I cried and cried for weeks.'

The elderly lady kept her eyes on Lilly's face. 'Mrs Rivers is your mother.'

'No one is supposed to know but everybody does.'

'The family resemblance is strong, but you have far more' – she seemed to search for the word – 'substance.'

Lilly took a seat by the window. 'My mother would disagree with you on that.' She said it very low. 'She finds me a rather inert, colourless character.'

'What of your acquaintance at Cawnpore? You will have received many a compliment, I am certain, from the ladies at your Club.'

Lilly gave a distracted smile, intending to deflect further questions. The last thing she wanted to do was talk about herself.

Miss Pearl appraised her from behind the eyeglass. 'You may feel better if you tell me about it. It's obvious you are not happy.'

'How is it obvious?'

She gave a tiny hitch of a shoulder. 'You have such sad eyes.'

Lilly sat with her hands in her lap, trembling a little. 'I'm in disgrace. These three months in the hills are my punishment.'

'Whatever did you do?'

'It's not important.'

Miss Pearl ran her fingers over the threadbare cover on the chair. 'It must have been something quite serious to be sent away by yourself.'

Lilly shook her head. 'Could we talk about something else? Such as where my mother is just now?'

'She has gone off for a carriage drive with Commodore Brownlee and then I understand they are going to see about engaging a dog-boy for her tiresome pet. This afternoon they are playing golf at the Residency.'

Lilly wondered how she had extracted this information from her flighty parent. 'Does Binnie even know how to play golf?'

Miss Pearl picked up her needlework and peered at her stitching. 'You are asking the wrong person, but I suspect she has no intention of participating, simply of being seen in that elevated circle. I'd hazard it's more about being seen with the Commodore than participating in a round of golf.'

Lilly drew her eyebrows together at this. 'She only met the Commodore at the séance last evening.'

'No – in that you are quite wrong. They go back at least several years. I believe their adulterous entanglement was cited in the grounds for her divorce from Mr Rivers.'

'Binnie sees a husband merely as a provider of luxury goods. She said Frederick had to go as he'd run short of funds.'

'Well, I think, dear, we both know that what Binnie says is not always the exact truth.' She waved a hand at the dog on the hearth rug. 'You should take Poochie for a walk. Up to the Yacht Club and back is a good stretch of the legs. I heard you playing the pianoforte when Noel came yesterday – you should offer your services for the theatrical performance to celebrate the King's coronation.'

'What is it to be?'

'Sullivan's Cox and Box, I believe.'

Lilly shook her head. 'Sullivan's music is notoriously tricky and I'm woefully out of practice.'

'Do something about it. We have a piano here. Conti Moore has one at home and there is another at the Club. Between the three of them, you should find one that suits you. Go up to the Club and find out what's cooking. Throw yourself into something.'

'Like the lake?'

The look on Pearl Pinkney's face was a picture. She clearly hadn't anticipated a joke. 'Why not? Go for a swim.'

Lilly wiggled her slipper-clad feet. 'I didn't pack my flippers and walking in proper shoes is out of the question this morning.'

Miss Pearl threw up her hands in exasperation. 'Then take the bicycle. It's in the yard at the back. You can freewheel down to the church and then the mall is flat until you get to Ram Lals – the nice new dress shop – and then it's a bit of a slope up to the Yacht Club. You'll find the exercise invigorating and it's also beneficial for one's – um – *ligne.*'

Lilly looked down at her waist. 'I never lost the weight after Caroline was born and nothing seemed important after she died.' She felt her throat close up and choked back a sob.

'The order is all wrong if a child dies before its parents. The loss of one's baby is devastating.' Miss Pearl scanned the desk. 'Is there not a photograph of her as well as your little boy?'

'She died before we got around to having one taken.' The tears began to well up again. 'Beyond her clothes and toys, I have nothing to remind me of her and I'm terrified I will forget what she looked like.'

The older lady placed a hand in the vicinity of her heart. 'She is here and you will never lose that, but you must try to get on with your life. The best thing would be to have another one quickly, even if you feel you could never bear to replace her.'

Lilly fished a handkerchief from her sleeve and blew her nose. 'You must think me very weak.'

'Tears wash away the pain. Take the bicycle and go to the Club.'

'I'm not sure I'd be able to bicycle that far.'

'Oh, my dear.' Pearl Pinkney pushed her needle in and out of the cloth. 'I don't think anyone has the notion of what is really possible until one sees if it is. If you throw yourself in at the deep end, you might be surprised how well you can swim.'

Lilly allowed her embarrassment to surface. 'Never mind me. I've forgotten the art of small talk.'

'It's a ride on a bicycle to the Yacht Club. I can't see an argument against a little harmless exercise.'

'I'd rather stay here with you,' she sniffed.

Miss Pearl kept her head bent over her work and did not look up. 'I hope you don't think that we are a nuisance, but it seems to my sister and me that you're not making the most of your time in Nainital.'

Pearl Pinkney's comment startled her. 'I beg your pardon?' Lilly said.

'You don't attend the socials at the Club or the evening concerts at the bandstand. People come to the hills to get out and about and you're not joining in.'

'Did neither you nor your sister ever marry?'

The old lady massaged the small rings embedded in her mottled fingers. 'I see you wish to divert the conversation. My sister was married but that all fizzled out and she reverted to our family name. Her private tragedy was that there were no children, you see, and it was easier to pretend she had not married at all than to have the, um, social awkwardness of explaining that she was childless.'

'And you?'

'Oh! There was someone years ago, in my salad days, but he was married.'

'You didn't want the scandal?'

'It was not that so much and like you just now, I don't wish to pursue that discussion. But you're a young girl and should try to have fun while you're here. It's the season and Nainital is full of bachelors desperate to flirt.'

'I'm not very experienced with men and I am married with a five-year old son.'

'No one need know that, unless you tell them.'

'If I'm kicking up my heels, my husband will find out. I told you I'm in disgrace and he's sent me here with Binnie so she can keep tabs on me and report back.'

'It seems unlikely she'd be bothered to sit down and write.'

'If not her, he'll have someone in his service who he's paid to spy.'

Miss Pearl snipped the thread on her sewing. She looked matronly, pink, clean. 'It seems to me that you have a golden opportunity to do something about that. You have three months in which to learn stealth; like a tiger in the undergrowth.'

'Make sure I'm not seen?'

'I would think that sort of thinking would hit the nail on the head to perfection.'

Lilly found the iron-framed bicycle at the back of the boarding house. By now the morning had deteriorated further; overhead, the clouds were dark. She felt a few flecks of rain as she hitched up her skirts and freewheeled down the hill to Mall Road. Within minutes, the heavens opened and she was soon soaked to the skin.

To her left, the lake seemed black, and discarded corn husks – yellow bobbing blobs in the angry water – butted their heads against the shore.

As she set off, Lilly had no confidence in her physical condition but soon, wobbling only slightly as she pedalled through puddles, chin to chest to shield her face from the rain, she found herself enjoying the exhilaration of a freedom that had been years in the lacking.

She'd ridden as a child, round and round the tennis court, hands out to her sides, laughing to her grandmother that she could balance and steer with her legs. Where has that carefree girl gone? she berated herself.

When she reached the Yacht Club, she leaned Miss Pinkney's bicycle against the wall and stood for a moment, looking at the wooden hulled yachts with their stiff triangular sails, wishing for all the world that she could scoop Teddy up and sail far away.

She turned back to the front door, again horrified to read the notice nailed onto the woodwork, painted in thick gold letters on a shiny black background. That Indians were barred after dogs seemed to reinforce how low they were thought of in India:

MEMBERS ONLY
NO DOGS
NO INDIANS

Lilly pushed the door open, walked past the turbaned official who sat behind his desk at the entrance, past a board that recorded the past winners of the Commodore's Cup and, screwing up her courage, climbed the staircase to the upper deck.

Noel's sister was sitting by herself at a baize-covered card table, playing a game of Patience. She looked up and watched Lilly's approach across the planking. 'Hello you! Come and join me in a game of cards.'

Lilly stopped and contemplated the deserted room. 'I thought there was a coronation concert meeting this morning. I came to offer to play the piano.'

Conti took a sip of her drink. It was difficult to know exactly what it was from the fruit and foliage in the glass. 'Haven't you heard? The coronation is cancelled because King Edward is unwell. Noel says that a telegraph has been sent around the Empire. There's a sign on the wall over there.' She jerked her head towards the notice board.

Even from where she was sitting, Lilly could see clearly the notice typed in bold black print: JUNE 24TH 1902. THE KING ILL – CORONATION POSTPONED.

Lilly took a half step towards her. 'In that case, what are you doing here if there is no rehearsal?'

Conti picked up her cards and shuffled them with ease. 'I came down to get out of the house.'

Lilly felt a jolt of disappointment that she was alone. She allowed herself one glance about the room and did her best to sound indifferent. 'Is Noel not with you?'

'He was going to come, but he's taken to his bed, unwell.'

The cool, wood-panelled clubhouse smelled of wood ash and stale beer. It was sickly and made her feel nauseous. 'He was right as rain at midnight.'

'It's always sudden, here. While we were clearing up, he said he'd had a lovely evening chatting to you and told you about his plans for the village and his tenants. He's very wary who he tells because, well, you know how folk here think about the natives. And then, with no notice at all, he clutched at his stomach and ran off to his room.'

'Was it something he ate?'

'Who knows? One moment one is perfectly fine and the next' – she drew a finger across her throat – 'dead as a dodo.'

Lilly wondered at her flippancy. 'That's a cheery outlook.'

'Realistic. A lot of fellows come to Naini suffering from bouts of cholera. The town was developed as a sanitorium after it was discovered by a sugar trader in the 1840s.'

'Noel lives here, so surely he is acclimatised.'

Conti flung a look at her. In all seriousness she said, 'No one is immune.'

'That's true. I lost my little girl to cholera. It's a pernicious disease.' She swallowed hard and fought the tremble in her lip.

'I'm so sorry to hear that.'

Lilly shook her head. 'I'm not the first woman to lose a child in India.' Trying to keep her voice steady, she went on. 'Is Duffy still up at the house with Magic Mary or whatever her name is?'

Conti gathered up the cards and gave them a comprehensive shuffle. 'Are you sure you don't want to play?'

'I'll watch you, if that's all right?'

With expert fingers, Conti dealt out the cards onto the table and looked at her shrewdly. 'I think you can do better than Magic Mary. One might even suspect a little envy. Margot's often up at the house with Duffy so you should come up and meet her. I don't think you had a chance to talk to her last night and she really is nice. Get her to read your palm.'

'Does she do that in her spare moments between séances?'

'Why don't you like her?' Conti's expression was friendly, smiling, confused.

They faced each other across the card table and Lilly could not help feeling like a child being pulled up over a poor performance at school. 'I never said I didn't.'

Conti gathered up the cards and swept them into her palm. 'You didn't have to, Lilly. It's written all over your face.'

Chapter 6

Three weeks after Lilly and her mother arrived in Nainital, the Assistant Superintendent of the District's Forestry Department summoned them to a little gathering for Sunday tiffin on the Residency lawn. As always, it began with mulligatawny soup, which was followed by some variation on a curry he'd left his cook to dream up.

The guests sat around a long, low table and ate their food off Spode china, drank wine from a Venetian decanter and, in between the courses, smoked cigarettes from a heavy silver box.

Noel, who showed no lingering effects from his illness, and his sister were amongst the party, but to Lilly's surprise, his house guest had not been included.

Binnie was sharing a joke with the Commodore who was sporting a straw boater, spotless white trousers and a naval blazer with shiny gold buttons. Every so often she pressed her parasol handle against her lips in some curious affectation, looking at him with an eagerness that Lilly found alarming.

The pair had arrived shamelessly late, the meal already in full swing. Their apology was insincere and impressed no one. 'What's an hour either way?' The commodore threw his head back, spluttering with laughter, and almost dislodged his eyeglass. 'Try dining with a Nawab. Add half a day to the time you're invited, and you'll still be early, what!'

Unusually, her mother was hatless, with not a hair out of place; she wore a gown Lilly did not recognise. Her lace gloves were elbow-length, and over the left-hand cuff she wore a strap watch, which she glanced at too often to have gone unnoticed.

Lilly shredded the rose petals that floated in her finger bowl, envying her mother her ease, too inhibited herself to say very much. She had never felt more awkward, more tongue-tied in her life. I'm dull, she thought. Grandmother would hate to see what I've become. A dullard. In her head she began to compose a list of words that began with dull. Dullish, dull-brained, dull-witted. She was so absorbed in her mind game she missed the start of the conversation.

Noel leaned forward, his elbows on the table. 'I'm going to disagree with you, Mrs Rivers. It's only by getting off the beaten track that you see the real country. I'd like to broaden her horizons, so could you please spare Lilly to come on my tiger hunt?'

Lilly looked back and forth between them. 'Tiger hunt? Am I allowed to know more before I'm committed to anything so dramatic?'

Conti touched her arm. 'Noel is the resident tiger-hunter in the area. When a tiger comes into a populated area, they turn to my brother for help.'

Lilly saw the pride in her friend's green-blue eyes and smiled. 'I can imagine there's no one more capable to ask.'

Noel's brow furrowed. 'I'm against shooting anything that I'm not going to eat but occasionally a tiger turns nasty and will predate on people. That's when I am asked to assist. I kill out of necessity and not for sport.'

'Are you hunting a man-eater this time?' Lilly asked.

He reached for his pipe. 'Happily not on this occasion, as I have a rather gloomy view of the future of tigers in

India. I'd estimate even now that we have a scant three thousand.'

Lilly was surprised the number was so small. 'Is this the trip to help Duffy find an animal for his act?'

Noel took his tobacco pouch from his pocket and began to fill the bowl. 'Yes. We'd be a party of four. Duffy, me, Conti and you.'

Binnie sat back and crossed her arms. 'Where would you stay? In a *dâk* bungalow?'

'There are no government rest houses where we are going – no real human habitation at all, to be honest. It's thick jungle so we'll have to camp. The roads are bad – narrow and stony – and there is water to negotiate.' He stopped to puff on his pipe. 'Not to worry, though. We'll only be gone for a few days at most.'

Noel went on to explain that they had arranged a camp and an advance party had set off two days earlier with a cage on a bullock cart, tents and camp supplies. 'A skeleton crew, boy to wait, cook and water carrier but we'll manage all right.'

Binnie gave Lilly a sidelong look. 'Shall you ride? I'm not sure if she knows how.'

Lilly saw the hint of speculation in her mother's eyes and knew she had no idea. She opened her mouth to set the record straight, but Noel jumped in first.

'We'll take an elephant, not hill ponies, because Conti is not a confident rider.'

Binnie seemed confused by the idea. 'Where will you find an elephant in Nainital?'

'The trunk road, of course,' the Commodore quipped, his monocle flashing in the sunlight.

Binnie rapped his knuckles with her tasselled fan and pushed out one of her falsetto laughs. 'You are too amusing, Puffs.'

'Aim to please, Kitten. Aim to please.'

Puffs and Kitten?

Even the ever-patient Noel looked exasperated. 'There are elephants in the animal enclosure near your guesthouse. The British visitors hire them for their moonlit picnics in the Ayarpata Hills.'

Binnie looked faintly horrified. 'Lilly wouldn't be bold enough to go on anything like that.'

Perhaps I would, thought Lilly. Binnie wouldn't acknowledge her parental role, yet wanted to take control of her anyway. She eyed her mother and smiled, 'I'd be delighted to tiger-hunt with them both, I just need to know where and when.'

Apart from the elephant at Warren's Circus, Lilly had not encountered an elephant up close. The giant beast was being ridden by a man who sat just behind the creature's ears and was advancing down the lower side of Mall Road, a wooden construction on her back. When she was within ten or so yards of them, the elephant stopped and plucked a trunkful of grass from the side of the road and smacked it against a leg.

Lilly swung round to Duffy. 'What's it doing?

'Her name's Pinky.'

Lilly shrugged. 'What's Pinky doing with the grass?'

Margot gave a heavy sigh. 'She's shaking off the insects before she puts the grass in her mouth. It's peculiar to Indian elephants. African ones don't do that.'

'How do you know?'

Margot threw a hand towards the animal. 'When you're around them for nine months of the year, it's hard *not* to know. The chappie getting down from behind her head is the *mahout*, Ashok, and before you ask, he's the one who works with, rides, and tends an elephant, as if it were his baby.'

Lilly flinched at her tone. 'I do know that people are known by the job they do, but in respect of elephants in particular, I am a novice. You should bear that in mind and explain how I am to get up into that.' She pointed upwards with her furled umbrella towards the wooden box, feeling a mounting regret at her wild impulse to tiger-hunt with Noel. 'Is there no ladder to assist us?'

Margot rolled her eyes and gabbled on for some moments until at last she said, 'The *mahout* will instruct the elephant to kneel and then you can climb aboard.'

With studied interest, Lilly watched as the elephant sank to its knees to bring the *howdah* – she now knew this to be the box – lower down. 'We are agile enough to jump in but you may find it a little more challenging. That being the case, Pinky will be asked to lower her trunk and you can use that as a step, if you can't manage by yourself.'

Over my dead body, Lilly thought, as she watched the agile spiritualist vault aboard. Muttering under her breath, she scrambled up without extra assistance, vowing to herself that she would coax some flex into her limbs if it was the last thing she ever did.

The *howdah* looked like a four-legged upturned table, divided by a central partition with one seat in each of the four sections. It was strapped onto the elephant's back by a length of thick rope. Lilly squeezed onto the front bench, wedged uncomfortably close to Noel, while Margot and Duffy sat on their cushions behind. Whispered words from Ashok raised the elephant to its feet, the angles at which they lurched entirely unexpected.

'Hold onto the sides with both hands and try to relax.' Duffy bent forward and spoke into her ear. His dark curls brushed her cheek and the nearness of his face aroused thoughts in her she found quite confusing. 'If you fight the motion, you'll find yourself seasick. You too, Noel.'

Lilly gave Noel a quick sideways look and saw that behind his glasses his eyes were narrowed with concentration, his knuckles white where he overgripped the *howdah*'s sides. She thought he looked like a drowning man in turbulent water, clinging onto a life raft.

She leaned towards him. 'Look at the scenery, Noel. It will take your mind off the motion. I did that coming out on the P&O when I was horribly sick.'

Noel clenched his teeth. 'I never track tiger on elephant back, so this is a new experience for me. Not one I am thinking of repeating.'

'I didn't think we had an option, did we, when Conti was coming too?'

'We could have taken hill ponies and when Conti changed her mind about the trip, I did think about it for a bit. That's the best way, but it's slow going and we don't have the luxury of time. As it is, it will take us the better part of the day on this lurching thing and the going will only get worse. We're not proposing to stop other than to answer the call of nature, so I hope you had a good breakfast.'

Lilly sat back in her seat and gave in to the motion of the elephant. With each lumbering stride, the vast expanse of wild, green country seemed to roll before her.

This was real jungle, dense and thick, but, even so, Lilly was surprised at how quickly it became impenetrable. Exchanging dry heat for a sticky humidity, she felt suffocated beneath the forest's dense, dripping canopy. She no longer imagined the jungle as a place of soft mists and mystique, nor had she imagined it would be so quiet, so darkly damp and – if she was being honest – quite so threatening.

Over and over, Noel took off his spectacles and wiped at the fog with his sleeve. He peered into the green depths as he took them on and off, but she had no idea what he saw amongst the tangle of vines and saw-toothed leaves.

Twice a low-flung branch almost parted her from her pith helmet; thorny vine tore at her sleeve if she forgot to keep her elbow in as the *mahout* hacked his way through the tangled branches with the machete he wore in his belt.

All day, they rode on in the silent half-light amongst the giant rough trunks of deodar trees, the elephant responding to a nudge from the *mahout*'s foot or a hand on its ear. Just as the evening was drawing in, they came to a wide, grassy space in the heart of the jungle with three tents set up around it. A wooden hut stood to one side of the clearing where she supposed camp supplies were stored. Noel said the site was ideal for tiger-hunting at this time of year before the main rains came. It was ringed on the east and west by an outcrop of large boulders towering up like a blockade beyond a riverbed where the water level was low. As soon as the monsoon rains fell on the hills in Nainital, he explained, the river would become a torrent and the whole place would be underwater.

He stood up and stretched his hands up over his head. 'Tigers will come here to drink when the water is benign. They like to swim, too, and beyond the rocks they can disappear into dense jungle as if they'd never been here.'

Lilly assessed the placement of the tents relative to the water and her mouth went dry. She licked her lips, hoping to regenerate some saliva. 'I would have thought the water might be a deterrent and that's why you chose this spot to camp.'

'The usual misconception of a city dweller.' Margot's voice was witheringly sharp.

Duffy said nothing either to confirm or contradict.

Its tail wagging, a dog ran up barking and Lilly recognised him to be Noel's dog, Goose. Two bearers wearing loin cloths and very little else followed the dog and placed a stool by the elephant. Obeying the *mahout*'s quiet command, Pinky knelt down.

The two men were off first, then Margot got to the ground with a clean, bold jump, which Lilly found impressive after hours confined in a narrow box. She hitched up her skirt in one hand and stumbled down from her cushion, muscles stiff from sitting, using first the elephant's trunk then the stool as a step.

Duffy gave her his arm to steady her descent. 'You must be dead beat. I fancy you might like to lie down for a bit or refresh yourself or whatever it is you girls do.'

'Just don't suggest a cup of tea.' Margot clasped her hands together as if imploring him to save her life.

Noel conversed with the two men in a local dialect, organising, he translated, for the elephant to be taken to the river to drink. 'The camp bearers have set up outside for our dining arrangements as the weather is good and they already have a decent blaze going. The ladies are to have a tent apiece and Duffy and I will share. First, though, a reviver around the fire will be just the thing to buck up our spirits.'

Lilly took a seat in one of the wooden framed chairs and stretched out her legs. 'I feel I should be walking around camp having sat down all day.'

'I didn't think you were a devotee of exercise, Lilly,' Margot said.

'I haven't had the opportunity to indulge myself.'

'Some of us earn our living by keeping physically fit. We can't afford to let ourselves slide.' The thrust was swift and hit its mark.

'Do you have an act in the circus, Madame Margot, besides summoning up the dead?'

Margot's mouth curved into a smile. 'I'm a bareback artiste. My horses are stabled at the high-altitude enclosure and I have practised every day since we've been at Naini. We're not on holiday and it takes a mere five minutes to get out of condition. Where would I be stumbling and tripping through my poses? Before you knew where you were, we'd be losing out on ticket sales and frankly, who wants to see a mediocre circus? Duffy's been up there daily, too, putting Mister Stripes through his paces. He'll teach the new cat the ropes, if we find one.'

The proprietorial *we* made Lilly bristle and her protest was out before she could bite it back. 'One less live cat roaming in the wild.'

Margot smoothed her wind-blown hair. 'What do you mean?'

Noel consulted the label on a bottle of whisky. 'Lilly means that this hunting trip is rather different to what I usually do.'

Margot's face changed. 'Oh?'

He poured a measure into four tall glasses and pushed them across the table. 'I'm normally called in to kill man-eaters, not to capture a tiger who's minding its own business, but I think our modus operandi will be the same. Tigers are creatures of habit. They use the same paths and trails. Drink at the same waterholes. We have plonked ourselves here in the middle of nowhere because we're hoping for a tiger that's not habituated to humans so won't have started to eat them.'

84

'Tell me you're joking.' Lilly swallowed, feeling quite shaken and picked up her glass and peered into the depths.

'Not one bit. There are plenty of man-eating tigers around, but we are not in danger here. A tiger will not attack you in your tent and the jungle will tell us when we need to be on our guard.'

'Really?' Lilly watched a troupe of grey monkeys playing in the trees and wasn't sure that could be true.

Noel threw back the contents of his glass. 'Take those monkeys. They will scream and stare at the ground if there is anything to alarm them and if you watch and listen carefully, there are plenty of signs to help the hunter. Sambar and chital leap into the air when a tiger is near. Birds call, deer bark. The jungle houses a cooperative society, each warning the other.'

Margot shooed a fly away from her face. 'My horses are very sensitive to disruption. It makes perfect sense that in the wild, animals would warn each other of danger.'

Lilly wondered if Margot could have learned all this in the circus but was not going to ask.

A drift of ink-black cloud passed over the sun and made Lilly shiver. The trees shook as a gust of wind chased through the camp; a fizz of lightning and a crackle of thunder followed.

Noel jumped up as the first fat drops of rain hissed on the fire. 'Come on, ladies. There's a storm brewing. Let's take cover in our tent as it's the closest.'

He ushered them towards the khaki canvas and lifted the flap; another gust almost blew them into the tent as the storm burst overhead.

In one corner there were two guns – a muzzleloader similar to the one her grandfather had used to teach her to shoot and a rifle – plus two or three saddlebags and a pair of rough boots. In the opposite corner two string camp beds placed side by side bore a selection of shirts and socks. Lilly wondered which *charpoy* belonged to which of them.

A battered trestle table on long spindly legs was covered with papers and books, and a camp table and four camp chairs stood on top of a rug. A corner of the tent was partitioned off; a bathroom lay beyond, Lilly presumed.

Lilly sank onto one of the string beds and looked back at the guns. 'You're not going to shoot the tiger, are you?'

'We don't plan to. We'll use a wooden box-trap baited with goat meat to encourage the tiger to enter. I don't favour the metal grille cage as the tiger can break its claws on the bars trying to get out. The box is the most humane way to capture a tiger without stressing it unduly and should also stop the tiger from overheating. The guns are simply for back-up if something goes wrong.'

Somewhat relieved, Lilly asked, 'Who's the better shot out of the two of you?'

'Are you a little nervy?' Margot crooked one beautifully shaped eyebrow.

'Nervy?' Lilly considered the word. 'Not at all, but I am wondering about the muzzleloader.'

Noel leaned forward in his chair. 'Do you know guns?'

'My grandfather used to stalk deer on his estate in Scotland. He preferred to shoot with the individually hand-loaded muzzleloader because it gave him the challenge of having to get close for a single, well-aimed shot to the head or heart. He liked a clean kill.'

Noel smiled. 'I agree. If you are shooting to kill, the animal mustn't suffer.'

Margot sat back in her camp chair and crossed her slim ankles. 'You said this tiger wasn't going to be killed. I hope you're right.'

Lilly tilted her head in agreement. 'Is this a permanent camp?'

Noel said it wasn't.

'But we've only just arrived and already the place seems lived in.'

'My tracker came ahead to stock up the larder with goat meat and he'll have started to unpack. The servants will have dealt with your luggage too but remember we're generally a bachelor crowd, so they might have got things wrong.'

Lilly smiled. 'I'm not likely to scold them, if that's what you're worried about.'

A faint hint of colour tinged Noel's cheeks. 'No, but my sister doesn't care for men servants to handle her, um, more personal items.'

Margot gave a snort of derision. 'I'm grateful for any helping hand; no one's that precious in the circus. I'll hand my tights over to anyone who is prepared to wash them.'

Noel sat back, his hands locked behind his head. 'I think that's what Lilly just said.'

A crash of thunder and rain beating on the canvas announced the storm was directly overhead. Noel's dog sat beside him, shivers running through his body but rather more excited than fearful; Lilly, too, thought the weather rather splendid.

Noel patted Goose's head. 'We're going after tiger tomorrow morning, so we'll make an early start. Knock knock at 4 a. m. Then we walk.'

Margot made a face. 'I'm not getting up at that time to eat tea and toast then walk about in the jungle where dangerous beasts are a-roaming.'

Lilly glanced at her. 'Isn't that why you came?'

She pursed her lovely lips and fixed her gaze on Duffy. 'I came to watch the caging of a tiger.'

A distant grumble of thunder raised Duffy to his feet. He lifted the tent flap and peered out. 'I think the worst of it has passed. I'll walk you to your tent, Lilly, and Noel can show Margot to hers. I'm sure you'll want a bit of a brush-up before dinner.'

He stared at her so fiercely that she felt the flush of panic stir her stomach.

'I'll certainly be glad to wash off the dust.'

Duffy motioned her towards him and held up the canvas to help her through. 'Whatever Noel says, I doubt anything wild will cross our path.'

'Or come into my tent, I hope.'

A hint of amusement brightened his eyes. 'Not a wild animal, but a wild animal trainer is another beast altogether.'

'Charming,' Lilly said drily. 'You'd be more useful standing sentry outside the tent flap.'

Duffy chuckled by way of response.

They stepped outside to see that the storm had deluged the camp, turning the soil into thick, brown gloop. Lilly hitched the hem of her skirt out of the mud with one hand.

Slipping and slithering across the camping ground, he said out of nowhere, 'You're a woman.'

'You are keenly observant, Mr Puttnam,' she laughed.

'I need your help with Margot.' The playful edge had gone from his voice.

'In what way?' She stopped and felt the mud suck at her boots.

'You know.'

'I'm afraid I can only guess that you intend to woo her, and Noel said that you had no business to be entertaining such thoughts.'

He shook his head, seeming agitated. 'When did he say that?'

88

Lilly unstuck her right foot and continued to walk. 'When I saw you looking at her at the séance.'

'Can you judge a man by his looking?'

'Isn't that some sort of proverb?'

'I don't know. But I'm not seeking an entanglement with Margot.'

Lilly narrowed her eyes, confused at his words. 'Then I'm not sure what it is you're asking of me.'

'She's very possessive,' he whispered and then in a more normal register added, 'Think about it, would you? That's all.' His look and tone gave her a peculiar ache inside. 'Here you are. Delivered to your door. Women need protecting so sing out if you need anything and I'll come running. Dinner is at eight.'

A week ago, she would have said with certainty that Duffy had romantic thoughts towards Margot, but what was he saying now? That he had shifted his attentions to her? She shook her head. She was in no position to get involved with anyone. Even if he was quite dashing.

As he strode back to the tent he was sharing with Noel, she held open the flap of her own tent and watched him, in two minds about whether to go after him.

There was no moon that evening, but the stars glittered bright in a jet-black sky.

Outside, illuminated by a pair of spirit lamps, they sat around the camp table on chairs still damp from the rain; around the edges of the camping ground, Lilly saw that fires had been lit. There was not a breath of wind and beyond the burning circle of fire, the jungle was still, dark and indistinct, and seemed to press in upon them.

They dined on jungle fowl under a cloud of tobacco smoke to keep the insects off, and the evening slipped away.

By ten o'clock Noel slapped a hand on his thigh. 'We've had an arduous day and we have an early start before us in the morning. Time for bed, people.'

As they rose from their seats, deep in the distance, something barked.

Lilly started. 'What's that?'

'Jackal, but a long way off,' Noel said.

'You're not nervous about sleeping in a tent, are you?' Duffy asked, still sipping his drink.

'There isn't the smallest reason to be.' Noel picked up a lantern and hitched the rifle over his shoulder. 'I'll walk you ladies back. You stay here, Duffy, and enjoy your drink, unless you want to do the honours?'

Duffy's face was cast in shadow and impossible to read. 'I'm happy to finish my brandy and then I'll turn in. You sort out the girls and I'll see you all in the morning.'

With the help of a hissing lamp, the smell of damp canvas in her nostrils, Lilly slipped out of her clothes and sought refuge in her bed.

As she lay alone in her temporary home, she acknowledged that she had not been truthful with Noel; she was more nervous about sleeping in a tent than she wanted to admit and only got under the covers as she deemed it a safer alternative to sitting up all night in a chair. She chided herself for letting her parent goad her into coming along on this trip. *A tiger hunt, really? Must try not to let Binnie get the better of me again.*

Alert to every whining insect, to every rustle beyond the tent walls, to the footsteps that passed and re-passed her tent, Lilly drifted in and out of sleep.

She awoke many times that night, until at some brutal hour, a portentous cough followed by a native voice outside her tent pulled her from her dreams. 'Time for knock, knock is coming, *Memsahib*. Best that you are getting up.'

She dragged herself out of bed and, not bothering to wash, dressed quickly in her clothes of the previous day, with little regard for her appearance. Outside it was still dark, but dawn was not far off. In the chill of tropical early morning, they took their first breakfast under a large India Rosewood tree that stood near their tents. The *khansama* in charge of the camp brought them tea in a chipped brown teapot and poured it out in big, thick cups.

Duffy sat by the fire, collar open at the neck and his shirt sleeves rolled up over his arms, the curly hair on his exposed skin making her quiver.

'Are you cold?' he asked her.

'No. You?'

'Not I.' He rubbed at the stubble on his chin; too early, it seemed for extended conversation.

Noel appeared wearing shorts and long socks as she was finishing her toast. She knew straight away that her clothes were all wrong; that in her tailored suit and petticoats, she was ridiculously ill-attired.

'I don't have the proper outfit for a tiger hunt. That's what comes of making impulsive decisions without due reflection.' *I sound like Royce.* 'But I'm still glad I came,' she continued weakly.

Noel sat on a camp chair, took the glasses from his nose and wiped them on his shorts. 'We heard a tiger in the night, so Ashok has already set off on his elephant with a net and an assistant and we're just waiting for the second of the guns. You could have gone with him if only we'd known you were bothered about your clothes. Too late now, though, so here's the form for the day. Ranjeet will lead carrying the muzzleloader. Lilly, you keep close behind him, then Duffy and I'll bring up the rear with the rifle. We walk in single file, sticking together and no talking. This is Ranjeet's show, and we respect his rules if we are to catch up with a tiger for Duffy.'

By the side of the men's tent, Noel's tracker, Ranjeet, was cleaning the muzzleloader. Noel leaned forward and lowered his voice. 'When he was eleven years old, he was mauled.'

Lilly saw that one side of his face was higher than the other, his mouth raised at the corner as if hitched up by a string.

'The bones on one side of his face were crushed in the tiger's mouth. One eye stands permanently wide and he is unable to blink, but he's a first-class fellow. Knows his stuff.'

As if he felt her gaze upon him, Ranjeet put his hand to his cheek, to cover his ruined face. She lowered her eyes, ashamed. 'Was he one of the childhood chums you told me about?'

Noel tried to smile but she saw the effort it took him. 'My best friend. And his disfigurement is entirely my fault.'

'I'm sure that's not the case.' She touched the back of his hand, hoping to reassure him.

'I dared him, you see. To put his head inside the tiger's mouth because I thought it was dead. But it was only playing, like Ranjeet and I.'

Horrified, she sat still, testing her response. 'You were both boys. Playing together. Children make errors of judgement all the time.' Unfortunately, she thought, some are more consequential than others and you both have to live with that.

There was a sick, almost shamed look on Noel's face. 'If I could turn back the clock and change places with him, I wouldn't hesitate for a second.'

*

A thin white mist hung above the ground when they set off from the clearing, too early yet for the sun to have burned it off. There was a stillness about the jungle that she found unsettling; there was no noise from bird or beast, no murmur of wind in the trees nor even a chirp from a frog. It was as if the mist had blanketed the jungle in silence and nothing was permitted to speak. It gave her an eerie feeling, not welcomed in the least by someone recently beset with nerves.

Before they had gone ten paces towards the riverbed, the dew on the wet grass had soaked through her boots and the bottom six inches of her skirts were damp and heavy.

The trees grew close together and beneath the thick canopy, the air was dank and smelled of last year's leaves. Noel's dog trotted by her side, his tongue lolling from his mouth. Occasionally he pushed his nose into her palm as if he sensed her unease. A distant roar sent a shiver down her spine and not for the first time, she wondered at the folly of this expedition. Against a new flurry of nerves, she was forced to consider whether she had any business being there at all.

'Hold your skirts well up, Lilly,' Noel whispered. 'This grass is just the place for giant millipedes.'

With a total disregard for her ankles that would have been unthinkable had Royce been anywhere near, she rolled over the waist band of her skirt three times.

For fifteen minutes they walked in silence, Ranjeet inspecting the underbrush and Lilly staring at the ground, wishing she had gone with the elephant in the dry safety of the *howdah*.

Eventually they came across a pug mark in the soft mud, sunk down low showing the weight of the animal they were tracking.

Ranjeet squatted down on his haunches and poked with his fingers. 'Big tiger. Female. Fresh. Fresh. More than four hundred pounds. We need to make a distance with her. Better is we are taking shelter,' he whispered and shook his index finger towards a dilapidated watchtower on the farther side of the riverbed.

'That's rather handy,' Duffy said facetiously. 'We should have brought a tiffin basket, collapsible table and chairs.'

Noel squeezed out a faint smile, but it faded almost at once. 'Maharajas used to sit in those *machans* all day. A live goat would be tethered to a stake, the tiger would be beaten out of deep cover to an easy firing distance and all the prince had to do was pull the trigger. The rest was done for him.'

'It doesn't look like it's been used in a while.' Though Lilly was glad the practice had died out, she had to wonder if the structure could still be sound.

Noel must have seen the uncertainty on her face. 'It will be perfectly safe but walk now and don't talk. We need to get up high.'

Barely had they reached the steps when a peacock cried out. Noel pushed at her back. 'Hurry up, the peacock's alarming. The tiger is coming close.'

The dog ran to the top of the steps, his tail wagging, and they followed him up the splintered wooden treads and stood on the platform, straining to catch sight of their quarry.

Ranjeet pointed. 'There. Are you seeing?'

Lilly peered at the grass. 'No.'

Duffy moved towards her and stood close. She could feel a tension in the air that had nothing to do with the proximity of the tiger.

'Follow the line of my finger – she's there, underneath that bush with the little white flowers,' he said, his breath warm on her cheek.

Lilly closed one eye and fixed on the spot where he was pointing. More than half her body hidden, a langur dead but not yet eaten by her side, the tigress lay stretched out in the long grass.

'She's beautiful,' Lilly murmured.

'That she is,' Noel said. 'And lethal. The tiger plays dead until the langur approaches. The langur's an inquisitive fellow and starts to play with her tail and then the tiger grabs him.' Even as Noel spoke, the tiger stood up, the langur dangling from her mouth. Her bottom incisor teeth stood up sharp, like yellow tusks.

The shout for the tiger to run died in her throat. It's not your business, she told herself. You can't get involved.

Noel straightened. 'She's going to find somewhere to feed. So now we can get down and follow her. The langur's too big for her to carry so we'll follow the drag line along the ground. She'll not want to run when her belly is full and that's the moment we'll trap her.'

Looking ahead but not at him, Lilly wiped her knuckles across her mouth. But it hasn't eaten yet, she thought, willing her to escape the cage they had planned.

Ranjeet led them a different route back to camp.

It took over an hour, weaving around great trees that rose from the thick undergrowth, calling a halt now and then to allow Lilly time to regain her strength. At the second rest stop, sitting side by side on a log, Noel's voice broke in on her thoughts.

'You are very quiet. Not too pooped, I hope.'

She shook her head. 'I was just thinking what Teddy will be doing right now.'

He bent over and relaced his boot. 'Are you thinking of going home?'

Lilly picked at the mud on her skirt. 'I can't. At least not yet.'

Half turned towards her, he sat so close that she could see the first dusting of grey at his temples, the tracing of tiny lines around his eyes. 'You must be missing him dreadfully.'

For a moment, misery caught at her throat and rendered her silent. 'I never stop thinking about him, but I've a long time to wait before I see him again,' she said at last. 'I'm finding it really hard.'

His eyes were full of understanding. 'You'll see him again before you know it. Time has a habit of racing by. Speaking of which' – he looked at his watch – 'we should get a move on and get back to camp. They'll be wondering where we've got to.' He got to his feet and, smiling with his eyes, extended a hand. 'Need a leg up?'

She rose and shook out her skirt. 'No, thanks. I'm not done for yet.'

At length, the dense jungle gave way to thin brush and they reached the clearing from where they'd set out.

Ranjeet handed the muzzleloader to Duffy, warning him that it was still primed. 'Maybe tiger's gone to ground but with animals we are never absolutely knowing. Keep gun with you while by water.'

Noel hitched the rifle over his shoulder. 'That's sound advice. Ranjeet and I will check with the camp boys to see if Ashok has been back with the elephant. Given the early start, you two might want to have a doze and put your feet up for a bit. Breakfast will be at least an hour.'

Lilly set off towards her tent, keen to scrub the dirt off her clothes.

'Vanquished or victorious?' Wearing spotless white muslin, Margot rose from the chair she had stationed outside her tent, shading her face with a parasol. Lilly stopped in front of her, unsure what to say.

Margot quirked an eyebrow in Duffy's direction. He had taken up position on a big white boulder set into a thin wedge of riverbed.

For a second, Lilly wondered to what she was referring and assumed she meant the tiger. 'We did see a tiger so in that respect we were victorious but we didn't catch her so in that respect we were vanquished, if that's what you mean? Noel and Ranjeet have gone off to see if the camp boys have any news. He said breakfast won't be too long.'

Voice raised, Margot called across to Duffy, although he was hardly twenty paces away. 'Do you want to join me for a second breakfast?'

He shook his head. 'I'm going to sit here for a bit. Ranjeet has gone with Noel to check in with the boys. I'm keen to find out if anyone's seen the tiger so I'll get something to eat later on, thanks all the same. You can give me a drink before lunch though; I'd be delighted to join you for that.'

Margot collapsed the parasol and disappeared into her tent, but Lilly found herself confused by the exclusive implication of their exchange. Weren't they all supposed to be on this trip together, not splitting up into separate groups? Privately, Conti had told her she'd given up her place so Lilly could get to know Margot better but so far, they'd hardly exchanged a word.

Now might be a good moment to pick up on whatever Duffy had started to confide, she thought, and squelched her way back to the water, across the soggy terrain.

She saw that he had propped the ancient muzzleloader against a rock, the barrel pointing to the sky and all thoughts of Margot flew out of her head. 'Put the gun flat. It's primed and could go off if it topples over. That's how gun accidents happen. You can't be casual around them.'

Duffy rasped his nails along the line of his jaw but laid the weapon on its side. 'I forgot you were an expert with firearms.' His tone was not admiring.

Lilly felt a prick of irritation. 'Wouldn't it be easier to find a tiger that's been reared in captivity than to put ourselves through all this tramping through the damp undergrowth?'

Duffy reached into his pocket for his cigarettes. 'Easier, yes, but a jungle-born cat is ready for training months sooner than a captivity-bred animal and is ultimately less dangerous.'

'That seems a contradiction.'

Duffy swatted at a cloud of mosquitoes hovering in front of his face. 'A wild animal never loses his fear of man and can be intimidated into doing what you want of it. Prolonged contact with humans makes a cage-bred tiger contemptuous and eventually it will seize on his captor's weakness. So that is why we are "putting ourselves" through this and will try again this afternoon. No one's forcing you to come and, frankly, I doubt Margot will bother.'

Lilly felt sick at the thought of it. She wished she'd screamed at the top of her voice to scare the tiger away. Intimidating a creature to the point of submission felt too close to home and if the opportunity arose again this afternoon, well she'd make sure she took it, even if it cost him his prize.

She tried to make a joke of his words. 'I didn't spend all

yesterday swaying on an elephant to lounge about on a chair in a clearing.' She turned to where Margot had been sitting when suddenly she heard a noise. 'Did you hear that?' She swivelled back towards the rocks and spoke in a whisper.

Duffy looked at her. 'What?'

Lilly raised her hand. 'Shhh! There it is again. Didn't you hear a growl?'

He tipped his hat back off his face and laughed. 'Too much tiger talk, I'd say. I think you're being fanciful.'

She shook her head, wishing that Noel would return to the camp. Goose, though, was sitting on his haunches in the wet grass, ears pinned back flat against his neck. 'The dog's spooked. He's staring at the bushes at the edge of the clearing where we were walking earlier.'

Duffy would not be persuaded. 'Stop imagining things and give me some credit. I ought to know if I heard a rumble or not.'

In the canopy above, monkeys shrieked and stared toward the ground. Lilly focused her attention on the thick scrub. There was definitely something moving.

Keeping the edge from her voice, she said very quietly, 'Stay where you are and don't move. There's something in the bushes to your left.'

Duffy whisked round. 'Hand me the muzzleloader.'

As she reached down for the weapon, a tiger padded out of the vegetation, silent as a shadow. At a distance of less than a hundred yards, she watched it climb onto the rocks to face her, its black-tipped tail flicking from side to side.

As it stepped into a patch of sunlight, she saw the tiger clearly: small ears atop its enormous head, the delicate black and white stripes on its face, its long white whiskers. Crouched down, shoulders hunched, it flashed its long yellow fangs, staring her down with implacable, pitiless eyes.

Lilly could not have said for certain whether this was the animal they had seen with the langur but what she knew in her soul, when it swished its tail from its lofty perch, was that the tiger was going to spring.

'Keep still. The tiger's on the rocks above your head.'

Even as she spoke, the tiger gathered itself on its hind-quarters. With a mighty leap it launched itself upwards, flying through the air with paws stretched wide. As the tiger's massive form flew down in Duffy's direction, Lilly snatched up the gun, raised the stock to her shoulder and squeezed the trigger.

The muzzleloader went off with a vicious kick, the report a strident sound in the rock-strewn riverbed that brought Margot from her tent, Goose from the bush and Noel and Ranjeet running. 'We heard a shot,' Noel shouted. 'What's going on?'

Duffy lay stretched out on the ground, his face shiny with sweat, the sleeve of his shirt soaked in blood. 'I think you just shot me,' he joked.

Margot's eyes, wide with shock, revealed far more than she realised. 'I don't understand what happened.' She stared at the gun Lilly still clutched in her hand. 'You must have hit him, you silly woman.'

Willing herself not to say something she'd regret, Lilly breeched the gun and laid it on the ground. 'I took one shot at the tiger. It must have nicked him with a claw as it flew over his head. He was never in any danger from me.'

Margot dropped to her knees, cradling Duffy's head in her lap. Her complexion was grey, almost the same bleached-out shade as Duffy's own. She clutched at Noel's ankle, her eyes pooling with tears. 'Can't you get help before he bleeds to death?'

Noel tried to reassure her. 'There's not enough blood

to have touched an artery but we'll get him to the tent and apply a tourniquet for a bit, just to be safe. Mop up your tears, Margot, and go and find me a stick.'

For a moment Lilly didn't move and stared at the lifeless animal, its magnificent body crumpled and still. *Poor tiger. You wouldn't be dead if we'd all stayed at home.* She exchanged a steady look with Noel. 'It was going after Duffy. I didn't have a choice.'

He ran a hand over his tawny stubble. 'No one's blaming you. Any of us would have done the same thing. It was a very plucky thing to do, Lilly – taking a pot shot at an animal at a higher elevation. The outcome for you could have been deadly serious if the tiger had landed its weight on you. But' – he motioned at Duffy – 'we could do with the disinfectant from my tent, if you wouldn't mind.'

Lilly started forward but she caught her toe in her skirt and it caused her to stumble, landing awkwardly on her knee. Noel held out his hand, and helped her to her feet. He nodded at her, then drew away his hand and flicked at her clothes with his handkerchief.

She thought that he was about to say something further but he turned back to Duffy. 'Come on, old chap. Let's get you up and see about making you more comfortable.'

A little before mid-afternoon, Noel was waiting for her by the campfire, a half-smoked pipe in his hand. 'I've patched him up as best I can but there's not much I can do for him here. He's got a nasty scratch on his arm which is now bandaged, but he needs proper medical attention.'

Lilly's mind was racing. 'Infection?'

'From the tiger's strike, yes, because bits of meat get stuck under their claws and soon turn rancid in the heat.'

'Then we must get him back to Nainital and no more

tiger-hunting.'

He knocked out the ashes from his pipe on the heel of his boot. 'I agree. We'll let the arm settle for now and move him tomorrow morning.' He pulled a flask from his pocket and held it towards her. 'You looked a bit shaken up earlier. Want a stiffener?'

Lilly shook her head. 'No, I'm all right thanks. I'd rather look in on Duffy and see if there's anything I can do.' She turned to go. 'I am so sorry you lost the tiger. What will happen to the remains?'

Noel shrugged and sloshed a fingerful of alcohol into the lid. 'The boys will take care of the tiger. They'll drag her into the bush I imagine and let nature take over. Not the result I'd have liked but we don't always get what we want. I stick by what I said earlier, by the way – you're a very decent shot.'

Lilly looked at the spot where the tiger had lain. 'I did have a lot of practice as a girl. My grandfather taught me a lot of things he would normally have taught his son. Although he never said, I know he missed my father dreadfully. When I saw the tiger above Duffy's head, years of practice kicked in and I picked up the gun and fired.'

Noel knocked back his drink. 'And yet you seem so . . .'

'So?'

He gave her an odd look. 'Vulnerable. Beaten up by life. Most of the time you look so unhappy, I sense there is more to your story than you want to let on.'

Lilly looked up into his frank, grey eyes. His tone was persuasive and in that moment she could almost have trusted him with every secret she kept hidden away. But she'd only known him a few weeks and dared not make a confidant of him yet. For all she knew, Royce could have the man in his employ. And so she hesitated, turning the words over in her mind.

'Yes, well.' She broke off, shying away from the truth. 'We are all the sum of our experiences, aren't we? One way or another.'

Inside the tent, Lilly found Duffy lying on the string bed, his eyes closed and lips compressed. His face was leeched of colour and his blood-stained shirt sleeve was ripped up to his shoulder, the mark where Noel's tourniquet had been an angry red welt on his skin.

Margot sat stiffly on her chair, dark shadows beneath her beautiful oval eyes. Oh my goodness! thought Lilly. She looks like a devastated wife awaiting news that her husband might die. Blinded by her tears, her hands made little pitiful movements until she dropped them to her lap. 'What must I do, Lilly? Give me a task or I fear I'll go mad.'

Lilly put out a hand and rested it gently on Margot's arm. 'Try not to make too much of it. Noel says he's all right. But we must get him back to Nainital and have him checked out at the hospital. He's given him what medicine he can, but in the morning we're going to strike camp and head back to Naini.' She handed Margot a basin of warm water and went on reassuring, calm. 'Take over from Ranjeet. He's an admirable tracker but a very poor nurse.'

Chapter 7

The following morning, just after nine, they struck camp.

Lilly remembered little of the journey back. All day long, as she clutched at the sides of the *howdah* with more gratitude to the swaying beast than she could have thought possible, she was fighting back the concern that Noel was wrong, that a young man might die.

It was early evening when they reached Nainital.

Stiff-limbed, Lilly scrambled out of the *howdah* in front of the Yacht Club; from there, Noel said, he would take Duffy to the Ramsay Hospital to have his wound tended.

Margot clung onto his arm. 'Take him to the Lady Dufferin Hospital. It's closer.'

Noel shook his head. 'I can't, Margot. It's staffed by female doctors for female patients only.'

'The Ramsay's at the other end of town.'

'I know, but it was built by the English for European men. He will be very well looked after.'

Margot blew out a resigned breath. 'I'll organise a rickshaw in that case. It's too far to walk and I'm not leaving his side until I know he'll get better.'

The lamplighter was already about his business.

There was a tint to the sky, a stain more red than pink, along the jagged outline of the mountains, which deepened as Lilly made her way home to the guesthouse.

The town had closed down for the day. Shops that overhung the route were dark and empty. Cooking fires had burned down to their embers and up ahead, a pair of stray dogs snuffled through the dirt.

Halfway along the Mall, she stopped and put down her portmanteau, regretting the impulse to walk. Her ankles ached and her boots still felt damp from the jungle. Where they protruded from beneath her skirt, she saw they were crusty with mud. *Clean and tidy at all times, Plumpty.* She shook her head to clear his voice from her mind and was on the point of picking up her bag when a movement caught her eye. In the lengthening shadows, she felt there was someone hidden. She took a breath as alarm squeezed the air from her lungs, and she snatched up her bag, her palm slippery with sweat.

Just as she was reaching the slope that rose behind St Francis Church, a rickshaw *wallah* came up behind her, his feet pounding, too close. He let out a long wail of warning and instinctively, she jumped to the side. She gave a scared little laugh. Why are you so jittery all of a sudden? she chastised herself as the man hurtled past. She stared for a while at the retreating wheels as if they might give her the answer, and then set off again, putting one foot in front of the other.

Although she was now accustomed to the rarefied mountain air, the lane to the guesthouse still presented a challenge. She took it in stages, but rounding the last bend, where the path rose more steeply, she had the eerie sensation she was indeed being followed.

She gave an involuntary shiver, as she felt it again – the prickle of certitude that trembled the hairs on the back of her neck. She wheeled round but there was no one there and yet, deep down, she *knew*. She wanted to yell

'Did Royce send you?' and demand that he show himself, but she kept the words to herself. Gripping her bag more firmly, she turned back and walked on with the stuttering chest of the hunted.

She saw a lone lamp burning in the guesthouse window and for some inexplicable reason Lilly thought of smugglers luring a ship to the rocks. Barely had she dropped her bag on the top step than the front door swung open and lamplight flooded the porch.

Something in the set of Pearl Pinkney's face warned Lilly that all was not well. She had an uneasy feeling that the old lady had been waiting for her and had taken ownership of the shocking news she was soon to impart.

Miss Pearl peered at her through her silver rimmed *pince-nez*. 'Oh, my dear, there's been quite a scandal. Your mother has run off with the Commodore and no one knows where they've gone. All Nainital is talking about it. I know that it's not supposed to be known that she's your mother, but it is. Already it is being talked about at the Residency and the Club. I really thought she was better than that. Her having been here before and all, she should have known how to behave.' Miss Pearl was almost breathless with indignation.

Lilly wondered how long she had been mounting guard. The whole three days she had been away? She picked up her bag and stepped into the hall.

'When was she in Nainital before?'

'She was at the other end of town, not with us.'

'At the Grand?'

Miss Pearl hesitated. 'I'm not exactly certain where she put up.'

Lilly wondered at the lie. Nainital was a small town. Miss Pearl had just said that everyone knew each other's business. She would know exactly where Binnie had *put up* and puzzled over why she had said she did not.

'When did she take off?'

'Oh, yesterday. She did a moonlight flit and owes us money.'

'She said the rooms were paid for.'

'Yes, they are, but all her little extras have mounted up.'

'Such as?'

'Special food for the dog, her evening tipples, temporary loans for this and that.'

'Where *is* the dog?' Lilly realised the house was silent.

'The one blessing is that she's taken that awful creature with her.'

'Pearl!' Her sister's voice called down from over the banisters. 'I'm clearing out that woman's room. Can you come up and give me a hand?'

For want of anything better to do, Lilly dropped her bag to the floor and followed Miss Pearl up the stairs.

The smell in the bedroom was overwhelming, opening up a door to a past she yearned for, and for a moment she let herself walk back. The bitter citrus smell of 4711 cologne and mothballs was pure Granny Wilkins. The room itself was overcluttered with heavy, awkward furniture; there was also a marble washstand with a scrunched-up towel dispatched to the floor and a dressing table littered with Binnie's tangled mess.

Her gaze wandered to the bed. There was something seamy about the crumpled sheets, the bedside table dusty with face powder and hairpins. She had a brief flash, an unsummoned image, of the Commodore in striped flannel pyjamas and squeezed her eyes shut. Binnie's bed was covered with clothes, discarded magazines, and *Lady Audley's Secret* – the novel she had been 'reading' since she got here – still as yet in its uncut state. Lilly picked up the book, having read it several times. I have half followed the plot, she thought to herself. Heroine deserts her child, runs away somewhere else. Why on earth didn't I think to push my husband down a disused well?

The older Miss Pinkney – Opal – was a darker version of her sister. Also petite, she wore a long black ruffle-hemmed dress with a band of velvet around her neck, from which hung a heavy gold locket. An evening dress seemed an improbable choice of outfit in which to clear out a room.

'I don't suppose she left me a note?'

Miss Opal shook her head. 'I wish I could reassure you. But perhaps you would care for a cup of tea. Or a schooner of sherry. You must feel so let down.'

As Lilly took in the chaos, a mood of bitter resentment locked horns with the pain of another betrayal.

'I'm sorry, Lilly.' A hand touched her shoulder and she turned to find Conti beside her.

'You've heard?'

'I was at the Club just now when Noel came in. I came straight down to see what I could do to help.'

'Is there any one in Nainital who doesn't know?'

Conti cleared a space on the bed and sat down, patting at the space beside her. 'I wish I could be more of a comfort but it's a hill town. People talk.'

The two Miss Pinkneys excused themselves, and went down the stairs in search of a drink.

Lilly sat on the bed and stared at the back of the bedroom door. Her mother's dressing gown hung from a hook. It was so typical of her impulsive nature to leave such ruin in her wake. 'Why did Binnie not care enough to tell me herself?'

'She's whimsical.' Conti threw an arm around her shoulder and hugged her close. 'It's not just you. We were all deceived.'

'Whimsical!' Lilly cried, uncharitable thoughts towards her mother gathering in her head. 'She's a coward. She waited until I was safely out of the way so she'd not have to explain why, yet again, she has passed me over for a man.'

Conti fell back on the bed and laced her hands behind her head. 'I agree it's a rotten thing to do, but you could look upon what's happened as an awakening.'

Lilly shifted her position so she could see her face. 'How can you possibly say that?'

'Well . . .' Conti smiled, a twinkle in her aquamarine eyes. 'It's good to see you have some starch in your corsets.'

Lilly felt her hair slipping from its usual tight control. She pulled out the pins and threw them on the eiderdown, shaking her hair loose. 'Did Duffy get to the hospital?'

'He went in a rickshaw almost as soon as you'd left.'

'Alone?'

'No. Smothered by a fussing Margot.'

'Your words or his?'

Conti raised her eyebrows. 'That's an interested remark.'

Lilly had totally forgotten that Noel suggested Conti entertained thoughts in Duffy's direction. 'Not for me – but maybe for you?'

Conti sat up and hitched a shoulder in a half-shrug. 'On the face of it, he rather has it all, doesn't he? Chiselled good looks, physique, the sort of man who looks like he'd sooner sweep you into an embrace than shake your hand. But he'll be off back to the circus in a matter of weeks so I'm not getting involved. Noel also says he has a wife whose existence he is keen to conceal and there's something about him that doesn't seem quite right. Maybe you should have let the tiger have its way if he's that much of a bounder.'

Lilly nodded her agreement, feeling she'd had a lucky escape. Duffy had no business to be sniffing around Margot, but she hadn't imagined a wife. 'Does Margot know he's married?'

'Oh, I should think so. Concealing a secret in the hills is nigh on impossible. Imagine what it would be like for circus folk in and out of each other's business day and night. I'd say she intends to have him, wife or no.'

Lilly made an effort to get off the bed, but it was half-hearted. She sank down again and said, 'I think there's a bit more to it than that.'

Conti nudged her with an elbow. 'Did you two have a jolly good heart to heart? That was the point of me giving up my place, after all. You sharing a tent and gossiping in the dark like a couple of schoolgirls.'

'It wasn't like that at all. We each had our own tent and she kept herself to herself rather. She didn't join us on the morning walk. I couldn't see why she had bothered to come really but then from the way she behaved after Duffy was injured, I'd say she's deeply in love with him. I think he was going to talk to me about her but the accident got in the way.'

'The plot thickens but you'll never find out now. Up at the house, before the tiger hunt, I heard them say that they would be packing up soon. That's why it was so much of a rush to get to the jungle.'

'Where are they off to?'

'Lucknow, I think someone said. There's nothing much to keep you here now Binnie's gone, so why not think about going with them? It might be rather fun.'

★

After refusing refreshment, Conti didn't stay long, and downstairs in her sitting room, Lilly paced up and down, balancing the pros of Conti's suggestion against the cons. Miss Pearl, a silent silhouette by the window, eventually suggested Lilly sit in the sofa corner she had been occupying, before she wore out the rug.

Lilly toyed with the lace antimacassar on the chair arm. 'I can't run away to the circus. I never heard of a woman doing such a thing.'

Miss Pearl fingered her waistcoat buttons. 'You could always go to Noel. You'd have another man's protection if your husband hears that Binnie has left you on your own and appears on our doorstep.'

'The minute Royce finds out, that *will* happen. I am exiled here with my mother as my gaoler. He said my punishment would be far worse if I broke the conditions he set out.'

Miss Pearl removed her *pince-nez* and stared at her with quizzical eyes. 'I'm sure he didn't mean it.'

'You can't reason with a tiger if your head is in its mouth.'

The sharp eyes softened. 'Then all the more reason to go to Noel. He's had his eye on you since you came up to Naini with your mother. Many a girl would consider him a catch.'

'I am married, Miss Pearl.'

'But I sense you have feelings for him.'

'He's a dear, lovely man but the fact remains I'm not free and while Royce still has Teddy, I'm powerless to do anything other than what he tells me. I wish I could just run away or disappear in a puff of smoke.'

'You could do both, if you had a mind to.'

'That's nonsense,' Lilly sniffed.

Miss Pearl gave a little shrug. 'I was in the same position once with my Wilfred. I was going to leave with him and we had it all planned. When push came to shove, though, I couldn't go through with it.'

'Did you lose your nerve or did you not believe he really loved you?'

'Neither of those things. He was married to my sister and however much I loved him, I didn't have the heart to break hers.'

Miss Pearl walked over to the mantelpiece and straightened the brass fire guard. Looking up at the gilt-framed mirror, Lilly watched her face in the polished glass as she registered the letter propped against it. She turned on her heel and held it out at arm's length as if to distance herself from the reality of it.

'I completely forgot to say that the Indian mail came in yesterday. There's a letter for you.'

Lilly took hold of the envelope and looked first at the handwriting, then glanced at the postmark. She ripped it open, desperate for news of Teddy. Instead there were two sentences, scratched so deep into the paper that the pen had almost cut it through.

HOW WAS THE SÉANCE LILLY? THE ONE YOU FORGOT TO MENTION? There was no signature. There was no need. The handwriting was his. The message was his. The rage was vintage Royce.

Lilly's mind ran back and forth like a beetle under a jar. 'I told you my husband has spies.'

Miss Pearl shook her head. 'He writes with a furious hand.'

Lilly felt her mouth drop open. 'Did you open it? Do you know already what he's written?'

She saw by the way the old lady avoided her eyes that she had.

Lilly tore the letter into fragments and threw them in the fire. 'If he knows about the séance, he will know about the tiger hunt, that I can shoot a gun and exactly who I went with. And just now, coming up the hill, I had the strongest feeling that I was being followed.'

Miss Pearl's eyes met hers. 'In that case you must leave him.' She sounded nervous and her disquiet caught her like an infectious disease. 'No one has a prescriptive right to bully and I don't think you can afford to wait.'

Chapter 8

It was late by the time Lilly went up to bed, but agitated by the receipt of Royce's letter and the suspicion she'd been followed, she couldn't drop off to sleep.

In the space of a few hours, Nainital was no longer a safe little corner of India but a threatening British hill station, where no one she knew could be trusted. Who had written to Royce and told him about the séance? And if he knew about it, why hadn't he come for her? She cursed the impulse that had her toss his letter in the fire. The date on the envelope would have told her how many days it had been since he etched his anger onto the paper.

She stretched out on the left-hand side of the bed, close to the edge, and stared at an unpainted wall. She fingered the bump on her wrist that Royce had broken more than three times and the dent in her skull when he'd almost caved in her head.

She looked through the window at the three-quarters moon and folded her arms across her face. She knew exactly what he'd do if he came for her and if she tried to escape him again, she'd never get away.

Miss Pinkney was right – she had to leave her husband.

Engrossed in her thoughts, she did not hear the door open and only became aware of Miss Pearl when the train of her dressing gown snagged on the coarse Mirzapur rug.

'Are you awake?' Miss Pearl leaned over the bed, looking like a character from a novel by Mr Dickens, with her lace-edged nightcap and candlestick, which she held out with one hand, cupping the flame with the other.

Lilly pushed herself up on an elbow and tucked the eiderdown around her shoulders. 'I couldn't sleep.'

Nervously, the old lady looked about her. 'I have something for you, but I don't want my sister to see. That's why I am creeping about like a thief in the night.'

Lilly watched the small figure in her geranium-red dressing gown as she crossed over to the door and poked her head out into the corridor. She didn't close the door, but turned back to the room, the candlelight reflecting off her glasses. 'I think she's asleep, but she has the hearing of a bat, so we need to be quiet.'

'Is everything all right?'

'Like you, I couldn't sleep. I've been thinking about that husband of yours.' She crossed to the bed. 'Come with me. I have something to show you.'

Lilly pulled back the eiderdown and swung her legs to the ground. Picking up her heavy cotton robe from the foot of the bed, she fastened the corded belt and pushed her feet into her slippers. 'Where are we going?'

Miss Pearl put a hand on her arm and nudged her towards the door. 'Your sitting room.'

She led Lilly down the stairs and opened the door for her. 'Take a seat and I'll be back directly.'

Miss Pearl returned carrying a Huntley & Palmers' Arcadian biscuit tin with two ball feet and a curved handle. It was full of papers, letters tied with string and that same smell of 4711 clung to its contents. Miss Pearl lifted them out and underneath picked out a rectangular teak box, inside of which were items of jewellery, each piece individually wrapped in tissue.

'Wilfred gave me these. Every last piece. Of course, I could never wear them – my sister would have asked questions – and they were given as an investment against our future together.'

Lilly dropped into a chair. 'What happened to him?'

Her voice faltered a little. 'He died in the Mutiny at Lucknow, like so many of his regiment. He never knew about this.' She looked up, a sudden tenderness in her eyes and held up the hand-painted portrait of a new-born.

For a moment, Lilly couldn't trust herself to speak. 'Yours?'

'I have never shown anybody this. Not even my sister.'

Lilly rather doubted that Miss Opal didn't know, given the sisters' propensity to snoop. 'Do you want to tell me?'

Miss Pearl shot a quick glance at her watch, then turned and looked Lilly deep in the eye. 'We adored each other and made a child out of our love, but I had to give him away.'

Lilly felt deeply moved by this disclosure and stood up, putting her hand in Miss Pearl's. She led her to the sofa and settled her against a cushion. 'How ever did you manage?'

Miss Pearl sighed. 'I went away to a friend in Calcutta. Her husband worked for the East India Company's Council, and I stayed with them until the baby was born. After that, they arranged for the child to be sent to strangers. It was thought that severing all ties was the best arrangement. An unfortunate child brought into the world by a shameful woman should be set adrift.'

Lilly found her lip was trembling. 'What did you call him?'

A look of pure love passed over the old woman's face. 'Wilfrid, after his father, but I doubt his new parents retained that name.'

'How did you bear giving him up?'

Miss Pearl shrugged. 'The ache of loss still flares but sacrifices had to be made.' There was a mixture of love and longing in her voice.

'Binnie said that about Teddy. She said he will be sent away for his education. I have no idea how I will bear that when the time comes, as these weeks away from him now are torture enough.'

Miss Pearl crossed her ankles and settled back a little further into her seat. 'I believe sacrifice is a catch-all word we can use about almost any aspect of life that causes us great pain.'

'But you were Wilfrid's mother.' Lilly could not mask the rise of indignation in her tone.

'And Binnie is yours. There are times when one has to put oneself first.' Miss Pearl's voice was level.

Lilly pulled the cushion from behind her back and hugged it against her middle. 'She always does. Rejection and parental neglect are second nature to her. How many mothers track their daughter's development by letter for sixteen years from half a world away?'

'I think your mother is more complex than you might suppose.'

A circular swatch of light from the gas lamp outside the window fell onto the floorboard. 'What are you not saying?'

'It might be wise for you to talk to Noel. I am an old lady now, but one's thoughts and feelings are the same as when one is young. From what you say, you have very little to do with your child as it is, and you will learn to manage without him for the time being. Leave him where he is for now and chase your own happiness.'

'I am childless and yet I have a child. That makes me as poor a mother as Binnie.'

'Define yourself by what you are now rather than what you are not. Eventually you will find a way to reclaim your son.' She pushed the biscuit tin towards her. 'Nothing of what I have told you tonight is to be repeated, but I do want you to have the jewellery.'

Lilly shook her head. 'You barely know me. I can't possibly accept your treasures.'

Miss Pearl's chair scraped on the floorboards as she stood up. 'You have hinted at what your life is and I can imagine the rest. If you return to Cawnpore after your sentence is served, nothing will have changed. You son will be sent away and you will carry on trying not to displease but fault will always be found. Accept the jewellery because it will give you options. Women must look out for each other and, for what it's worth, I think your mother would approve of the gift.'

Wondering at the reference to Binnie, Lilly watched her as she crossed to the door and went out. Miss Pearl might look bent and frail, but underneath she was shot through with steel.

Chapter 9

Early the next morning, the guesthouse was silent as Lilly inched up the latch, trying not to breathe at the click of the door when she let herself out. Living with Royce, she'd learned how to close a door without a sound, easing it shut using her fingers to guide it into position then slowly release her hold on the handle until it sat silent in its place. She'd also learned to place her feet so that the sound of her shoes would not rile him. *You tramp about the house as if you're threshing corn.*

Fingering the gold cross around her neck, she walked down the hill to Mall Road, as the moon gave way to the pale rising sun. Royce had been brought up as a Catholic and did not believe in divorce. She knew he would never agree to one and allow her to leave with their son.

She stumbled on up the road, tramping over the Flats and up the winding hill. It was still a long climb up to Lake View, but even at the steepest pitch of the road there was no need now to stop, chest bent to knees as she fought for every breath.

Barely had she reached the last of the four stone steps to the rear veranda than the words were out of her mouth. 'I'm sorry to intrude on you so early but I fear I must ask for your help.'

Noel untucked his napkin from the neck of his shirt and looked up from his plate. He smiled and held out a hand. 'Come and sit down. Have you had breakfast?'

'I have no appetite,' she said and, walking up and down floorboards that were slightly tacky underfoot, filled Noel and Conti in about Royce's letter and how he could possibly have known about the séance.

'The thing is,' she finished up, 'even though I miss my son every minute of every day, I'm scared to go home.'

'You must try to avoid a knee-jerk reaction. Sit.' Noel pointed to a green rattan chair that had seen better days. 'I don't think you should panic just yet. The séance was weeks ago and if your husband was coming to fetch you home, he'd have been here by now. Carry on as normal with your letters. Say you didn't mention the séance because it was so lacking in novelty it completely slipped your mind.'

Conti fetched a cup from a glass-fronted cabinet and filled it with coffee. She put it on a low table by Lilly's chair and squeezed her hand. 'Noel's right. He may have written the letter in a fit of pique and means to do nothing further. Try to put it out of your mind.'

Lilly braced herself for the first ghastly sip. In no way did Conti's coffee mirror her sweet personality; overbrewed and bitter, it was never less than a trial. 'It's not quite as straightforward as that. I write seven letters on a Sunday afternoon and Miss Pearl posts one every day. But the news I send him recounts the week we have just had so everything I tell him is out of date, but I pretend it is happening currently.'

Conti's forehead creased to a frown. 'Then surely that's all right then. You *have* told him about the séance.'

Lilly ladled sugar into her cup. 'You are missing the point. He knew about the séance before I'd written to him about it. So, someone had to have told him. If he finds out about the tiger hunt, that I went off with two men into the jungle, I am not going to get away with a casual explanation.'

'Are you completely certain you're not overreacting? What did he think you would be doing here? Sitting in the guesthouse with your tatting?' Noel's manner betrayed no alarm.

She shrugged her shoulders, dismissing the question. Close down this conversation, she counselled herself. Do not confide in these two.

Noel sighed when she offered nothing. 'What are you not saying?'

She braced herself and looked into his eyes. He stared back with such infinite compassion that, scarcely aware of how it happened, she heard herself say, 'Royce barely lets me out of his sight and my opinion is never sought. About anything. Ever.'

He leaned in her direction. 'You are required to be seen and not heard?'

'It's more than that. I am required to listen and not speak. He tells me what to do, what to wear, what to think. If he hears that Binnie has run off with the Commodore and left me by myself, he'll be here before you can blink.'

Noel shifted uncomfortably in his seat. 'Isn't your imagination running away with you a little? This is the twentieth century and I don't know any man who would behave like that towards his wife.'

Lilly took in the concern on his face and realised how blessed she was to have such a staunch, warm-hearted ally. Noel was generous with his time, his house, his affection. Miss Pearl was right to have sent her in his direction.

She gave him a tight smile. 'I have Teddy to think of and have borne everything because of him.'

'You could divorce him for cruelty. Two impartial European witnesses to corroborate your story would do the trick.'

'I've often thought of that, but it wouldn't necessarily mean I'd gain custody of Teddy.'

Conti drew her feet beneath her and leaned back in her chair with her head among its cushions. 'Who could have told him?'

'Does anyone remember who was there?' Duffy had wandered onto the veranda, face pale through his suntan, his arm securely holstered in a sling. His deep brown eyes met hers and Lilly felt an alien fluttering in her chest that had nothing to do with the coffee.

Her cup rattled against the saucer as she misjudged its return to the table. 'There were eight of us around the table: Binnie, the Commodore, the four of us, Margot and that woman who has the scandal hanging over her head.'

Duffy took the seat next to hers. 'It could have been anyone.'

Noel ran his tongue over his teeth. 'It wasn't me.'

'I would never betray a friend,' Conti put in.

Lilly tapped a finger against her lips. 'The day we arrived in Nainital, I asked Binnie if Royce had asked her to spy on me. She said not, but she tells so many lies that it's impossible to get at the truth.'

'What about the Commodore?' Noel said.

Puffs? Lilly looked at him and shook her head. 'I don't know him well enough to say.'

'Pillow talk?'

Lilly turned her head away. 'No. She doesn't admit to me being her daughter for fear it will pin down her age. She's flighty, untrustworthy and dishonest, but one thing I can say with absolute certainty is that she won't have had that particular chat with the Commodore.'

Duffy let out a low whistle. 'Is there anything else that you want to get off your chest?'

Lilly shook her head. 'I'm sorry. Her running off has got me a little ruffled, that's all.'

'What about Margot?' Conti queried.

Wrestling between curiosity and envy, Lilly couldn't quite mask the spike in her voice, 'Can we call her in and ask her?'

'She doesn't live here with me.' Duffy's eyes were steady on her face. 'Would it bother you if she did?'

Lilly felt the flush creep up her neck. 'I thought, well, with you being here and after her reaction to your acci—'

'She has lodgings in town. Noel's mother rents out a couple of her houses during the season, which is how I found myself here. Margot went back there last night when I came home from the hospital.'

'And that's how I afford to live in this place.' Noel waved his arm about. 'Amongst the residue of someone's past glory. Mother buys properties at auction for a song, mainly from Britishers leaving Nainital, along with their effects in whatever state they happen to be in. We've thrown a few personal bits and bobs on the walls and shelves but the rest of it was a job lot. It needs a bit of spiffing up, but – pardon the expression – I barely own the pot we piss in.'

Lilly could not help but make a comparison between the house in Cawnpore where the servants measured the distance between the walls and rugs each morning with a stick. It was probably the most English home in India and the irony did not fail to strike her.

'Can your mother not help out?'

Conti shook her head. 'We don't see her very much. She feels she's done her bit providing the house and the rest is up to us.'

Lilly felt no small connection with that sense of aban-donment. 'I didn't realise that people would come and go quite so much. The Miss Pinkneys have been here for ever.'

Noel looked at her, a faint wrinkle on his brow. 'The British come up for the summer months between April and November. It's a transient community; people move and their properties become vacant. Ownership is a peculiar English obsession so there's always plenty of stock to buy, sell or rent out. Very few people stay in winter because it's freezing in the hills. Those who can, move down to the plains.'

Lilly brushed a stray hair from her cheek. 'If it's not too vulgar a question, where does Margot get her money? She's always so beautifully turned out.'

Duffy leaned back in his chair and balanced a foot across his knee. 'There's money to be made in the circus if you're any good and she's a big star. The show is mobbed wherever we go. I'd have thought you might have seen us when we came to Cawnpore at the end of April.'

Lilly shook her head. 'I was in a lot of trouble for taking Teddy to Warren's. I wasn't allowed out of the house after that even though I would have loved to have taken him.'

Duffy's smile was wide, his eyes bright slits of shining conker. 'A shame you didn't get to go. There's nothing in the world like the circus, which is why people run away to join it. It's a chance to jump out of your everyday and chase down new dreams. We criss-cross the country, somewhere new every month, and if you've a mind to disappear, you'd never be found.'

Conti stretched out her hand and touched his arm. 'Not everyone is so starstruck, but I do think that Lilly should move up here with us. That way she will have the two of you to look after her if Royce turns up and' – she turned and smiled at her brother – 'I know Noel will be thrilled to have her stay.'

'I'm not going to be here that much longer.' Duffy cradled his arm against his middle.

Noel watched him for a long moment. 'You'll be here longer than you think, old chap. Tiger scratches can be a bit tricky.'

Duffy narrowed his eyes. 'The doctor was pretty gung-ho up at the hospital. I've no broken bones and he says that by the end of the month, we'll be packing up the animals and heading down to Kathgodam, as planned.'

Noel stared at him and appeared to be collecting his thoughts. 'If Lilly leaves her things with the Miss Pinkneys and Royce arrives unannounced, he might think she's gone off on an impulse with her mother but intends to come back. If he asks around, we must all stick to the same story and say that she has.'

Lilly shook her head, wishing she'd said nothing. 'You are very lovely to offer but I can't stay up here. Surely you must see that by taking me in, you will be putting yourselves at risk and even if they do not mean to give me away, someone will say they have seen me. No.' she shook her head again. 'I must leave Nainital as soon as possible but it must appear to Royce I'm still here.' She paused for a moment as the realisation struck her. 'Which means I will have to continue with the letters.'

Conti's snub-nosed face lit up. 'It will be rather fun trying to outwit the fox. Like a mystery play and we are the actors. I'll buy a stack of picture postcards from the general store. There are still loads commemorating the passing of Queen Victoria, so you could write to Royce and say that there is so little going on here what with the cancellation of the King's coronation and so on that you are switching to postcards to fulfil your daily obligation. I'll post them for you as the Miss Pinkneys have done.'

Noel nodded enthusiastically. 'And if, say, you wrote three weeks' worth, that would buy you time while you quietly "disappear" somewhere.'

Conti spoke, her tone slightly lower. 'What about the house at Choti Haldwani?'

Noel gave a single shake of his head. 'Not a good idea, Conti. If Royce comes, he'll pass through the village and stay overnight at the Murray Hotel. Everybody does. We can't rely on folk keeping their mouths shut.'

'That's true,' Lilly agreed. 'Binnie and I stayed there on our way up. It's too small a place to go unnoticed.'

Duffy's gaze was on her again, questioning. 'Can you ride?'

Lilly wrenched her eyes away. 'I haven't for a while.'

'Margot rode one of her horses up the mule track from Kathgodam. You could hire a hill pony and come down with us when we leave at the end of June.'

Noel held up a finger. 'First thing wrong with that plan is if Royce came up in the other direction, you'd have a head-on collision. There's only one route up and down. We'll have to think of something better, foolproof, so that even your own husband won't suspect you've given him the slip.'

Chapter 10

Not until late that afternoon did anyone come up with a plan that might work.

Duffy went out after lunch, leaving her alone with Noel and his sister. It was now a beautiful evening; the air cool and still, the sun a huge orange disc slipping slowly down the sky.

They were sitting on the veranda sipping a cocktail Noel called a gin rickey from long, heavy tumblers.

Lilly folded her hands around the glass, enjoying the woozy feeling from the alcohol. Margot came around the side of the bungalow and stood unsmiling on the bottom step, her jacket unfastened, revealing a dove-grey dress with an intricate lace collar. 'Oh, hello. We thought by now you'd be back at the guesthouse.'

Noel rose from his chair and began mixing her a drink as she came up towards him. 'Is Duffy not with you?'

'He said to meet him here. He's been giving Mister Stripes a good workout at the high-altitude enclosure.'

Conti tutted. 'He's supposed to be resting his arm.'

'Circus performers work with injuries all the time. Anyway, Duffy works the tiger with his voice not by brandishing an upturned chair.'

The gin had loosened her tongue and the words were out before Lilly could hold them back. 'On the tiger hunt he spoke about intimidating the animals and using their fear to control them. Wasn't catching a wild beast the purpose of the trip because it will be quick to subdue or did I totally misunderstand?'

Margot turned her cool gaze upon her. 'You know nothing about circus life, Lilly.'

'I wasn't referring to the circus as such. It would be like Noel saying he whips his dog to make him behave. No one with a sense of decency would willingly instil fear in another living being,' she said, flushing at the truth of her words.

Margot's face tightened. 'What do you think the circus is, Lilly? It's not a dressing-up box, a tent and a few moth-eaten animals. It's bloody hard work. You make your own costume out of whatever you have to hand. Have you ever cut up a pair of curtains or sewn sequins onto your riding jacket? You can't just step into the ring and entertain. The practice is endless, which is why Duffy is not here right now drinking cocktails with you and Noel, and the hours are long and conditions miserable. It takes graft and grit and I'm not sure you have either.' She spoke without heat, but Lilly pondered what she'd done to offend.

'I'm sorry,' she heard herself say out of long habit. 'You're quite right. I know nothing about circus life at all.'

Conti leapt to her defence. 'Why are you being so horrid to Lilly? We've just found out her marriage is ghastly and it's up to us to help her. That's what friends do, if you count yourself as one.'

Margot accepted her drink and shrugged. 'I'm trying to be realistic. Duffy said you might ride down with us at the end of the month but I don't think you'd survive five minutes in the circus and I'm trying to spare you that.'

In her mind Lilly conceded the point with a nod. What she said was true but at that moment she was not interested in hearing her inadequacies spelled out in detail by someone who knew nothing about her.

'I mean, what could you do if you did come with us?' Margot went on. 'I know you can fire a gun at a target but we don't have that act in our circus. You're the wrong shape for an aerialist. Duffy says you can ride but could you perform on horseback? Could you ride two galloping horses with a foot on each without falling off? You're not the type and there's no question of me lending you one of my string to trot down the hill to Kathgodam, before anyone asks.'

'What type am I, Margot?' Lilly said, speared to the quick.

Rings sparkled on the hand that brought the gin to her lips. 'Soft. Unused to hard work. You've had servants all your life so even a job in the cook tent would be beyond you.'

'That's a harsh judgement, given you barely know me at all,' Lilly said, even though in her heart she knew that Margot had spoken the bitter, unflattering truth.

'Did you tell Royce about me being at the séance? We've ruled out everyone else who was there and here we all are discussing where I might go to hide. How do I know I can trust you not to blab to the entire Yacht Club?'

Noel smacked his palm on the table. 'Stop bickering, girls. The more pressing need right this minute is for Lilly to disappear from view and we can decide where she is to go after that, don't you think? It doesn't have to be the circus. It could be anywhere.'

Lilly tented her fingers. 'I've been thinking I'll go back to the convent in Bandra where I was at school. There are retreats for those wanting to remove themselves from everyday life and I know I'd be welcome.'

'Didn't I hear that the nuns there run a racket of marrying off their charges?' Margot leaned forward to set down her glass.

'Yes. That's where Royce found me.'

'That would be the first place I'd look if I was in his shoes. If he paid the convent for their services once, it's likely he'd bribe them again and to be clear, Lilly, I didn't tell Royce about the séance.'

Noel twisted towards the kitchen and shouted 'Khansama!' at the top of his voice. He turned to Lilly. 'A better occupation by far would be to sort out a disguise and remove you permanently from the guesthouse to here.'

Conti clapped her hands. 'We could dress you up as an Indian lady in a sari and you could travel down in the *howdah*. You have dark hair, we could rub your lovely olive skin with walnut juice to make it darker, plait your hair, apply some eyeliner – an Indian in India is of no remark whatsoever.' She tapped the tips of her fingers together. 'When he gets here, we'll ask the cook if his wife will help you with the clothes and swear them both to secrecy. That goes for everyone in this room as well.' She put finger on her lips. 'Mum's the word.'

Half smiling, Noel nodded his head, his clear-eyed gaze lingering on Lilly's face. 'A white doesn't notice a native unless he's forced to. I am certain that if you did come face to face with Royce, he wouldn't recognise his own beautiful wife.'

Lilly looked down at her wedding ring and pushed the image of her husband away. What must it feel like, she wondered, for someone to say 'I love you' and for you to mean it back?

★

The following morning, when breakfast at Rohilla Lodge had been cleared away, Lilly broached the idea with Miss Pearl. 'Noel has suggested that I move up to Lake View right away so, if you are in agreement, I'm going to pack up my things and leave you as soon as I'm done.'

'I think that is a wise precaution. If your husband turns up, we'll say that you've gone off to join your mother. I'll bring my sister in on the secret.'

'I'd appreciate that very much and I'm going to transform myself, too, with some sort of disguise, so next time you see me I might not look like me.'

Miss Pinkney rummaged in her sleeve for a handkerchief and polished a speck on her *pince-nez*. 'I suppose one has to kill off the person one was to become the person one wants to be.'

Or kill off the person you've become to find the one you once were.

It took almost all day to get herself organised and the light had started to fade when she reached Noel's bungalow and found Duffy and Margot by the fireside drinking tea.

The unexpectedness of seeing them together caught her off guard. She was already aware of confusing feelings towards these two but they were as yet unexplored and troubling.

Duffy lounged back in a red velvet chair with cream tassels at the ends of its arms and Margot sat in front of a scuffed rectangular table. A fox fur was draped about her narrow shoulders and an oversized hat stacked with feathers, flowers and lace was secured to her head with a pearl-tipped pin.

Margot picked up the strainer and made a comment in a voice too low for Lilly to hear. Duffy laughed at whatever she had said and held out the cup for his tea. She wondered just how long they had been sitting there and felt ruffled, inside and out.

He half rose from his seat when he saw her come into the room. 'Ah! There you are, Lilly.' His tone was casual, as if he'd been expecting her for a while.

Margot yawned behind her hand. 'Tea, Mrs Myerson?'

The stress on the honorific, she knew, was to remind Lilly that she was married, and that Margot was free as a bird.

Lilly dropped into a low chair and glanced across at Duffy and saw the look in his eye. It was gone in an instant, but it flipped her heart over that he had communicated something personal to that woman. There was warmth of more than friendship on his face and confirmed an intimacy between them she'd already suspected.

It was fortunate that Noel chose that moment to bluster in from the garden and distract her from her musings. He kicked at the wooden peg that propped open the door and tossed his terai hat towards the sofa. 'It's chilly in here. You should stoke up the fire.' He threw a log into the hearth and puffed vigorously at the pale ash with the bellows. He took the chair next to Margot and announced he was parched.

Lithe as a young cat, she sprang to her feet. 'We hadn't really noticed the fire, had we, Duffy?' Margot lifted the teapot. 'Let me pour you a cup.'

'Noel doesn't like tea,' Lilly said in a rush.

A pair of beautiful violet eyes flashed with irritation. 'Coffee then?'

Lilly hopped up with less elasticity in her step than Margot's and sought out the gin bottle. 'Noel's more of a peg person at this time of day,' she said and poured a three-finger measure into a glass and shoved it into his hand.

Noel twitched his eyebrows and downed it without a blink. 'What's going on?'

Margot returned the teapot to the table. 'We were discussing Lilly, actually, and might have come up with a plan.'

Duffy looked up. 'We've had a telegram from the circus, advising we are leaving at the end of the month.'

'Isn't that sooner than you were expecting?' Noel pressed a palm against his temple.

Duffy nodded. 'It's all to do with the postponement of the King's coronation. We are being recalled early because we need to be ready when the new date is published. Money's tight at the best of times and we only work if Tiffert has funds. We were thinking if Lilly does want to come with us and disappear for a bit, there's an opportunity going but she'll have to earn her keep.'

'Whizzy Delroy is looking for a property girl.' Margot withdrew the pin from her hat – which seemed the length of a small spear –and tested the tip with her finger.

Lilly stared at her in horror. 'Am I to be strapped to a target with Whizzy the Knife throwing blades at me?'

Margot stabbed the spear back into the pile of feathers on her crown and pulled on her leather gloves. 'He's a trick cyclist. He's looking for an assistant to hand him his props. It's not an experienced performer he's looking for, so it might be just the ticket for you – at least *pro tem*.'

Duffy got up, held out his good arm and pulled Margot to her feet. 'Think about it, that's all. We'll send him a note to say we've found someone who'll do and you've got till the end of the month to decide one way or the other. And now we must go.' He slid a hand under Margot's elbow and manoeuvred her to the door. 'It's cocktail night at the Club followed by dinner and a carpet dance. Conti said she would meet us there and you should come, too,

Noel. People are starting to forget what you look like.' He nodded for a moment in Lilly's direction. 'I'd love you to come as well and slow-waltz you cheek to cheek around the dance floor, but better not or gossiping tongues will wag.' His words would have seemed light, an excuse for not asking her along, but his look seemed only for her. It lasted a heartbeat or two and then he blinked and it was gone. If it had ever been there at all.

Noel walked them out and when he came back, Lilly could see he was troubled. He lit his pipe and sat down beside her, taking her hand between the two of his.

'Have you got five minutes? I have something I need to say.'

She felt a tremor of foreboding. 'Fire away. You may as well say what's on your mind.'

'I'm not very good at this sort of thing and it's probably none of my business, but you must try not to give yourself away where Duffy's concerned.'

'In what way?' She breathed in and out. Too fast. Too fast. Too fast.

Noel looked uncomfortable. 'Playing at happy families with Duffy and Margot. Taking tea. You're wary of Margot, that's plain as day, but Duffy is a different kettle of fish.'

She bit her lip and held back for a moment. 'He didn't invite me to join you all at the Club.'

'That's true but even so, your eyes give you away when you look at him. You weren't like this with him when we were camping in the jungle.'

Lilly picked up one of Conti's magazines and peered at him over the top, trying to frame her defence. 'At the tiger hunt, he asked me for help with her and I got the impression that—'

'What?'

She glanced towards the door where they had both gone out. 'Never mind. I obviously made a mistake. I don't understand what's going on between them so it was a shock to find them taking tea together and seeing them so comfortable with each other when I thought he was trying to distance himself from her.' It was said before she could hold the words back. She could feel his disapproval and guilt washed over her.

'Is there something I've missed?' Noel asked.

She didn't want to tell him that her feelings towards Duffy had changed and tried to turn her mind away from foolish thoughts of his houseguest. She put on a smile. 'Nothing at all.'

He stretched out his fingers towards his pipe. 'Be careful there, Lilly. He has a wife in South Africa. Children too, probably, although I've never asked. And you are not free.'

'Don't you think I know that?' She spoke sharply, more annoyed with herself than she would admit. Teddy's small face, all dark eyes and long lashes, flashed through her mind.

'Margot's on manoeuvres and will not be elbowed aside. She has a knack with men and likes to bounce between them and Duffy's no more immune to her advances than a man in the grip of Peshawar fever. He'll not give you a second glance if Margot gets her way.'

'It's easy to dole out the advice when one's not emotionally involved but don't degrade her feelings towards him, Noel. She was beside herself when Duffy was mauled.'

Noel gave an odd short laugh and put a light to his tobacco. 'Don't play with fire, Lilly. I couldn't stand to see you burned.'

Lilly bowed her head, her heart racing. 'I wasn't talking about me. As you rightly said, I'm not free and I have a small son to take care of.'

Chapter 11

That night, sleep came in broken snatches.

Before six o'clock the following morning, Lilly lay awake in the semi-darkness taking in the contours of her new home as the tawny yellow light of an Indian dawn seeped in through the curtains.

It was a long, narrow room, overcluttered with redundant furniture, chairs covered with crumpled muslin squares that had come from the bazaar; whoever had been responsible for the décor, it was credit to a disorderly hand.

She forced herself to remain in her room and concentrated on the tick and whirr of the clock. When the clang of cooking pots and clattering of crockery, which signalled the breakfast hour, had passed and the house had once more fallen silent, she ventured into the hall.

By midday, the atmosphere in the empty house had become oppressive. She paced about, straightening cushions, rearranging drooping flowers in vases, then settled down with a book but couldn't focus on the print.

She whistled up Noel's dog and stepped down into the garden, the animal hard at her heels until, distracted by an intriguing smell, he scampered off towards the lake. She walked along the side of the garden, which rose against the hill, and amongst the rhododendron and oak trees, before sinking down on a grassy bank. The dog nosed its way through the rear bamboo hedge and stretched out by her side, head resting on his paws.

Lilly watched the drift of clouds overhead as they curled over the great shoulders of rock that formed the peaks of the mighty Himalayan mountains. She tried to recall their names but today only Nanda would come to mind. For over an hour she looked alternately at her watch and the front of the house, allowing herself a peek a minute, willing the crunch of feet on gravel, less convinced with each glance, that *he* would come. She had contrived to be alone, but now it was too much. What would she say to him in any case? Her throat felt dry, Duffy's voice tight inside her head. *I'd love to slow-waltz you round the dance floor, cheek to cheek.* And there had been a look between them, she was certain of it now.

Did that mean he really was attracted to her? Had she only imagined he had feelings for her? Or maybe she had misunderstood completely and he was inextricably involved with Margot?

She sat alone, dropped her head to her knees and allowed her mind to race.

By late afternoon, a thousand thoughts had coursed through her head before Lilly found her answer.

She returned to the house and slipped around the back of the bungalow and up the steps to the veranda. She moved into the hall where, from the panelled walls above her head, trophies of antelopes some previous owner had shot stared at her with shiny glass eyes. She threw her hat onto the table and turned towards the drawing room. The door was ajar, the room evidently not empty.

Noel was at the piano with his back towards her. Goose sat beside him, his ears erect, head tilted at an angle as if he was waiting for a cue to sing.

137

She stepped back into a patch of shadow as he began to play and for a few moments she listened through the half-open door as the Adagio of Beethoven's Moonlight Sonata transported her back to England. She could hear the sound of her grandmother's practised touch as she performed her scales and arpeggios on the Steinway. *A tennis player will warm up before a match. Playing an instrument is no different, Lilly. Practice is essential.* Granny Wilkins carried a lifetime of dedication in her head; she played *all the big boys* – Wagner, Chopin, Grieg and Mozart, and rarely reached for the music.

Why didn't you fight for me and spare me all this? Lilly's inner voice screamed at her grandmother.

Then, as if an invisible finger hooked her away from this unsettling thought, she was drawn back to Noel's playing. She pushed open the door and went in.

Conti sat on the fender seat, a cup and saucer on the carpet beside her, a basket of darning at her elbow. 'You see, brother? I told you the music would bring her.'

Noel swung around on the music stool. 'We've been back for ages and looked for you everywhere.'

'I was in the garden. Look, I'm glad you're both here because I've made a decision.'

A glimmer of surprise crossed his brow. 'About what?'

'I'm leaving in the morning.'

He looked at her in confusion. 'Are we allowed to ask why?'

'It's the best thing for all of us.'

Conti delved into the mending basket and held up a sock, the hole in the heel marking it a very old friend. 'Tell her she's being ridiculous, Noel. And say about the other thing as well.'

Lilly sat down at Conti's writing table, which apart

from the piano, was the only decent piece of furniture in the room. 'Where is the sharp shoe of the dance floor, by the way?' As soon as the words were out, she wished she could have bitten them back. She felt the scrutiny of Noel's gaze through her own lowered lids and the sear of embarrassment in her cheeks.

'Duffy's out on an errand.'

'For Margot?'

He drew up his stool before her, leaning forward on his elbows which rested on his knees. 'Leave it alone, Lilly. We've both spent the day giving him what for, for leading you on with his inappropriate remarks last night. He was out of order flirting and making overtures towards you and he's been trying to make amends today.'

Scorn gave her courage. 'Has he really? Whether he finds me attractive is neither here nor there and, as I just said, I'm packing up and going back to Rohilla Lodge.'

'Duffy's organising a surprise,' Conti blurted out. 'That's where we've been all day.' She looked across at her brother, her eyes searching his face. 'I'm sorry, Noel. I had to tell her.'

He nodded, the smile for his sister fond. To Lilly, he said, 'When we came back from the Club last night, we'd thrashed things out. He's terribly conflicted. On the one hand, he has Margot, and a wife in Africa and on the other, he has feelings for you.'

Lilly felt her heart begin to race. 'You don't approve.'

He was unable to look at her. 'I can't see a happy ending. I've told you that before, but I'm not your keeper.'

Conti abandoned her darning and tossed it in the basket. 'So, we went out this morning and bought you some things.' She got up from her seat and fetched a bulky package from a drawer in her desk. 'Instead of wearing a sari, we thought if you dressed as a Pahari hill woman you would look more ordinary. We went to the cloth stall at the market on Mall Road and found you an outfit but then had to take it to the tailor at his shop.' She held up a pair of trousers. 'The sizing might be a bit rough and the fitting a little haphazard, but the bottom is called a *churidar* pyjama and you tighten it with a string about the waist. It's supposed to be baggy so I don't think anyone will really notice. The top is a knee-length, full-sleeve *kameez*. The material is a heavy cotton cloth as the hills are very cold, but this is traditionally what the women wear. The next thing but one' – she shook out another length of cloth – 'is a head scarf which is also made of thick cotton and lastly . . .' From the bottom of the package she pulled a pair of sandals. 'We got these.'

'They are not new,' Noel apologised, 'but we thought they might be easier to wear if the leather was already worn in.'

'Hill women don't normally wear shoes,' Conti added. 'It marks them as unchaste, but we thought you could kick them on and off if you have to cross someone's threshold.'

Lilly didn't think that was remotely likely but was too choked up at their generosity to speak.

'You must wear your hair in two tight braids which you dress with mustard oil and secure with black thread.' Noel tapped a finger against his cheek. 'What else did we buy, Conti?'

'I have them here.' Duffy strode into the room, a beedi cigarette balanced on his lower lip. He was wearing a long, black unbuttoned coat, a white crumpled shirt that fell to his knees outside loose orange trousers. Strands of hair escaped from the folds of his inexpertly tied turban, with which he had muffled up his head. Lilly thought he looked like a child in dressing-up clothes.

'You look fairly ridiculous,' she said.

He hitched his shoulders towards his ears and grinned. 'A demonstration of how not to transform oneself in the costume department, should one want to disappear unnoticed into the crowd. I have been out so long,' he said, pulling two packages from an inner pocket of his coat and holding one out towards her, 'because Noel and Conti have organised the proper costume and asked me to provide the props.'

Lilly undid the brown paper he'd placed on the table beside her and unwrapped two pale glass bangles and a third, slim circle of gold.

She stared at him. She couldn't help it. 'From you?'

He swept his eyes over her face. 'Married natives of any standing in any type of dress will have this jewellery. Put them on your wrist. If push comes to shove and you find yourself in need of funds, you can always sell the gold. But I had to wait at the jeweller's for this.' He gave her the second parcel.

'This one's from us,' Noel put in. 'Conti and me.'

Lilly unwrapped the tissue paper to find a necklace made of small black beads separated with little gold ones between. At the end of the necklace there was a filigree gold locket in the shape of a butterfly. The craftsmanship was exquisite.

Noel looked at Conti, who nodded her approval for him to go on. 'This belonged to a close friend of our father's and when she died, it came back to us. It's called a *mangalsutar*. *Mangal* means auspicious and *sutar* means thread.' He took the necklace from her. 'Let me put it on for you.'

Lilly turned her back and bent slightly forward, pushing a loose strand of hair up off her collar.

'It doesn't have a clasp,' Conti said. 'You need to stand up.'

Lilly straightened, pulling back her head just as Noel leaned forward and dropped the strand of beads around her neck. A smart blow to the back of her head made her gasp.

She pressed a hand to the spot where they'd collided and swung round, cradling the butterfly in her palm.

Noel stepped back, holding his chin, and started to laugh. 'That's a nice thank you for our present,' he teased.

'I'm so sorry, Noel. Have I knocked out a tooth?'

He shook his head. 'No harm done.'

Conti looked as if she wanted to laugh, but instead said, 'Is your head all right, Lilly?'

Lilly gave her scalp a little rub and dropped her hand, feeling a flush of embarrassed heat at her cheeks. 'I'm fine, thanks.'

In a voice still tinged with amusement, Noel said, 'Before you go in for round two, I want you to know how dear you are to us both and if fortune does not favour you in whatever you go on to do, the thread will tie you to us and bring you back to Nainital.'

'Where you'll always have a home.' Conti nodded and reached out a hand. 'We'll keep your room for you just as it is.'

Lilly grasped her fingers and held them against her cheek, her chin trembling with emotion. Noel and Conti had been everything to her in the past weeks: brother, sister, friends.

She smiled up at Noel but his eyes were full of sad knowledge. He suspects I'll never come back, she thought, and nothing will be the same.

Chapter 12

For the next couple of days, Lilly donned her new clothes, gradually habituating herself to the feel of the coarse cloth against her skin and the reality that she was now, for the first time in public, wearing trousers.

From watching her mother-in-law, she knew it was important to heat the mustard oil pomade to lessen the musty odour. Even so, as she combed it through her hair, the smell was far from pleasant. She touched her hand to her scalp, which still hurt where she tugged her hair into plaits and bound them tight with thread. She had been sparing with the walnut juice, only sponging the stain onto her feet, hands and face. Noel told her that besides making baskets, the Pahari women earned a living carrying stone and wood from the hills or by selling firewood to the British residents. She began balancing small loads of wood around the garden until she could carry them on her head without support from her hands, but she had not yet been into town.

After lunch on the third day, Noel came into the sitting room where Lilly was reading. 'Miss Pearl's had a letter from Binnie,' he said.

'What does it say?'

'Why not trot down and see for yourself? It would be good to see how you get on with your disguise. Go before teatime when the town will be crowded.'

Wearing her second-hand leather sandals, Lilly shuffled her way down the hill from Lake View, past the gothic style church of St John in the Wilderness and crossed the Flats towards the temple.

A grey monkey sat on a stone pillar, picking nits from its fur. Monkeys were unpredictable and this one suddenly began to bark. She backed away and almost tripped over a young man whose right leg ended just shy of his hip bone. She let out a small gasp and fanned her fingers against her chest as she took in the lack where his leg should have been. He'd positioned himself at the entrance to the temple, his site well chosen as it was impossible to avoid him if one wanted to enter the holy ground. He shuffled towards her on his bottom, his begging bowl outstretched, and eyed her expectantly. Beggars should be fed; it was the currency they used for their basic needs and they trusted to strangers to provide them with it. He patted his naked stomach and pointed at his open mouth and said that he was hungry.

But, besides the load on her head, Lilly had nothing to give him so fell back a step, thinking that this mutilated man was likely one of the myriad reasons the British kept to the upper side of Mall Road – to protect their delicate sensibilities from the harsh reality of India.

As she met the man's expectant eyes, Lilly was overcome with impotence that there was nothing she could do to help. *I'm sorry*, she wanted to say. *I'm so sorry I have nothing to give you.*

She turned away and retraced her steps to the far side of the Flats towards the more palatable side of town, where brick and timber houses held onto the hillside, like daubs of coloured paint.

In the narrow, crooked streets of the native bazaar, a swarming population went about its business; this was the real Nainital. No longer did natives stand aside to let her pass. They held their ground, forcing her into the open drains to swerve around whatever lay in her path.

All manner of small businesses competed in the overcrowded lanes. Hundreds of low-roofed shops huddled together but there was order in the twisting alleys. Tailors sat cross-legged on the threshold of their establishments, tape measures around their shoulders, a sewing machine to one side as if to attest to their profession. The cloth merchants formed the next quarter, grouped on either side of the street, displaying their brightly coloured fabrics on woven grass mats. Jewellers clustered together, then grocers and an assortment of shops selling spices piled high in colourful pyramids.

It was congested, the drainage non-existent and the smell appalling.

Grey with dust, an old woman making *kachauris* was hunched over a glowing charcoal fire. She was nothing but a bag of bones, her hair matted, her face lined and dirty.

Lilly took her wood pile from her head and handed it over, saying that she had too much. *'Ma aap yeh lakari rakh lo, aap ke kaam ayengi. Mere pass bahut lakari hain.'*

'Beti thu khushi raho.'

The old lady's blessing that she should find happiness brought tears to her eyes as she swung on her sandals to go.

In her oversized footwear, walking with feet turned out to keep the sandals in place, it took her almost an hour to reach Rohilla Lodge where she found herself knocking on the Miss Pinkneys' front door.

Miss Pearl peered out from the hall, a frown on her brow. 'Can I help you?'

'It's me. Lilly.'

Miss Pearl adjusted her *pince-nez*. 'You sound like her,' she whispered, her voice uncertain. 'Say something we would know. Before we let you in.'

Lilly paused for a moment, staring at her stained, brown fingers. 'My mother is called Binnie and her dog is Poochie. It's completely demented.'

Miss Opal emerged from the shadowy hallway. 'It *is* you, Lilly. You must come in for a schooner of sherry and tell us all your news.'

Miss Pearl peered again through her eyeglass. 'You make a very convincing native, I must say.'

'I've just spent an hour in the bazaar, and I don't think I raised an eyebrow of suspicion. I gave the pile of wood I was carrying on my head to an old lady and she called on God to bless me.'

'Noel says you have fluent Hindi.'

Lilly shook her head. 'If that language is the only means of communication between one person and another, you would be very lonely indeed if you didn't make an effort to learn it. But I am far from fluent, though the odd slip here and there should go unnoticed.'

Miss Opal placed a linen square on the sitting-room table and handed out the drinks. 'Does this disguise mark the death of Lilly Myerson?'

'For now, it has to. At least till I leave Nainital. I can't be seen out in public in Western dress as everyone thinks I left town with Binnie. Speaking of whom, Noel said you've had a letter.'

Miss Opal gave a warm smile and said that they had. 'I hid it away because as a piece of evidence, it could be considered quite damning if it were to fall into the wrong pair of hands.' She got up and pulled an envelope out from under the cushion where she was sitting. 'I think you need to read it to yourself get the full force without us paraphrasing the content for you. The first thing for you to know, though, is that she is in Mussoorie, staying at the new Savoy Hotel that has just opened.'

Vague memories stirred in Lilly's mind. 'I stayed in Mussoorie once, but at the Charles Ville, and from there went to Dehra Dun because Royce's grandfather is buried in the cemetery.'

Miss Pearl dabbed at her mouth with a napkin. 'We didn't know where she was going but I didn't imagine it would be Mussoorie. The Commodore lived there with one of his wives, you see, and I can't imagine he'd care to run into her from what I heard.'

Lilly would have liked to pursue that comment but did not get the chance.

'Here.' Miss Opal held out the letter and it reminded Lilly that other than the letter she had sent to Cawnpore to invite her to the hills, it was one of the few times she had seen Binnie's hand. 'Read it for yourself.'

Lilly pulled the note from the envelope and saw that it was embossed with the hotel's monogram. It didn't surprise her at all that Binnie had not used her own writing paper – if indeed she owned any – and the letter was undated, in her usual slapdash way. That her mother was so particular in other areas of her life – clothes, appearance, connections, and so on – made the sweeping aside of this sort of etiquette all the more difficult to reconcile.

There was no formal greeting, nor explanation for why she had left Nainital without word. Lilly scanned through the opening sentences. They were having a marvellous time at the new hotel which was the height of luxury and set in eleven acres. It was absolutely the place to be seen and had a charming place to eat called the Beer Garden. They had dined at the Assembly Rooms, been to the theatre, *bla, bla, bla.*

And then:

'*It's pure selfishness that she has not written to me,*' Binnie wrote in her childish loopy hand. '*You know how I crave her letters and there's been nothing – not so much as a single word.*

I want you to tell her to pay the money I owe you – about ten rupees I should think – and I was indeed sorry to run out on you just like that while she was off on that tiger hunt but, goodness, it was a whirlwind decision. The Commodore clicked his fingers and what was a girl to do? It was rather fun though, creeping out in the dead of night!

Lilly is so negligent in this respect – writing, that is. One could totally understand that I would find it hard to find the time to write because my life is so full – there's always something going on and I never have a minute to sit down and put pen to paper. Goodness, who does if one is a catch socially and one's company so busily sought?

Unless she got eaten by a tiger (ha! ha!), Lilly has hours and hours to spend writing letters. She manages well enough with writing to Royce but what about me? Her mother. Not a single peep. I expect she is occupied enough with those books she reads and the socials at the Club – oh I forget she is too dull to go there. Are they putting on a spectacle for the rescheduled coronation in August? I was to perform Penelope Ann in Box and Cox *at the Yacht Club. Quite the most important role.*'

Lilly looked up and shook her head in disbelief.

'Which particular bit have you got to?' Miss Pearl enquired.

'She's complaining I haven't written to her, but I have no idea where she is.'

Miss Opal snorted. 'She's completely irrational and wrapped up in her own little world. There's not even a female role in *Box and Cox*, but carry on. It gets better.'

'It's such a business not to know what is going on with her. Has Royce come yet? I can't enjoy Mussoorie properly – not one least little bit until I know that he is not too peeved I left his wife to cope on her own. He's such a crafty character – always six steps ahead of everyone and just when you think you are catching up, he's started a second set of steps before you even realise he's moved his feet at all. Really and truly, I think she might consider me a little for once in her life. I'm a little strapped at the moment and as her mother – oops I should not have written that word down on paper – but as her mother I have as much right to her husband's money as anyone. He said he would not see me starve but has he dipped his hand into his pocket? He maintains his own mother after all and she's a native, for pity's sake. The Commodore and I are off to Simla for the rest of the season and then to Lahore for Christmas week, which is the social event of the cold weather – I know that's months away but how am I to manage with no dress allowance? It's so much smarter than Nainital and the company more diverting. It's not so very easy to juggle one's pennies when one is between husbands. Does she want me to end up working as a seamstress? Tell her to dip into her allowance and send me five hundred rupees.'

Lilly could picture the frown above the thinly plucked eyebrows, could almost catch the tone of her petulant outpouring. She tossed the letter across the table.

'She's not getting a penny from me. In the sixteen years I was in England, I never had one letter from her, addressed to me in person. I think my grandmother had a scant two a year. If she is short of funds, let her apply to Royce herself. I've no interest in her financial woes, particularly as she cannot be bothered to ask me herself.'

Miss Opal reached for her glass. 'She told me she was about to marry someone from the ICS and now she's run off with a retired Commodore who has worked his way through three wives.'

Lilly raised her eyebrows. 'I have no idea what goes on in her head.'

'I think your mother is a riddle no one will ever solve,' Miss Pearl concluded.

'But you know more than you have told me. You told me Binnie has been to Nainital in the past and that she once lived in Bombay.'

Miss Pearl's loose tongue was not to be had. 'I also said that I am silent as a mute if needs be. If I am party to information that is not mine to pass on, I am sorry, Lilly, I will not pass it on. Now tell me, when are you thinking of leaving?'

'There is a possibility of leaving with Duffy and Margot and joining up with the circus for a bit as a trick cyclist's assistant. They leave very soon and are busy working their animals up the hill.'

'That sounds terribly exciting, doesn't it, dear?'

Miss Opal clapped her hands. 'Oh yes, but I don't think you should limit yourself to giving the limelight to the star. You should learn some cycle tricks of your own. Borrow the bicycle. Take it up to the high-altitude zoo so you can practise in secret now you have such a convincing disguise.'

Lilly found herself caught up in the idea that riding a bicycle would be so much easier if it were not necessary to grapple with heavy, layered petticoats and long skirts that caught in spokes and around pedals. It would be more akin to riding in bloomers, like Duffy's orange trousers, and she caught herself laughing out loud.

'What's funny?' Miss Pearl asked from across the room.

'I was just thinking of Duffy. He got himself some silly trousers from the bazaar to detract from something he'd said.'

'Be careful of that man, Lilly. We do not admire his reputation.'

Noel had said exactly the same. 'We are friends. That's all.'

Miss Opal folded her hands in her lap. 'There's no such thing as a platonic friendship, Lilly. You might find him dashing. Exciting even. But he will always be looking over your shoulder for something better to come along. He's not a man to pin your hopes on. Trust me on this. I know from bitter experience.'

Chapter 13

Most afternoons over the coming days, on the way down the hill from the high-altitude enclosure where Lilly was teaching herself to balance on the back wheel of the Pinkneys' bicycle, it was her habit to stop on the corner of the cobbled lane while Noel knocked on the door of Rohilla Lodge.

And then one afternoon, on the last Monday in June, there they were: Teddy with *Ayah* – a neat, slim girl who wore her hair in two long plaits down her back, her robin's egg dress long and unbelted – and Royce, feet spread wide on the concrete steps, talking with Miss Opal.

Whatever Miss Pinkney was saying, she saw the tight-lipped disapproval on her husband's face, his thick lips drawn back like a snarling dog.

Royce leaned down and said something to her son. She took in the slight droop of his shoulders and watched as Teddy wrenched his hand away from his father's.

For several seconds she was unable to catch her breath, feeling the bile rise to her throat, the snap of fear at her heels. She loathed Royce with a bitterness it was hard to articulate.

And yet.

A blend of both his parents, Teddy was along the street, barely thirty paces from where she stood, stick-thin legs, so like his father's, showing below his knee-length shorts, an overstretched sock collapsed at his ankle. His little hand clutched at the stiff celluloid collar and miniature bow tie that encased his childish neck, his dark hair shiny with oil and falling into his eyes. When he turned his head, she saw the kajal dot that *Ayah* daubed on each cheek every morning to protect him from the evil eye. From Lilly's side of the family, he had inherited the beaked Wilkins nose.

The temptation to run to her little boy almost overtook her. She loved him and would have done anything in that moment to feel the warmth and softness of her child in her arms.

Teddy's name was already forming on her lips when Noel took her arm.

'Lilly,' he breathed in her ear. 'Carry on down the hill – or everything we have prepared for the past weeks will have been for nothing.' He placed a hand at her back and urged her forward. 'Now is not the time. Go.'

Squinting through her tears, she put one foot in front of the other until she reached Mall Road. She turned left towards the rickshaw stand and followed the road to the far side of the lake where the dress was native, not white.

The wind blew across the water, whipping the calm surface to agitated ripples. Rigging clanked against boat masts, fly catchers wheep-whistled in the rushes, the incessant chirruping of cicadas in the long grass was too shrill.

Eyes cast down, she pulled the front of her scarf over her forehead and walked along the side of the lake where the sun never shone.

Stall owners who were carrying huge baskets of produce strapped to their backs or pushing wooden barrows squeezed past her, the weedy track too narrow for two people to pass comfortably. A wrinkled peasant in a filthy loincloth urged a bullock forward, alternately slapping its hide with a length of bamboo and whistling through *paan*-stained teeth. Lilly hitched up her pyjamas and stepped round a pile of fresh dung.

There was activity all along this side of the lake; women squatted beside the muddy shore, filling clay bowls with lake water or washing up dishes with mops attached to sticks; men fished, casting their lines from skiffs on the water; hawkers with trays hung around their necks sold samosas, piled high on chipped plates.

Dressed as a native, she was as invisible as thought.

When she drew level with the Yacht Club, she raised her eyes for an instant and stared at the far side of the lake. 'Oh Teddy,' she wept to herself, drowning once more in a well of deep loss.

Dusk was falling when, finally, a rain-drenched Noel mounted the veranda steps to Lake View with his soggy hound at his side. Goose trotted to the far end of the veranda, had a comprehensive shake and lay down on the floor.

With an unsteady hand, Lilly slapped at a mosquito on her arm. She began in desperation, 'Where have you been? I thought you'd never get back. I've been half out of my mind, conjuring up what's been going on down the road.'

He shook the water from his coat, and held up his hand, palm towards her. 'I got caught in a random shower, but first things first. I need a drink and so do you. You look done in.'

He went to the cloth-covered camp table that bore the spirit bottles and poured hefty pegs of Shelby's gin into two long glasses. Squeezing fresh lemon into the glasses, he topped them up with soda water and placed one in her hand. 'Get that down you and then I'll bring you up to speed. Where are the others, by the way?'

Reclining back full-length in her basket chair, Lilly took a sip and set the glass down beside her. 'They've gone down to the Club. Duffy went with Conti as they said she needed to chitter-chat with the members and promulgate the fact that I really have left Nainital.'

Noel nodded. 'If anyone has seen Royce and started to speculate . . .'

Her worry got the better of her. 'Did you speak to him?'

'That's where I've been all this time. After you went down to the Mall, I trotted along to Rohilla Lodge, pretending that the Miss Pinkneys are my aunts. They were absolutely magnificent.'

'They are the dearest ladies.'

'He was not what I expected.'

'In what way?'

'From what you've said, I thought Royce to be clear-cut, but he's not. He speaks with a perfect English accent, impeccably dressed as for an afternoon at his Club and he's only slightly darker in complexion than you. He could be any Mediterranean nationality and if I did not know to the contrary, would have pegged him as Italian or Greek.'

Lilly had the same view when she'd met him. He spoke with an accent she had grown up with and his manners were flawless. There was no reason on this earth to suspect he was none other than the gentlemanly version of himself he'd presented to the nuns.

'How was Teddy? Did he talk about me?'

'He was rather taken with Goose, but your husband wouldn't let him touch the dog.'

'Teddy adores dogs but Royce won't let him near one. His business partner's little boy was bitten by a pariah dog that got into his compound and now he's neurotic that the same will happen to our son. The poor boy ended up at the

Pasteur Institute in Coonoor and had over a dozen injections to his stomach, which was agonising, I understand.' She bit her lip. Of course she didn't want Teddy to go through anything like that, but she ached at being unable to give him his dearest wish. 'I'm in two minds about it.'

Noel's tone was grim. 'You never forget the bark of a mad dog and its foam-flecked lips. He's right to be cautious.'

'What did Royce say when he found out I wasn't there?'

'Miss Pearl told Royce that he had missed you by a mere couple of days as you had left to join your mother in Calcutta. She talked expansively about the town and of what there was to see and the hotel where Binnie is staying.'

Lilly nodded. 'She lived there for a while a long time back. That was a clever ploy of hers.'

'He was vastly displeased that you were not at home and furious Binnie had gone so far away without telling him.'

Lilly sat up a little. 'Why should she have?'

Noel lit a cigarette and handed it to her. 'That's a very good question.'

'I didn't think they were in touch. I never saw Binnie put pen to paper the whole time she was here. Could she have been the mole all along?'

Noel scratched his forehead. 'I can't comment on that, but Royce seemed suspicious. From the way he stared at each of us, I don't think he believed a word we were saying.'

Lilly balanced the cigarette on the edge of an ashtray. 'He does that.'

'Even I found him threatening and if I could have backed away, I think I probably would have.'

Noel's encounter with Royce did nothing to ease her mind. 'Did you tell him that Binnie had done a bunk?'

'No. Miss Pearl said Binnie's husband-to-be had sent for her. There'd been a letter and no time to tell anyone properly that she was off. Not even her own daughter. She said you'd gone to join her when the telegram came.'

Lilly squeezed her eyes shut. 'So many lies, Noel. I hate that you are all perjuring yourselves for me.'

He groaned, shame-faced. 'I think – well, we all thought at the start that maybe you had exaggerated Royce a little, but the Miss Pinkneys said they'd seen behind your mask straight away. Miss Pearl said that you were very guarded about what you did say about him and I said the same. But by the time we had spent some time with Royce, we all felt we'd have sworn black was white to keep you clear of him. He's a volatile bomb with a very short fuse.'

Goose got up and trotted down the veranda, laying his chin on her knee. Lilly ruffled his damp fur. 'I shouldn't have allowed myself to leave Teddy behind.'

Noel looked down at his dog. 'Your son seemed happy.'

Question after question rose in her mind but she pushed them all down bar one. 'Where are they staying?'

'One of the Miss Pinkneys – I can't remember which one – told him they don't accept children. I thought that was brave, considering it was obvious they were both scared stiff of him. She said he would have to take a room at the Grand.'

'Royce already knew about the child embargo because that's why he sent me here – knowing full well I couldn't bring Teddy.' Lilly kept her eyes on his face. 'How did he seem?'

Noel swallowed. 'Teddy asked his father if Plumpty had got in a muddle and forgot they were coming.'

She clutched her stomach and leaned forward in her chair. 'I feel sick, Noel. Can't you see what he's doing?

He's poisoning my son against me. Goodness knows what Royce has been saying about me. What if he's told Teddy I don't want to be his mother any more? I can't just sit here knowing that my son is in a hotel on Mall Road and I'm hardly a mile away from him.' She got up and straightened her *kameez*. 'Enough is enough. I'm going to change my clothes and—'

Noel jumped up and laid a hand on her arm. 'No, Lilly. Think!'

She gave a slow shake of her head. 'I have to get Teddy away from him. I have to take him and get him home.'

'But where is home?'

'Wherever I am.' Her voice caught in her throat.

He settled her back in the basket chair and sat on the edge of another. 'You have to be practical. If you snatch him here, where will you take him? There's one road in and out of town. He'd find you in five minutes.'

She lifted her glass and took a few sips. 'And that's the problem I can't seem to solve. I come up with a new plan every day but each is as desperate as the last. I've been thinking of going back to England but have no money for the passage and even if I managed it, I can't count on my grandparents. Snatching Teddy from under his father's nose is my best option but even if I got away with it, you're right – I have nowhere to take him and no money to support us. To have a viable plan in place there has to be some hope of success, and . . .' She bit her lip. 'As hard as I try, I can't seem to find one.'

He looked away from her, towards the open window. 'Tomorrow they are leaving, and I have offered them the use of the house in Choti Haldwani while Royce sorts out transport to Calcutta. Initially, he'll have to take the train from the railway terminus at Kashipur that runs the line from Punjab to Calcutta. He'll stop at Bareilly and travel back past Cawnpore via Varanasi and on to Calcutta. The thousand miles or so will take him about a week. For the time being, while we know exactly where Royce and Teddy are, you must also leave as soon as the coast is clear.'

Again, she shut her eyes as a picture came unbidden. She saw Teddy's face, creased up in concentration as the tutors came in relays, a half-hour allotted to each subject. She had been forbidden to intervene, to stand between their son and his education, as the tutors drummed sums into his head, coaxed English spelling onto the page and extracted the Hindi verbs from his mouth. Royce had insisted that education was everything. Given the storm he'd blown up over a few hours at the circus, she couldn't believe he would have abandoned that plan.

'Is he not to take Teddy home to Cawnpore? What happened about sending Teddy to school in Darjeeling?'

'Oh Lilly. I don't believe that's his intention at all. He talked about his leather and bristle brush business and his emporium in Cawnpore and that he has an admirable assistant most capable of running the show in his absence. He came to reclaim you and when he gets to Calcutta and finds you're not there, I believe he'll use Teddy as bait to lure you back to his side.'

Chapter 14

By the following evening, the moon had elbowed any hint of rain from the sky. A gin cocktail and plate of nuts at her elbow, Lilly was sitting in her favourite place in the corner of Noel's study. She looked around at the well-worn furniture, the glass-fronted bookshelves behind which his library was housed and the desk below it on which stood his pipe rack and a photograph of his father, mother and sister.

Jittery at the thought that she would soon leave Lake View, her hands were so tightly interlocked that her wedding ring cut into her finger. For a moment, she squeezed them tighter thinking how the Bandra nuns would ease their soul through torments of the flesh and then dropped her hands into her lap. Physical pain and punishment were memories she did not cherish.

Noel's deep rumble startled her from the doorway. 'You look lost in thought.'

She turned and leaned her head against the wingback chair. Lilly worried at the state of him. He looked shattered, his face pale and drawn.

'Just trying to get my head around things. Royce turning up yesterday made me realise that in staying here, I'm putting all of you in danger. How long will it be before he discovers I've not joined up with Binnie?' She worried a finger in a hole on the chair arm.

'We need to talk about that.'

Lilly could see behind his spectacles that his eyes were troubled.

'It largely depends on who has been supplying him with information. When he leaves, he may not get as far as Calcutta if he has arranged for telegrams at the railway stations as he goes.'

'What do you mean?'

'All the major railway stations have a telegraph office. He can pick up word wherever he stops.'

She drew in her chin. 'You said *when* he leaves. Did he not go this morning?'

His eyes never left her face. 'The Miss Pinkneys said Royce came back this morning. They were like two little girls afraid of being left alone in the dark. Even though he tried to use Teddy as a charming distraction, they were frightened out of their wits.'

Lilly thought of all the times Royce had slammed her head against a door, threatened her with a knife, yanked her by the hair. 'No cheap reassurances, please. Pour yourself a drink and come and sit down. I want the truth of what went on.'

Noel began to pace around the room, his footsteps echoing as he passed from rug to floorboards and back. 'He didn't believe that you had left to join up with Binnie. He ransacked the house for anything that would disprove what we'd said, pulling items from drawers, sweeping books off shelves. The place looked like a tornado had passed through. Miss Pearl said that she'd never seen anyone so angry.'

Lilly twisted her fingers in her lap, dismayed that he could generate such terror into two innocent old ladies. 'They shouldn't be scared witless in their own home.'

'Nor should you, Lilly.'

'This is all my fault. If I had behaved in Cawnpore, they wouldn't have had to come face to face with that monster.'

He stopped in his tracks. 'What do you mean "behaved"?'

'I took Teddy to the circus without asking Royce first. That's why he sent me away without him.'

'I would never dream of telling you what to do but, Lilly, this has got to stop. Royce is ferreting about at the bottom end of town, so tell me what you are going to do and I'll do my best to make it happen.'

'I still don't know.'

Noel bent over and helped himself to a handful of pistachios. 'What about going with Duffy and Margot to the circus? I think that job is yours if you want it.'

She shook her head. 'It's a ridiculous idea, Noel.'

'You've been practising at the high enclosure. You're getting quite good.'

'That's very sweet of you, but we both know I am no performer. My best bet is to hole up in the *bustee* and find work somewhere.'

He settled into the chair by the fire and picked up his paper. 'Seeing Royce has clearly warped your judgement. The native quarter is not a solution. It would raise more questions than answers. Indian society is bound by caste and family, and how would you explain Teddy having no father? No, Lilly. You'll have to do better than that.'

Lilly got up and walked across to the French doors. It had been raining all week and it still hadn't let up. She stood for a few moments staring up at the sky and then let her gaze slide down to the lake.

'It's still light outside. Could you bear to get wet? I'm in need of a walk.'

Noel looked up, his expression surprised. 'It's not very nice out.'

'I know. But we've been cooped inside for days and I have to clear my head. I'll go by myself if you'd rather not.'

He folded his paper and laid it on the arm of the chair. 'Conti won't come, I'm sure.'

'Then let's just go, the two of us.'

Noel look at his dog who was in his basket snoring in front of the fire. 'I suppose Goose could burn off some energy.'

Lilly laughed. The dog was like an infant who could switch from deep sleep to full wakefulness in the blink of an eye. Sensing an outing, he was fully alert, watching Noel's face, his ears pinned back with hope.

'Ready, boy?' Noel said and almost before the question was framed, Goose bounded from the room barking joyously at the prospect of his walk.

Armed with a couple of mackintoshes from the cupboard in the hall, they descended the stone steps beyond the lawn and took the path that wound down to the lake. They walked along companionably, Noel holding an umbrella over her head with Goose trotting ahead, his nose to the ground.

They ambled on, saying very little, until eventually they came to a clearing in the woods. A small army of grape hyacinths stood stiff beneath the trees and dwarf daffodils, their leaves a luxurious green, looking soon to flower. The air was full of their scent.

Noel collapsed the umbrella and stabbed the tip into the soft earth. For the next quarter of an hour as he bent and straightened, flinging out his arm for his dog to chase after sticks, she told him what she'd decided to do.

★

The next day, it was well after eleven before Lilly emerged from her room and found Noel in the study, puffy-eyed, his breakfast laid out before him. She was glad he was on his own.

She felt half a degree more cheerful than the night before and yet the shadow of her predicament seemed to hover in the air like a thick black cloud.

Panels of yellow light tracked across the hearth rug on which Noel was standing, revealing bald patches where the pile had worn thin. He was studying a letter with a deep furrow between his brows. At the sight of her, he hastily folded it and stowed it in his jacket.

Lilly made an attempt at flippancy. 'Death threat from Royce?'

'It's not something to joke about.'

'I know. Sorry.'

He crossed to the gate-legged table and began to ladle guava jam on to his plate. 'Help yourself if you're hungry.'

'I'm fine for the moment, thank you.'

He took his toast to the sofa and sat with the plate on his knee. 'At the séance, I told you I have some land at Choti Haldwani where we have the other house and that I'm creating a model farm there for the locals. I'd like them to be able to grow their own fruit and vegetables but I don't have the skills to manage it properly. The land needs clearing, fencing in and so on and Conti has been applying on my behalf for training.'

'Goodness.'

'The letter I have in my coat pocket tells me that I have an appointment with the Revenue Department at Raj Bhavan in a week's time.'

'At Government House?'

'Not a picnic on the lawn this time. I'm negotiating a position with the Imperial Forestry Department.'

She sat in the armchair next to the fire. 'Why the Revenue Department?'

'Revenue is a sub-section of the Home Department, which operates out of the Post Office at Government house. If I'm successful, I will be accepted for training as an officer.'

'Conti will be pleased as punch.'

His face bore an expression she didn't understand. 'If I'm successful, I will be sent to England to train at Cooper's Hill, the Royal Indian Engineering College in Surrey.'

Lilly looked about his manly domain, at shelves stuffed with dusty ornaments, then let her eyes rest on the framed picture of the Queen Empress Victoria hanging on the wall. 'I was to be presented at Court before I came to India.'

'I thought you had to have kissed the Queen's hand to have that honour.'

'My grandmother had and so was able to nominate me.'

'Aristocracy in our midst?'

'No. My grandfather was a banker – a member of the Stock Exchange. That qualified them, I believe.'

'You never had any intention of coming to India, did you?'

'No. I'd had my formal dress fitted, my plumes and veil were on order, and I was practising my deep curtsey when Binnie's letter came.'

'I see now why you are so bitter.'

'That was to have been my life. I've had to silence that person, or I would have gone mad with shouting. And . . .'

Noel caught the hesitation in her voice. 'And?'

'I don't know how to say this as I don't want to cause you offence, but my grandparents are dreadfully prejudiced against the Indians. They think the British should clear out and leave India to stew in its own juice.'

'And yet they sent you to India.'

Painful memories came to her uncensored. 'There was a letter. My mother said she missed me and I was sent here.'

'After all those years?'

She waved away the question. It was territory she couldn't explore. 'Enough about me. Are you to become an engineer?'

'No. I will train at the forestry school. Not only will I learn how to manage my own patch of turf but there are wider openings. To do what I want to do at Choti Haldwani, I will need funds and that entails me finding a salaried job. The Indian Public Works Department are anxious to recruit personnel – and I quote – "for the protection and participatory sustainable management of natural resources".'

'Meaning what?'

'We learn how to manage the forest for the production of timber, which eventually will allow me to sell trees off my own land.'

The door opened and Duffy appeared in the space and seemed to be reasoning with himself. 'Am I in the way?'

'Not at all,' Lilly said.

Noel beckoned him forward. 'Come on in. We're just chatting.'

Having welcomed his company, Lilly felt suddenly shy and busied herself with the coffee pot.

He came to her side and picked up a cup. 'Just because I haven't talked to you about Royce doesn't mean that I'm not feeling for you.'

'I can't talk about him either. Probably, though, for different reasons from you.'

Duffy took a cigarette from the box on the desk and sat with his coffee on the fender seat. He glanced at Noel before saying, 'Noel says he's dangerous. How on earth could you not have seen that? Before you married him.'

She shrank from the interrogation as she watched him light his cigarette. 'I only knew him for a few days before the ring was on my finger. I was totally ignorant of the man he really was.'

He smiled at her encouragingly, but she would not let him hold her eye.

'I was sent to the Loreto Convent School in Bandra. One of the nuns' specialities was finding husbands for their matriculating girls. Out of a number of candidates, Binnie selected Royce and that, as they say, was that.'

She heard him draw in a breath. 'Why?'

Lilly hitched a shoulder towards her ear. 'Only Binnie has the answer to that, but she is not for saying.'

Duffy crushed out his cigarette and tossed it in the fire. He got up and stretched out his back. 'What I came in to tell you is that since you told us at dinner last night you're definitely joining the circus, Conti's come up with a plan but it means a rather swifter departure than you might have been anticipating.'

'When?'

'Tomorrow.'

Lilly had counted on another forty-eight hours, possibly more, to give Royce time to get clear.

Duffy turned to Noel and in a brisker tone said, 'Conti says you would be safer taking the route to Bhimtal where your mother has the fishing lodge. The footpath will discourage any but the most determined traveller and if the lodge has a tenant in it, there's always the *dâk* bungalow. From there you could descend directly to Kathgodam and join up with the circus train from a different direction.'

Noel thought for a moment. 'It's a much longer route – at times hardly more than a bridle path – but that's in its favour, I suppose.'

'How far is it?' Lilly looked out of the window and saw that it was still raining.

Noel helped himself to more toast. 'It's a really pretty route from Naini to Bhimtal –about twelve miles give or take. And then from Bhimtal to Kathgodam, where the circus train is waiting, is about another seven. You wouldn't be able to do it in a day.'

Lilly felt her pulse quicken. 'Am I to go alone?'

Noel brushed dry crumbs from his shirt. 'Of course not. I'll stay on and do a couple of days' fishing but I'll take you to the train to make sure you get there in one piece.'

Lilly changed her mind about breakfast and loaded up a plate. 'I can't leave without saying goodbye to the Miss Pinkneys.'

'Out of the question. If you want to pen them a note, I'll trot down with the letter this afternoon. But we have no idea where Royce is so, no, you cannot leave this house.'

Anxiety for the two ladies nagged at her heart. 'But what if Royce threatens them again?'

'Duffy will keep an eye until he leaves with Margot the day after tomorrow. I don't think Royce will hang around once he's established that you really are not here.'

The following morning, after an early breakfast, they set out in the cool dawn.

Conti handed Lilly a package. 'A proper pashmina. It might be cold when you stop tonight. Have confidence in Noel. He's utterly dependable.'

Conti walked with her to the veranda and wrapped her in a hug.

Tears pricking at her eyes, Lilly made an attempt at cheerfulness. The kindness of these two, she thought. Their unremitting kindness. 'How will I get it back to you?'

'Don't be silly. It's a gift. I don't want it back.'

Lilly removed herself from Conti's embrace and ran down the steps.

The hill ponies were waiting in the lane with the hill men who would accompany them. Wisps of cloud hung like cobwebs in the endless blue sky. Despite the early hour, the mountain sun was already strong when Lilly and Noel climbed into their saddles. They had agreed to leave by seven to reach the *dâk* bungalow at Bhimtal by late afternoon.

'We must get to the government resthouse before sundown. Mother says there is a tenant in the lodge and these places are run on a first come, first served basis. I can't imagine that we'll have competition for the rooms but as we can't book ahead, I'd rather be safe than sorry.' He shifted his leg and adjusted the girth under his saddle. 'But we do know the *dâk* keeper – he used to work at the Yacht Club so I'm sure that'll count for something. Coolies have gone ahead with the bedding, cooking pots and kerosene cans. They're at least three hours in front of us and they'll let him know we'll need food when we arrive.'

Duffy walked a little way up the road with them along the bamboo boundary of Noel's garden leading Lilly's horse by the bridle. When they reached the bend at the top, he dropped his hands from the harness and turned to her, his smile non-committal. 'See you in Kathgodam. Noel will take you to the railway terminus where the circus train is in the siding. Ask for Mr Tiffert. He knows to expect you.'

As they continued up the path, feeling slightly faint with excitement, Lilly swapped the reins to her right hand and turned in her saddle; she stared and stared, willing Duffy to turn back, until the trees hid him from view.

Chapter 15

At first, their descent from Nainital to Bhimtal was easy riding.

It was beautiful verdant country, the air crystal-clear. The sun filtered through the trees and every now and then, Lilly caught a glimpse of snow-capped mountains, brilliant white against the sparkling blue sky.

On either side of the track, the deodars grew tall and water flowed down steep ravines, but as they began to lose height, the forest gave way to sal trees and teak.

Occasionally the terrain levelled out and they were able to canter for a stretch.

I'm doing this, Lilly said to herself. I am really leaving Royce, but she did not quite believe it.

The freedom of riding with Noel in these vast surroundings was exhilarating. Every uninterrupted view seemed to encapsulate rural India: a cow wearing a necklace of daisies; a vulture on a tree, its shoulders seeming to sag under the weight of its feathers; a flock of scrawny goats tended by a half-clad boy.

And yet.

By the middle of the morning, they had ridden several miles and Lilly was bone-weary, her lower back jarred and aching. The terrain was no longer easy-going, the constant adjustment from light to shade was hard on the eyes and for a while she'd been fighting the pain in her temples.

When the halt was called for morning tea, for Lilly it wasn't a moment too soon. Not only had it been years since she'd sat on a horse, but it was the first time she'd ridden astraddle.

Noel had apologised. 'We ride hill ponies astride. I'm not sure how you'll manage for clothing. The pyjamas won't give your legs much protection.'

'I'll make do. I have side-saddle breeches that I'd normally wear under a riding habit. I'll just put them on underneath.' What she didn't add was that side-saddle breeches had decorative buttons on the outside of the left leg and on inside of the right, which dug uncomfortably into her skin as she squeezed her thighs against the leather.

They drew up their horses beside a mountain stream where larkspur grew in clumps at the water's edge.

Noel tethered the ponies and Goose bounded off to nose out smells in the soft, lush grass. Hanging from a branch in a basket filled with damp straw, bottles of lemonade had been left for them by the bearers in the forward party. A young man sat beneath the tree, swinging the basket back and forth by a rope tied to his toe.

'Aren't the birds magnificent?' Noel said as he pulled the basket from the branch.

Musical she might be, but Lilly's ear was not tuned to birdsong. She shook her head. 'What can you hear?'

'Where to start? Hundreds of migrant birds come up to summer in the Himalayas. Already this morning I've heard a green barbet, a drongo and my first Indian cuckoo of the year. Listen.' He tipped his head to one side. 'Can you hear that beautiful bell-like clear sound? That's the golden oriole. It's a gorgeous bird but it hides in the branches and you'll hardly ever see it.'

His sun helmet tipped back from his forehead, Noel settled himself on a moss-covered stone and reached for his pipe and tobacco. Clamping the stem between his teeth, he whistled for the dog. Within moments Goose was sprawled at Noel's side, his nose resting on his paws.

Enjoying the smell of the newly lighted tobacco, Lilly bent over and fondled Goose's silky ears. Pulling at the fabric of her riding breeches with her spare hand, she said, 'Why did you call him back? Is anything the matter?'

'No, but I don't want him bounding off. He's a devil if he gets a hint of a jungle fowl rustling in the undergrowth.' He pointed at a corner of rock, seeming to understand her reluctance to sit. 'You might want to stretch your legs while we have a breather, but do have a rummage in the haversack and fish us out something to eat. Conti's packed a basket that will feed an entire army.'

Lilly winced as she hefted the bag to the stone.

His puckered forehead told her he knew. 'You're in trouble, aren't you?'

'The riding breeches were made for riding side saddle. They have buttons down the left side of both legs so the ones on the right leg dig in as I ride.'

He thrust his hand in his trouser pocket and pulled out his silver penknife. 'I could cut them off.'

The shock of his suggestion almost unnerved her, and Lilly felt the blush warm her cheeks. 'I'd need to take off my pyjamas. You'd see my legs.'

'Lilly. You are running away to the circus. You will be dressed in a tutu and tights every night when you perform. I think you must not mind if I catch sight of your ankles.'

She wriggled out of the pyjamas and forced out a laugh. 'I suppose you're right. I may as well begin with someone I know who has the manners not to ogle.'

His moustache twitched with concentration. 'If you pull the button upwards, it will expose the stitches and I can snip it either side and pull it free.'

She took hold of the topmost one, wishing the decoration had stopped at her knee. 'Is that high enough?'

'Perfect,' he said and began to saw. He worked quickly, refraining from comment until the last one was free. 'There. All done. I'll do the left leg tonight so both sides match.'

Lilly folded her hand over his. 'Thank you, Noel, for being a darling friend and coming to my rescue.'

He smiled at her with encouragement in his eyes. She saw that he had little gold flecks in his slate grey eyes. 'Do you need a minute or are you ready to go on?'

She gave a brief nod. 'Let me put my pyjamas back on and then I'm all set to ride.'

Down and down they went, the path narrowing until it was barely wider than the pony's shoulders with a high rock wall to one side and a sheer drop to the other. She sagged in the saddle; she was too tired to sit up straight and the dull pain behind her eyes had become a sharp ache. Caught up in her misery, for a moment she lost Noel round a tight turn and panic gripped her heart.

Lilly felt her palms begin to sweat and briefly lost hold of her reins. The pony stood still, one ear back, and pawed at the ground, its hooves scraping on the stone.

'I hate heights, Noel,' she called. 'I'm really scared.'

He was back in view and called over his shoulder. 'Let the pony do the work. If she tugs at the rein give her her head and she'll pick her way down. It's inbred in them. Just don't fight her.'

For the next few twists and turns of the route, Noel was unusually talkative. It seemed he knew every legend of every peak in sight. He explained that Bhimtal was the best route between the Kumaon mountains and the plains of India. It was a stopping place for traders from Tibet travelling down with caravans of sheep loaded with borax, to trade for goods that couldn't be obtained in the high mountains. It may well have been part of the Silk Route, he thought, but wasn't entirely sure.

Lilly knew his chatter was his way of distracting her from the sheer drop on one side of the track, but his rambling monologue didn't disguise the tinkle of loose stones as they skittered over the drop-side of the path. She leaned back in her saddle lying flat on her spine, the pony almost sitting on its haunches as they negotiated the slope. She could feel the pulse pounding in her temple.

'Noel, can you stop? I'm going to get off and walk.'

Again, he swivelled in his saddle. 'Stay where you are. It's more dangerous to walk. Hang on in there. We haven't much further to go.'

But she dropped her feet from the stirrups and swung her leg over slid off the saddle and squeezed herself between the pony and the rock face. She edged her way in front of the animal and holding the reins in one hand, she braced herself against the rock with the other, and inched her way down the path. Eyes misted with tears, she didn't watch where she was going and stumbled on a sharp stone, falling flat on her face.

In a second Noel was out of his saddle, by her side, scooping her up towards him, his arms tight around her.

Lilly could feel his heart jumping in his chest against her own. 'Any damage?'

She compressed her lips for a moment, but her eyes must have given her away. 'I don't think so,' she murmured.

'Where's my plucky girl of this morning?'

'My head began to swim, and I just fell.'

'You probably need something to drink.' Keeping his arm around her, he pulled a water bottle from his pocket and unscrewed the cap. 'Take a few swigs.'

When she had drunk, he wetted his handkerchief and dabbed at a graze on her forehead. She gasped at the pain and forced herself not to cry out.

'Look here. You've got a bit of a gash but we're going to have to carry on. It'll take another couple of hours or so of steady going to reach the bungalow. Do you think you can manage?'

Margot's words rang in her head. *Circus performers work with injuries all the time.* 'I'm fine,' she lied. 'I just think I'd rather walk to the bottom or to where the track is wider. It's looking over the edge I can't bear.'

He dropped his arm and took a step back. 'Are you sure that this is what you want? In the space of ten minutes two days ago you rushed into the circus thing. Given more time we might have come up with a better way forward to free you from Royce and secure a future with Teddy.'

She looked at his patient face. 'I can't stay in Nainital, Noel. You know that. It's why we're on our way to Kathgodam.'

'It's your call,' he shrugged with a return of conviviality. 'You always have a room at Lake View and I'll always take your side, however things pan out for you. Just don't base all your decisions on fear. Let hope get a look in too.'

'I don't feel hopeful of getting to the bottom in one piece.'

'Get back on the horse. I'll walk beside you down the track on the drop-side and lead my pony. It's not long till it's easy going again and then we can pick up the pace. I promise this is the worst of it.'

On and on the ponies stumbled along the narrow stony path. Goose the faithful companion trotted ahead, ears erect, his pink tongue flopping from the corner of his mouth.

They continued in silence, the hammering in her temple incessant. When the path widened a little, he dropped behind her until eventually they reached the plain.

Noel raised his foot to the stirrup. 'Do you want to kick on? Let the horses stretch out their legs?'

She watched the sky as a dark cloud blotted out the sun and wondered if it might rain.

'All right,' Lilly said and urged her horse to a canter. 'The sooner we get there, the better.'

At Bhowali, they stopped for another break. A different man sat beneath a different tree and flapped the wicker basket back and forth.

Lilly smiled at him to show she was grateful, and he stared back. There was something about the intensity of his gaze that caught her unprepared, his eyes watching her so intently. The toe swinging the rope dropped to the floor and he stood up and took a step towards her.

And then, she was sure.

She froze in her saddle and whipped her head round to Noel. 'I've seen him before.'

A question widened his eyes, but she shook her head and said no more.

Noel swung out of his saddle and took the bottles and a pack of sandwiches from the wet straw nest. Goose sat on his haunches and stared at the paper package with hope in his eyes. This dog didn't steal. He would sit and wait until he was told that he might eat.

Noel tore a sandwich in half and signalled to his pet. 'We've about another half a mile to the crest of the ridge and then you will see Bhimtal down beneath us.' He glanced towards the bearer. 'And then we can talk.'

'Is it very much further?' Almost at the limit of her endurance, Lilly watched the gentle way the dog took the food from his hand.

'We're about halfway. Did you know Bhowali is renowned for producing the finest fruits? If we're lucky, we might stumble across a wayside seller. Something sweet would be good for your fatigue.'

She eased the pain from her back and shoulders and looked at him without a word. At that moment she couldn't have cared less if Noel had told her the houses were roofed with gold. She stuffed down a sandwich and drank her lemonade, too spooked to get off her pony.

They covered the remaining miles at a rising trot and just as she was wondering how much more she could bear, a clearing in the trees brought Bhimtal into view.

The lake was a sparkling sea of emerald water lying in the fold of a tree-clad valley.

It could have been a Scottish resort – somewhere she had been to shoot grouse with her grandparents when she was a girl – a million years ago.

Set in its own gardens and full of flowers whose names she did not know, the *dâk* bungalow was larger than she was expecting.

There were three pairs of rooms, separate and independent from the others, each accessed from its own door on the front veranda. Lilly had been allocated the pair in the middle and Noel had the two rooms to the left. The front room was freshly whitewashed and contained a table and two chairs and a rug on the floor. In the corner, her bedding had been placed on a *charpoy*, the traditional woven

Indian bed. The second room was a bathroom of sorts: a cool spartan room containing a solitary chair, a hook on the wall and a brass basin for washing, balanced on a wooden tripod. There was also a bathtub set on the floor surrounded by a line of bricks about six inches high. The principle was straightforward. When the bath was finished, the tub was upended and left to drain through a hole in the floor.

Lilly lowered herself into a chair, hardly able to move, while through the wall, she heard Noel ordering up a bath.

Moments later, he knocked on her door although she'd left it wide open. 'Are you decent?'

'Come in, Noel.'

He took two strides into the room. 'Tea's waiting on the veranda but before we sit down, do you want to tell me what went on back there, when we had the rest stop at Bhowali?'

The throbbing in her head was relentless. 'I recognised the man from the cast in his right eye. He struck a chord in my memory, but I can't place him. I've been sitting here racking my brains.'

'Are you absolutely certain?'

She nodded and with that conviction came a sense of fear. 'Where are the porters now?'

He took a handkerchief from his breast pocket and blew his nose. 'I couldn't tell you. They disappeared into the woodwork and will only come back the day after tomorrow when I head for home.'

'Oh God!' she whispered, pressing her hand against her temple. 'Royce could be here.'

'It's too soon. If the fellow has been paid to pass on a message, it will take him a day to get back to Nainital or to push on to Kathgodam.'

'If you're sure.'

'I am, and what I also wanted to say is that if you want to give me your breeches, I could cut the buttons off the other leg?'

Gingerly, she lifted a leg. 'Can we leave it for now? I haven't the energy to move and I think I'll have to soak them off in the bath. The fabric is stuck to my skin.'

'I hadn't realised that things were so bad. You must make sure you wash thoroughly with soap and water. It's the best thing. Your forehead as well.'

'I don't suppose you have any ointment?'

'I'll see if I can rustle you up some turmeric powder to pat on. That would be much the best thing and obviously you can't ride tomorrow and probably not the day after that either. We should take a couple of days to rest and leave after that.'

Lilly stiffened. 'We have to be in Kathgodam by tomorrow. Before the circus train leaves.'

'I know but the distance is almost the same as today, and you're not fit to go on.'

She wondered why he was so against her going, but said only, 'I really don't want to lie in a stifling sling for the better part of a day.'

He hitched a shoulder towards his ear. 'It's that or walk, Lilly, if you want to make the train.'

That night, she lay on her string bed, distressed almost to the point of weeping. The disagreement she'd had with Noel raged round in her head and she felt entirely at fault, as if he had caught her stealing money from his wallet.

After supper, they'd settled themselves in long chairs on the veranda and stretching their legs out on the extending leg rests, his face was hard and held a look she had not seen before.

'I think you've changed,' he said in his quiet way.

Unsettled by his comment, she thrust out her chin in a show of defiance. 'Since when?'

There was a perceptible pause before he went on. 'Be careful, that's all.'

'How have I changed? If you're going to level accusations at me, you need to back them up.'

He reached under his chair and held out a burlap sack. 'Conti has asked me to give you a stack of postcards. She has addressed and stamped them. She just asks that you let us know where you are and how you are doing from time to time. She says we should have an emergency signal – just in case the worst happens with Royce.'

'If he comes back to Nainital?'

'Or if we get a sniff of him from somewhere else and need to warn you.'

'All right. What do you suggest?'

'Something no one could interpret but us.'

'The greyhound is out of the trap. Would that do?' It was one of her grandfather's pet expressions for when Granny was on the rampage. It had kept them out of trouble many, many times.

He nodded. 'Very British.'

She could see there was more in the bag. 'What else is in there?'

'My father's service revolver. I want you to take it.'

'Whatever for?'

'Behind every tree lurks a tiger. If one jumps out at you, don't be afraid to shoot.'

Lilly wasn't sure if he was speaking metaphorically or whether he meant there were tigers in the surrounding hills. 'You don't mean we're going to run into tigers here, do you?'

He looked down for a long moment and then said, 'No, not here. But you are going to a circus.'

She studied him, wondering what he was getting at. 'Caged tigers are not much of a threat, I wouldn't have thought.'

He nodded once, pressing his lips together. 'Let's hope you're right.' Then he got up from his chair and tucked in his shirt. 'I hope everything pans out as you want it. But if it doesn't, you know where I am. In the meantime, take the gun. You never know when you might have to pull the trigger.'

She took it, felt the weight of it in her hand and spun the chamber.

It was fully loaded and ready to fire.

Chapter 16

That night, Lilly tossed and turned, sat up and lay down, but sleep would not come.

It seemed she had barely closed her eyes before Noel was outside her door, knocking gently, announcing the new day. 'I'm awake,' she called.

The door opened but it wasn't Noel who came in.

The *dâk* bungalow keeper placed a tray beside her bed. '*Chota hazri.*'

She watched him pour tea into a cup. '*Suniye Noel babu uth kar taiyar hogaye hain kya?*'

'Oh yes, *Memsahib*. He is long since up and has gone back to Nainital. Sahib says you must wear your English clothes. When you are ready, the bullock cart is here to take you to the train. That is what he told me to say.'

She felt a shock in her heart at his leaving her there on her own. Her mind numb, she picked up the teacup, and took a sip, allowing the hot drink to give her some comfort. As she set it back down on the saucer, she noticed a piece of paper tucked beneath the pot on the tray. *Lilly* was scrawled on the front, the writing almost illegible.

She unfolded the scrap of paper and read his words: *Forgive me for my early departure. I'm no good at goodbyes. Keep safe, Lilly. Noel*

★

A bullock cart, Lilly knew all too well, was a loose description for any type of cart pulled by an ox and some were considerably more uncomfortable than others.

The cart that Noel had secured for her was the most basic of its type, a two-wheeled, wooden-framed conveyance that was little more than a wooden platform yoked to a pair of oxen by a plaited hemp rope. This one, however, had a woven roof structure that gave the cart the appearance of a gypsy caravan or one of those bathing machines she'd seen on the beach at Brighton.

Wearing a grubby, battered hat, the driver sat on the ox-bow yoke in much the same way as the *mahout* had sat on his elephant, his short, skinny legs dangling on either side of the wooden collar, a long, thin whip in one hand.

He jerked his head at the back of the wagon, indicating she should put her belongings there, and sat on his perch while she scrambled into the cart.

She braced her back against the side of the cart and, with her heart in her mouth, tapped the cart boards with her foot. '*Challo! Challo!*' she called. 'Let's go! Let's go!'

As the day wore on and the cart lurched along the rutted track, she pitched between the sadness that Noel had left without saying goodbye and relief that she was leaving her husband behind.

By mid-afternoon, the sun was high in the sky and they had been creeping along in the swaying unsprung wagon for hours. She had no real sense of where they were but guessed they couldn't be far from Kathgodam.

She framed her eyes against the sunshine with the sides of her flattened hands and focused on a distant tuft of smoke that rose above the teak trees.

'Is it much further?'

He eased the oxen to a halt then squatted on his haunches, elbows on knees and waggled his head from side to side. '*Kya aap bhookhe hain?*'

Not just hungry, she was starving.

He hopped up and a *dabba* – a brass tiffin box – appeared beside her. She released the handle and pulled out the three tins that were stacked up on top of each other. Inside the first was roti bread, the second contained rice and the third potato in a fragrant sauce.

She took some rice, rolled it into a ball with her fingers and soaked it in the potato dish then put it in her mouth with no spill or mess. Royce's mother had shown her how to eat with her hands, saying that it was just practice, that even a British person could manage.

The driver nodded his approval. 'You eat like an Indian.'

'This is delicious. Did your wife make it?'

'Oh yes. She is a very fine cook. Noel Sahib asked me to bring you food. He said you eat like a horse.'

She laughed. 'When did he ask you to take me to Kathgodam?'

His huge dark eyes locked on her face. 'Last night when he paid for the cart.'

Lilly tried to ask more, but the words would not come.

Nothing could have prepared her for the fresh wave of wretchedness that suddenly engulfed her. More than once during the night she had been tempted to knock on his door, wondering if he, too, was sleepless. He was the very best of men but she knew as she sat eating the food that he'd given her, that she could not have stayed in Nainital without risking everyone she cared for.

Their friendship was at an end. She would never see him again.

For most of the afternoon, they descended steadily through the wooded lowlands, the foliage shimmering greenish-blue in the heat until, just before five o'clock, the cart driver pulled up at Kathgodam railway station, a long thin building behind which were two platforms and an old bandy-legged man who didn't look up to the job of portering her luggage.

Wearing a sleeveless cotton coat, his dhoti looped between his legs, and tucked into the waistband behind his back, the man placed a little round cap on top of his wiry, greying hair. He hoisted her trunk onto his head and gathered up the rest of her baggage, his elbows squeezed in tight to keep everything secure.

'Do you need me to help?' Lilly feared for his well-being. 'I could carry something.'

'It is my job to be carrying these loads. I have pride in carrying these loads,' he said in a tone of voice he had copied from the English. Slow and deliberate, as if talking to the mentally impaired. 'We go now. You are keeping up till the other side we are reaching. We are not stopping.' He waggled his head to indicate the direction they would take, but the trunk seemed glued in place. He set off at an alarming pace, cutting a straight path down the crowded platform as a farmer might furrow a field.

Lilly launched herself into the throng, following the red of his cotton coat through the station concourse, elbowing her way through the milling masses, the heavy pre-monsoon air a brutal reminder that India seared, away from the cool of the hills.

★

As Duffy had said, the circus train that moved the show from one stand to another was parked on a railroad siding, the letters 'TIFFERT'S CIRCUS AND ROYAL MENAGERIE' emblazoned in gold on its purple baggage cars. At every designated destination, he said, the wagons would be hauled to the circus ground and lined up behind the big top like a mobile town.

The circus wagons were already mounted on a long line of railway flatcars, ready to move out the following day.

Mr Tiffert sat behind the desk in his office wagon car. A heavy-set man, he wore rimless wire glasses and was almost bald apart from a fringe of silver hair that half-circled his head. Despite his lack of head hair, his moustache was full, and his grizzled beard closely cropped. Wearing an expensive, mouse-grey tailored suit, the cuffs of his crisp white shirt fastened with mother of pearl buttons, he was fully engrossed in a magazine, *Berliner Leben*. A rottweiler sat on its haunches, eyes fixed on her, its head slightly raised and ears erect. A menacing growl grumbled in its throat.

Lilly rolled back her shoulders and put on her best, English drawing-room accent and held out her hand. 'Mr Tiffert. It's terribly nice to meet you.'

'Who the shit are you?'

'I'm Lilly Myerson. Duffy Puttnam said that you would be expecting me.'

He sat up from his desk and set his reading material aside. He slapped a welcome on his face with great speed, but it was obvious his smile was perfunctory.

Pulling a packet of Muratti cigarettes towards him, he flipped up the lid and put one between his lips. He lounged back in his chair, and as he spoke, it waggled up and down like an admonishing finger.

She stepped towards him, but the dog gave a predatory snarl and looked ready to pounce.

He reached for a wooden match and struck it on the side of the box. He tipped his head back against the chair and pulled on the cigarette, blowing perfect circles of smoke towards the ceiling. '*Feinster türkischer Tabak.*'

'I'm sorry?'

'Finest Turkish tobacco. My wife brings back packages of cigarettes when she goes home to Germany and the matches too. German matches with phosphorous tips are the best. Wax matches are too prone to damp.'

Lilly took a second, more cautious step. 'I didn't know that.'

The dog curled its lips and gave a savage growl. Lilly shrank back.

'Don't mind Clara. My wife's trained her to behave like that when a woman comes in to the office. Any funny business and she will go for your neck. She's a great guard dog.'

Lilly wondered for whom – Mr Tiffert or his wife?

'Should I not move?'

'You're fine as long as you don't touch me,' he said, patting the dog's head with a large sinewy hand. 'Sit down on that packing case.' He pointed his cigarette at a trunk that was pushed hard against the wall.

Lilly backed towards it and lowered herself down, keeping her eyes fixed on the growling dog. 'Is Mrs Tiffert not here?'

'Not Mrs Tiffert. She's a Busch – born into one of the best-known circus families in Europe – and Ines is there now, sourcing potential new ring performers before the off-season. Then she'll sign them up if she likes what she sees. Ines handles the business end of the circus and I take care of the technical side. So . . .' He finished his cigarette and ground it out under the heel of his shoe. 'I hear you need a job.'

'I do. Rather urgently.'

'What's your story?'

Lilly remembered Duffy asking her that very same question when they met on Noel's veranda and wondered whether he had coined it from this man. 'I have to disappear for a while.'

'Everyone in the travelling circus is running away from someone or something and chasing after a dream that probably doesn't exist.' He shrugged his shoulders. 'If you want to disappear, the circus is the perfect place. Make no mistake though, the circus is an exacting bedfellow. It will take its toll on your personal life.'

She folded her hands in her lap, squeezing her fingers together until they hurt. 'I'm married, Mr Tiffert.'

'I remember now. I have a letter about you somewhere.' He fished it out from beneath a pile of papers. 'It says you need to bide your time for a while.'

'Yes. I have some things to sort out.'

'What is the circus to you, Mrs Myerson, other than a place to hide?'

Lilly scratched her cheek and it was then she felt it, something taking hold at the back of her neck, tickling hairs; a quiet realisation that she had it in her to impress him.

Images raced through her mind, of glitter and glamour. 'I saw Warren's not so long ago. Circus is showmanship. A spectacle for entertainment. Magic takes place inside the ring.'

A frown appeared on his brow. 'I have no idea what you've been told about Tiffert's but this is not Barnum's American circus with spectacles, freak shows, razzle dazzle and a cast of millions. There are enough physical deformities on the streets in India without displaying them in the ring.

'Animal acts are a big feature of this circus and we have many performing animals. A stud of Arabian horses and Java ponies. Tigers. Ten elephants.' He spread his arms wide to demonstrate the enormity of his menagerie.'

'You have Whizzy Delroy and his trick cycling.'

'Yes, and clowns, a contortionist, acrobats and aerialists. Eighteen acts in total. Fifty performers, a hundred working men and a circus band.' He swivelled in his chair and took a bottle off a shelf. 'Want an IPA?'

She leaned towards him to get a look at the label and provoked a volley of growls from the dog. 'I don't know what that is.'

'India Pale Ale. This one – Jeffery's – comes from Edinburgh. It's too hot to brew beer in India so they ship it out. They advertise on our circus programme and we get crates delivered in return.' He held out the bottle. 'Take it.'

'No thank you, but I would like to know when I will meet Whizzy?'

'He's not back yet from his engagement in Lahore. Most of the performers take other work in the layoff season. They can't survive financially otherwise. He's been playing Stiffles.'

Lilly shook her head.

'Fancy nightclub. He takes his act there. A lot of them have different contracts for the hot weather.'

'Do you think he'll be away for much longer?'

He tipped his head back and drank from the bottle. 'What's the fascination with Whizzy?'

'I thought I was to work with him as his property girl.'

'I agreed to give you a job. I didn't say what it would be or with whom.'

Lilly tried to keep her voice level, hoping he could not hear the note of desperation in her tone. 'But that's why I came. I've even been practising with my bicycle.'

He took a long pull on his beer bottle. 'Look, dear. There's not a lot in your favour as I see it. The letter says you can shoot but we don't have that act in my circus. As I favour, I said I would help you out for a few weeks, but I didn't realise you'd look like a native.'

Lilly stared at her hands. 'It's walnut juice. Underneath, I'm the same as you.'

Mr Tiffert seemed not to register her comment. 'We only have European artistes in our circus because natives come to the circus to see white people. No Indians lying on beds of nails or charming snakes out of baskets in our show. We are guests in this country, and it is our responsibility to respect its people, unlike you British who do your best to demean them.'

'Not everyone is like that.' Lilly spoke the words but knew he was right.

He tipped the dregs of the bottle into his mouth. 'The Maharajas like to have their photograph taken with the stars — quite often they will ask for a private performance — so before you even entertain a notion of stepping foot in the ring, get rid of the brown colour.'

'The stain will wear off in a few days.' Chest tightening, she swallowed hard and braced herself. He's going to turn me away, she thought. And then what? If I can't earn my way, I'll be out with nowhere to go.

He threw the bottle into a basket by his desk. 'Can you muck out a horse?'

'At home we had two gr—' She broke off in time and stopped herself from telling him Grandpa had employed grooms for his horses. 'We had two greys. I mucked them out all the time.'

He raised an eyebrow. 'In that case, you'll have no trouble doing an elephant.'

'Marvellous,' she said. 'I'm very fond of elephants.'

He nodded approval. 'Pay is fifteen rupees a month, board and lodging found.'

One English pound? The maids earned twenty pounds a year at her granny's house, almost double what she was being offered. She clamped her lips together to keep the protest inside.

'We travel by train with the elephants taking the prop wagons and animal dens to the ground. Elephants are much revered in India, and by us, too, because for this show they are the pegs upon which the circus is hung. I said we have ten, give or take. You can start at the bottom end and work your way up. If you show any promise, I'll think about getting you a permit to perform.'

Chapter 17

The living quarters she'd been assigned were in wagon fifty-nine. Not the full wagon, it turned out, but the left-hand half through an entrance marked *Women*.

'You'll be sharing with the Schinkel sisters. Dodo does an iron jaw act and Nattie works the trapeze,' Mr Tiffert told her. 'They'll show you the ropes, if not quite literally.' He stared pointedly at her middle.

Lilly struggled to hold onto her carpet bag and bedding while bumping up her trunk as she mounted the steps. She pushed at the door, realising that this was the first room she had ever shared with people she didn't know.

'Hang on,' a voice called from inside. 'I'll have to move a couple of things before you can get in.'

The door swung in a little more and a face appeared in the space. 'You in here too?'

Lilly nodded. 'Mr Tiffert said there was room for one more but by the looks of things he must have made a mistake.'

It was full of clutter, piled up in corners, suspended by strings from the roof.

'It's how we live. Everyone shares unless you are a showstopper act and then you can pretty much dictate your own terms. The American railcars are called sixty-fours because they hold that many berths. We're quite private with our little home for three.'

Lilly felt her jaw drop.

'First time in the circus?' The woman pushed at a box with her foot to create a little more space.

Lilly dumped her rolled up bedding on the bottom bunk. 'Is it that obvious?'

'First things first. Size of your trunk. Circus regulation size is twenty-six inches and one piece of hand baggage. You're over the limit and if we had more time, I'd make you drag it to the luggage wagon along with everyone else's. What's your act?'

'Property girl for the trick cyclist, but in the temporary absence of Whizzy Delroy, I'm to muck out the elephants.' Lilly took a deep breath expecting mockery, but the woman merely nodded.

'We all have to roll up our sleeves unless you—'

'Are a big star,' Lilly finished.

'Exactly.' The woman with delicate features and hair the colour of apricots held out her hand. 'I'm Dodo Schinkel and on the top bunk is my sister Nattie. We take it in turns to stand up.'

Lilly eyed the stack of three beds, one on top of the other. Three women, plus belongings and a tiny brass burner in a one-windowed space barely ten feet by twelve was going to take some complicated choreography. It was stifling in the wagon and Lilly was grateful that she had chosen to wear a cotton blouse and serge skirt rather than her heavier travelling suit. Dressing in English clothes that morning for the first time in a long while, she realised that she had shed some weight. The blouse sagged over her chest and the skirt slipped over her hips.

'Are you in disguise?'

'Why do say that?'

'You look like you've borrowed someone else's clothes. You're wearing European dress but your hair looks like you are wearing a bearskin hat. You have stain on your hands and face, but your accent is pukka English.'

'You're German?'

'Of course. Coffee?' Dodo offered Lilly a cup of coffee.

Lilly accepted it gratefully but when she looked down at the inky black liquid, she had to wonder whether a teaspoon might stand up in the cup by itself.

'The best of British luck,' Dodo laughed. 'Nattie's coffee is always a challenge.'

'I am that Nattie.' The second lady sat on the top bunk, her legs dangling over the sides. Her head was bent forward owing to the lack of clearance between the top of her hair and proximity of the ceiling. She was in every way identical to Dodo. 'Short for Renata.'

'Is Dodo short for anything?'

Dodo looked faintly outraged. 'No. What is your name?'

'Lilly.'

'Is that short for anything?'

'No.'

'Well then. Yours was a silly question.'

Lilly swallowed. 'Are you always this direct?'

'What other way is there?'

Unable to think of a suitable response, Lilly decided to changed tack. 'Your English is excellent.'

Dodo lifted one shoulder. 'English is the common language in the circus. If you want your point of view to be heard, you need the words to voice it. So, I repeat. Are you in disguise?'

Lilly smiled at the joke, took a sip of bitter coffee and set the cup on the stove. 'I was for a while, when I needed to be.'

Dodo's stare was unnerving. 'You are wearing a wedding ring. Where is your husband? Or is he the problem?'

The lie was instinctive and ready on the tip of her tongue, but Dodo's unexpected frankness pushed her to tell the truth. She twisted the slim gold band on her finger. 'My family is Catholic and would disown me if I took it off. But you are correct. I have left my husband and for the time being that means losing my son. That is beyond hard.'

Dodo sank down on the bottom bunk. 'I have two children. They are with their grandmother but leaving them behind, I agree, takes the spirit from you. Could your mother not be of use?'

Lilly almost laughed out loud. 'My mother is about as useful as a parasol in a tornado.'

'Grandparents?'

Lilly looked around for somewhere to sit but immediately drew a blank. She leaned her back against the window and shook her head. For years she had not spoken about her upbringing, but in the past few months, she'd retold it again and again and with each retelling she realised how spineless she'd been. 'I was brought up with them in England but when I was sixteen my mother wrote saying she wanted me back in India. I sailed into Bombay eight years ago.'

Dodo rolled onto her side and propped her chin under her hand. 'Where next?'

'Convent school for two years in Bandra.'

'Home for the holidays?'

'No, but it wasn't unusual to be unclaimed from school. There were a substantial number of girls like me and when I was eighteen, I married Royce.'

'Why?' Curiosity widened her eyes.

Why indeed? thought Lilly. 'I was sent to the convent to improve my matrimonial chances. The nuns prospected for husbands, and my mother selected Royce.'

Dodo laughed but her expression softened. 'I'd have refused.'

Already, in under an hour, Lilly felt a keen attraction towards these two. Dodo was undoubtedly the stronger personality but she noted that Nattie was no mouse. A tiny thrill of excitement whispered at the back of her mind that these two might become her friends.

'I made a bad choice with my husband. What about you?'

'There is no husband. Nattie and I joined a travelling circus when we were twelve years old. It was a one-wagon, one-horse circus show that toured isolated villages in Eastern Europe. Every night, after the performance, the circus director pressed his very close attentions upon me.'

'Our parents had no money and could not afford to keep us,' Nattie continued. 'They had run their own aerial circus acts until our father could no longer work. He was given a substantial payment in advance and we went with the director, sold to the circus.'

Dodo ran a hand across her stomach. 'I had my little girl when I was a month shy of thirteen and Achim came a year later.'

Lilly wondered at her candour. 'That is truly awful. How can you bear to talk about it?'

'In the circus, even if you are top bill and high earning, everyone will be eyeing your slot to steal it from you. Telling lies. Creating stories. Fabricating fictitious events. Sabotaging your equipment. I am explaining our story – Nattie's and mine – so that when you hear jealous tongues wagging about this and that you will remember the truth. Our parents sold us to the circus to put food in their mouths, allowed a man my father's age to abuse me and accepted the two resulting bastard children as a reasonable return on their investment.'

'Was there no one you could tell?'

She shook her head. 'We were in the middle of nowhere, moving all the time and had no money. But eventually, if you are good at what you do, you can create your own luck. In 1893, we were spotted by the manager of a circus who wanted to replace one of her aerial acts. She agreed to take us both.'

Lilly frowned. 'Ines?'

'Yes.'

'What's she like?'

'An excellent lady golfer like Nattie. She'd hoped to spend the off-season playing golf at the Residency in Nainital, but work drew her to Europe. She won't come back now until the circus finishes in Europe for the winter.'

'I rather meant as a person,' Lilly said, lifting her chin.

'Make your own judgement if you're still here when she gets back, and don't apologise for your opinion. If you have one you should state it.'

I'll bear that in mind, thought Lilly. She cast around the tiny wagon, looking for a space to sit and hide behind her embarrassment. 'Is all this paraphernalia part of your act?'

Dodo nodded. 'Rigging. We carry our own. A carpenter carries his own tools, a hairdresser her own scissors. This is no different. An aerial artiste carries her own equipment.'

More and more, Lilly liked this German lady with her loud voice and sparkling, intelligent eyes. She radiated energy with a personality far in excess of her height. 'What do you do in the circus? Precisely?'

'Precisely, I climb up a dangling canvas-covered rope suspended on swivels from the top of the tent and hang from a strap by my teeth.'

'And I am suspended below on a trapeze.'

'You're joking.' Lilly almost laughed.

'I never joke,' Dodo said. 'I am billed as The Golden Bird.' She stretched out her legs and closed her eyes. 'You'll see when you watch me perform. Now I am going to sleep. Ideally, we travel at night as the animals find the dark and the cooler temperature reassuring. The sway of the train lulls them to sleep. This is a long haul though, to Lucknow. We'll pull in sometime tomorrow, depending on how many stops we make and whether Tiffy wants to offload the livestock.' She yawned more deeply. 'My advice is to hunker down and get some rest, because that will be in short supply when the big top is up and the circus operational. You can take the middle bunk as your legs are longer than mine.'

Lilly sat on her upended cabin trunk, grateful for its rigid reliability. It had cost forty-eight shillings at Henry I. Box and Co. on Kensington High Street and she recognised, as she often had, that Granny Wilkins had never skimped in matters of necessity. Made of brown waterproof canvas and bound round with four cane hoops, the advertisement had claimed it to be lighter and more durable than its compressed fibre equivalent. It was doing excellent duty, just then, as a chair.

Even though she had barely slept for the past few nights, her mind was wound up like a clock. Hour after hour, she sat by the open window, her forehead pressed to the glass, as the labouring train creaked and groaned its way through the night. Every fifteen minutes or so, the train shuddered to a halt at small, whitewashed stations whose unfamiliar names were painted on oblong signs in large black letters. She had been sitting thus, watching the lifeless wastes of central India glide past, since the train had pulled out of the siding at Kathgodam the previous evening.

The train thundered heavily along the track and every yard they covered brought the circus closer. Soon I will see him again, Lilly thought, doing her best to quash the memory of Duffy as she'd ridden off on the hill pony; he'd not turned back nor had he waved goodbye. She brushed aside a chill of doubt. If she was going to make a change in her life, she'd need to be firm. She'd challenge him on that when she saw him.

Screeching brakes and a jolt of enormous force flung her off balance and instantly Lilly thought they must have hit a cow. She craned her head through the window and saw the stars, pale before the dawn, and a sign hanging above the station platform announcing that they had pulled up at Bareilly.

Almost immediately, the stillness of the early morning was broken by a turmoil of sound. Men, women and children carrying flat wicker trays laden with food swarmed down the platform, a tide of surging humanity solid as a wall. Tea and peanut vendors wheedled through the windows, shoving their hands through the slats like pistols; the *paniwallah* carrying water in a dripping goatskin rapped on the bars, pulling anyone still vaguely sleeping from their dreams.

Dodo sat up as far as she could, taking care not to knock her head on the berth above her. 'Where are we?'

'Bareilly.'

'We should get off the train. Stretch our legs. Find somewhere to pee and get something to eat.'

'Are we going to be here a while?' Lilly leaned her head against the wall.

'I don't really know. There's a good restaurant building here. We'll all take it in turns – those of us, of course, who don't have private quarters in the wagons.'

'Big stars?'

'And management. The stars won't associate with the supporting acts. It's fiercely competitive – everyone vying for the top spots, their place on the programme is keenly contested and fought over. I told you before that back-stabbing is rife and no secret safe. Oh! And keep your valuables with you at all times. Make yourself a grouch bag to keep your treasure in your pocket. Even when you are out there performing.'

'You're not selling me the lifestyle,' she joked.

Dodo shrugged. 'You made the decision to be here. I'm just telling you how it is. We could have created merry hell having you in here with us if you are working with elephants and are not a performer.' She swung her legs over the side of the bunk. 'But we didn't, and I am hungry.'

Lilly stood up and worked the crick in her neck. Out of the corner of her eye she saw a rickshaw *wallah*, stretched out across the seat of his conveyance, his legs dangling over the sides. 'Do you think I should go and see if I am needed to help with the elephants?'

Nattie leaned down from the top bunk, her pale butter-scotch hair tousled and her face creased where it had pressed into the pillow. 'Let me give you some advice. Do not volunteer for anything. If they want you, they'll come looking for you. Time off is only ever measured in minutes, so make the most of what you have. Tiffy won't remember from yesterday that he's assigned you to the elephants, but someone will wake up to it when we get to the circus ground.'

Lilly tilted her head towards the ceiling and contemplated the dangling ropes. 'I'm starting to feel out of place.'

'As a first timer I'm sure you are. Let's go and find something to eat and between us, and over the course of today, we'll do our best to settle your nerves.'

They trooped up the platform, snaking their way through the shrieking hordes. Rather than shout, Dodo pointed to a red tiled building and elbowed her way past stands selling brass pots, jewellery and embroidered cotton, cheap books and peacock feather fans. Lilly followed on behind and, several minutes later, was standing in line for the *Refreshment Room – European* amongst the rose bushes of the station-house garden.

They sat down at a table and a waiter set a china-white crockery bowl of thick, spiced stew in front of them with a plate of oven-fresh bread rolls.

Dodo dipped in her spoon and smacked her lips. 'Goat.'

'I can never tell the difference between mutton and goat.' Lilly rubbed at tired eyes with the back of her hand.

'Flavour and texture. What else is in this would you say?'

'I wouldn't know.'

'You're an English *memsahib*. You should be able to tell me. Don't you instruct your servants every morning what to cook before they polish the silver?'

Lilly shook her head. She'd hardly cared what she ate since she stopped caring for herself. 'I never get involved.'

Dodo banged her spoon against the dish. 'You British have such a condescending and contemptuous attitude towards the local people. You are like religious missionaries who try to thrust their version of Christianity down people's throats in the name of civilising the heathens. I am certain India did very well before that greedy villain Robert Clive starved a third of the population to death and sold them out to the crown.'

Lilly felt the rebuke was personal. 'I can only apologise on behalf of the Empire.'

'Taste the stew and tell me what's in it.'

Lilly broke open a bread roll and dipped a chunk of it into the sauce. She took a large bite then stirred the liquid with her spoon. 'At a first glance, meat cubes, potatoes, carrots, cauliflower florets and beans, onion.' She sucked on the bread and considered. 'There's heat from green chillies and whole spices; *jeera, haldi* and *imli* to prolong its life.'

Dodo stared at her for a long time, clearly making a judgment. 'You have a good palate for someone who does not associate with proper India, and a vocabulary that suggests you are more intimate with the country than you would care to admit.'

Lilly did not reciprocate her gaze but ate two mouthfuls of stew then laid down her spoon. She noticed that neither of the sisters had bothered the bread plate.

Nattie placed her spoon on the table. 'I want to know why you are running away from your husband, so we can put rumours straight.'

I'm sure you do, Lilly thought, and closed her eyes briefly, shielding herself from curiosity, sympathy or pity. The sisters hadn't dwelt on the past and neither would she. Her sole focus was to keep hidden from Royce then regain her son. Lowering her head towards the bowl, she began to ladle up the hot, fragrant stew. She was surprised the food was delicious, and more particularly, that she was enjoying it in the company of strangers.

All that day on the train, Lilly and the Schinkel sisters talked. Lilly admired their ease with each other as they shared their stories. She gazed out of the window as the train crawled through the sunburned country, feeling at times that she could count the tail feathers of the birds as they sat on the telegraph lines and the pale stalks of straw on the squat thatched dwellings. They stopped periodically as they had during the night to allow the engine to cool.

Dodo rose from her bunk and indicated, by flicking the tips of her fingers towards the window, that it was her turn to stand. 'You need to find yourself an original act if you're to stand a chance of fitting in. You can't steal someone else's turn.'

Lilly and Dodo squeezed past each other in the centre of the wagon and while Dodo assumed the trunk perch by the window, Lilly worked out how she would get into her berth without the aid of a ladder. Eventually, stepping onto the lower bunk at the foot-end and reaching up to the horizontal bar overhead to which a frilled pink curtain was suspended, she heaved herself up and crawled into her domain. Thrilled at accomplishing such a gymnastic feat, she lay back on her pillows and grinned.

Dodo glanced over, a pitying expression on her face. 'The problem is not just a matter of fitness. Individual acts will never share and certainly not with an unskilled newcomer. Bareback riders are rated top and command the top money. They have honed their skills since the cradle and when you watch them perform you will see why they are considered the best.'

From the creaking above her head, Lilly knew that Nattie was exercising her muscles.

'There are family acts who will not admit an outsider,' Nattie said.

Dodo played with the suspended rigging. 'Animal acts work with their animals and wild animal trainers work alone.'

Nattie sat up but smacked her head against the roof. '*Verdammt und zugenäht!*'

'Don't swear, Nattie,' Dodo chided.

'I was going to say, before I hit my head on the blasted roof, that aerialists will only work with other aerialists. Can you actually do anything, Lilly? Juggle clubs or hoops? Throw knives? Anything at all?'

Lilly was fascinated at the line of hand-sewn pockets tacked up against the wall inside her berth and was on the point of asking their purpose. 'I can ride.'

'Margot owns the horses she works with. She will not let you borrow any of her stock.' Dodo laced her fingers together and raised her hands above her head.

It seemed to Lilly that the two sisters were unable to sit still. 'Duffy said as much.'

That caught Dodo's attention. 'You know Duffy?'

'He was in Nainital at the same time as me. Margot was there too, but not staying in the same place. It was he who suggested I come to the circus.' Or was it though, she wondered. She couldn't remember now.

Nattie tutted. 'Poor old Duffy. Margot's been hounding him for a couple of seasons. Liaisons between sexes are not permitted in this circus and Ines will fire you in a heartbeat if she finds out you've been carrying on behind her back. She runs a very strict establishment, and no romantic affairs are allowed.'

Lilly raised herself on her elbow. 'That's ridiculous.'

Dodo narrowed her eyes. 'What is ridiculous is joining the circus because a man thought it a good idea.'

'Is it ridiculous to want financial independence and to claw back some control of one's life? From today I am earning my own living and making my own decisions,' she said, working to keep the heat from her voice. 'They have nothing to do with a man.'

Nattie called down from the upper bunk. 'Me now please, to stand. These bunks are hard as a plank and I've had my fair share of lying on my back.' She took hold of the curtain rail and swung herself down from her shelf with the ease of a monkey from a branch.

Dodo shifted across the trunk seat and gave up her place. 'I am thinking that if you are to muck out the elephants, there's maybe an opportunity to develop something with them. Your best bet is to enlist with a troupe so you could ask Tiffy to let you understudy someone's routine. Exploit every opening that comes your way. If you are going to perform in this circus and get your name on the programme, you are first going to have to dig in, show some grit and then come up with something pretty quick. Generally, he'll allow four weeks to bring a new act into anyone's repertoire.'

'The snag is,' Nattie cut in, 'you only have one week.'

At some antisocial hour in the cool, early dawn, the Lucknow-bound circus train juddered into a siding. The stops and starts throughout the night as the train paused to catch its breath were enough to part teeth from their sockets. Lilly realised she must have dozed off and sat up with a jolt.

She leaned over the edge of her berth, looking first up, then down. 'Should we pack our things?'

Dodo pressed her fingers to her brow. 'Where do you think you are going to be living?'

Lilly leaned out a little further and watched her face closely. 'Is there not a hotel in town?'

'Factually there are four. Unless you are flush with money or desperate for a hot bath, this is your home – here with me and Nattie in this wagon – for the next however long you last at the circus. And in any case, smart hotels are closed at the moment. They only open from October to March. I thought you'd know that – living here as you have.'

Nattie swung down from the horizontal curtain bar and landed softly on the floor. 'Even headline acts live on the wagon train. When we're told, we'll get off and walk to the lot. That's why we always use freight yards because they have loading ramps to get the wagons off the train. The elephants unload first because they will pull the wagons off the flatcar and haul them to the showground.'

'Margot too?'

'Of course, Margot too. She's a spoiled madam but successful and a crowd puller. In addition to her stateroom, she has her own private dressing tent with platform floor, soft furnishings and carpet.'

Lilly swung her legs over the side. Soft furnishings and carpet didn't seem so extraordinary. She stabbed at the rock-hard mattress with two fingers. 'You sound envious.'

Nattie nodded. 'Of the accommodation, yes. Of what having it entails, no. Between shows and what-have-you for the salary she commands, she is expected to promote the circus.'

'And herself,' Dodo added.

Nattie hopped to the window and stuck her head between the bars. 'She entertains whomsoever: news reporters and advertising representatives from the local papers, local dignitaries and literally anyone who wants to throw money at the circus. It's a business and at the moment Margot is at the top of her profession, Tiffy's ace up his sleeve.'

Dodo dropped her hand to the floor and felt about for her shoes. 'Until someone produces a joker, that is.'

'Are you saying the pack of cards is on the verge of collapse?'

'The circus is barely solvent, Lilly,' Dodo said, flexing her jaw. 'We fear for our jobs all the time.'

Chapter 18

Nattie was wrong about the elephants.

Mr Tiffert had not forgotten in any measure whatsoever that she was to be assigned to the doling out of their food and the ensuing consequence of their eating.

He stood outside the wagon door and rapped loudly with his silver-tipped cane. 'Where the shit is the shit shoveller?'

Lilly jumped down from the wagon without using the steps and, destabilised through lack of sleep, misjudged the drop. She let out a startled yelp, which she masked with the back of her hand. 'Here I am,' she said, hopping on one foot.

He puffed on his cigarette and gazed towards the sky as if reading a signal in the smoke. Then he looked her up and down, from head to toe, taking in the skirt and blouse and shaking his head.

She stood up a little straighter and pushed back her shoulders, challenging him to comment.

'Here. You'll find these more practical to work in.' He held out a bundle of clothing. 'Get back inside and change into these. The blouse will be all right unless it's a family heirloom. Take off your jewellery. Working with elephants is mucky and their manners not always polite. The men don't bother but I don't want you moaning if you spoil your fancy clothes.'

Lilly shook out the bundle and screwed up her face. Overalls were workers' garments, trousers attached to braces were men's clothes.

Mr Tiffert raised the corners of his mouth and Lilly was not sure if she had witnessed a grimace or a smirk. 'You can't work in a skirt. Elephants are playful. If they hoist you up in their trunk, you don't want to show the world your bloomers. And fix your hair. It's too . . .' He shaped his hands around the sides of his head. 'Big. They might think you're wearing a hat and try to take it off you.'

She looked at the ground then turned towards the wagon. 'Give me a minute,' she said, climbing the stairs. 'The sisters aren't here so there's plenty of room.'

An hour since, Dodo and Nattie had walked to the lot in search of some breakfast.

'Will there be food available already?' Lilly could hardly believe it.

Dodo opened the door of the wagon. 'The cook tent is always first on the lot. It has its own team of cooks and dishwashers. The elephants offload their wagons before anything or anyone else.'

Lilly ignored the protest from her stomach and swung down from her bunk. 'Do they carry the food with them?'

Dodo flapped the door back and forth to circulate some air. 'It's a huge logistical operation. But all the provisions for staff and feed for the animals is seen to by the twenty-four-hour man — so called because he travels twenty-four hours ahead of the train. In addition to that, he organises the delivery of wood shavings for the ring, bales of straw for bedding, hay and grain by the hundred weight; and permits for the pre-show parade, performances and water of course.'

'For the elephants?'

Nattie scoffed. 'Non-circus people always ask that and it's a complete myth. All our venues are sited near rivers in so far as that is possible. The water is for us. Two buckets a day for all our requirements.'

Dodo waggled a finger in Lilly's direction. 'That's something you'll have to do later on. Sort yourself out with a bucket from the commissary.'

Twenty-four-hour man? Commissary? Lilly stood still, her heart beginning to race. She hadn't realised that the circus would have a language of its own. She hoisted her shoulders, her eyebrows raised.

Nattie came to her rescue. 'It's the mobile equivalent of an emporium. Everything you would buy at a street shop, you can buy at the commissary, from a postage stamp to a zinc-lined bucket. If you don't have cash, you can sign for it and pay when you get your money at the end of the week.'

Lilly ran her hand across the front of her chest. Underneath her blouse, she was wearing a second, tighter one, down the front of which she had stuffed a roll of notes. A grouch bag of her own in all but appearance.

Nattie began to unhook rigging from the ceiling. 'We're going to be out all day. Tiffy has called general assembly this afternoon to watch and time our acts and work out a running order for the programme.'

Lilly reached under the bunks for her shoes. 'Can I come with you?'

'It's only for people under contract with the circus.'

'I am too.'

Dodo stared at her, the expression on her face frosty. 'Three cheers for you.'

Nattie attempted to dilute the slap of her sister's words. 'She's only grumpy because she needs food and exercise.'

Halfway down the wagon steps, Dodo said over her shoulder, 'There's a blue flag over the cook tent. When it's flying, they are serving; otherwise you'll have to do without.'

Lilly eyed the work clothes with distaste and threw them on her bunk. The Pahari hill clothes would have served very nicely but she knew he wouldn't approve. Amongst the many things he had said to her about his circus, Mr Tiffert considered white women wearing native clothes disrespectful. *Too bad.* She gave a shrug, unbuttoned the fastening of her skirt and dropped it to the floor. She wiggled out of her calico petticoats and reaching behind her back, she untied the bow at the back of her stays and worked open the laces with her fingers until the corset was loose enough to slide over her hips.

Lilly pulled the overalls over her thin-soled boots, the coarse fabric chafing her blistered thigh, and secured the straps over her shoulders. With no mirror to reflect her appearance, she felt strangely liberated as she pulled at her hair. Her carpet bag was at the foot of the bed but the search for her brushes was fruitless. She felt a bubble of panic bloom in her chest and breathed in and out, trying to pinpoint the time she knew she had last used them.

The *dâk* bungalow at Bhimtal.

She could picture them in the whitewashed room when she brushed her hair before supper. She'd sat at the table, holding the hand mirror in one hand and brushing hard with the other. A hundred strokes per night to stop her hair falling out. Or to keep her hair thick. She didn't remember which. She pressed her hands hard against her ears straining for the echo of a voice, but her grandmother's words were silent, held inside like an oyster safeguarding its pearl.

'Where are you?' She heard the impatient bounce of Mr Tiffert's stick on the step.

In one stride she reached the door. 'I was as quick as I could be. But now I'm ready and if you show me where the elephants are, I can get to work.'

'Did you shut the window?'

'It's stifling in there.'

'Go back and shut the window and make sure you draw the outside bolt on the door. There are monkeys everywhere and baboons. If they get into your quarters, you'll not be popular with the sisters.'

'I'm already sensing Dodo is not my greatest fan.'

He cleared his throat with a gruff 'ahem'. 'She won't let you get close. For many of the performers and with someone like you who has declared already that you are not here for the long haul, they can't afford the emotional investment. For now, you'll live your life in close company, eating, working and sleeping together for months at a time but next season you'll be gone. They'll never see you again and you won't write.'

'I just want to do my job to the best of my ability. I'm not hoping to find a best friend.'

'Realistic expectations are good. Now we need to get going as the elephants are not in the railroad yard. They've hauled the wagons to the circus ground and will be going back and forth all morning getting all the circus equipment to the ground.'

Lilly wondered why he had made such a fuss about her hair and clothes if the elephants were somewhere else.

As they walked, he went on with his explanation. 'First you clean their wagons and sluice them out. Second you come to the show ground, and watch the elephants work through their act. After that back to Bibiapur, which is about half a mile from here on a bend of the river, so they can bathe and drink without us having to haul water. We've contracted to keep the horses and elephants in a couple of riding schools down by the Cantonments. Horses go in one stable block, the elephants in the other, so don't mix them up. Horses have a natural fear of elephants so it's important to give them separate accommodations when they are not working the ring.'

'Do elephants really need to be stabled at night?' She was thinking of the elephant that had swayed its way through the jungle on the hunt for a tiger and had spent its down time tied to a tree.

'They are too valuable to the circus for us to be slack with their care. They pull the wagons, help erect the big top, pull the wild animal cages into the ring. Ours are well trained and you are not going to mess that up.'

Lilly felt a quiver of excitement that she might soon be a part of this world. 'Is this to be my job?'

'We are short of a sitter so you can do that for now while we are regrouping the show. Elephants are naturally curious and will egg each other on. They are also hugely intelligent. If they watch you draw a bolt, they will copy and let themselves out of their stall. They can untie knots – regular Houdinis, the lot of them.'

'What is that?'

'It's a person. Houdini's an escapologist and his act involves extracting himself from handcuffs and other restraints, but it's all supposed to be an illusion. Ines says he's in Europe, doing the rounds. I believe Margot's also seen him but you should ask her. She has a keen eye for a good act.'

'Are they here yet? Margot and Duffy?' Lilly tried not to sound too interested.

213

'Margot was on the same train as the rest of us but Duffy is not back yet. Some local chap has found him a beaten-up tiger and he's doubled back to fetch it.'

She strode on ahead of him, his last remark unwelcome. She said nothing but her heart was full of regret for the animal and its captor.

By now they had reached the elephant wagons, the ramps to load and unload them, lowered and resting on the tracks. A green-painted wheelbarrow bearing the wording TIFFERTS, inside which were a fork and spade, waited on the path. 'When you're done here, come up to the big top. I've called Assembly this afternoon and you can meet your charge.'

'What shall I do with the muck?'

'Fork it into the barrow and wheel it to the pit by the fence over there.' He pointed towards a line of trees behind which she imagined stood the fence. 'It's lighter and drier than horse dung so easy enough to transport. As the elephants are stabled elsewhere for the next month, this is a one-off job. Do it properly or you'll attract rats.'

He looked in her direction but avoided her eyes as if he felt ashamed in some way. 'I should warn you that this job is not popular because of the very nature of it. You'll spend your whole time with the elephant because it can't be left to its own devices. The sitters get fed up with the lack of freedom and soon move on to something else. We lost a fellow two days ago who just upped and left. Didn't even stop to collect the money he was due.'

'Are you saying that I'll live with them?'

'Her. Belle. Elephants work one on one with their trainers, who do for them like servants. The elephants thrive better with a single keeper. They prefer it.'

Lilly recalled the argument she'd had with Margot over Duffy's rapport with his tigers. 'Do they tell you?'

'Not in so many words,' Tiffy said. 'But they'll let you know if they are unhappy.'

Chapter 19

It took Lilly several hours to deal with the wagons, by the end of which she was faint from hunger. *Will I have time for lunch?* She looked at her watch. *Or will the blue flag have stopped flying?*

As she walked up towards the Big Top, the heat of the midday sun flung itself in her eyes. The light was blinding, the air seemed to shiver in the heat and made her stagger.

A boy driving an ox cart almost ran her down. He spat red betel juice through his reddened teeth. 'Watch where you're bloody going,' he shrieked in Hindi.

Snippets of conversation danced in the quivering mirage. *Remember you are British, Plumpty. Three square meals a day and don't forgo your afternoon tea. Got to keep your strength up, old girl. No married chap likes a bag of bones for a wife.*

Her fingernails cut into her palms.

People swarmed like bees: in and out of alleyways, from darkened shop fronts, from the piles of driftwood that lined the banks of the river. Children and animals were everywhere; huge wild pigs with pointy noses snuffled amongst the dirt, eating everything in sight. Elephants didn't like pigs. That was a fact she did know.

Lucknow, like Cawnpore, was a military town and as she walked along the banks of the river, soft and thick with yellowy earth, soldiers rode at a trot throwing up clods and scattering everything in their path.

Mr Tiffert had told her to walk towards the flags and billowing blue canvas he pointed out in the distance. 'The circus is on a bend of the river. Follow the Gumti upstream and you won't get lost.'

'I thought the tent would be white.'

He jerked his chin up, a gesture she knew to mean 'why?'

She had no experience beyond English tea tents, fund-raisers with her grandmother for the annual fete and blustered on, like the village fool. 'I've never seen a blue tent before.'

'What colour was the canvas at Warren's?'

Before she could embarrass herself further, saying she didn't recall, he said, 'The service tents are striped brown and black. Another first for you, I dare say.'

'How have they got the tent up so quickly?' she stammered out.

'Practice,' he said. 'Everything to do with the circus is practice. Like shovelling shit. The more you do it, the better you'll become.'

The road to the Big Top was under repair; the workforce entirely female. Lilly watched as a chain of dark, muscular women laboured with picks. Backs bowed, they hacked at the rock-hard earth while others filled woven baskets with rubble, which they strapped to their backs and carried away. A third team carted the spoil to mule-drawn carts, balancing their loads, their hands free, on the crowns of their heads.

I could do that, she acknowledged to herself. A skill I have acquired, in Noel's garden, through practice.

She carried on along the road until she was almost at the circus gate.

A little boy walked past, clasping his mother's hand. Lilly's heart leapt at the sight of them. He might have been

Teddy; he was the same age, about the same height and had a fringe that fell over his forehead, as it did with her son.

She could almost feel Teddy's fingers warm and small folded within her own. Her heart filled with such tenderness it almost made her choke.

Stop it, she cautioned herself and turned her steps towards the gate. Get on with your new life because that is the only way you will get your son away from his father.

The circus tent was pitched on a bend of the river near the Residency – a cluster of crumbling buildings which, according to the plaque outside, had been under siege for eighty-six days in the Mutiny of 1857. Originally built as the residence of the British Resident General in the nineteenth century, the walls were scarred with bullet marks and cannon shot and Lilly couldn't help but wonder whether it was here that the military officer that both Miss Pinkneys loved had lost his life in battle.

After ten minutes of silent walking, she saw the lunchtime flag had been lowered on the cook tent yet, tantalisingly, cooking smells still lingered in the air. She guessed at lamb and ran her tongue over her parched lips. Your fault, she told herself. Dodo gave you advice that you didn't take on board. Make sure you listen carefully in future, or you won't last five minutes.

Lilly wandered past a water wagon and fingered the roll of notes inside her blouse, making a mental note to acquire her wash bucket after the afternoon assembly. She raked a hand through her matted hair. Her skin was dry and itchy and a pungent odour of dung clung to her clothes that almost made her retch.

Inside the Big Top was an alien world of canvas poles, ropes and swinging sledgehammers.

Workmen were building the circus seats, arranging them in steps that rose behind a circle of boxes directly behind the edge of the ring, some of which were screened with curtains. On one side, the steps were covered in blue carpet, on the other the steps were bare. A section was partitioned off with cheesecloth, stretched taut on bamboo poles. The ladies in purdah would have to sit here, away from the men, as their faces could not be seen. The Europeans, the Eurasians and wealthier Indians would take seats according to their caste and the size of their purse; there was also a roped-off section where the audience could stand.

Sawdust arrived on the back of horse-drawn carts and an army of men spread and beat it into place, sprinkling it with water to tamp down the dust. Dodo had told her it was not practical to cart tons of it on the train as they traversed the country. The circus ordered the ring covering in every place it performed.

In a far corner, the circus band was tuning up.

Lilly flapped a hand in front of her face and scanned the interior.

An acrobatic troupe was forming itself into a human pyramid and overhead a young girl carrying a frilled yellow umbrella was walking on a wire.

To one side of the ring, Nattie was talking to a tall man in brown overalls, who was raising Dodo into the air by a rope attached to the trapeze on which she was suspended by a hook. Holding on by a leather bit she had clamped between her teeth, she had turned her face upwards, relying on the strength of her jaw to keep her from falling. Her neck tendons stood proud as the man hoisted her towards the roof.

'That's high enough for now,' Nattie called. 'She has enough clearance to swivel from there.'

Lilly gulped as Dodo snapped her legs and began to spin, alternately extending her arms and legs out, then bringing them in close to her body to speed up and slow down.

Lilly rubbed the side of her jaw wondering at the strength of the bone. 'I've never seen anything like it.'

Nattie nodded. 'She's just warming up. She suffers from vertigo, so she has to work her way up to the full performing height.'

The laugh came out unbridled. 'She's an aerialist, for goodness' sake,' Lilly said.

For a moment, Nattie said nothing. 'Don't ever let her hear you say that. A lot of artistes have issues with height and that is what makes them all the more extraordinary – that they are able to overcome their fear and perform these complicated tricks high up in the air.'

Lilly felt unsteady and breathed slowly, her hand pressed to her chest. She felt ill-equipped to respond. Her present circumstance and longer-lasting predicament had brought her to the circus because she could not conquer her fear.

'Of course,' Nattie went on, her expression wry, 'when she's comfortable she'll hang from the trapeze with her knees and hold a second trapeze in her teeth. That's when I join in and perform my poses on the bar she's supporting from above. The act goes on after that.'

'I thought she was joking when she said she dangles from a hook by her teeth.'

Nattie sighed and kept her eye trained on her sister. 'Dodo told you she never jokes.'

Lilly turned her face away, sensing an eddy of disapproval and felt she must talk it away. 'I know and I'm sorry,' she said, fiddling with the buttons on her blouse. 'I couldn't imagine that Dodo might be less than confident in the air – with anything really.' She could see that Dodo couldn't afford to be afraid. It would jeopardise their act. A distant memory of a saying plucked at her. Something about courage being rooted in fear.

Lilly let her gaze stray to a tall man with a soft, clean face and moustache dark as ink who stood outside the sawdust ring juggling handfuls of clubs. A clown, his face painted with streaks of colour, strutted on stilts. A young girl wearing tights and a leotard was doing a series of somersaults on the feet of an older acrobat who lay upside down on his back in a wooden construction that might once have been a chair.

She studied a woman who was training cockatoos to drink from a glass. One of the birds was trying to reach the bottom but its head had got stuck. 'What's in the glass?' she called across to the juggler.

His eyes never left his props. 'Liquor most probably, but those birds learn fast.'

Already it had tilted the glass and pulled it free from its head with its claws.

'What else do they do?'

The juggler was still juggling. Wooden balls now – five, maybe six. He was too quick for her to count. 'No idea. She's new. I've never seen the act before.'

With an ache in her heart, Lilly wandered off, feeling she had no place here, and then, through the artists' entrance, Lilly saw a familiar figure walk in.

Ridiculously pleased to see him, she watched him work for a while. Bending down, taking equipment from crates, straightening to carry it across the ring. She could tell by the fluidity of the movement that he was at ease in these surroundings – that he had done this work thousands of times in the past.

Perspiration glued his shirt to his back and there were wide circles of it under his arms. The top three buttons of his shirt were undone and she could see that a wall of hard muscle dissected his chest.

'Hello,' she called, slightly short of breath.

His face broke into a smile. 'How's it going?'

'I'm working with elephants. Literally starting at the bottom.' She stopped, hopeful that he might ask her something more personal but he took a quick step backwards, an expression of pure delight stamped on his face.

She began to laugh. 'It's not that wonderful.'

He rubbed the back of his neck. 'Can't really talk now. Not a good time. Later maybe? Or catch up tomorrow?'

She frowned, not understanding but she soon worked it out.

He waved and flopped down on the chipped wooden ring fence, his legs stretched out, the right crossed over his left at the ankles, as Margot cantered her horse in a circle.

No one seemed to be orchestrating the white horse's manoeuvres as Margot balanced on its back, pirouetting and performing handstands. Every now and then she threw in a backwards somersault landing on its rear quarters. There was no mistaking her skill; every eye in the tent was upon her.

'She's magnificent,' Lilly said out loud.

She watched his gaze soften and bit her lip.

'Yes, and she's only warming up,' she heard him say. 'This is not her only act. When Margot properly performs, she needs no one else. She is the circus all by herself.'

Chapter 20

'Attention, people.'

Mr Tiffert joined them at the side of the ring, dabbing at his brow with a blue checked handkerchief, and climbed on a wooden crate. He held his arms wide, turning slowly so that everyone in the tent would notice his shiny golden coat. The rottweiler Lilly had encountered in his wagon sat at his feet and watched his every move.

She remembered that Goose did that with Noel and a smile rose to her lips. In her mind she went back to the week when it had poured steadily each day and sheltering under the umbrella, she walked with them down the steep path that led to the lake. The dog was running before them and when they came to the clearing in the woods, and stood together under the dripping trees, she could smell the rich odour of moss and damp earth. She watched Noel's smile and the arc of his arm as he launched sticks into the air for his dog to chase, and the look of loss on his face when she told him she'd decided to leave.

Something brushed against her leg. She started so suddenly, she almost tripped over the ring wall. And then she saw it was Mr Tiffert's dog who looked up, wagging her tail.

'Hello Clara.' Lilly knelt down on the sawdust and tickled her behind the ears. 'I thought you didn't like women,' she said as the dog shivered with pleasure at her touch.

'Quiet!' Mr Tiffert blew on his whistle three times. 'I've been looking at the content of your acts and here's the bottom line: you're dull. What the shit have you been doing for the past few months?'

The juggler dropped his coloured balls to the ground. His stare was hostile, his eyes unblinking. 'Working my arse off in a nightclub because the pay here's so crap.'

One or two heads nodded but no one else felt the urge to chip in.

Mr Tiffert locked his hands on his hips and shrugged. 'Don't even bother with your complaints. The British King has got over whatever it was he was suffering from and we now have a show to put on in double-quick time. We lost a lot of bookings when the King took ill, so the tour – your jobs – are dependent on us staying solvent. This circus needs some imagination, or we won't last the season.'

Margot slid off her horse. 'I prefer finesse to sensation.'

Mr Tiffert shook his head. 'Normally I'd agree, but it's not what the public want. The more danger you give them, the more engrossed they will be. This is a one-ring circus, so everyone sees everything. To make people clap, you must risk your lives.'

The juggler pulled at his moustache. 'What does it matter what they see if we have taken their money at the ticket office? This circus has never been much more than a horse show with a few extra artistes thrown in.'

Mr Tiffert threw his arms in the air. 'People come to the circus because there's the grisly possibility that they may witness something shocking, such as a tiger mauling its trainer or a trapeze acrobat mistiming a manoeuvre and falling to his death.

'Outside of what people can provide for themselves, entertainment is what we can give people. We are not the only circus in operation in India; Warren's are always trying to snatch an audience from under our nose, but we are better. Everyone from the District Collector downwards will be sitting round the sawdust ring and it is our job to give them what they've come to see.'

'I already give them skill and daring,' Duffy huffed.

Margot brushed a thread from his sleeve with the back of her hand. It was an intimate gesture and by it, Lilly understood that Duffy and Margot were more than just troupers in a travelling show. Lilly also guessed that Margot knew she would have seen, that everyone would have seen, showing circus rules did not apply to herself.

Margot smiled. 'You have an inbuilt suicidal streak, Duffy. No one could ever say that your act is dull. Who else would be brave enough to sit on a tiger as it jumped through a burning hoop?'

Again, Mr Tiffert raised his palms to the roof. 'We must give them more. Diversify. Add to your acts. Join up with another act. I don't care what the shit you do but you must dazzle like the sequins on my coat. We have twelve bookings on the route card, but we won't get past the first venue if our show is shit.'

'What's a route card?' Lilly whispered to the cockatoo lady.

'Like a postcard but with the itinerary of the show's movements printed on it instead of a picture. We send them home, so our families know where we'll be at any one time if they need an address to write to. You can get them at the commissary.'

Lilly wanted to show off that she knew what this was, that she wasn't a total greenhorn. 'I must pop by later to pick up my water bucket and a hairbrush as I left mine behind.'

'Dodo's started a tab for you at the commissary and ordered one for you. She told a property man to paint the letters G R I T on the side and leave it in the dressing tent. She'd said you'd understand that. Now be quiet, before we get into trouble.'

Dodo rapped her leather mouthpiece on the ring wall. 'I do not care to do anything I have not been trained for. I work in one discipline and I'm not doubling up at slack-wire walking or prancing about on a horse. Moving outside something I have learned since I was a child is not happening with me.'

'I agree,' Margot echoed, as did the assembled company of circus performers. 'We are likely to get ourselves killed if we add an unfamiliar discipline to our work.'

The barrier to Mr Tiffert's proposals was thick; an almost tangible, impenetrable wall.

Yet at that moment, something took hold of her, a flash of a former self, who was not the timid puppet she'd become. Or was it Dodo, a woman so utterly confident in her views, that encouraged the daring that made her jump up and say, 'May I make an observation?'

The proprietor cocked a scornful eyebrow. 'What is this? Do you have words of wisdom from the elephants?'

The words began to dry in her mouth. *If you want to be taken seriously, show some grit. Just say what you have to say.* 'Why not invite the public to participate in some way? Involve them more with what is happening inside the ring. Let them enjoy the full circus experience.'

He waved his hand about his ear to indicate he was listening.

'I saw Annie Oakley in Buffalo Bill's Wild West Show in England. She was a great drawing card because she was a woman in a man's world. She would have members of the public come into the ring and she would shoot cigarettes out of their mouths – not with real bullets, obviously, but no one knew that at the time. She showed that women were able to handle firearms and even outshoot men.'

Lilly saw Margot and Duffy exchange a look and wondered what they were thinking.

Mr Tiffert stared at her for a moment. 'Margot is our star here, even if you could find me a woman who's a crack shot.'

Lilly realised he thought she was joking and thought it politic to keep her ability to shoot to herself. 'The other thing they did at the Wild West Show was to offer prizes if people entered their own horse in a competition to, say, jump over obstacles in the ring. As Lucknow is a military town, there would surely be a few willing entrants from amongst the officers. Also—'

'The wild west has no relevance in India. That's a ridiculous idea.' That was Dodo. Obviously.

Lilly brushed off the unwarranted reproof. 'That's not the point I was trying to make. You advertise yourself as Tiffert's Circus and Royal Menagerie. Why not show the animals separately before the performance and charge a fee to view the exhibits? Duffy's tigers and Margot's horses. And the elephants, because you told me people like to sit on them and have their photograph taken. And the parrots because they can talk? It wouldn't stress the animals because they are used to performing.'

Margot shook her head. 'Animals are stressed by contact with people they don't know. The fact that they're used to performing is irrelevant.'

Her bravado began to ebb and suddenly she felt self-conscious. 'I don't know,' she trailed off. 'It was just an idea.'

Mr Tiffert held up a finger. 'There is some merit in floating the idea of a horse competition with a few flyers in town but I'll think about the other.' He pulled his watch from an inside pocket of his jacket. 'I'm going to look at the acts not involving animals before supper. Animal people can eat first and when I've finished with the aerialists and wire walkers, we'll swap over. I'll have a first stab at a running order at eight o'clock when I've seen what you've got.'

'Tomorrow morning?' Lilly was already at the tent flap, the pull of food too strong.

Mr Tiffert shook his head. 'Tonight. We work, we work, and we work some more until we are perfect. You'll do well to remember that if you survive more than a week.'

As Lilly reached the cook tent, she was intercepted by a white-jacketed waiter who asked which act she was with so he would know where to seat her. Behind him, she could see that there were performers already in the tent, scattered about as if they were keeping their distance.

'I have been working with the elephants.'

He stared at her chest. 'You're not one of the girls.'

'I think you'll find I am.'

'No, you're not. I know all of them. And your face is just not familiar.'

'You're not looking at my face.'

He closed his eyes, shook his head, then raised his eyes to the sky and coughed. Lilly knew she had caught him out. 'I've been looking after the elephants, rather than sitting on them doing poses.'

His voice was much louder when he spoke again. 'You need a meal ticket if you're a workman. Mr Tiffert won't have anyone cadging food. Money's too tight – I 'spect he's told you that already.'

'Then what am I to do? He's busy looking at the aerialist acts so he's hardly going to break off and write me out a chit.'

The waiter raised his shoulders in a shrug. 'Rules is rules. I'm not going to lose my job because you haven't had the wit to see him earlier. Didn't you have breakfast or lunch?'

'No, I didn't have time for those meals so technically you've saved on two because I didn't eat them.'

She was about to turn away when Duffy appeared beside her, Margot nowhere in sight. 'It's all right, Reggie. This is Lilly. She's new here and doesn't know the ropes. But she's certainly not a cadger. She can sit with me for now, until you work out what to do with her.'

Reggie looked uncertain but stood to the side as they went into the tent. Duffy led her to a long table, covered with a starched white cloth, with all the plates and cups upside down on the table to keep off the dust. He stepped over the bench seat and indicated that she should do likewise. Reggie trouped behind and began to right the crockery before them, wiping it down with the cloth he had draped on his arm.

'We've chicken thali or vegetable thali.' For some reason, his voice was hostile.

Drily, she said, 'When in Rome . . . I'll have the chicken but no roti.'

Reggie's face was a mask.

'Make that two,' Duffy said. 'But I'll have everything.' He reached for the basket of bread. 'Everyone has their own place. Nothing is random in circus life. There's a pecking order and you have to respect it. You can't just pitch up and plonk yourself next to anyone you fancy the look of.'

229

'A shame you won't get to sit next to Margot, in that case.'

He pushed the basket of bread towards her. 'What made you say that?'

Before she could answer, Reggie returned with their food and set the platters down before them. Lilly looked at the array of small bowls, containing the chicken, dry and wet vegetable dishes, roti, lentil wafers, rice, pickle, curd, and a sweet. She took the chapatis off the metal tray as well as the *gulab jamun* − a fried milk-based dessert − and slid them to one side.

'I don't understand what's going on between you two.'

He raised his eyebrows at her. 'Is anything ever as it seems?'

She had no idea what he meant. 'Earlier when we ran into each other in the tent I got the impression you two were, shall we say, having a moment? I just wonder . . .' She cast him a sidelong glance.

He tore a strip off a chapati and dunked it in the chicken. 'It's so much nicer catching up with you over supper than chatting in the tent, or with Noel standing guard over you like Tiffy's dog.'

She stabbed at the dish of vegetables in sauce. 'That's not an answer and please don't say horrible things about Noel. He's been a wonderful friend to us both.'

He sat two feet from her, their eyes level. 'But now you're away from his protective clutches and' − he threw her a couple of winks − 'who knows what we might get up to?'

She flapped at him with her napkin. 'Don't be so silly. Mr Tiffert gave me a morality lecture when I signed on with him, so I am wondering why Margot is not bound by the same rules? I saw her lay claim to you in the tent before the entire circus just now.'

'I told you in Nainital that Margot is a big star.' He wiped a drip of sauce from his chin.

And you have again side-stepped my question, she thought. But not before she'd seen the rapid tapping of a finger on the table and that he'd stiffened when he mentioned her name.

Puzzling this for a short time, she ate her food before her thoughts turned to Teddy. Chicken in its tomato and yoghurt sauce was one of his favourite meals and she could picture him eating it, his small fist wrapped around the handle of his spoon.

'What are you smiling at?'

'I was thinking of Teddy. He loves this dish.'

'So do I,' he said, licking his lips.

She stared at him, wondering why he could never be serious. 'Coming back to Margot. On the tiger hunt, you asked for my help with her.'

'Did I?' Duffy kept his focus on his food. 'I've forgotten all about it if I did. But a far more interesting topic though is what happened with you and Noel. He came back to Naini in a right old state.'

Her stomach tightened. Was there some more to him leaving than saying he hated goodbyes? 'What did he say?'

He looked up from his dessert. His eyes were on her, watching. 'About what?'

There was something in his look that stopped her from asking more. Lilly set her fork across the metal platter and looked at her watch, remembering that she had to send a telegram. 'Sorry, I've got to go.'

'Is there somewhere you'd rather be other than with little old *moi*?'

The bench scraped the floor as she stood up. 'Actually

yes, just now there is. I left my silver brush set at the *dâk* bungalow in Bhimtal. I have to get it back.' She dropped her voice to a whisper. 'Think about it, Duffy. If Royce does have spies and I was followed from Nainital, finding something that is monogrammed with my name is not going to have a happy outcome, is it? He'll know straight away that I'm not with Binnie. If I'm quick, I'll have time to dash to the railway lines, send a telegram to Noel and be back in good time for the walk through at eight o'clock.'

He stacked the empty dishes on his tray. 'You're picking up the language already, I see. We'll make a circus trouper out of you yet.'

'I don't know about that but for now, I have to go.'

'You'll be in trouble for leaving the lot.' He waggled his eyebrows.

'So don't tell anyone or come with me.'

His face turned a little red. 'Margot is expecting me later.'

She stepped over the bench, balled up her napkin and tossed it on the table. 'Have a nice time and give her my best.'

Chapter 21

The telegraph office at Lucknow sat along the side of the main entrance to the station.

Lilly wavered in front of the grimy window, wondering if she had been rash; the fact she was even sending a telegram was outside her experience and she had little idea how to accomplish it. There had always been people – men – to do these things for her.

And now there were none.

Squaring her shoulders, she took a step forward and rapped on the glass.

At the sound of her knock from somewhere close within, a man lifted his head and looked her up and down, his mouth working as if he were parting a cherry from its stone. His uniform was dazzlingly white with *British Indian Telegraph Company*, embroidered in gold thread on his coat. Lilly judged him to be in his early thirties, his shirt buttons straining over a paunch, which bulged over the belt of his trousers. He wore a wedding ring and looked kind, a family man, she thought, with two small children and a wife who sent him to work each day, washed and pressed with his lunch packed in a three-tiered tiffin box.

As Noel had done for her.

She rubbed her forehead with the heel of her hand, her mind casting back to their discordant parting. Was it in Bhimtal that Noel told her that the railway stations all had a telegraph office as a means of monitoring and controlling the movement of trains and the sending and receiving of news?

Or was it before?

He had asked her to let him know, via a telegram, where she was in his country. While this was her first opportunity, it was not her primary purpose in sending it.

'Come round side entrance,' the telegraph man called, leaning towards the glass.

The long dark room was stifling, a half-hearted *punkah* fan doing little to stir the air. She looked around to where the *punkah wallah* might have been sitting and noticed then that there was another person in the friendless brown room. Stacks of papers teetered on every surface, charts lined the walls and folders held together with string were crammed on shelves that were too high to reach. A line of telegraphic instruments – originals, she supposed, from when the telegraph was first introduced into India – lay on the bench, covered in dust.

As her eyes got used to the half-light, her attention was caught by a wooden frame that held an advertisement for a career in the telegraphic service.

Are you literate?
Could you learn Morse Code?
Are you able to spell?
Men and women are sought to learn to operate the telegraph key.
Annual salary: men 150 rupees per annum, women 40 rupees per annum.
After four years of excellent service a woman will be entitled to an annual increase of two rupees eight annas up to a maximum salary of eighty rupees.

Do not delay.
Apply in writing today.

'Is very fine career for women, telegraph office.'

Lilly snapped her head round and stared at the fellow, struggling to comprehend that a woman would earn a quarter of a man's salary for an identical job. She calculated it would take twenty-four years for a woman to reach the top of the pay scale, which would have her earning just over half a man's starting salary. She hadn't even known that women did this type of work.

Although scandalised at the injustice, she managed to push out a smile, feeling a hostile demeanour would not be to her advantage. 'Is this where I may send a telegram?'

Disappointment spread across his face; his mouth stopped working, as if he'd finally freed the stone from its fruit, and twisted into a reluctant smile.

There was an extended pause while he looked from her face to his desk to her face once more. He lined up his collection of pre-inked stamps and straightened the stack of forms before him.

'You are wanting a letter or a message telegraph?'

'Could you explain the difference?'

'Letter is fixed rate and number of words is fifty. Message is charged by word and there is being no limit.'

'I think I would like a message telegraph.'

'You must fill message on form.'

He tapped his finger up and down on his Morse telegraph key, but he did not slide a form across the desk.

'Please may I have the form for my telegram?'

A few seconds passed.

Lilly's heart pounded as she waited.

The disapproval remained in the workings of his mouth, but a smile hovered about his eyes. 'I am wondering what the purpose of your visit to this office is being.'

'I would like to send a telegram to a friend in Nainital.'

'Who friend?'

'An English friend who lives there. Do you normally quiz your customers in such a manner?'

In the matter of a blink of an eyelid, the smile slipped from his face. He wouldn't look at her. He put on his peaked cap with the British Indian Telegraph Company insignia pinned to the front and centred it on his head.

Shaking his head vigorously, he said, 'I am not able to assist with your wishes.'

Lilly was confused. 'If there is a problem, can you not help me to put it right?'

'Are you attempting to bribery?'

She placed both palms on her back and massaged the crease in her spine. Her husband would have slipped some rupee notes in the clerk's direction and quietly greased his palm. It was what he called 'facilitating business between countrymen'. He would play the chummy Indian card when it suited him or the standoffish British one if it would match his purpose better. He dressed as a European from the stiff wing collar of his shirt to the perfectly polished shoes. Only the colour of his skin and the volume of his hair gave his mixed origins away.

And yet.

Royce was a man on the periphery of society, a half-Indian who lived with his mother and English wife; however much he thought he could, he could not pass himself off as white.

Lilly looked at the wall behind the clerk's head and saw that the paint was peeling off in huge pale flakes and that his desk was pitted with rust. What would Royce have done with an inflexible employee, a petty rule-following functionary who stood in the way of what he wanted?

As he might have, she felt an overwhelming urge to shout. 'I am British, and I want to send my friend a message. I fill in the form, and you will read the message that I want to send before you convert it to Morse code on your machine. There is no mystery as to my intention in sending a telegram and what I want to say.'

His head began to sway like a balloon dancing on a string and seemed drained by the explanation. He passed the questioning to his counterpart, a nice-looking boy who appeared barely old enough to shave. 'And you are not understanding, young madam. The content of your message is not for discussion but there is a mismatch in how your voice is sounding and how you are looking.'

He joined his palms together as if to petition her to accept his explanation. 'Only Britisher persons may send telegram from this office.'

A trickle of sweat made its way down her spine. Why on earth had she not changed into Western dress and scrubbed the dye from her skin. 'What do you mean?'

There was no mercy in his stare. 'You being half-baked woman with a pretend convent accent and all is why you are not allowed. Even if you shout from rooftop.'

Lilly knew the expression. It was one of her mother-law's favourites. She was as prejudiced as the British towards the Eurasians and looked down on them because to her, they were neither one thing nor the other. *Kutcha butcha* - half-baked bread - she called them; *teen pao* being three quarters native or *adha seer* half a pound if you were nearly white. Lilly had pointed out the hypocrisy of her comments to Royce and had received a slap in the face for her trouble.

The man wearing the telegraph company cap smoothed the paperwork in front of him. 'How long you are living in this country?'

She let out a breath she hadn't realised she was holding. Perhaps they were about to relent. Lilly forced a smile, trying once more to get them on side. 'I have lived in India for eight years. I am married to a businessman from Cawnpore and I'm English.'

'Why is husband not sending telegram? Very not normal for wife to be doing.'

'Because he is not in Lucknow.' *And I've left the controlling bastard,* she longed to shout.

Another tidal wave of discussion ensued with his colleague.

'Again we are not understanding your objections to our most reasonable questioning. Why is he not with?'

Grit, Lilly.

She shook her head and rolled up her sleeves. 'I do not believe you have the authority to block my request. See for yourselves. I am not one of the half-baked. My skin is white. My husband is well acquainted with the District Collector who dines frequently at our home.'

Both heads bobbled slowly, showing respect but little comprehension. 'Then all the more we are not understanding.'

She put her hands on the counter and leaned over so they could see her face clearly. 'I'm with Tiffert's circus. I work with the elephants. For the book I am writing,' she added. 'I would like your names, please, and that of your superior, to report this disgraceful lack of cooperation.'

The older telegraph operator seemed uncertain for a moment then smiled, shaking his head from side to side. An emphatic decision had been reached. He stood up and came out of his booth. 'Here is telegraph form.' With his hand held to one side, he guided her across the floor to a separate counter. 'You fill in address of friend in Nainital.' He stabbed at the top left-hand corner of the paper with a finger that was none too clean. 'You put here your name. In right corner where "From" is written.'

Lilly stared at the sixteen blank boxes and didn't know where to start. She had several false starts before she was happy with her message.

Left hairbrushes Bhimtal stop.
Could you retrieve stop
Lucknow one month stop
Will write soon stop

'Are you not signing name?'

'It's on the form.'

He looked at the name she had written at the top of the sheet.

'Thank you, Memsahib Victoria Regina. Your handwriting is most clear to be reading.'

Chapter 22

The wagons had all been towed by elephant to the circus ground and now stood in rows, like terraced houses on a London street. The numbers were even configured in the same way, with the evens on one side facing the odds on the other.

Inside number fifty-seven, Lilly looked around, confused. 'Where's my trunk?'

Dodo snapped the rubber band against her wrist. Lilly had already learned it was a danger signal, that she was irritated, and trouble was brewing. 'Over there.'

Lilly looked at the box covered with brown sail canvas; it was barely two-feet square.

Sitting on the hard, bottom bunk, Nattie did not blink. 'It's a proper circus trunk made by the Tailor company especially for circus use. Hence the name. Tailor-made.'

'It is zinc-lined so it can stand on the ground and still keep your personal things dry.' Dodo kicked the box with the toe of her boot.

Irritated that they had not consulted her, Lilly formed a tight-lipped smile. 'It's smaller than I thought.'

Dodo snapped the rubber. 'There's no allowance for personal possessions in a box the size of a tiger cage. It's impossible for the three of us to be in here at the same time so we had your trunk removed to the dressing tent.'

'When?'

'When you walked off the ground.'

'Did Reggie tell you?'

The circus had been entirely surrounded by a fence to deter ticket dodgers from slipping under the canvas. There was now one entrance in and out of the circus for performers, workers and public.

Dodo looked at her with contempt. 'He didn't have to because you were seen. Tiffy's eye is everywhere. You'll have your pay docked for that.'

'That's ridiculous,' Lilly shot back, furious. 'I didn't think I'd swapped one cage for another.'

Dodo made more of an effort to explain. 'You are expected to be on hand. What if there'd been a dump of shit to shovel in the ring and you were off on a jaunt in town? You have Sunday off. That's when you go on your little errands, to do whatever it is you have to do.'

'How am I supposed to change my clothes when everything I own is in that trunk?'

Nattie dismissed her protestations. 'All the performers dress in the same tent – unless you are Margot. She has her own arrangements.'

'Everybody undresses in full view of each other?'

Dodo stood back from the trunk. 'Don't be ridiculous. It is separated down the middle by a canvas sheet – men to the left, ladies to the right.'

Nattie shook her head and sighed. 'Space is limited, which is why you now have a new trunk. Yours was too big for the circus.'

'It cost an arm and a leg in London so I'm not throwing it away.'

Dodo hunched her shoulders. 'They've found a place for it in the dressing tent along the sidewall. Unpack what you need day to day and put it in the new "two by two".

If you manage any spare time in the day, that two feet is your private space where you can sit, until you come back to the wagon at night.'

'Mr Tiffert says I have to sleep with the elephants.'

'You need to learn his sense of humour.' Nattie got up from the bunk and stretched down to her toes.

'I think he was serious.'

'No, he wasn't,' Nattie said, her face close to the floor. 'He's very protective of the women performers. He'll not have you sleeping at the other end of town. You might take the elephants down after the evening performance, but you'll be back here to sleep.'

Dodo took the place her sister had vacated. 'Your bucket's there as well. It will be filled twice a day and you'll have to get the hang of bathing yourself, washing your hair and clothes in two buckets of cold water.'

'I don't think I'm going to be able—'

Three times Dodo snapped the band. 'Grit, grit, grit.'

'I've never undressed in front of anyone before. Not even my husband.'

'You won't in the dressing tent,' Dodo said.

'Absolutely no nudity,' Nattie put in. 'I'll show you how to wash wearing your bathrobe which you must not, at any moment, take off. There's a knack to it but it's quickly learned.'

Dodo got up from the bunk and shook out her skirt. Until that moment, Lilly hadn't registered that she had changed out of her practice clothes. 'Are you not joining the rehearsal later on?'

'Of course, but performers may not wear work clothes to the cook tent. You have to change.'

'And then change back for work, which is why all our clothes are by the Big Top. It's a practicality that saves a lot of walking,' Nattie continued. 'We have to be off in a tick so you might as well walk across with us.'

The trunks were arranged end to end in two parallel lines.

Dodo raised a finger. 'Don't just dump your trunk where you fancy putting it. Here's the rule of thumb. Horse performers sit nearest the lamps which are hung from the centre poles. It's a question of prestige, you see. Foremost stars get the best light, then aerialists. Extras, like you, will have to slot in where there's space to put on your make-up.'

Only women of disreputable character wear face paint. If you could see me now, Royce, you'd never believe your eyes.

'Put your trunk on the end of a row and don't block an aisle,' Nattie cautioned.

'Where will I find my bucket?'

Nattie pointed to a flap in the tent. 'Outside. It's got your initials on it so don't just take one randomly. We tend to wash ourselves first and then our laundry. When you are finished, tip the remaining water onto the straw to keep the dust down. It's etiquette so don't forget.'

Dodo sat down in front of her trunk and lifted the lid. 'The stool you need to buy from the commissary, but make sure it's the collapsible version, so it fits in the trunk. Otherwise you'll be charged porterage when we move on the train to the next town.' She unhooked a tray from inside the lid. It was neat as a pin and contained all the essentials she would need in her life as a performer.

Suddenly it dawned on Lilly that this was real; she was not a spectator at a travelling show but was now a part of it, a minuscule cog in a huge piece of machinery. She located her travelling trunk and set to work, sorting the essential from the non.

'Am I likely to need evening clothes?'

Lilly regretted the question as soon as it formed on her lips. She heard the snapping of the bands on Dodo's wrist and knew what was coming with the exact same certitude that a clock will strike when the whirring begins.

'Are you planning on joining the ladies at the Lucknow Club for tennis and cocktails? Maybe hand out cups of tea from the refreshment table to the polo boys after the last chukka in your silk and ribbons?'

'I was thinking more of when an invitation to dine arrives from a millionaire Nawab,' Lilly shot back. 'It might be prudent to keep the froth and feathers near the top of my trunk.'

Spluttering with laughter, Dodo clapped her hands. 'Our British friend is finding her courage. I think you might relegate the evening wear to the bottom of the London trunk. You should have clean underwear and a towel, soap and your toiletries, practice and performance clothes and a couple of skirts and blouses. That's going to be your working wardrobe for the next short while. And keep a nail file handy for those new talons you're growing.'

Smiling to herself, Lilly returned to the reordering of her affairs. In amongst her clothes, she found the jodhpurs minus the buttons on one leg that Noel had removed, his father's gun and Conti's pashmina and the stack of post-cards. Teddy's drawing of them both at the circus stared up at her from its place in the trunk. He had drawn her nearly as tall as the big top tent, the stick fingers of her hand entwined with his. Hot, angry tears rose to her eyes, although she knew she had no right to feel anything but guilt. Even though it was because of Royce, it was still she who'd walked away from Teddy's life. She swallowed hard and swivelled round and saw that both sisters were climbing into their costumes and transferred the burlap sack to the tailor-made trunk. She recalled Noel's words, *Behind every tree lurks a tiger*, and cringed at the memory of that last awkward evening.

'How do I go about sending a letter?'

Using her little finger, Dodo applied gloss to her lips. 'The box for sending is by the entrance to the dressing tent. If anyone sends post to you, Tiffy has a man who makes a couple of trips a day to the post office and it will find its way to you. He's not paid for this so it's customary for each performer to tip him a few annas at the end of the run.'

Lilly felt the stirring of anxiety in her stomach. There were so many items to pay for and her supply of cash would soon run out. Miss Pinkney's jewels were sewn into the lining of her trunk against the moment she might need to sell them. She hadn't thought it would be so soon.

'Stamps and paper?'

'Commissary.' Nattie patted white powder onto her neck.

'Who are you writing to?' Dodo rolled her lips together and peered into her hand-held mirror.

'No one you know.'

Dodo replaced the mirror in her trunk. 'You'll blab eventually.'

I won't, thought Lilly. Noel is no one's secret but mine.

Chapter 23

Lilly had never looked after an animal in her entire life, let alone one the size of a small mountain.

She stepped away from the terrifying beast, dabbing at the perspiration on her face. 'What do you mean I'll be unable to leave her for a week?' She'd thought to spend an hour each day in the stables and then idle her time, as usual.

Mr Tiffert jerked his chin at her charge. 'Belle wasn't born in captivity, so she has had to become used to working with people.'

Belle was beautiful – the colour of ash and approximately eight feet tall from foot to shoulder. Her huge ears were freckled with the palest pink dots, her eyes brown and gentle and she smelled of fruit; apples, she thought.

Lilly was consumed with sadness to think she might have been physically abused. 'Was she beaten to make her tame?'

'Not with a stick, if that's what you mean. In the wild, elephants live in hierarchical groups with a dominant beast in charge. Effectively, as her groom, you are assuming the role of that matriarch and it will take you a week, more or less, for her to get used to you. You can't just turn up and have her to do as you say. It takes time. As in the wild, if she is naughty, she must be reprimanded so give her a stern slap on her bottom with your hand. But then reinforce with stroking, talking to her all the time. She understands "Yes", "No", "Good". Give her a reward for doing something well.'

'Does she live in fear?'

'No, but bad behaviour has a consequence.'

As painful images surfaced, Lilly shivered and wrapped her arms around herself. 'I don't think I could strike her.'

He shrugged his shoulders. 'Then she will walk all over you and that could be very messy indeed.'

Vowing to be strong, she turned away, breathing in and out through her mouth.

She focused on the wide, open space behind the stable block. The trees were thick with twittering parrots, which smacked their wings in the branches, and towards the top of the twisted trunks, long-tailed grey monkeys swung beneath the canopy. Belle reached up with her trunk and latched onto a branch pulling it towards her, twisting it back and forth until it parted company from the trunk. She opened her mouth wide and stuffed in the swathe of leaves and wood with a guilty look of pleasure, reminding her of Teddy shovelling sweets into his mouth.

She turned to Mr Tiffert. 'Isn't India full of *mahouts* looking for jobs?'

Mr Tiffert's expression was resigned. 'A *mahout* will expect to have sole charge of his elephant but here responsibilities are shared, and it dilutes his authority. Elephants know the commands they need in both their working life and in the circus ring but on occasion pretend that they muddle them up.'

'Are the commands that different?'

He smiled before continuing. 'Essentially, no, but they do not come from the same person. Her groom – you – teaches her to stand patiently and to present different body parts on command so that the circus vet can conduct his inspections quickly. It also helps with their work in the ring where they are taught some tricks.'

'Who presents their act?'

'Me. The elephants know that cooperation results in treats. Belle can be a bit playful but, by and large and if in the mood, she should do what you ask her to do.

'But do not be deceived or ever let down your guard. One day – without warning – your docile charge may turn on you so treat her with respect. We don't tether our animals either.'

'Really?'

'There's no point. They can lift their stakes out of the ground, go off for a wander, and then replace them in exactly the same position. We had one elephant not so long ago who pulled out her stake, let herself out of the stable, picked her way across the yard that separated her from the grain store and let herself into the barn. She spent the next hour or so siphoning up the oats before returning to her stall and putting her stake back into the ground.'

Lilly couldn't suppress a flash of admiration. 'That's really clever.'

He nodded. 'It is indeed. She broke out night after night until she was caught with an empty sack. She'd even taken to removing the evidence and hiding it in her stall.'

'Was it Belle?'

There was a silence before he laughed. 'She's one on her own is Belle. I think you'll get on just fine.'

Each morning, when the dawn sky was still tinged with pink, Lilly forked out the dung that accumulated each night in her stall and got Belle ready for work in the ring. She was surprised at the cracks and fissures in the elephant's dry, wrinkled skin from which, intermittently, thick hairs protruded. The pad of her foot was hard as a plank, but it was the tail Lilly found the most curious. Disproportionate to her size and as thin as a whippet's, it was scarcely three feet long and tipped at the end by hair as coarse and hard as wire. Belle's tail swung efficiently to the right, the hairs sweeping her broad bottom but barely reached as far as her thigh on the left. As an insect swatter, Lilly thought, Nature had sold her short.

Over the next days, Lilly learned that Belle ate between one hundred and one hundred and twenty pounds of food each day. She pooped between eight and ten times a day, the fresh dumps were semi-solid and green in colour and smelled musky but not unpleasant. She quickly discovered that dry droppings had no smell and one elephant produced a pile that looked like six or seven balls of straw every two hours. She spread these out so that anyone who had a mind could help themselves; dry elephant dung was an excellent mosquito repellent when set alight with a match.

Most days, in the bristling heat, the elephants lumbered along the narrow path in single file from the stables to the river, and as they drew close to it, lengthened their stride and ran together towards the water. On command, Belle would lie down on her side, and using a hog hairbrush to remove mud and dust, Lilly scrubbed her clean. Besides their physical well-being, elephants needed mental exercise to keep them in good health and Mr Tiffert's herd knew their job.

'Could I watch the rehearsal this afternoon? I'd like to see Belle perform.'

'Did you not see her the other day?' An eyebrow rose over the top of his spectacles.

Lilly had not returned from the telegraph office in time. She had slipped into the tent as the closing acts were presenting their turns. The lie she produced would be convincing enough. 'Margot asked me to wash her tights. I wasn't in time for the elephants.'

'All right then. If you've got through your chores, after lunch you can sit in and watch.'

'I need meal tickets. Apparently, you should have given me them when I signed my contract.'

'Who told you that?'

'Reggie.'

'Did he now?'

'He said I need an act to qualify for free passage into the cook tent otherwise I have to ask you for tickets, or he'd end up serving food to half of Lucknow and the circus can't afford it.'

'Did he now?'

'So could I have tickets?'

'Tell Reggie when you go for your food that you are working with the elephants and you can sit with the girls.'

'I did.'

'And?'

'He stared at my chest and said he didn't recognise my face.'

He considered her answer for a moment then said, 'Pass him a message from me. If I hear one more complaint that he's trying it on with the girls, he's out on his ear without notice.'

That afternoon, the dress rehearsal started well enough.

Mr Tiffert introduced and orchestrated the five-elephant act. Lilly gasped in delight at the sight of the elephants plodding silently into the tent, stirring up the sawdust in yellowish puffs so that they seemed to walk through a mist.

From his position outside the ring, the cues he used were gentle, the idea being, he said, that the elephants were performing by themselves, without human intervention.

'We don't jab and poke with a bull hook. Our elephants are working animals as well as performers and if you get them off-side, they are unpredictable. I told you that I oversee their training and present them in the ring. Each knows exactly what she has to do.'

'I've seen a *mahout* urge on an elephant with his toes. And he spoke to her.'

'It's pointless everyone speaking in the ring. It will confuse the elephant, so we work by touch, gesture and a lone voice, mine, to remind them. Watch now. You will see they know their jobs.'

The elephants began by running around the ring, each holding the tail of the preceding elephant in her trunk.

Mr Tiffert trained his eye on the performers. 'I prefer to showcase their strength and how fleet they are of foot. I am opposed to showing tricks that are unnatural for elephants.'

Lilly sat down on a tub and nodded vigorously. 'Give me an example.'

'Standing on their hind legs is not typical elephant behaviour and our females are not comfortable doing this. Only copulating bulls or, in nature, ones trying to feed from a tall tree would do this.'

'Presumably they can be taught to raise up on their hind legs?'

'Yes, but only with extensive use of the bull hook and I won't do that in my circus.'

Mr Tiffert gave another cue and Lilly watched while the elephants turned in a circle and raised their right forelegs. As they put their legs down five girls dressed in brightly coloured clothes ran into the ring, striking different poses as each elephant lifted her up with its trunk.

Belle wore a saddle-shaped cradle on her neck, and on Mr Tiffert's command, the showgirl placed a foot on the elephant's knee, caught an enormous ear with one hand and swung up onto her back. In one single seamless movement, she landed soft as a fly behind the elephant's ear and rode with one hand in the air, the other on her hip. All the girls rode in the same hands-free fashion, sitting easily on their mounts.

Mr Tiffert smiled his approval. 'Notice what they are doing, Lilly. Every move is relevant. They are not overperforming. The professional works with intense self-control, for the less you move, the more focus you will hold. Nothing is wasted. You must transport the audience for that is why they come – to be taken out of their lives for a few hours. Mistakes will be spotted and will reveal you as an amateur. To be a brilliant artist you must create the magic. You must smile and perform. The more danger you give them, the more engrossed they become.'

As Lilly was watching, caught up in the mood of the performance, a tent man sauntered past, whistling and twirling an iron peg as if it were a baton.

Fear clouded Belle's light brown eyes as she saw the object in the workman's fist and, swishing her trunk, her ears fully forward, she shrank back squealing in terror. The showgirl swung down from the elephant's harness and hopped out of the ring.

'Belle's afraid,' Lilly said, and began to walk towards her, arms spread wide. 'If she can smell me, it might calm her down.'

Mr Tiffert disagreed. 'She needs to be disciplined. It's up to you to show her that her reaction to the distraction is unacceptable. She must concentrate.'

'No, she's afraid,' Lilly repeated. 'Please let me try to calm her.'

Mr Tiffert held out his arm to block her. 'For your own safety, you must keep back. She's dangerous when her ears flap.'

Lilly pushed past him, fishing a lump of jaggery from her overalls and holding it out in the flat of her hand, inched towards the elephant clucking as she had heard the groom do with the horses in England. She stopped two yards short of the wildly flapping ears. 'Please, Belle,' she whispered. 'Make this easy for both of us. You'll avoid a beating and for once I'll be taken seriously.'

Belle stood still, her ears flattened against her head and Lilly took a step forward. The elephant was visibly trembling, her trunk extended upwards, sensing and probing the air.

'Get back!' Mr Tiffert cried. 'She's going to charge.'

'You're not going to charge, are you, Belle?' Lilly crooned. 'You're just frightened to death but I'm here and you're safe.'

Belle shook her head violently from side to side. Lilly was breathing hard, wretched with the sense of failure.

And then.

Belle lunged forward, whipped the sugar from Lilly's hand and popped it into her mouth. Trumpeting loudly, she lifted her front leg and wound her trunk around Lilly's waist, lifting her into the air. With a spine jarring thud she was deposited on Belle's neck, holding onto her ears for dear life.

Belle dug her feet into the sawdust and Lilly lurched forward squashing her head in the folds of Belle's neck.

Mr Tiffert began to laugh. 'As I was just saying, any extraneous movement detracts from the overall performance, but I think you've, quite literally, landed yourself a new job.'

★

The following day, Lilly began to understudy the elephant's routine.

Mr Tiffert had no inclination to teach. 'The way to learn is to watch. We have to train this way because there's no time to rehearse a stand-in. If you're needed, you'll have to jump in there and then. Work on your mounts and dismounts and practise your hands. Watch the showgirls' mannerisms and gestures and get the sisters to show you how to bow, smile and play to the audience. Sort out a costume. Someone is invariably injured and unable to perform. That will be your moment to step up.'

Over and over, Lilly slipped and fell forwards, grazing her wrists on the links of the elephant's harness. The ache in her legs was unremitting as she tried to steer Belle with a flick of her toes. It was akin to moving a mountain with a feather and after hours behind the harness, weak with exhaustion, she was swaying in her seat.

Mr Tiffert strode across the ring. 'Why are you holding on with one hand? It ruins your symmetry. You must present yourself.'

'I don't know what you want me to do. I'm just trying to balance.'

He huffed with impatience. 'Didn't you learn ballet as a child? Or any form of dance?'

Lilly blinked her eyes wearily. 'Yes.'

'Then you'll remember that you were taught to be aware of how you look. Of what your body is doing, how you carry your head and the shapes you make with your hands.'

'If I take my hand off the harness, I'll lose my seat.'

Mr Tiffert pressed his lips together, seeing that she was

shaking. 'Are you frightened of falling? Or just generally frightened?'

She wanted to explain that, by itself, it wasn't the fact that she had slipped that had spooked her. It was more that it had brought six years of fear to the surface. 'Just give me a moment,' she said.

'I may be an insensitive German bastard, but what exactly is it you are frightened of?'

'Everything.'

'Get down off the elephant.'

Lilly peered at the ground, tears running down her cheeks. 'I don't know how.'

As if anticipating her difficulty, Belle raised her trunk.

Compassion softened his eyes. 'She's showing you a way down. Wiggle over her head and slide down her trunk.'

'The showgirls don't get off like that.'

'Then ask her to raise her leg and use it as a step.'

'Utha!' Lilly gave some life to her command.

Mr Tiffert stood back as Belle lifted her leg and Lilly stepped to the ground. He looked at her for a long time, his head on one side. 'If I could give you some fatherly advice?'

Lilly looked at him through a mist of tears.

'When my mama died, my heart was broken with grief and I was scared of being on my own.' He put an arm around her shoulders. 'Involve yourself in the circus, Lilly. Immerse yourself in activities that require you to give so much energy and dedication to what you are doing that your thoughts are directed away from those things you find so troubling.'

'Did it work for you?'

'One day I woke up and realised I was no longer afraid.'

'How long did it take?'

Mr Tiffert stepped away and gave a ghost of a smile. 'All wounds need time to heal, but I don't think anyone can predict with any precision how long that will take. In the meantime, Whizzy Delroy says he'll try you out for his act.'

She was silent for a moment. 'That as well as the elephants?'

He handed her his handkerchief. 'You have too much time on your hands, which is allowing you to dwell. Immerse yourself. Keep busy until you are so tired you will sleep where you drop.'

Stunned, Lilly stared at him. 'I don't have a permit to perform.'

'I know. Leave it with me. You'll be legal before you ever set a foot in my ring.'

Chapter 24

Whizzy Delroy was a showman.

A tall, lean man with a bony, weather-beaten face and a moustache as thin as a pipe cleaner, he twirled his unicycle about his head as if he was a drum major in a brass band. He laid the bike on its side and ran with it, holding the saddle down between his legs. He hopped onto the right pedal and threw his weight forward until he was aboard, propelling the bike with first one foot and then the other.

Lilly began to clap. 'Is riding with one foot difficult to master?'

He broke into a smile. 'It's the easiest trick, really, once you've learned how to balance. Ride as fast as you can, lean forward and take your front foot off and let the momentum carry you forward.'

'I can ride a bicycle. Do you think I'd be able to do that?'

He spun in a circle, his arms held out to the sides and nodded to Lilly; she tossed up his five coloured clubs, one by one, as he started to juggle. It was accomplished and looked easy. 'Let's get this part of the act slick and then we'll see.'

'Are you going to throw them down?'

'Do you have another suggestion?'

'I can balance a basket on my head. I could catch them in that, which will keep my hands free to toss up the hand sticks for your next stunt. That way, there won't be a gap.'

'Good idea,' he said, dropping the clubs to the wooden flooring they had dragged out to cover part of the ring. 'Get hold of a basket from the commissary and we can work that into the act.'

Next, Lilly threw up the two hand sticks and then the devil stick that Whizzy caught on the cord that stretched between them. 'The skill with this is to keep the movement slow and even, then build it up with an extra push into a single flip and then with a bit more force you can attempt the double flip.'

'That's really impressive. You can toss those into the basket as well.'

'Good girl. Take the long rope over there' – he jerked his chin towards the wooden curbing that edged the ring – 'and tie the end of the rope to the quarter pole and grab hold of the other end.'

'Which pole is that?'

'The pole supporting the middle section. I'm going to try skipping over the rope.'

'Juggling at the same time?'

'Of course, juggling at the same time. Tiffy says he wants the audience at the edge of their seats, but do you know how hard it is, Lilly, trying to appear fresh, having to constantly reinvent your act so that you never grow stale?'

Lilly could not decide how the skipping would work. 'If I am to swing the rope round you, you're going to have to be utterly precise in how far you jump and toss the clubs. You'd be better off with the wooden balls because they aren't as high. And how are you going to lift the unicycle?'

Whizzy pedalled backwards and forwards a few times. 'Another good point. Just swing the rope for now so I get used to hopping the wheel up and down.'

'Why don't you have your own skipping rope and forget the juggling? You've already shown the audience you can do that. If you stand on the pedals, you could grip the saddle between your legs and lift it up that way.'

His eyebrows lifted towards his hairline. 'You sound like you know what you're doing.'

'When I first heard that I might be your property girl, I started to practise with my bicycle. Duffy showed me a few stunts. Hopping was one of them.'

'I don't need you to perform as such on a bike. Can you do cartwheels?'

'When I was about five.'

He began to hop the cycle on the spot. 'You could do that to add a bit of colour to the ring while I move from this trick to the next.'

'I thought the clowns are supposed to segue between the gaps.'

He made a face. 'I don't work with clowns. I will move from the low to the high seated unicycle and you could provide some acrobatics while I transition.' He motioned towards a second cycle he called the giraffe.

'How do you get on it?'

'Bounce up from the tyre onto the pedals. It's a bit of a manoeuvre but the audience like the fact that I'm up high, doing daring stunts and placing myself in danger. The possibility that I could fall at any moment while doing this for them keeps them interested.'

Lilly attempted a pirouette. 'The obsession with putting one's life at risk is difficult to understand. It's morbid, like waiting for a fatality so you can stare at the body.'

'The circus is a place where remarkable people perform daring feats with inexhaustible enthusiasm. It's what makes us tick.'

'For next to no money.'

'Exactly. I love the fact that I own very little except the thoughts in my head and that at any moment I can leave.'

'Were you born in the circus?'

Whizzy reached up towards the saddle. 'I was one of very many who ran away to join it and like most, one day I will leave either through choice or because I cannot earn my keep. Rarely do performers make old bones and circus operators cannot afford passengers on their payroll.'

'How hard is the unicycle to learn?'

'I started when I was a child and I'm still improving.'

'Would you let me try?'

He seemed to think for a while, then wiped an arm over his sweaty brow. Dropping the giraffe to the floor, he picked up the unicycle and held it towards her. 'All right, but only so you can see how tricky it is. To start riding, hold onto something. This will show you how to balance on a unicycle. That's the key at the start. Riding forwards and staying up will be your first goal.'

'I can ride a bicycle.'

'So you've said. That tells me you have balance, but this is not at all like riding a bike.' He thrust the unicycle towards her. 'Adjust the saddle but don't have it too high and work alongside someone's safety net as it will give you something to hang onto if you feel yourself wobble.'

Lilly swung herself onto the saddle and grabbed at his arm, but her gaze was fixed in the far corner, where she had caught sight of Duffy and a tiger in its cage. Her heart was beating so fast, she could barely swallow.

Whizzy tapped her thigh. 'Concentrate. Keep your eyes straight ahead as if you're looking at a beautiful view. It's natural to want to look down, but that'll only make you fall.'

She relaxed her grip on his forearm. 'I bicycle looking at the ground ahead of me.'

'Does your elephant walk looking down?'

'No.'

'Exactly. It's disorienting to run while looking straight down. Elephants look straight ahead and so must unicyclists.'

She half glanced towards Duffy again and said, 'That's true. When they go to the river for their bath, they stare at it and run towards it. Nothing else matters in the world at that moment but getting into the water.' Lilly stole another look at Duffy, wondering if he'd seen her.

Rocking backwards and forwards on her wheel, Whizzy seemed to know her mind was elsewhere. 'Do you want me to go on?'

Drawn to him, but fighting it back, she wanted Duffy to notice her. Like a child showing off, she wanted him to see that she had mastered something difficult and should be applauded for her efforts.

'I'm sorry, yes.'

'Don't be afraid to wave about with your arms. You'll see the high-wire artist doing it to keep his balance. It's no different on the ground as arms are essential to keeping your balance when you first start out. You'll find it works and everyone does it.'

Duffy turned in her direction, raised his hand, a faint smile dancing in his eyes.

With a jolt, she pulled her thoughts back to her lesson. 'You don't.'

'I don't need to. You'll find as you get more comfortable, you can ride along with your hands at your side, but it might take a little time. And don't forget to lean forwards when you get on.'

'I never saw you do that.'

'I've had years of practice to perfect a running mount. But for you, your unicycle should be tilted in the direction you want to ride. By pedalling forwards, you keep the unicycle from falling over. This takes some commitment at first; if you throw your weight too far forwards, you can always just step off onto the ground. It's when you don't lean forwards that you end up falling off the back and getting hurt.'

He gestured for her to set off. 'Hold your back straight and suck your stomach in. If you're sagging in the middle, you're not going to be able to hold your balance. Keep your eyes on the safety net and see if you can reach it.'

Lilly set off towards her target, but her mind began to drift and before she was aware what had happened, she was face down in the sawdust.

'What happened there?'

'I don't really know. Suddenly I was in England, riding my bicycle hands-free around my grandparents' tennis court.'

Whizzy helped her to her feet. 'Riding a unicycle is a matter of understanding what works for you, and then doing it enough times so that you don't forget. You did this when you learned to ride your bicycle and once you've got the hang of it, you'll never forget how to do it. Practice. That's the key. And keep your eyes off Duffy, as well. He'll do nothing for your equilibrium.'

'That word is starting to get on my nerves.'

'Duffy?'

Dust was rising, lifting towards the top of the tent. It seemed to dance in the heat. 'Practice. I don't even know if it will ever benefit me.'

'The circus has given you an opportunity, but it doesn't always translate to a career.'

'What is the point of all that practice if it's not going to get me anywhere?'

'The practice is the point. Imagine you are learning the violin. You can make some agreeable-sounding notes quite soon on, but to become proficient you have to work at it every day, doing dull, repetitive exercises to progress beyond what is merely pleasant to the really beautiful.'

He began to walk away but Lilly called to him. 'Is Whizzy your real name?'

'No.' His head jerked round at the question.

She waggled her eyebrows, encouraging him to go on.

He held off for a while, and then 'Waldo Watkins,' he said briefly.

Lilly had the impression it was a question he hadn't wanted to answer, that she had a forced a response he was reluctant to give. She did not want to let the moment slide.

'Anyone else with a made-up name? The Schinkel Sisters?'

'They are real, but most of us have a different name for performing. If you are hiding out in the circus, the last thing you'd want to do is advertise who you really are. A little secret for you though: Madame Margot is Lesley Ramsbottom.'

Lilly could see the absolute sense in that and admonished herself for not also changing her name. 'It's an intriguing name.'

'Have you asked her to read your cards?'

Lilly shook her head. 'I went to a séance of hers, but it seemed too far-fetched, almost as if it had been put on to place her in the spotlight. I'm beginning to think that I got it wrong.'

He pulled her down beside him on a golden bale of hay. 'Margot isn't a crank but she's a very private person and won't read for you unless you ask her yourself. She has a gift. She sees things. You have to remember that a lot of true performers started out in a one-wagon, one-horse gypsy affair that toured Europe in the closing years of last century.'

'Dodo said that's how she began.'

He nodded. 'The show would amount to nothing much more than a few folk in a roving caravan, touring a series of far-flung hamlets. There were no ticket sales and these outfits depended on voluntary donations, whatever people could spare.'

'What sort of acts would they have done?'

'Much the same as we do here but they would have all taken a turn at everything: horse-back riding, foot juggling, acrobatic routines. Possibly an act featuring a dancing dog or playing an instrument while dressed as a clown. To the people they were entertaining, just try to imagine. Their day-to-day existence was drab and unexciting. Seeing these performers dressed in their spangles, executing amazing feats must have seemed almost supernatural, like bejewelled ghosts coming out of the fog.'

'Margot looks like a sprite.'

'She's a princess. Imagine her as a small child equestri-enne on top of a horse, pirouetting and jumping through paper hoops from the back of a loping beast.'

A fairy, Mama!

Lilly shook her head to clear Teddy's voice. 'How does that explain the fortune-telling?'

'Don't ever let her hear you call it that. It's referred to as cartomancy, or otherwise put – divining by cards. It was likely one of the ways people were attracted to the show. Tiny Margot and her Petit Lenormand Cards.'

'My grandmother used to say fortune-telling was nothing more than trickery designed to relieve the gullible of their pennies. The medium asks you questions so she has a fair idea of what you want to hear.'

'I don't see how when the cards have faces that all mean something. If you are cynical then I don't think it's for you.' He stood up and dusted off his tights. Then he pulled her to her feet. 'We have to get back to it if we're going to be ready by the weekend.'

Lilly took a step back and stared over his shoulder. Wondering how to frame her question so that it would appear casual, she gave a nervous little cough. 'One last thing.'

A frown appeared on his forehead. 'Make it quick.'

'Is Duffy Puttnam made up as well?'

He gave a snort. 'That fellow is a one hundred per cent fiction. From the gossip in the world of circus, his name is merely the tip of the iceberg.'

Lilly swallowed, a lump of unease lodged in her throat. She had heard all about his failings from Noel, but until now, they hadn't seemed to matter. 'What is he called if his name isn't Duffy?'

'The last time I heard, his name was Charles B. Franks.'

'Wild animal trainer?' She was conscious of holding her breath.

Whizzy spun the unicycle by its saddle. 'Not even close. He was billed as The Flexible Wonder and could fold himself into a tailor-made trunk.'

'But that's almost—'

'Impossible,' he said.

'So why did he change his act?' She shook her head, not wanting to know.

'That, dear Lilly, is something only he can answer.'

Chapter 25

Lilly's days were full, every moment leading up to the timing of the show. What she did in the morning related to the unshakable deadline of the evening performance. No one took time off for fear of finding themselves unemployed.

Circus nights, though, were a time to talk of things other than the day-to-day running of the circus – to drift in other directions. Nights were not for sleeping much; it was too hot, and folk dragged their bedding outside their wagons or sat about on foldable chairs, while piles of elephant dung smouldered beneath a sky as black as a horse's nose. Few performers wound down enough after the show to sleep before one o'clock.

Seeing Duffy every day was proving harder than she had imagined; a tenuous, treading-on-eggshells relationship that ought to have been easier than it was proving to be. Lilly was surviving on crumbs of stolen time when Margot's back was turned.

Dodo had noticed, of course. Nothing got past her. After the performance that evening, shielded by her kimono, she was taking a 'bath'. She had taken off her costume, while the robe hung loose from her shoulders, then fastened the robe under her arms. 'You've been making cow's eyes at the tiger trainer. Even a simpleton with one eye missing and a squint in the other would notice.'

Lilly watched in fascination as Dodo sponged under her arms. 'We were friends in Nainital. This is not some new infatuation.'

As often as not, Dodo's reply doused her enthusiasm. 'I thought you'd have more self-respect.'

'What do you mean?'

Dodo had finished her arms and face and raised the garment, securing it around her neck. Screened by this protective layer, she began to wash and dry the rest of her body. 'Didn't your husband limit the time you spent with your son?'

'Yes.'

'And you didn't fight for what you wanted. You let him tell you how it was going to be between a mother and her child. He gave you his permission to read a bedtime story and you said, "Thank you very much. I'm terribly grateful."'

Lilly kept her eyes on Dodo, the familiar squeeze in the pit of her stomach taking hold, and anticipated the burn of the bullet before she fired.

By now Dodo had washed down to her feet. She sat down and dunked them in the bucket. 'Well, didn't you? He had you cornered, and you let him snap at you.'

'You have no idea what it was like to live in fear of his tread on the floorboards.'

Dodo squeezed the water from her sponge and returned it to her trunk. 'And now you have taken up with a wisp of grass.'

'Is that a German expression that you've translated badly?'

Dodo dried between her toes. 'I have no difficulties with my English, thank you. That man bends with the prevailing wind. Backwards and forwards, backwards and forwards. It could go on for years.'

Lilly bit the nail of her little finger and looked at the floor. What Dodo said was true. Duffy did behave like a straw in the wind. Margot blew up a tornado and he leaned in her direction. When she made a claim on his attentions, he sprang back to her.

When eventually she looked up, she saw that Dodo's feet were done. 'Is there a point to this?'

'Knock Margot off her pedestal if Duffy's the one you want. People walk all over you so often I'm surprised you're not as flat as a strap.'

It was past midnight, as they sat beneath a sliver of yellow moon that hung low in the sky and listened to the dull drone of insects. The long-awaited monsoon rains had started and were a temporary relief from the heat, but they had stopped again at a cost. Humidity was at such a level it was difficult to breathe and, just as the blisters from her ride with Noel had finally resolved, an itchy rash of small, raised red spots prickled all over her body. Lilly plucked at her collar and ran her fingers beneath her sleeves yet found little to give her relief.

She flapped listlessly at her head then placed the back of her palm against her forehead. 'It's stifling. You could almost fry an egg on my face. The rains shouldn't have stopped for weeks.'

Duffy looked pale in the moonlight. 'The same happened years ago. The rains started in July and bucketed down for days and then dried up. We've been lucky because normally our season would have finished in June but for the King's coronation.'

'Even so, it would be nice to clear the air.'

He had taken her back to his wagon – a spot in the furthest removes of the circus stand, behind the cages where he kept the tigers. 'The cages block the breeze so we must suffer for our privacy.'

They sat side by side on the wagon's steps, their backs against the painted door, and looked at the stars. Duffy turned to her. 'There's no chance in the world that anyone's going to sleep in this heat, but no one will find us here.'

He slid an arm around her, and she leaned her head against his shoulder, just for a moment; it was too hot to stay in contact for long.

He withdrew his hand, pushed his hat back from his forehead and massaged his temples. 'What did you think of the performance?'

'I didn't really see much of it, to be honest. Margot had me running around after her with her cloak and slippers until I was on with Whizzy.'

'Where did you get that costume? You looked different. Glamorous.'

Lilly's heart quickened. If he'd seen the costume, he must have watched her work. 'Did you see me perform?'

'I did. Who showed you how to compliment the audience?'

'Mr Tiffert told me to copy the sisters.'

'They never bow to the audience. You'll have to do better than that.'

Lilly was on the point of saying that, indirectly, it had been Margot. That she had spent hours studying her from behind the velvet curtains as she skipped into the ring wearing a long satin cloak, blowing kisses to the audience, smiling as if thrilled to see old friends, her elegant, shapely arms held out to the crowd. If she was completely honest with herself, Margot was rather marvellous.

'I watched and saw it's not like accepting applause at the theatre. You acknowledge your audience and thank them in different ways. So, I've tried to develop my own style

269

and not copy anyone else.'

He nodded his approval. 'Are you practising your unicycle with Whizzy?'

Lilly breathed in the tobacco scent of his hair. 'No. It's far harder than it looks and I'm not good enough to do anything other than throw up his props. Nattie lent me that outfit I had on tonight, but I have to make my own, so she always has a spare.'

'Did she tell you to get fleshings?'

Lilly shook her head. 'No.'

'She probably thought you'd know. Flying performers wear them, you see. The ladies need to protect their modesty so wear flesh-coloured tights that extend upwards like a man's vest to cover the whole body under the costume. The commissary doesn't carry much for ladies beyond soap and basic underclothes, but they will have tights. They're a must if you entertain thoughts of acrobatics in the ring. Margot never performs without them underneath her tutu.'

His concern sent a thrill through her but the reference to Margot spoilt the effect of his words.

Lilly lifted the hem of her skirt and flapped it against her legs. 'I have some good news. Mr Tiffert's offered me a slot with the elephants. He's applying for a performing permit, which he says is a mere formality.'

Duffy eyed her critically. 'Really?'

She gave his arm a playful punch. 'Yes, really. You might be pleased for me at least, even if you don't approve.'

He took hold of her hand and squeezed it; his forehead creased into furrows. 'I'm concerned, that's all. Firstly, you are already working in the ring so the permit should be in place and the whole point of coming to the circus was for you to disappear. Sitting on top of an elephant and actively participating in Whizzy's act wasn't really what we had in mind when we were discussing all this at Noel's. You're too visible. What if Royce does have a man on your tail? He'll spot you a mile off.'

Lilly tossed her head. 'There's no way he could have tracked me here and even if he had, he wouldn't place me in this context.'

Duffy was looking at her properly now and it was not the intense heat that was causing her to melt.

He pulled her towards him, his eyes softening into hers. 'Have you heard back from Noel, you know, about your dressing-table set?'

Lilly felt a little breathless. 'There's been nothing. Are you sure he didn't say anything when he came back after Bhimtal? You said he was upset.'

'I think he was glad to have the house back to himself. He asked Conti to clear out your room and he shut himself in his study to concentrate on his forestry applications.'

Lilly thought that odd. Conti had applied to the Forestry Commission on his behalf and the interview was already in place. They'd both said she'd always have a home in their house and keep her room as it was. Why then would they want to wipe it clean?

'Do you think he was upset about catching your new tiger?'

'Write to him and ask him yourself if you're that bothered.'

'I've been meaning to and, truthfully, I've been putting it off but I've promised myself I'll do it tomorrow. In the meantime . . .' She hesitated before finishing her sentence. 'I sent one of the Queen Victoria postcards to Conti and one to the Miss Pinkneys.'

'Was that entirely wise?' His eyed widened and she saw she had given him a fright.

In the space of his four words, the dread was back. 'Conti

had already addressed it. I didn't send a message. It was to reassure them that I am all right, so they won't worry.'

'The old ladies were rattled when you left without word.'

'Noel told me not to go to see them.'

'I know, but those two old dears – they've taken you into their hearts. Miss Pearl in particular.'

Lilly blinked and swallowed. 'What did they say when you delivered my letter?'

'They clutched each other for support. One seeking strength from the other.'

She felt a flutter of alarm. 'Like Dodo and Nattie.'

'Still missing your son?'

'All the time.' She was deeply touched he asked and yet she folded in half, both hands pressed against her abdomen. 'I can hear his name without welling up, but missing Teddy is like a bruise on my arm that is too agonising to touch. I don't feel it all the time but it catches me up and . . .' She put her head on her knees and shut her eyes. 'I am run through with pain.' And guilt, she thought. So much guilt. I've been here for weeks and I have no more idea of a plan how to get him back than the day I arrived.

Duffy gathered her to him and kissed the top of her head. In the circle of his muscular arms, she breathed in the stale animal odour caught in the fibre of his clothes that sparked a different ache within her. She wanted more than snatched moments. She wanted some happiness and to fulfil a physical need that had been missing in her relationship with Royce. One way or another, Lilly vowed she would do as Dodo suggested and push Madame Margot off her perch.

She pulled away and turned to face him. They were so close their noses were almost touching. She spoke in a voice that had a mind of its own. 'Kiss me properly,

Duffy – I've been waiting long enough.'

Before dawn had pushed back the night shadows, Lilly raised her fingers to his mouth. 'I have to go,' she said.

Duffy wrapped a sheet around her shoulders. 'Use it to cover your face. It is dark out but there are eyes everywhere. The circus never sleeps, remember, and you mustn't drop your guard for a second.'

She rubbed her cheek against his arm.

He put a hand to her face. 'Do you want me to walk with you, to your wagon?'

'Not necessary. I've no sense that I'm being watched and am certain I'd know if I was. So, lie down and rest. You need to sleep. I'll see you tomorrow afternoon at some point.'

Duffy took her to the door, his arm about her waist. 'I'm not sure I can wait till then. I'll walk down to the stables tomorrow morning when I've sorted out the tigers, if you'd like that.'

'I would. Very much indeed.'

'You haven't left anything behind? Everything you took off you have put back on?'

Lilly laughed a little. 'Yes.'

She gave one long, lingering look at the bed, took in the rumpled sheets and felt a shiver down her spine. This is what you have chosen, she said to herself and clicked the door shut behind her.

The night outside was hot, damp with the suspended monsoon, a new dawn fighting its way through the thick air.

There was no one about, no crowds now. She flattened herself against the perimeter fence and kept to the shadows as she made her way back to the wagon.

Chapter 26

Dodo pummelled her feet against the underside of Lilly's berth. 'You stay out all night and now you are fidgeting so much we're both wide awake.'

'Pinch punch, first day of the month.' Lilly almost shouted the saying.

'*Das kommt mir Spanisch vor.*' There was a bad-tempered edge to Dodo's voice.

'What?'

Nattie peered over the edge of her bunk, her face blotched with sleep. 'She has no idea what you are talking about.'

'We say this on the first day of the month. For especial good luck. Today's the first of August so pinch punch.'

'Why should the first day of the month be lucky?' Nattie's voice rang down from above.

From the bunk below, Dodo let out a snort. 'It's ridiculous. What does it mean, "pinch punch"?'

'It's from medieval times when it was thought that salt made witches weak. People left out a pinch of it, then it was easy to punch them away.'

'In Germany we have no saying to welcome the new month,' Nattie said.

'You have nothing to solicit good luck?'

Dodo turned over and smacked her pillow. 'That is the only thing I want to punch at this hour on a Sunday morning. Apart from your face, that is.'

'Charming as ever,' Lilly murmured. But as she swung out of her bunk and landed softly on the floor, she was sure she heard Dodo laugh.

The circus lot was silent when, dressed in her Pahari clothes, Lilly scooped up the bag containing her writing materials and let herself out of the wagon.

Dodo and Nattie had no plans for the day other than to wander into town, find somewhere swish to eat kebabs – a Lucknow speciality, Dodo said – and work on a refinement to their act.

Mr Tiffert had called an assembly in the performance tent at six o'clock as he had an announcement to make. The rumour was that the show was either going to stall, or that performers would be shed, and Lilly felt sure the Schinkel sisters would not be the only ones working flat out to impress the boss.

Duffy was to give his new tiger a workout and then he'd come down to find her, to carry on where they'd left off the night before, he said.

For the animals, however, Sunday was no different from any other day. They still needed to be fed, cleaned and exercised. Somewhere on the circus ground, Duffy would be with his tigers and Margot her horses; she was pleased, that, in this, they had something in common.

It struck Lilly then – as she made her way to the elephants' quarters, along neat streets and bungalow gardens to the military part of town – as a strange irony that it was now the human shackled to the beast. Or was this some sort of karma? she wondered. She'd been abandoned herself by her parent, had done the same to Teddy, and Belle was now her responsibility, a dependent child who needed its mother.

Leaving her bag in the stable yard, Lilly slid back the bolt that fastened the door to her stall; Belle spread her huge ears outwards and extended her trunk upwards, sweeping it from side to side to smell the air.

Lilly talked nonsense while she mucked out the stall and fed the elephant stale roti. It was forbidden to remove food from the cook tent but, as Reggie unfailingly ignored her request to remove them from her tray, Lilly smuggled out the giant, redundant flatbreads for her charge. Belle belched loudly as she gobbled down the plate-size treats, but Lilly sensed there was something amiss.

Even after so little time with the circus, Lilly realised that the comments she had flung so carelessly at Margo in Nainital were misplaced and ignorant; animals did communicate with humans and while not actually able to talk as such, they were perfectly able to express how they felt. Today, Belle was in a mood.

Lilly patted her big leathery bottom then fondled her ears. 'What's going on, Belle?'

The elephant spread her feet and looked her up and down with her long-lashed brown eyes.

'Is it Duffy?' The heat in Lilly's stomach lurched its way to her toes then up to her face. Her heart began to race as she relived the previous night.

Belle moved her front right foot through the straw and blinked, seemingly fascinated by the dust that rose up and danced in a stripe of sunlight.

'Utha!' Lilly tapped Belle's left leg and when she had lifted it up swept underneath. 'Don't you like him?'

Belle dropped her foot to the ground and stretched out her trunk, reaching into Lilly's pocket.

'Are you jealous?' Lilly laughed, rubbing oil onto Belle's head to protect it from the sun. 'Last night was the best night of my life – if you don't count having my children. The best bit of your day, though, is coming now.' She rolled up her sleeves and picked up the brush she used for the daily scrub bath. 'This is what we do, just you and me. You don't need to be jealous of Duffy. You know as well as I that I've hardly seen him since he arrived back at the circus. He's been too busy with training.' And Margot, she added to herself. 'But last night we lay together and now he belongs to me.'

Belle knocked the brush from her hand. It took a great deal of coaxing with handfuls of jaggery to entice her to the river. Jaggery was her favourite treat – refined molasses, utterly irresistible to this elephant; an edible balm to soothe troubled waters.

But the river was still swollen from the early monsoon and boiled, thick and angry. Overhead, in the heavy canopy of trees that lined the water's edge, swarms of crows flapped and rattled amongst the leaves and the air hummed with crickets.

The elephant stood by the water's edge, one baggy back leg crossed over the other, her trunk swinging from side to side.

Lilly stood at Belle's shoulder and placed the sugar into her mouth. 'What is it, sweetheart?'

Belle shifted her eyes uneasily and gave a low rumble in her chest.

Lilly suspected she was afraid to go into the water without the companionship of the herd. On this one day of the week, keepers chose their own time to tend to their animal. 'Go on,' she cajoled, 'it's perfectly safe to swim.'

Belle stepped back and held her coiled trunk above her head; it was a defensive gesture. If her trunk were to be damaged, she would be unable to drink or feed and eventually she'd starve to death.

'Do you want me to come in with you? Is that what the problem is?'

Belle swung round and, trumpeting loudly, eased her trunk over Lilly's arm. Lilly patted it gently and Belle wound it round her waist as tight as a steel corset and hoisted her onto her neck.

Lilly knew she must not waver and give any hint that she was other than fully confident to take an elephant into the river by herself. 'All right then, my precious. *Agit!*' she commanded and Belle, knowing she was no longer alone, obediently lumbered in.

By the time Lilly had scrubbed the elephant clean, taken her back to the stables and forked a mini mountain of fresh fodder into her stall, her clothes no longer clung wetly to her body and she was almost too tired to think.

She flopped down under a large peepal tree, and for over an hour, lay on her back, arms crossed behind her head, her brain taunted with memories of Noel and their last night in Bhimtal.

She pulled her bag towards her. The letter loomed, the composition of it seeming trickier and more unassailable than the grey cliff of Belle's backside.

What was she to write?

Fragments of conversation scuttled like trapped rats beneath the rafters. Lilly shut her eyes and waited for the words to stop their ghastly scratching.

She smiled as she imagined Noel relaxing in a long wicker chair on his veranda, leaning forward with his elbows on his knees, pipe clamped between his teeth. A gin rickey at his elbow, he would barricade himself behind *The Times of India*, his eyes sparkling beneath his shaggy brows as he pretended to disapprove of the husks of gossip Conti brought back from the Club. In the drawing room, she heard him playing the piano with Goose at his feet, the dog's ears pinned back, nose lifted up as his whole body pulsated with the ecstasy of his master's music. The photograph on his desk of the man himself; the light catching the shine of sweat on his forehead.

She winced when that awkward meal came to mind, when friction had crackled in the hot night air as they'd tried not to look at each other, conversing silently with the demons in their heads. And then the gun. *Watch out for tigers, Lilly.*

She shook her head as she remembered him pleading his case for British India. '*Don't lay the blame of your unhappiness at her door. She deserves another chance.*'

'England's not like this. I hate it here.'

'*Emotionally you've never unpacked your bags.*'

'I can't stay in Nainital.'

'*Something about Duffy just doesn't add up.*'

A tendril of doubt uncurled itself. She put her head in her hands and squeezed her forehead; the pain of him not saying a proper goodbye still dismayed her, undid her for a while until she fought back and climbed out of that dark place.

The temptation to abandon the letter was overwhelming.

Noel was her confidant, her voice of reason, the person she could always count on; the risk of losing him as a friend was unbearable. She took out her writing paper and unscrewed the top from her pen. She would be sincere and keep her tone light; she would thank him and wish him success with his farm. She wrote slowly, weighing every word. Language was powerful whether written or spoken; the idea that words could never hurt you was nonsense; sticks and stones could do so much damage. Now, more than anything in the world, she wanted him to give her his blessing.

Dear Noel

At last I'm standing on my own two feet.

I have two jobs. I work with the elephants, which will make you laugh if you remember how scared I was of Pinky on the tiger hunt. Elephants need a great deal of attention and I spend many hours each day caring for Belle to build a relationship with her. I find I like feeding her and keeping her stable clean. I know where she will be at any hour of the day and night and that gives me a stability I've rarely had from people. I feel she has been given to me to help with the loss of Teddy; I have become her carer; the provider of her food, the one who puts her to bed at night and tells her stories so that she can sleep. Voice is everything, I have learned; I have also learned I am very fond of elephants!

It's just as well she can't speak as she would tell me what I should not want to hear: that we did not part on the best of terms and for that I can only ask your forgiveness.

So, I am here at the circus, breaking away from everything familiar, living in a tiny wagon with two outspoken German ladies, which is a tight squeeze. We have no washing facilities apart from a bucket that we fill twice in a day in the dressing tent. But I don't want to sound put out because I truly am not; the bustle of the circus will hide me for as long as I need to be hidden, but I don't know how long that will be. I am living from day to day and by night-time am exhausted but that is what I need. It stops me from dwelling too much on myself.

I don't know how long I'll be able to stay. I haven't worked out a way to do what I need to do but I am sure that one day, it will be clear.

I have sent the Miss Ps a route card – a friend wrote the address for me – and hopefully it won't raise suspicions at the post office in Nainital. I told the dear ladies that I would stay in touch and I mean to keep my word.

I'm considering a third communication – not to Binnie, for goodness knows where in India she might be – but to great friends of my grandparents, and maybe I will write it. The German ladies – twin sisters with whom I am sharing the wagon – think that I lack grit. Their words, but I think they fit me very well. You even hinted at it yourself after the tiger hunt when I fired the gun. I'm going to try to learn the real circumstances of why I came back to India because I don't believe what Binnie told me. Slowly I am finding my courage; I had it once but have misplaced it over the years and now I want it back.

I can't imagine, dear Noel, how you and Conti put up with me so well. Pearl Pinkney had my measure within moments and told me I had to wake up from a deep sleep, like Sleeping Beauty. Perhaps dormant was what I'd become.

So, this is the new me. Taking charge. Trying not to hate India as much and laying blame for all that is wrong in my life at her door. Not relying on a man – any man – to tell me what I must do.

I need to plan, to have some idea of the future, but the road ahead is not yet clear, although one thing is certain: I will get Teddy back and I will free myself from Royce.

Do splendid work with your model farm; you will be such a success with the Forestry Department that before very long I will read your name in The Times of India and be so proud of the dear man who fights the good fight for everyone who crosses his path.

Think not too badly of me,
Lilly

She laid down her pen and hid her face in her hands. The relief she expected to feel in writing the letter did not oblige her; instead, she felt even more profoundly alone.

Chapter 27

Later that morning, they crept into one of the crumbling stable barns, one that was no longer in use. The door had half dropped off its hinges and the lock had given up its job and hung slack like a dislocated jaw. The place was lofty, clean, yet smelled of soiled straw and horses.

It was intolerably hot.

Slick with sweat, they lay together on their sides nose to nose, gazing squint-eyed at each other. Lilly ran her hand across the wiry hair on Duffy's chest. His face was as red as fire, but he seemed distracted and his preoccupation unsettled her. *Every time I get closer to knowing him,* she thought, *he slips further away.*

'What are you thinking about?'

He kissed her for a while then said, 'Nothing important.'

She entwined her fingers with his, trying to reclaim him. 'I've asked Margot if she'll do a reading for me after the assembly later on.'

'Good idea. She thinks you're drifting,' he said with a smile.

'Margot said that?'

The smile deepened. 'It's no good being wishy-washy, Lilly. A reading will give you focus. Ha!' His voice rose with enthusiasm, as if he'd solved a difficult clue in a crossword puzzle. 'Focus. That's exactly what you need.'

She heard the confidence that he clearly knew what was best for her and thought, *never again.*

She raised her eyes to Duffy. 'And Margot will help?'

He smiled again and sat up. 'She practises divination with a pack of cards. I'm glad you've approached her because I know she's been hoping you might.'

Lilly let go of the fact they'd discussed her and kept the real reason for the reading to herself. Finding out more about Duffy was her objective and the reading had become the excuse. 'I don't actually believe in all that hocus pocus. I think we all navigate our own paths and don't need cards to tell us which life turning to take but she might have something useful to say. I'll accept any help I'm given if it helps me decide what to do.'

'Margot has clients who hang on her every word and ' – he reached into his trouser pocket for his cigarettes and matches – 'you can't stay here for ever.'

Admonishment was a tangible feeling: a sharp spike in her breast that slid down her body and took root in her gut. 'Are you saying I should leave?'

He drew several times on his cigarette, sending intermittent puffs of smoke into the air. Lilly imagined he was transmitting a tribal message to Margot. *Tell her to go. Just tell her to go.*

'Take a hard look at yourself. You've plonked yourself in the circus, but you are just marking time until you can think of some way to reclaim your son. It's making a mockery of all the performers who make a career out of this life that you are just playing at.'

'You must have thought it was a good idea at some stage. Why else would you have championed my cause to Mr Tiffert in that letter you wrote?'

She saw the surprise on his face just before he looked away. 'That was Margot's doing. She gave you a character reference and explained the circumstances of why you needed to disappear for a bit. There's no way Tiffy would have taken you on if she hadn't. She saw something vulnerable in you in Nainital and just wanted to help. That's all she's ever wanted to do.'

Lilly tried to laugh but her throat was tight and it came out as a groan. She knew she'd been guilty of a misapprehension and that the assumptions she had made about Margot were all wrong. She had spent so much time watching but not really seeing, that she hadn't acknowledged the truth: that Margot was sensitive and kind; possibly even a friend.

'I'm also going to ask her about that night when she spelled out the word "imposter" on the sheet of paper. Whether she actually believed that there was a fraudster in the room or whether it was all a bit of fun.'

'It wasn't a prank. She believes wholeheartedly in what she does and it could have been any one of us or all of us.' He sent more smoke into the air.

'Or none of us.'

Duffy leaned over and stroked her cheek with two fingers. She sat up – she couldn't help it – to check they hadn't been seen. 'We must be very careful. Mr Tiffert will sack us if he finds out,' she said.

'You worry too much.' He pulled her back down and kissed the tip of her nose. 'Last night was just the beginning. I've wanted so much more for a very long time.'

'Since séance night?' She felt a little faint in the airless barn.

He nodded, his eyes bottomless and transfixing. 'Séance night.'

Breathing hard, she forced herself to say, 'I have to know what it is you have with Margot. I felt sure that you were trying to distance yourself at the tiger hunt and yet almost immediately after you were injured, you were thick as thieves. Are you in love with her?'

His eyes shifted. Lilly sensed his hesitation and felt the hairs on the back of her neck start to lift.

He lowered his voice a little. 'Margot knows things about me that she threatened to divulge. It would end my career at the circus in India if they got out.'

She held his face between her hands. 'Did she read them in your cards?'

'No.'

'She's blackmailing you.' She kept the inflection from her voice. She didn't query what was clearly fact.

Without her prompting, he went on, 'A handful of years ago, I did her a favour. She'd been touring in Pilsen with the circus, but it wasn't doing well so she signed contracts with a succession of outfits in Europe, developing the act she has now. In Paris, when she was performing at the *Cirque d'hiver*, there was one gentleman who was very persistent in his attentions.'

'Were they reciprocated?'

'Not at first. He was in the audience every night, wined and dined her, put on a public show of courting her until she found out he was married.'

'You came to her rescue.'

'Yes, and he gave up visiting the show.'

Lilly picked up her pyjamas and tied them in place. 'Just like that? Whatever did you say? I can't believe he'd back down on the spot because a wild animal trainer told him to.' The words came out at a run.

'But he did when he knew Margot and I were involved, and sent her a white colt and me a five-word note.'

'Five words?'

'Call the stallion *Sans Rancune.*'

'Her horse Ranky?'

Duffy nodded. 'He told her that to be truly spectacular

she would need to break in her own horse, so that it knew it was a ring horse, and not an import pretending to do a job it would never have the skill to pull off.'

'That's a rather pointed remark.'

He must have read something in her tone because he continued. 'You're right. The comment was aimed at me, but he wasn't wrong about the horse. Margot trained him so that he doesn't lope like most circus horses. He trots so that his gait is even, to minimise the rise and fall as he circles the ring. His back is as flat as a billiard table. He knows what his job is and doesn't try to do anything else. He's a perfect platform for every aspect of her act which is why she will never let anyone else near him.'

'What does the French mean?' She shook out the tunic and put it on.

'No hard feelings.'

'I'm guessing you told him Margot was your wife.'

He reached for his shirt. 'Correct.'

'Even though you have a wife.'

'Even though I have a wife.' He smiled at her, his white teeth gleaming.

'Who is where?'

'I have no idea where she is or with whom. I met her in Cape Town when we were young and then I jumped on a ship to Bombay.'

'Are you hiding here?' She drew in her breath and waited.

'Not from her.'

'What was your act in Paris?'

He smiled again. 'Training wild animals, like now. Why would you ask?'

Lilly bit her lip. There was a sense of menace behind the brilliant smiles that unnerved her. 'Something I heard but I must have got it wrong.'

He looked at her, his eyes narrowed to slits, and he whispered in her ear. 'What did you think you heard, Lilly?'

Lilly swallowed as he curled his arm about her waist. 'That your name is Charles Franks.'

For a bare moment she thought she saw surprise or even shock in his eyes, but then it was gone. Binnie had a similar look when whatever she said next was a lie.

'That is not my name,' he said casually. 'I'm surprised you even asked.'

It was not a truthful answer, she knew, and tried to twist away, to pull herself free but he held onto her wrist, circled between his thumb and forefinger.

'I've another practice session with the new tiger this afternoon. Come and watch. I'll be in the covered menagerie.'

'Where's Margot likely to be?'

'She's with Tiffy schmoozing some bigwig in her tent who's come forward as a potential sponsor for the coronation shows. They'll be busy for ages, so we don't have to worry about them.'

Lilly disentangled his arm and rolled over, weighing up his words. She wanted to believe him, but on the subject of his name, knew he'd just spun her a line.

In the heat of mid-afternoon, Lilly went to watch Duffy training the tiger.

It was crouching in the corner of its cage – a primitive wooden affair that looked barely fit for the purpose of keeping the animal inside. The tiger swished its tail from side to side then hurled its great striped body against the bars; it stretched through its paws and raked at the air.

Duffy approached the cage making a rumbling sound with his tongue.

'What are you doing?' Lilly tried not to let her anxiety show in her voice.

'I'm speaking to him in his own language.'

The tiger slapped over and over at the bars, its frenzied roars buffeting her heart. 'I don't think it understands your accent. That tiger is beside himself.'

'It's all part of the process.'

'What have you called him?'

'Bagh.'

'That's original.'

'What do you mean?'

'Bagh is Hindi for tiger. It's like calling a cat, "cat" or a dog "dog".'

'I forgot you were an expert,' he snapped.

'He doesn't want to be a circus tiger, Duffy. Captivity is driving him mad. Can't you let him go?'

'Early days yet. I'm going to be doing this for a long time before he'll completely trust me.'

'He's too wild to integrate him into your act.' She was still looking at the tiger; his yellow eyes burned with hate. 'Aren't you afraid of him?'

With a flick of his fingers, he waved away her fear. 'There's no reason to be. I've been feeding him myself since I got him, so he knows our association is positive, and I've managed to touch him a couple of times. He'll learn from Mister Stripes so I'm thinking he'll perform for the coronation show, billed as a savage man-eater – which is why I wanted him in the first place.'

He leaned across and nuzzled her neck. 'What are you thinking?'

The memory of Duffy's fingers on her body gave rise to an exquisite feeling in her belly; she found herself swept up in the thrill of it and squeezed her eyes closed to fix it in place.

With a huge effort, she peered back at the cage. 'You can see from his face he's livid. I think putting him in the ring is madness.'

He caught up her hands and held them against his chest. 'He'll give in eventually. Just as you did.'

She pulled her hands away and shook her head. 'Do you think it's right to exert your authority over a wild animal and tame it? At least with the trained elephants they do other work besides perform, and Mr Tiffert doesn't make them do anything in the ring that diminishes their natural dignity in the wild.'

'He'd have a better act if he wasn't so soft. If my tigers only did what was natural to them in the wild, they'd lie about in the steel cage with their heads on their paws.'

Lilly pulled at his arm. 'I can't really see a tiger amusing itself in the jungle by sitting on a pedestal until you tell it what to do. I personally don't think force over nature is right.'

He gave a derisive snort. 'Isn't that what British gardeners do? Exert their authority over nature?'

'It's not a realistic comparison. He's a wild animal. He didn't ask to be captured and forced into behaviour and poses that are not natural to him.'

'Nor does a wild field ask to become tamed by Capability Brown.'

She held up a finger. 'Do be sensible for one minute.'

He put his face close to hers, as if to show the sincerity in his eyes. 'But I am, Lilly. I know it's not easy asking an animal to bend to someone else's will and do something which is foreign to its nature. But that's what I do, and I'm good at it. Very few scars and still rather handsome.'

'It's a wonder you can get into the ring with a head that swollen.'

He mewed like a tomcat. 'You spend time with them and are kind – they do not forget. Already he recognises my voice.'

Lilly pulled her head back with a tiny shake. 'I think you are deluding yourself. He knows you feed him, but he doesn't like you.'

As if to endorse her words, the tiger launched another assault on the bars; the cage rattled and shook under its weight. 'That cat would rip you to pieces if he ever got the chance.'

Duffy impaled a chunk of raw meat on a long-handled fork and poked it through the bars. 'Everyone assumes that a wild animal must be savage but that's not true; take Mister Stripes. He's no harder to handle than Noel's pet dog.'

For a reason she couldn't have anticipated, Lilly's heart tumbled at the sound of Noel's name. 'He doesn't approve of subjugating anyone's will. You've heard his opinion on what the British are doing in this country.'

'Noel's too entrenched in India. He wouldn't squash an ant because it might better itself and come back in its next life as a cockroach.'

In contrast with Noel, Duffy was quick to judge. Lilly looked again at the tiger, which was now crouching in the corner of the cage. 'Noel has to live in this country – there's nowhere else for him to go. He doesn't agree with the caste system but respects it because he understands the people and their fundamental belief: be kind in this life because it might favour you in the next. Has your time in India made you nicer or not so nice?'

Duffy dismissed the question. 'The trouble with Noel is he doesn't know how to push. That's why he's living up in that god-awful hill town without a bean to his name. His sister has more idea with all that networking she does at the Club. Binnie too. She landed herself the Commodore, don't forget, and we all know how well that's worked out for her.'

'I'm not that interested in Binnie's behaviour.'

Duffy drew his wooden fork across the bars as a pianist might execute a glissando from one end of the keyboard to the other. The tiger launched another assault on the cage.

'Why are you set on antagonising him?'

'He needs to get used to distractions and noise if he's going to be able to concentrate in the ring.'

'Will he be any good?'

'Too early to tell. Some just can't be taught. They lack inclination and however much you encourage them, they forget from day to day what they've been shown.'

'What will happen if he has no aptitude?'

'I shall discard him.'

I don't doubt it for a minute, she thought. 'I have to go,' she said, after a pause, rather wishing she hadn't come to watch him work.

'Not quite yet, surely. Five more minutes or so won't hurt.'

His voice was intimate and tender as he put out his hand and pulled her towards him. She felt her insides quiver as his fingers melted into hers.

The burning afternoon had turned to dusk.

Still wearing her practice clothes, Dodo pulled the swivel mouthpiece from her rigging box. 'Tiffy has just blasted the bugle horn so we have three minutes.'

'What do you think this is all about?' Lilly sat down on her collapsible chair and drew her elbows in. Twenty-four inches in front of her trunk was not an enormous space to call her own.

'If he's called assembly, something will have happened and pound to a penny, he's not going to be happy. We've all been making tweaks to our routines and you were missed by the way. He's likely to want to see what we've improved so you've got to hope Whizzy is feeling generous.'

'I was helping Duffy with his tigers.'

Dodo coughed three times then paused, like a clock that is going to strike. 'The tigers must be on heat.'

'I'm sorry?'

Dodo fixed her with her pale grey eyes and stared as she spoke. 'You should take a bath before Tiffy gets a whiff of you. One of the elephant girls was caught carrying on and she was thrown out. That's why you've got her slot, not because you're any good.'

Suddenly the downtrodden girl deserted her, the words were quick on her lips. 'He's every bit as agile as his tigers.'

Dodo tested her teeth on the leather mouthpiece but there was laughter in her eyes. 'And from what I hear, he's better equipped than one.'

Nattie took Lilly's arm and ushered her towards the entrance. 'You should have been practising or sewing your costume. Did you get your fabric? And your tights?'

'I got white cotton tights. That's all they had at the commissary. The fabric I found for the costume is heavy, with silver thread running through it so it will shimmer under the lights like sprinkles of stardust.'

'The easiest thing is to buy a basic leotard or bathing suit,' Nattie supplied. 'You can personalise it how you like with straps, sequins and net skirt like Margot favours, and I can show you how to do that. But Dodo's right. You really do reek. Make sure you sit a long way from Tiffy.'

Chapter 28

Mr Tiffert stood in the middle of the circus ring, looking like one of the penguins Lilly had seen at the London Zoo. Rather than the red jacket and riding boots in which he was usually decked out when in the ring, he was wearing a full dress-suit, a starched white shirt and shiny black shoes. He might very well have been dressed for a dinner engagement and Lilly wondered if perhaps he was going out after he had dropped his bombshell, to drown himself in a sea of champagne. He seemed nervous as he looked about him, possibly composing the words of his valedictory in his head.

Some distance removed from the main body of performers, Lilly perched as still as she could on the ring curb, knees squeezed together. She was sufficiently alarmed to shift her position and caught a fishy whiff of herself. The sisters were right; as soon as she was able, she would take the bath they'd advised.

Mr Tiffert blew the whistle a second time; three short, shrill blasts that weren't easy on fraught nerves. Lilly wondered what it must be like to have such presence, such confidence that he could quiet a tent full of people with three puffs of wind.

'I hope you've had a profitable rest day and I'm sorry to pull you away from your evening,' he boomed. 'I know rumours abound so I will cut straight to the chase.

There are two things to tell you that will impact on us all. First, Margot has secured a new sponsor for the week of coronation performances – not here in Lucknow but in Cawnpore.'

Cawnpore? A surge of panic took hold of Lilly's chest.

'We will be providing a private show for the sponsor and his guests on the ninth of August – the actual day of the postponed coronation – and he will attend the circus on every night of that week. There is to be a public holiday on the eighth and eleventh of the month, so we are expecting high demand at the ticket office.'

Margot stood up smoothly from her chair; a queen rising from her throne. 'This is great news for all of us as it will swell the circus coffers and guarantee that we all have a full run in India. There is also another piece of splendid news that Tiffy has asked me to share with you all and the reason why he is looking particularly dapper tonight. As soon as we are finished here, he will sign the great daredevil Diabolissimo to Tiffert's circus.'

Whizzy leaped to his feet. 'That act will overshadow mine.'

'Quite literally,' Dodo butted in, dryly.

Lilly edged along the curb. 'I haven't heard of him.'

Whizzy windmilled his arms. 'He loops the loop on a bicycle dressed up as the devil. He's just about the most famous act on the circus circuit in the entire world right now.' He sounded awestruck.

Lilly turned to face him. 'What makes him so good?'

Whizzy wouldn't look at her. 'He uses a huge construction like part of a barrel but first climbs a ladder up to the top of the circus tent with his bicycle over his shoulder. There he mounts up, careers down a hundred-foot ramp picking up speed and then performs a full upside-down circuit of the side of the barrel, before he exits the loop and lands in a net. He's the only person in the world to try it.'

Mr Tiffert flapped his hand in a calming gesture, a note of apology in his voice. 'That's not entirely true, Whizzy. He's the only one in the world who hasn't killed himself doing it so far, so he has a novelty value until he breaks his neck. You'll still be doing your act long after he's turned to dust.'

Dodo began to tap the ring curb with the metal hook on her mouthpiece. 'What do we know about this saint who's decided to save us? Did anyone ask him *why*?'

Margot seemed to share her concern. 'We've only managed to sign him because of the sponsor's generosity. Diabolissimo will be a huge draw and we must profit from the time we have him with us.' She glanced over at Whizzy, who was kicking the ring curb with the toe of his shoe. 'I'm not happy about it either but I'm trying to act like a grown up, to protect all our jobs,' she added.

'Not mine,' Whizzy shouted. 'I'm not playing second fiddle to an Italian who wears sticky-up devil horns on his cap. I quit.'

Margot stepped out of the dark and slid into the seat across the table; the only light in her tent came from a lone, flickering candle.

Worn out, wanting to lie down and sleep rather than hear what Margot might foretell, Lilly didn't want to say out loud that her treacherous thoughts were better left where they were, firmly locked inside where no one could reach them.

Lilly ran her hands over her skirt. 'I thought you'd be dressed as a gypsy with a shawl on your head and your eyes on a crystal ball.'

Margot drew a breath but did not speak at once. At last she asked, 'Is this really what you want?'

It wasn't exactly because, even though she had determined to give Margot a chance, her feelings towards her were contradictory. 'I should really like to hear what you have to say.'

Margot propped her elbows on the table and rested her chin in her palms. 'I'm not the enemy here, Lilly. Relax and let me help you.'

'I haven't said a word.'

'You don't need to. You're wound up as tight as one of Dodo's spins.'

You wouldn't be surprised if you knew why I'm really here, thought Lilly. 'I'm not certain how you can help me. I don't see how randomly drawn cards can have any relevance to someone's life and what's happening in it but I'm hoping to learn.'

Margot's eyes narrowed as she spoke. 'The cards speak to each other much as letters form words when they are placed in a certain order. I don't read cards singly but as combinations and every card has an equal importance – there are no major or minor cards as in Tarot.'

Margot leaned forward and slid the deck towards her. A tiger's claw mounted on a gold clasp swung out from a gold chain around her neck. With thumping heart, Lilly pushed the thought aside that it might be a gift from Duffy; it was too unbearable, too intimate a reminder that they shared history together.

Margot nudged the pack. 'You must cut the cards.'

Lilly divided the deck in two. 'Do you not use all the cards?'

Margot placed one half on top of the other. 'There are only thirty-six cards in the Lenormand pack – these are all the cards. For me, this is not divination but prediction as to what is likely to happen. There are many ways to deal the cards, but I prefer a cross of seven.' She dealt out the cards face up from left to right: the first, a well-dressed woman carrying a fan, then a picture of a letter sealed with red wax, a house set in a garden, a dog holding a lead in its mouth and at the end of the row, a scythe resting on a sheaf of wheat. Above the middle card, Margot placed a fox slinking through grass and below it a leatherbound book on a table. Lilly saw that there were numbers at the bottom of each card.

'What does it all mean?'

Margot tapped the line of cards, one by one from left to right. 'I would say that you, as the seeker, will receive information or news – that's the letter card – from a woman at her home. It is a safe place. And it will be about someone close to you who you can depend on – the dog tells me that as does the rhyme printed on the card: *He is man's best friend, faithful and true, his soul he'd lend in trust to you.*'

Unexpectedly, Lilly was curious. 'What is the significance of the scythe?'

'Decisions have been made about your future. It is a danger card and can mean rupture, severance or a sudden accident perhaps. The unopened book contains stories that are concealed until the pages are read. Then the truth is revealed. Someone known to you is keeping secrets.'

'What about the fox?'

Margot traced the words on the card and spoke them out loud. '*The fox is sly; a friend is too. Someone you know may try to dupe you. With wily glances the renard snaps, evade deception and avoid old traps.*' That is a further reinforcement of what the book is saying. You are surrounded by lies, trickery, people trying to outsmart you.'

Lilly hadn't envisaged this. 'You're frightening me.'

Margot blinked in the flickering light. 'We can now interpret the cards in a different way by looking at the numbers.'

Lilly looked down at the cards, feeling rather sick. 'You believe all this, don't you?'

'I do, Lilly. Whether you think it's mumbo jumbo or whatever, I have never found the cards to lie. Yours is a strong reading. Your line across adds up to eighty-eight and when we add the eight and eight together, we arrive at number sixteen – the stars. It is the healing and destiny card. The central line adds up to forty-four. Four plus four is eight – the coffin – signifying endings and closure.'

'Could you guess at what it all means?'

Margot stared at the cards, her concentration absolute. 'I don't need to guess. To interpret it for you I would say that to be happy, you have to uncover the secrets that have been withheld from you by someone purporting to be a friend but who is sly and duplicitous like the fox. A friend who is not really a friend – just out for their own ends. The woman, the house and the dog are all positives in your reading. But you have some unravelling to do.'

'The coffin and the stars?'

'You will find peace. A happy ending if you like.'

Lilly breathed in and said, 'More than anything, I want my son back and a life for myself. I want to be able to say out loud the things that I think without the words being planted there by people who think they are more entitled. I need to know what my future holds, so I can plan a life with Teddy.'

In the dim light, Margot looked at her, a mixture of interest and horror on her face. 'I hadn't realised you were so unhappy.'

'I lost the art of speaking up for myself a long time ago.'

'Ask me anything, if you think it might help.'

Although Lilly had anticipated this, she still took a moment to choose her words. 'There is one thing. At the séance you spelled out the word "imposter" with your planchette board. I've been wondering for a long time if there was any chance that it was an after-dinner stunt?'

Margot sat with her chin cupped between her hands. 'It was not. Think about your reading just now. Someone close to you is untrue and has told you lies or concealed the truth. To find out who, Lilly, you must think back to who was sitting around the table that night and work out who might be the fox in your reading.'

And now the moment had come – the reason she was here – to voice her suspicions out loud. 'Do you think it might be Duffy?'

Margot sat very still and when she spoke, her voice was sharp. 'What makes you say that?'

Lilly had felt certain she'd leap to defend him. 'There have been things he's said that make me wonder about him and as you know him really well, I wondered – and I hope you don't mind – if we might talk about him for a bit?'

'What do you want to know?'

Temporarily wordless, she shook her head. 'It's not so much that I want to know anything. It's just things that he says don't always – forgive me for saying but this is really awkward – I don't think he tells me the truth.'

Margot began to collect up the cards. 'Why don't you just voice what's on your mind?'

'Earlier today, he told me something about Noel that I knew wasn't true so I wondered why he would make that up? And there have been other things as well. He has a habit of avoiding questions he doesn't want to answer and when we were all in Nainital, he gave me the distinct impression that it was he who put in a word for me with Mr Tiffert but I understand that it was you I have to thank.'

A little frown appeared between her brows. 'Oh, I see! The letter.'

'I'd always assumed Duffy wrote it.'

She shook her head. 'Not Duffy. He will never have your interests uppermost in his mind.'

'And this afternoon, he told me he'd lied to help you out with the married man in Paris who gave you Ranky and then acknowledged he has a wife in South Africa.'

Margot stared at her with unblinking eyes. 'I think you'll have to explain.'

Lilly picked up the picture of the fox. 'Duffy said in so many words that you're blackmailing him with his secrets because otherwise he cannot work in India with the circus. Because of what you know about him, he must dance attendance on you whenever you snap your fingers and that's why he can't spend as much time with me as he'd like.

'But then I remembered the look on your face at the tiger hunt when you feared for his life. I knew you loved him but then, if you loved him that much, why would you not keep his secrets and be happy to do so?'

Margot gave a deep sigh. 'I've never worked in Paris, Lilly, and neither has Duffy. I did have an admirer though, but that was in Rangoon, where this circus has its permanent home.'

Lilly bent her head and concentrated her attention on the table, breathing in and out, slowly, through her mouth.

Margot touched her arm. 'Is everything all right?'

After a long pause, Lilly looked up and when she spoke her voice was unsteady. 'Rangoon is where my father's first

301

wife came from. They had two daughters, but they didn't survive. Their grandfather was the lighthouse keeper.'

'That would be Walter Barnes. His only daughter Edith Mary did die in Bombay, but the granddaughters are there, in Rangoon. I am certain they are.'

'Is that your professional instinct?'

Margot smiled. 'A little more than that. I've met them, although I can't recall their names. They are very fair, the pair of them. They are not like you even though you do share a parent.'

'Would you have any idea how I might contact them?'

'If you can be patient, I'd write to the retired lighthouse keeper via the Marine Department, which has responsibility for the lighthouse. The letter will find its way to them eventually. Rangoon's not a huge place.'

Lilly fingered her lip, an unpleasant churning in her stomach.

Margot held her head to one side. 'What are you thinking?'

'I'm wondering if Duffy lies to you as well.'

Margot hopped to her feet. 'Shall we have one of Noel's gin rickeys, if I can remember what went in them?'

Lilly watched her move across the tent, arranging glasses and bottles on a side table, shaking her head as she peered at the labels.

Lilly could picture Noel mixing them. 'Gin, squeeze of lime and soda water. They were awfully good.'

Margot was busy with the drinks for a moment then returned to the table with two long glasses. 'Here you are. Can't guarantee they'll be like Noel's but tally ho! Down the hatch!'

Lilly raised her glass. 'Good health! I wasn't expecting to be socialising with you, if I'm honest.'

Margot settled back in her chair. 'I'm not sure that I was very kind to you in Nainital, particularly about your aptitude for the circus. After the tiger hunt, I knew you to be courageous but, with Royce, we all saw you needed protection.'

'Dodo told me I lacked grit. And she's right. She's been giving me some hard lessons in self-schooling.'

'She has always had my respect. How few of us have the courage to say what exactly is on our minds and hang the consequences?' Margot's good humour seemed unshakeable.

'She's earned the right. She's had a tough time.'

'As have you. You should take a leaf out of her book and just say precisely what you think.'

'That's a novel concept.'

Margot ran her finger around the rim of her glass and drew in a breath. 'We've spent very little time on our own to chew the fat, you and I, and I've often wondered which of the two of us has avoided that the most. In Naini we spent hours in each other's company and yet left so much unsaid.'

Lilly wondered at that. She hadn't consciously avoided Margot's company but had seen her as an obstacle to over-come. 'I don't know that I have, specifically.'

'Do you really like the circus, or is Duffy your reason to stay?'

Lilly relaxed her tight hold on the glass and took a sip of her drink, affecting not to have heard. Her feelings towards Duffy were newly complicated; she needed time to process the thoughts in her mind.

'But you are attracted to him,' Margot went on. 'I'd even go so far as to say you are a little in love with him yourself.'

303

Self-conscious as if judged and found guilty, Lilly was more rattled than she could reasonably explain. 'You mustn't repeat that.'

'So that Tiffy doesn't hear?'

'Even though I have run away from my husband, I am still married. I've given Royce the slip for now, but he'll be hunting for me and he won't give up. If he finds me and thinks I'm involved with someone else, there's no telling what he will do.'

Margot nodded briefly, as if she understood her predicament. She got up and walked over to the table and picked up the bottle of gin. 'Have you any reason to suspect he knows where you are?'

'I have no reason to suspect he doesn't. Once or twice, I've felt that something was out of place. A figure in a shadow where it shouldn't have been. That someone was following me, watching. He's out there, Margot, even though I can't see him. In my shoes, what would you do?'

Margot poured another measure of gin into her drink. 'Only you can decide on that but I will tell you what I think.' She leaned in to whisper. 'The real reason you came to the circus is fear. You have to come to terms with it if you are to have any hope of getting Teddy away from his father.'

Lilly watched her from her seat across the table. She had learned so much in the past few weeks she felt that she was a totally different person to the ignorant, weak creature who had boarded the circus train. Difficult words telling her she had yet more to address were not easy to hear.

Laying a cool, pale hand on her arm, Margot nodded towards the cards. 'It's time you went back to Nainital – to the house, the lady and the dog. That is where you will find the truth. Not here with the circus.

'Clear your head of Duffy. Whatever you may think, however attractive he may seem, you must not pin your future on him and I'll help if I possibly can.'

'Why are you being so nice?'

As she sat down, Margot sighed. 'Duffy has immense difficulty distinguishing between reality and fantasy. Take my horse, for example. He may think he's been to Paris and spun you a convincing saga of stories about me and whatnot, but if you challenge him, he will be adamant that he is right, or that he never said the words you accuse him of saying. He will tell you he's from South Africa, but he's not been there either. He has invented a wife and yet he's not married.'

Lilly asked the last question she'd been fearing. 'Whizzy said his name used to be Charles Franks and he worked as a contortionist. When I mentioned it to Duffy, he all but called me a liar.'

Margot adjusted the sleeves of her blouse. 'Reinvention can be a form of avoidance.'

'You could say that of me. I've changed my appearance but I'm no closer to getting away from Royce.'

'But you haven't lost the talent for telling the truth.'

'That's a fairly damning thing to say about someone you love.'

'Is it?' Margot cradled her glass against her chest. 'I've let you believe what you want to believe, that Duffy and I are entangled romantically, and yet nothing could be further from the truth.'

'I know what I have seen.'

'No, Lilly, you don't.' Her gaze was fixed on the far wall of the tent.

'Then tell me.'

Margot turned and seemed to collect herself. 'I wondered when we would get to this conversation and somehow, I thought it would have been sooner. In Nainital, perhaps, when you were both living with Noel.'

Inhaling deeply to control the hammering in her chest, Lilly waited for her to go on.

'Duffy is my brother.' Margot's voice was loud in the tent; it seemed to ricochet off the canvas.

Lilly's thoughts flashed to the day she'd seen Margot place a hand on Duffy's shoulder in the ring and then to her tear-stained face after Duffy had been injured by the tiger. Taking tea together at Noel's house, and the look of admiration on his face when she performed in the ring. 'Oh,' she exhaled, realising these scenes in isolation had painted a completely different picture.

Margot returned her gaze for a long moment and then said, 'You don't believe me.'

She studied Margot's face. 'I'd imagined something else.'

Margot steepled her fingers and stared in the direction of her drink, though she seemed to be looking away into a much more distant place. After a time, Lilly sensed a change in her breathing that seemed to bring her back. 'You have grown close to Duffy and I, too, am fond of you. I'm going to share a confidence so there is no future misunderstanding between us – that no one knows except he. It is one of the many reasons we stay together and it's better that I tell you, for you to understand why we are as we are.'

Lilly picked up the drop in her tone, watched her lips move and couldn't drag her eyes away from her face. 'Go on.'

'If you were to ask my parents, they would tell you that I am Duffy's brother.'

Chapter 29

Lilly stared at Margot, bewildered at first, and then shocked. 'His brother? But you . . .' She realised her jaw had dropped open and supported her chin with her hand. 'You're the imposter,' she murmured.

Margot was adamant. 'I am not. First, I channelled the message at the séance and as such could never be the recipient of it and second, I am true to who I am.'

Lilly felt dazed, a little off balance. 'Could I have another drink, do you think? I'm rather in need of the gin.'

'Finish up the one you have first.' Margot lifted a slender finger in the direction of her glass.

Momentarily flustered, Lilly saw that her glass was still half full and lifted the drink to her lips. Her teeth rattled on the rim, her mind revisiting everything she thought she knew about Margot. 'Is this why you have your own dressing tent and sleeping quarters? Why you didn't stay with us at Lake View? Why you didn't share a tent on the tiger hunt or get up early for the expedition?' She hoped the interest in her voice might mask the fluster from her tone.

'Yes to all of those questions. Somehow, I've always felt as though the gender I was given at birth was not mine. I felt uncomfortable in my skin – that the body I'd been given by God belonged to someone else. That it was a mistake somehow.'

Lilly couldn't imagine what that must have been like. 'Did you always feel that way or did it occur to you gradually?'

'I think right from the moment I became aware of how I felt. I can't put a specific date or age when I knew I was not male.'

'What did your parents say when you told them?'

'What did they not say beyond pack your bags and get out? Duffy left with me and we've looked out for each other ever since.'

I know the pain of that Lilly thought, when my grandparents sent me away. With an ache in her throat, she said, 'How old were you when your parents turned you out?'

'I was fifteen and Duffy twelve.'

Lilly's mind rebelled. How could a parent not accept their child for whatever they were, and love them unconditionally, without judgment? 'Is that why you came to the circus and presumably changed your names?'

Margot nodded. 'That's the beauty of circus. Illusion and skill, of course. Being at the top of one's game is a definite advantage because no one sees beyond the magic of what they want to see.'

Lilly trained her eyes on Margot's face, but there was nothing to see that might mark her as male. 'It must be hard, pretending to be something you're not.'

'I wear a costume of clothes to transform myself into someone else. You could say the same of yourself when you put on the Pahari hill clothes. A woman wearing trousers is not conventional, but you have donned them nonetheless.'

Lilly felt herself backing away from this logic. 'It's not the same.'

Margot sat back in her chair. 'You and I are more alike than you realise. Have we both not suppressed the person we really are to present a more acceptable public face?'

The tent felt suddenly oppressive and Lilly could barely breathe. You are right, she thought. I've not been the real me for eight years.

Margot opened a box on the table by her chair and took out a cigarette, which she lit with a pink-tipped match. 'What did you see in Royce?'

Lilly didn't need to think. 'He reminded me of my grandfather. He was the only man I knew growing up – a brilliant, successful businessman and he was dapper. Well dressed with thick, wavy dark hair and a drooping moustache but he was, above anything else, a kind and devoted family man. He was once asked to stand for Lord Mayor of London, but he turned it down because he would have had to spend too much time away from Granny.'

Margot took a pull on her cigarette. 'And your husband wasn't as attentive?'

Lilly sat very still but her hands were shaking a little. 'When I got married, I imagined I would be like my grandmother, who floated around in glamorous clothes with servants to ease her life and a husband who adored her. Perhaps it was my fault that everything went wrong but I hadn't expected to be so bored or for the days to seem so long and bare. I joined the Cawnpore Ladies Club and made a few friends but almost immediately I was expecting Teddy and Royce insisted I stay at home. At the time I understood his anxiety because in India, pregnancies often go wrong. Teddy was born and Caroline soon after but it was after she died that everything changed for the worse.'

Margot looked at her, her head to one side. 'Do you want to tell me how?'

Lilly was surprised at how easy she was to talk to. It made her want to offer more, a confidence in return for a confidence, so she opened up her heart. 'Without telling me why, he cancelled my membership at the Club and brought his mother to live with us. Rules were imposed about what I might or might not do and Teddy was the prize for good behaviour and the punishment for bad. I told myself that all would be fine if I stuck to his regime but Royce got worse, enforced discipline with his fists and so I cauterised my feelings and gave in.'

Margot appeared to be thinking, a frown fixed between her brows.

Have I now said too much? Lilly wondered. Does she consider me weak?

Margot continued to ponder, staring into the depths of her glass. 'It seems strange that your mother recalled you from England and married you off to a Eurasian.'

'And that my grandmother let her. That's what has troubled me the most in the years I've been here. When I was leaving, she said something on the dock at Tilbury, but however much I search my memory there seems to be no trace of it there.'

'Memory is a strange beast. The echo will come back when you least expect it – just don't force its recall. I do think, though, you have a sticky conversation to have with your mother.'

'I have asked her repeatedly but getting a straight answer out of her is like trying to pin down the wind.'

'Where is she now?'

'I have not the first idea.'

'Did she not go to Bombay?' Margot chased some cigarette ash from her sleeve.

'She wrote a letter from Mussoorie and sent it to Rohilla

Lodge instructing me to send her money, but it wasn't addressed to me. I very much doubt she's still there.'

'The Miss Pinkneys might know more. Binnie won't know you're no longer there unless someone has told her. Your cards say you should go back to Nainital and this is further proof that the answers you seek will be found there. Go to Noel. He will give you strength.'

Lilly leaned forward and took Margot's hand. 'I have misjudged you and I'm sorry. I can't imagine how much you have suffered.'

She stood up and pulled Margot to her feet, putting her arms around her, and held her tight in a simple gesture of human solidarity; it was natural, right, that one woman would reach out to another.

They stood together for a long time, chest to chest, as Lilly let her tears come. She cried for all that had been taken from them both: the people they loved, their basic human right to be the person they wanted to be.

As she cried, she raged. 'I am a coward, Margot. I'm hiding in a circus, too frightened to move.'

Margot disentangled herself from Lilly's arms. 'Sometimes it's not obvious what to do. I understand perfectly that fear can paralyse us to the point we become inert. Don't under-estimate your ability to conquer that fear. You have to quell it. Stamp it into the ground and don't look back. Realise that what you thought could never happen is actually happening. You have left Royce. That's a first courageous step.'

Lilly wiped her tears with her fingers and regained her seat. 'My fear hasn't eased with time and as yet another day passes, I dread that my son will forget who I am. On the one hand, Royce's voice is less often in my head, but I can't get on with my life until I know that I am completely free of him. I wish I had your conviction.'

'Unless you take control of the situation, you'll be looking over your shoulder for years. He will find you eventually so you must gain the upper hand. Do it now. Plot the revolution while you have the support of everyone at the circus.'

'Who would help me? I'm at the very bottom of the pecking order.'

Margot sat down. 'That's where you are wrong. Everyone will help you because that is what we do when the chips are down. No one's trying to win a pat on the back. You have stepped up to replace one of the elephant girls and have been prepared to shovel elephant shit. You have rooted in you, the ability to craft a life for yourself and your son that is just and kind. I'd say you are a trouper of the very first order and everyone – even Reggie in the cook tent – has seen what you are made of. He knows you smuggle rotis out for Belle, but he doesn't know how you do it.'

Lilly looked up and managed a thin smile. 'I'm scared to death that I'll run into Royce when the circus moves to Cawnpore for the coronation shows.'

Margot leaned in closer. 'A far better plan would be to lure him in so he's on unfamiliar ground.'

'Then what?'

'We'll bring the bastard down.'

Lilly was relieved to get back to the wagon. It was her refuge, where she felt safest, sandwiched in her middle bunk between the two German sisters.

But they were not in bed. She found them sitting in canvas chairs, smoking by the step.

Dodo sniffed loudly and pointedly. 'Not with lover boy tonight?'

'I've been drinking gin with Margot in her tent.'

'Since when did you two become friendly?'

'Since Nainital.'

Dodo ground out her cigarette beneath her heel and took another from the packet. She ran her fingers up and down the little tube and straightened out the tobacco. 'That's a lie. Margot doesn't entertain troupers in her tent. She's not generous with her time unless you can benefit her in some way or have enough money to embellish her jewellery collection. Not what I would call a gracious hostess.'

'She's not that shallow. What she does is for the benefit of all of us. Mr Tiffert says the circus is barely solvent and getting the sponsor in Cawnpore is a fantastic coup, entirely down to her.'

'Did you find anything out about the new act?'

Lilly slapped her forehead with the heel of her hand. 'It went clean out of my head.'

'I thought that's why you went. To set Whizzy's mind at rest.'

'I went for a reading.'

Dodo puffed on her cigarette. 'Palm?'

Lilly tucked her hands in her pockets and rolled her shoulders. 'Bible.'

'You're being really uncommunicative. It's like pushing water uphill with your bare hands.'

'Or getting blood from a turnip,' Nattie threw in.

Dodo stared at her sister. 'What sort of rubbish English is that? The expression is blood from a stone. Misusing your idioms makes *you* look like a turnip.'

Even in the dark, Lilly could see that Nattie's face was pink. 'Do you know what, Dodo? Could you for once keep your smart remarks to yourself and if you cannot find anything nice to say, just keep your mouth shut? For what it's worth, squeezing blood from a turnip is valid English – a perfect synonym for your own expression.'

With shining eyes, Dodo clamped her lips together and placed her forefinger in front of her mouth in an effort not to laugh.

Nattie beckoned with her hand and lifted her chin a couple of degrees towards the door behind her back. 'The post man came this afternoon. There's a telegram for you on your bunk. It's too dark to see inside so bring it out and if she can be bothered, Dodo will strike a match and that way you can read it.'

'Why would I share my private business with her?' Lilly found she was enjoying the spat.

Dodo almost choked. 'I'm beginning to like you, elephant lady, but to save you the bother I've already read it. Telegrams tend to be urgent.'

Lilly hardly raised an eyebrow. 'What did it say?'

'Bloody load of nonsense. Hairbrush here stop. Suspect greyhound out of the trap stop. Take extra care. Stop.'

'Do you remember who it came from?' Lilly tugged off her shoes and sat down on the bottom step.

'Someone from Nainital with a silly name.'

She felt her pulse quicken. 'Noel?'

'Christmas? I know the English are generally ridiculous when it comes to names but surely no one would call their child after a religious festival.'

'That's his name.' She looked down at her hands as she spoke, picturing his long, slim fingers on the keyboard of his piano.

'I'm starting to think you are a little fixated with men. Is that why you ran away from your husband – for more sexual freedom?'

Lilly let out an exasperated sigh. 'Noel is a friend, as is his sister, Conti. I stayed with them for a while.'

Dodo tapped her fist against her forehead. 'Ah! That's the stupid name.'

'It's short for Constance.' Lilly felt a flare of disappointment in her chest that the telegram had not come from him.

'Just as well that's not yours. You wouldn't be able to live up to it.'

'You are not even remotely funny.'

Nattie got up and shook out her clothes. 'It's getting late and you two need to give it a rest. Whoever sent the telegram and whatever the message means will have to wait. After the performance tomorrow night, they're tearing down the lot and we're moving off to Cawnpore.'

Chapter 30

Watching the tents come down was almost as exciting as raising the Big Top.

After the last person had been served in the cook tent, it was disassembled and hauled by the elephants to the railway siding and loaded onto the flatcars.

When the animals were inside the Big Top for the performance, the menagerie tent was struck and stacked into neat piles of poles and rolled canvas. Ten minutes later, it was on its way to the train. At the end of each act, rigging and apparatus was stored away and by the time the performance was over there was nothing left but the Big Top itself.

At a quarter to eleven, as the audience was leaving through the main entrance, workmen – each assigned to his particular job – began tearing down the seats and dismantling the central ring. Almost as the last person went out, the canvas dome was bare and ready to be struck.

The last structure to come down was the dressing tent.

Dodo unscrewed the lid from her cold cream and scooped out a fingerful. 'Make sure you have everything packed away. You can only take the performer's trunk to the wagon. There's no room for both.'

Lilly draped the washing kimono over her shoulders and shimmied out of her costume. 'Where will the larger trunk go?'

'Get someone to paint your initials on it – same as your wash bucket. When it is loaded up on the luggage wagon, it'll find its way back to you tomorrow. Don't be surprised if it is full of dents – they just throw the bags in – especially if the tear-down is running late.'

Lilly folded her costume and placed it on a chair. 'There are things in there I don't want out of my sight.'

Dodo wiped the cream from her fingers as she spoke. 'Move them now and I'll watch out for you. Be quick, though, before anyone else comes in.'

Lilly put her hand into the smaller trunk and withdrew a key. She slid it into the nozzle lever lock, opened the lid and removed the tray. 'Do you have any scissors handy?' she called over her shoulder.

Dodo pulled a pair of nail scissors from behind the length of elastic she had tacked to the lid of her trunk. 'Will these do?'

Lilly turned and held out her hand. 'Perfect.' She bent over the lip of the trunk and began to snip at the stitching on the striped lining.

'What are you hiding in there?' Dodo had moved to the doorway and was standing guard.

Lilly worked her hand into the gap in the lining and stretched down to the bottom of the trunk. It didn't occur to her for one second to withhold the truth from her staunch German roommate. 'The sort of thing you would keep in your grouch bag.'

'Worth much?'

'Yes. I was given the jewels in case of *extremis* and I can't afford – quite literally – to lose them.'

Dodo put her head to one side, which often presaged a question. 'Running away money?'

'In a manner of speaking.'

317

'Call it none of my business but why don't you sew them onto your costume? No one will think for a minute that the spangles are real. It's the safest bet if you want to keep them close.' She patted her chest as if to emphasise the point.

Lilly finished pulling the tissue-wrapped jewellery from inside the lining and knotted it in a handkerchief. The *mangalsutar* necklace from Noel she left where it was. *The thread will tie you to us and bring you back to Nainital.* 'That's an excellent idea, but I don't have time to do that now. I'll put it where no man would dare to rummage for treasure – inside the front of my blouse.'

'Not even the tiger tamer?'

Lilly gave a small smile. 'Not even him.'

'Nattie wondered why you wear that tight-fitting bodice in all this heat.'

'It's the safest place. Not comfortable, but practical.'

Dodo left her position by the door and laid a hand on Lilly's arm. 'Tell you what – we'll help you sew everything in place tomorrow. It will be quicker with the three of us.'

Lilly swallowed hard, overcome by this unexpected offer of help. 'That's a lovely thing to say, but I think what would be more helpful just now is if you could help me make a grouch bag like yours.'

Dodo pulled her a little closer, her tone urgent. 'We can certainly do that, but not right now. The last wagon is moving off at one o'clock. If we're not on the train, the circus will leave without us.'

The morning after the tent was struck in Lucknow, the circus set up in Cawnpore.

The coronation day of King Edward VII, postponed

318

from June on account of His Majesty's illness, was now only two days away.

It was stifling in the office part of the wagon where Mr Tiffert lived and slept. He was shifting papers around his desk as if searching for something among the chaos. There were files and ledgers covering every available inch of the scratched, unpolished surface.

Lilly knocked on the door. 'Do you mind if I come in?'

'No,' he said, not looking up. 'Please feel free.'

Saliva drooling from the corner of her mouth, Clara stood guard by Mr Tiffert's chair but seemed grateful to flop to the floor when she saw who it was.

Lilly squatted down and mussed her ears. 'I was wondering if you have a performing licence for me yet?'

'No,' he replied and continued to hunt. 'What's the urgency?'

'I was hoping that I might negotiate an increase in my wages as I've run up quite a tab with the commissary now that I need a costume and tights and so on.'

'If you lack the cash, credit's good until you can pay.' Mr Tiffert opened a drawer in his desk and continued to rummage.

'Is there anything I could do to help? I'm quite good at looking.'

There was panic in his eyes and she felt it too. 'A travelling circus is always in danger of an unexpected problem and our finances are precarious at the best of times. As I've said so often, money determines our future and as it stands at the moment, I'll be paying the performers with IOUs soon instead of their weekly cash. Unless you have unlimited access to a fortune, there's nothing at all you can do to help.'

'I thought the sponsor is paying for this week in

Cawnpore?'

He picked up a ledger and began to flick through the pages. 'I received a communication from a Sir Rivett-Moon saying that we are illegal.'

Lilly nodded. 'He's the District Inspector. I've met him a few times.'

'Well, in his letter your Inspector says our insurance does not cover private performances. The loss of revenue will cripple us and Diabolissimo – our star attraction – will not come. I'm trying to find the certificate in amongst all this paper so I can read the small print.'

'Have you had this problem before?'

'Never. Seems it's a new thing. Specific to the Collectorate in Cawnpore.'

'Could you not cancel the sponsor and just perform to the public? We could all go around the town and nail up posters.'

He looked out of the corner of his eye and gave the smallest shake of his head. 'The other more pressing issue is we have no licences. No one on this show does. I've been meaning to get around to applying but there is never enough time. Ines is supposed to see to the administration, but she's too busy sourcing talent in Europe to do anything practical to help.'

'As I said just now, I'm very happy to lend a hand. You only have to ask.'

'What you could do is think of a new performing name for yourself. I'm going to change the wording on the coronation programme if the show goes ahead.'

'Has someone dropped out?'

A shadow crossed his face and he was silent for a while. 'People have their private reasons for joining the circus and it's not my business to pry, but there were two men sniffing about the lot the other day. Asking questions about you.'

She stared at him, her heart jumping at his words and for a moment she could not speak. 'What did they want?'

'News of you. They had a photograph they were wanting to show around but they didn't get past the gate.'

Her heart was beating faster. 'Who stopped them?'

'Reggie. He told them they were wasting their time and there was no one who looked like you on the lot. We decided between us it was better you didn't know. Think of a new name for the programme. It'll turn you into a different person and throw the hounds off your scent.'

'Take me off the programme entirely,' she said. 'I think that's the safest for everyone. Royce knows a lot of people in Cawnpore and could destroy the circus if he finds out I'm here.'

He put his arm around her shoulders. 'We've weathered far worse storms than an aggrieved husband chasing his fugitive wife. So stop overthinking and leave the worrying to me.'

Chapter 31

The European part of the town of Cawnpore was decked out with bunting and despite what Royce prophesied back in April, the local residents seemed happy enough to dig deep in their pockets and hand over their hard-earned rupees.

Opportunity for entertainment was limited. Musical evenings were generally a result of plonking something out on a piano that was never entirely in tune. Amateur dramatic efforts were staged at the European Theatre or the assembly hall, but there was no society to organise their production. Generally, the idea to 'get up a show' was created at The Ladies Lawn Tennis Club, enthusiasm far greater than the talent to hand, but it was something to be looked forward to and its rarity ensured its success.

For the British in India, there could never be too much entertainment. Even with the official events planned in honour of King Edward's coronation – a military parade and service in Christ Church, a dinner and ball in the assembly rooms and an English fair in Queen's Park – the circus was the talk of the town.

Lilly walked on from the circus ground and skirted the old city, a shapeless agglomeration of ancient mud dwellings packed cheek by jowl in the rural tradition of close living. Separated by narrow lanes, it was overcrowded and filthy and its poor sanitation gave frequent rise to contagion. It was to her own family, here, that the *ayah* had brought her little girl, Caroline, where she had contracted cholera and fallen foul of the dreadful disease.

It was almost impossible not to compare it to the European district, where streets stretched to twenty-four-feet wide and masonry drains distanced its occupants from life-threatening filth.

Even beneath her parasol, the heat from the scorched land was unbearable; the sun glaring off the white dusty road burned her face as she hurried towards the shops in the old town. She had lingered too long with Margot and was anxious to reach her destination before the midday pause, when the heat was at its fiercest.

However, despite the discomfort of that broiling August day, she felt purposeful in a way she had not in a long time. Wearing Dodo's newly fashioned grouch bag concealed around her middle, and a hat from Margot's collection on her head, she was on her way to Sadar Bazaar, where the jewellers were every bit as impressive as those in the side streets of Delhi.

Earlier that morning, when she had finished with Belle, Margot had been the obvious person to ask. 'Mr Tiffert said there were a couple of men asking about me on the circus lot the other day.'

Margot nodded. 'I heard Reggie sent them packing.'

'Royce knows I'm here. I can sense him, watching. Waiting for me to slip up.'

'What can I do to help?'

Lilly paused and glanced over her shoulder. 'I have to go into the Bazaar later on and it's imperative I'm neither followed nor recognised. I'm hoping you can transform me into a different person entirely. Someone not even Royce would know.'

Margot took hold of Lilly's shoulders, twisted her round and pointed to a chair. 'Then we will take every precaution.' She took a step back. 'And start with your hair.' She squared herself in front of the mirror and extracted the pins from Lilly's head. 'Something soft and fluffy I think.'

Margot reached for a wire frame and when she had secured it to Lilly's head, swept the hair up over the edges. 'You have lovely thick hair but I'm going to use a couple of rats to create extra fullness at the sides. Open the drawer in front of you and hand them up to me if you would.'

Lilly slid out the dressing-table drawer and fished out a couple of fabric bags. 'I could never be bothered to collect my own hair from my combs and brushes even before I lost the dressing set. Let alone sew them into a pouch.'

Margot reached down her hand. 'But they turned up?'

'Yes. I had a telegram from Conti to say Noel had found them in the *dâk* bungalow.'

Margot teased her hair into shape. 'He's a good man, that one. One in a million. He always said that eventually someone would let you out of your cage and free you from all the bottled-up resentment you have simmering inside.'

Lilly acknowledged the truth of her words but hung her head, shame-faced. 'At Bhimtal, he gave me a gun to ward off tigers.'

'Did he think you were in danger even then?'

She shook her head. 'I don't know. He left before we had that discussion.'

'Where is it now?'

'My circus trunk in the dressing tent.'

Margot stood back again, her head on one side. 'What sort of hat?'

'Straw. It's too hot for anything more elaborate.'

Margot disagreed. 'I think we must be bolder. Elaborate is better as it will hide more of your face.' She selected a large, wide-brimmed hat decorated with plumes and flowers and pulled a long, jewelled hatpin from a padded cushion to secure the hat to Lilly's hair.

'I remember that hatpin from Nainital. You tested the tip with your fingers when you were at Lake View with Duffy.'

A hint of a smile flickered across her lips. 'I know. Your face was an absolute picture.'

'I was so envious of your poise and elegance and confidence – your easy relationship with Duffy. You had everything I longed for myself.'

For a second Margot let the words hang in the air. 'It breaks my heart to think someone made you think so little of yourself. You are beautiful, graceful and kind, and don't ever let anyone tell you you're not.' She rummaged amongst the clutter on her table. 'Swivel round and I'll put some tut on your face.'

It was on Lilly's lips to protest but instead she laughed, knowing she was not how she used to be; that she was no longer meek. 'Royce would have a fit. He hates me wearing face paint so slap it on. The thicker the better.'

Margot prised the lid off a pot of whitening cream and applied a generous layer with a sponge. 'That's the fighting spirit. Hold still while I dab on some talc to curb the shine and then we'll apply some colour to your cheeks and lips.'

Lilly thought of a garish doll she'd had as a child with a painted porcelain face. 'What do you use to create that vibrant shade?'

'Rose or geranium petals – anything red-coloured really. I'm concentrating the colour in the centre and fading it out towards the edges of your lips. It's a more natural look.'

Margot stood back, her hands on her hips. 'There. No one would recognise you now. Not even your husband.' Margot held out her hand to her. 'You have shed some weight with all the exercise you've been doing with Belle and Whizzy and your clothes are hanging off you. Stand up and I'll pin them and while I do, you can tell me what all this skulduggery is for.'

Lilly briefly closed her eyes then nodded. 'One of the Miss Pinkneys gave me some jewels against the moment I might need cash.' She patted the grouch bag she wore beneath her skirt. 'The purpose for all this "skulduggery" is because I'm on my way to sell them and it's vital I'm not seen.'

Margot tossed her a pair of cotton lisle gloves. 'Wear these. Don't take them off until you get back and then throw them away. Better still, burn them and leave your clothes out in the sun.'

'You have a habit of scaring me.'

Margot fixed her with serious violet eyes. 'In this instance, fear is a good thing and will keep you safe. Those back alleys are brimful of disease and you must keep your wits about you. Think of these gloves as a necessity to keep you healthy rather than a fashionable accessory to set off your outfit.'

Lilly pulled on the gloves, easing the cloth over her wrists and forearms, conscious that her fingers were not steady.

'As soon as you get back, come to my tent and strip off everything you've been wearing and wash yourself with soap. I'll take care of your hair.'

'I'm almost too anxious to go out.'

'Normally, I'd ask Duffy to escort you but he's not been feeling the best. I'll come instead if you need some support?'

Lilly shook her head. 'It would attract more attention if there were two of us. But what I do want you to do when I have come back from my errand is to use the money I give you to settle the circus's debts.'

Chapter 32

The night of the coronation performance was unbearably hot, almost too hot to work.

It was pitch dark as Lilly stood behind the dusty velvet curtains that separated the artist's entrance from the main ring. She breathed in the acrid tang of horse and elephant, the thick smell of sweat that gave the circus its distinctive odour.

She tried not to move in that airless space; everyone was dripping, fanning themselves, trying not to overheat.

The circus band began to play *Entrance of the Gladiators*, the music for the overture that signalled the start of the show.

Lilly felt the familiar lift of hairs at the back of her neck and the lump in her throat, a sort of choking sensation halfway between laughter and tears. The swell of sound was so moving; beautiful music had always made her cry. The overture finished with a crash of cymbals and Mr Tiffert stepped out through the curtains wearing his bright red jacket, black trousers tucked into high shiny boots, the band of silvery white hair freshly slicked. Lilly smoothed down the skirt of her new glittery costume, inordinately proud of the work she'd put in.

Someone in the band began a drum roll before they struck up 'God save the King', and everyone rose to their feet. When the anthem was over, Mr Tiffert cracked his whip and shouted through his megaphone, 'Welcome to the Big Top and the magic of the circus. Three Cheers for the King Emperor, Edward the Seventh, crowned today. Hip hip, hip hip, hip hip.'

While the band was still playing, Lilly watched through a chink in the curtain, and saw the last scramble of latecomers searching for their seats. The audience had turned out in their best: there were ladies in feathered hats wearing formal evening wear; heavy silk saris, bare feet and anklets were adjacent to high heels and silk stockings. Men sat straight in their tall evening hats with cravats and canes, wearing immaculate white gloves and polished black shoes.

The sides of the tent had been rolled up in the hope of catching some air and hundreds of twinkling lights hung from the quarter poles, casting a flickering yellow glow on the sawdust; the laughter and the hum of excitement became a roar in her ears.

The Big Top was packed, not a single seat unoccupied, and the unlucky had been turned away at the gate. Despite the ferocious heat and the sign saying that the show was sold out to a private party, the ticket office had been besieged. Hundreds had spent the afternoon standing in line in the hope that they might gain admission to the tent.

For the umpteenth time, Lilly checked the *Advise*, which listed the running order of the performance. The elephants were on before the intermission, trick cycling came after Duffy, The Golden Bird after Whizzy, who'd decided to stay on after all.

Margot opened the show. Tossing her cloak to one side, she kicked off the jewelled mules that she wore over her suede shoes to keep them out of the dust. Spangles clung to her hourglass figure, her lovely legs encased in tights as she sprang onto Ranky's back, alternately performing pirouettes, backflips and handstands. The sight of her was breath-taking as with utter femininity, she performed to the music that accompanied her act.

Arrestingly beautiful, Margot engaged with her audience, building up their expectations as she cantered round the ring, astride two dappled grey horses, taking them over six hurdles of fire. The crowd were mesmerised.

After her last lap of the ring, the curtain parted and Margot appeared, patting her horse on his sweaty neck.

'They're in a party mood out there,' she laughed, sliding to the floor. 'It's going to be a great night.'

From the other side of the curtain, Mr Tiffert blew on his whistle. 'Ladies and gentlemen, for the first time in its long and successful history, Tiffert's Circus is proud to present Diabolissimo, the dare devil rider from Italy, who will perform the Loop the Loop for your delectation. Keep your eyes trained on the red-horned devil who will scoff at death as he risks his life for your entertainment.'

'Are you ready to ride, Diabolissimo?' he yelled towards the roof.

From the top of the tent, caught in the spotlight, the cyclist waved at the audience and shouted down. 'Si Signor! All ready.'

The drum roll began as, from way up in the roof space, he mounted his bicycle. The audience gasped as he set off, pedalling furiously down a long runway that turned upward at its lowest point. Lilly wanted to turn her head away as the rider and his machine shot down the ramp but like the audience, the grisly possibility that he might not succeed kept her eyes trained on the man.

As he struck the loop, the momentum turned both rider and his bicycle upside down before he hit the ground and catapulted over the handlebars and into the net that caught him.

Scrambling to his feet, he bounced his way to the side. Performing a neat forward roll over the edge of the webbing he landed, feet together, on the sawdust.

There was an audible collective sigh of relief before the audience sprang to its feet, cheering and clapping, some stamping their feet on the wooden planking, others throwing their hats in the air. Some had even brought in tin trumpets, waved miniature Empire flags and banged on celebratory drums.

Diabolissimo raised his hands to the roof then bowed low to his screaming fans, scraping the sawdust with his hand. It was the most thrilling noise imaginable, and he milked it for all he was worth.

The music changed and Mr Tiffert announced the next act. Privately, Lilly thought the performing cockatoos bizarre but to give her credit, Mavis – their trainer – had coaxed a splendid performance from her tiny, feathered troupe as she brought them by name to the ring.

It seemed improbable that a parrot could chime a certain number of bells from a prompt in the audience or that it could tell the time from a watch. Another played 'Home Sweet Home' on bells and chimes and the cockatoo, which had been learning to drink from a glass, had finally mastered its trick.

The show was going well.

Mr Tiffert held up his hand to silence the crowd.

Eventually all was quiet.

Through the gap in the curtain, Lilly watched as the spotlight streaked the audience, picking out a sea of happy, excited faces, red and shiny with the heat.

And then the spotlight came to rest.

Lilly froze, and felt the blood leech from her face.

She turned sideways. 'Royce is in the audience. As soon as he sees the elephant act, he'll know for certain he's found me.'

331

Dodo spread her arms wide in a gesture of incomprehension. 'Do you think? Your name is not on the programme and you look fabulous. Circus is magic. An illusion. There is no way he will put you here.'

Lilly's chest had tightened so much she could barely breathe. She knew instinctively that Dodo was wrong, that it was no accident he was here at the circus. He'd tracked her down and would have his eyes on her from the moment she stepped into the ring. 'My heart's banging faster than the man on the drum.'

'Which one is he?'

Lilly pointed at the sponsor's box. 'The black-haired one in the centre. He's sitting with the Assistant Collector; the Manager of the Alliance Bank of Simla is on his left and Allahabad Bank on his right. The fifth man is from the Bank of Bengal.'

'Did Margot tell you Royce was the sponsor?'

'There's no reason she would know it was him. When Royce came to Nainital, she never met him.'

'She told me the sponsor was a native. Some vast Hindustani who said his line was in hog bristle brushes.'

Lilly shook her head. 'That's Paramjit, his business partner. Royce is far too clever to show his hand so overtly.'

'Where's Royce from exactly? He's very smart and looks Spanish, or Italian maybe.'

She watched him take off his spectacles and wipe them with a starched white handkerchief and found herself on the brink of a confidence. 'He's half-Indian and that's his frustration. He thinks of himself as thoroughbred British but is despised amongst those he most wants to join.'

Dodo conceded a nod. 'I see it's no coincidence he's here.'

The music for the elephant act was playing.

Ancient fears awakening, Lilly had difficulty breathing. 'He's come for me and I can't go on.' She swayed and clutched at the curtain.

Dodo wrapped an arm around her shoulders. 'Yes, you can. Do what you do. You're brilliant. Get out there and dazzle. You have the advantage because you know where he is. Work the crowd as normal but don't look in his direction.'

The band began to play 'Under the Bamboo Tree'.

Dodo gave her a little shove. 'That's your cue. Off you go and be the best elephant girl you can possibly be. Don't think about Royce or let him spoil your moment.'

Lilly squeezed her eyes shut, swallowed and drew in a breath. Then she threw back her shoulders and skipped into the ring, her step light and bouncy as Margot had shown her. *Show them the spring in your joints and the strength in your arms. Remember to smile and compliment the audience. You are doing this for them so draw them in. Capture them, Lilly, and show them you are performing for them.*

As Margot had done, she dropped her cloak to one side, and focused on Belle, her jewelled anklets and her sparkling headpiece. Lilly pirouetted on her soft satin slippers and extended her hands to her elephant inviting the audience to love her.

Mr Tiffert stood outside the ring curb, his silver-tipped cane in his hand, and turned to the entrance where the elephants were filing into the tent.

He raised the whistle to his lips and clapped a hand to his chest and brought five huge beasts to a halt. On cue, they turned to the crowd and posed, one foot on the ring curb, trunk curled high in the air in salute.

Applause rang out in the stands.

It was hardly necessary, but when he cued again, they

dropped the raised foot and turned in a half-circle before taking three steps across the sawdust.

Lilly danced towards Belle, who raised up her head and watched her approach.

Fanning her ears, her mouth dropped open and Lilly could almost have sworn that she smiled.

Belle extended her right leg for Lilly to mount. She reached up for the collar but her hands were slippery from the heat and she failed to take a firm hold. Belle seemed to sense her difficulty and dropped her trunk, cradling Lilly in its curve, and lifted her gently aloft.

Sliding into position between Belle's ears, Lilly straddled her head and planted a kiss on her grey, wrinkled neck. 'Thank you, my darling,' she whispered. 'I couldn't have managed without you.' Then with one hand in the air, the other on her hip, she arched her back and pointed her toes to the ground.

Belle gurgled in her throat. It was the noise she made when she was happy.

For the full ten minutes of the act, Lilly felt the band was playing just for them and a lump rose in her throat. Nothing mattered but the joy of performing with her beautiful, magnificent Belle. It was impossible to think about Royce. As she rode round and round, alive, exhilarated, and proud of what she'd become, she felt nothing could hurt her again.

When the act was over and they came out of the ring, Lilly raised her hands to the roof. Stretching up her fingers, hearing the swell of applause, at last it felt right to be loved.

The show went on.

Duffy's wild animal act was scheduled after the ten-minute intermission to allow time to wheel the tiger cage into place, without interrupting the flow of the show. The performance cage was made of two parts: a larger section for the tigers and a smaller one to allow the trainer to pass through an outside door, lock it behind him and enter the inner door to the animals. As usual, his watchers – two men, each armed with a sharp spear attached to a long pole – were on hand. They would step in to help if they saw that Duffy was in danger. They watched for atypical behaviour, any unrehearsed movement that could possibly lead to trouble.

Behind the curtain, Lilly continued to watch the show. The cycle act was billed after the tigers and even though she was wilting from the heat, she was ready, her cloak draped about her shoulders.

Duffy entered the wooden floored cage and clicked the gate shut behind him.

Mr Tiffert blew his whistle and snatched up the megaphone. 'Ladies and gentlemen, put your hands together for this most splendiferous of acts. Tonight, before your very eyes, our extraordinary tamer of tigers will put Mister Stripes, the largest Bengal Tiger in captivity, through his paces after which he'll introduce his new jungle friend, Bagh.

'The trainer will show you his skill, courage and mastery over these beasts of the wild and you will marvel at his ability to work with this pair of savage beasts.'

By the time Mr Tiffert had finished his accolades, the audience were delirious with enthusiasm.

On the ringmaster's cue, the band began to play 'Saint-Saens Dance Macabre', a dark mournful air that seemed to suggest something sinister was expected to happen and the audience appeared to love it.

Duffy's act began as usual with Mister Stripes performing his sit-ups, rollovers and hoop-jumping. He then stood on his hind legs and received a reward of fresh meat that Duffy held aloft speared at the end of a stick.

'Seat, Stripes,' Duffy yelled at him to sit on his metal pedestal.

On a second pedestal, at the opposite side of the cage, sat Bagh.

Again Mr Tiffert blew on the whistle. 'And now, for the first time in this circus ring, in honour of King Edward's coronation, our trainer will put Bagh through his paces. The only Indian tiger caught in the jungle and taught to perform in less than one month.'

Duffy was a charismatic performer who walked with style and elegance in the ring. Like a ballet dancer, his footwork was precise, as though it had been choreographed by a professional. *Got to keep on your toes with the cats. They spring, you jump out of the way.* That night, though, he seemed less assured and once or twice stumbled, steadying himself on the bars of the cage.

Bagh had been taught to jump over a gate that Duffy set alight before the jump. *It's an easy trick because tigers are frightened of fire. Bagh knows if he doesn't make the jump, he'll be punished. It may seem cruel but the height a tiger can leap is huge. He's never going to be in danger and the audience will love it.*

Somehow, though, Duffy had forgotten to set light to the gate.

Bagh jumped from his prop and paced up and down, snarling and lunging at the air with an enormous heavy paw. Stripes sat on his prop, watching, and Lilly knew he would stay there until he was told he could come down.

Folk moved to the edge of their chairs.

'Seat, Bagh.' Duffy commanded the tiger to his pedestal.

Lilly staggered backwards and held a hand to her chest, relieved that the tiger had done as it was asked.

Even though she knew Duffy was in control, there was always the possibility that something might go wrong; watching his act was turning into an almost tangible anticipation that he would soon be torn to pieces. Lilly wiped the sweat from her hands on the skirt of her costume and exhaled a pent-up breath.

The watchers took a tighter hold on their poles and moved a step closer.

Mr Tiffert had taken up a stout wooden fork that Duffy used for cuing the tiger and the band were poised to strike up a different tune. Lilly knew that the act was so far in trouble that it was on the point of being halted.

'Jump, Stripes,' Duffy bellowed.

It was not Stripes who jumped though, but the yellow cat with its long, pointed teeth and murder in its eyes.

It roared and flew straight at Duffy, its paws stretched wide. Crashing into his chest, it knocked him flat. *Never turn your back on a tiger, Lilly. A tiger stalks his prey in the wild and attacks from the rear. He'll have to be really upset or hate you like the devil to attack from the front.*

The audience also roared, thinking it part of the act.

Lilly could not recognise herself as a passive, accepting spectator. Animals should be outside in the wild, invisible in the grass. They should not be under a spotlight suffering inside a cage, maddened to fury by the man who controlled them.

But tonight Duffy couldn't. His act had turned sour.

The tiger had hold of Duffy's head between its claws but before it had a chance to get to work, Stripes leaped from his perch in a flash of orange fur and knocked him to one side.

For those who had the nerve to look, the scene was terrible as the tigers ripped each other apart to the tune of a brisk German march.

Clutching his ribs, eyes trained on the tigers, Duffy edged backwards towards the door as if he was quitting a royal presence.

'Fetch the gun,' Duffy roared, feeling behind him for the bolt.

Lilly saw the confusion on his face as it did not slide back. In the pit of her stomach, she worried that this was no minor mishap, no haphazard malfunction of a temperamental lock.

Chapter 33

Lilly ran to the dressing tent and pulled the split tray from her small trunk. Noel's gun was safely stowed in the pocket of her cloak, when a voice stopped her in her tracks.

'Hello, Plumpty.'

She reeled, feeling she was falling from a high, vertiginous place with no one to pull her back. She whirled on her heel to face him.

Royce was sitting in a metal-framed fold-up chair in the corner of the tent.

A long silence elapsed before he said, crossing one leg over the other, 'Do tell me why you chose the circus of all places to hide.'

Lilly lifted her chin, couching fear with flippancy. 'I felt like a change of scene.'

'Is this the tiger fighting back?' He cracked his knuckles one by one beginning with his thumb and produced the bleakest of smiles.

'What do you want, Royce?'

'I want my wife.' His voice was toneless but precise, as if he was addressing a child in small words, that it might perfectly understand.

'How did you find me?' she said. 'Have you had some paid lackey follow me from the moment I left Cawnpore?'

'Easy does it,' he said, holding up a hand. 'I don't think

you're in any position to be firing off questions at me. Get your things together. We're going home.'

The sound of a gunshot came from the main tent followed by a second. 'I can't talk now. I have to go.' She heard the sob in her voice as she turned towards the main tent.

He leaped to his feet and shot out a gloved hand, yanking her back. 'I don't recall saying you could,' he whispered in her ear and slapped her hard on the cheek.

She was knocked sideways by the force of the blow, too stunned for an instant to speak.

'Do as you are told, yes? Pack up your things.' He pushed her towards the trunk and shoved her hand inside the lid. 'There we are. That's better. Pack what you need, the motor is outside by the entrance.'

'You should not be in here, sir.' Dodo stood in the doorway and from the look on her face, Lilly knew she'd seen it all. 'This is the female dressing tent and male visitors are not permitted.'

Lilly pulled her arm from his grasp and nursed the tender place where he'd hit her. 'It's all right, Dodo. This is my husband.'

Dodo's eyes never left Lilly's face. They were cold, the grey steel showing. 'I don't care if he's the new King of England. We're all queuing up out here.' She shut the lid of Lilly's trunk and placed her zinc bucket on top, turning it round so the lettering G R I T was facing towards her. 'Belle wants to know if she can come in and change her clothes. She says it's too hot in her heavy headdress and wants to take her bath. Both the tigers are dead and Tiffy's cancelled the show. Everyone's started to leave.' She jerked her chin in Royce's direction. 'The man's got to go so we can change and call it a night.'

Lilly fingered the letters on the pail. She traced them slowly, one by one, so that Dodo would know she understood. She thrust her hands in her pockets to disguise the bulk of the gun and took a step towards the tent flap. 'Let's go outside, Royce. It's not fair to keep everyone waiting. There's nothing in my trunk I want to keep.'

Royce gripped her arm and half pulled her towards him. 'That's my girl. First thing I'm going to do when I get you back home is to scrub you from head to foot. I've told you only tarts wear make-up, but I hear that's what you've become.' He screwed his hand to a fist and punched her in the stomach. 'You're a tart like your mother, but at least she had the wit to offload her bastard onto the numbskull that married her.'

Wincing with pain, Lilly could barely push out the words. 'That's a despicable thing to say.'

'Your mother will drop her drawers for anyone and right now that old bugger Brownlee's paying handsomely for her services. Your mother was still doing it for money with the locals when she got married until your father saw her for the trollop she was. The shame was so great for a man in his position, he put a gun in his mouth and swallowed a bullet. Tarts, the pair of you.' He spat out the words, raining spittle on her face. 'And now we're going home to talk about your behaviour.'

The message was conveyed. She'd understood the words loud and clear. Goodness knew it was the same old song.

But she no longer felt like singing.

Was he telling the truth, though? She was almost sure he wasn't, but not quite. She stared at the four letters on her bucket. G R I T. It's time you showed some, thought Lilly.

'I don't believe you.'

'More fool you, then.' He propelled her towards the exit and laughed. 'Your mother's been the ace up my sleeve all these years. Like I said, she'll do anything for money.'

'You bribed Binnie to spy on me.' She didn't need to phrase her words as a question. 'But at some point, she said no and that's what you cannot stand.'

He spun her round, his fingernails digging into her shoulder, and was going to hit her again. She sensed it, but couldn't tell what changed his mind. Has he seen something in my face? she wondered, which wasn't there before?

He swung her back and jabbing her between the shoulder blades with his fist, bundled her towards the Big Top where Mr Tiffert was shutting down for the night.

As if nothing out of the ordinary had happened, he'd removed his jacket and the stock from the neck of his shirt and was raking the sawdust, humming under his breath.

Lilly cleared her throat. 'Did you see what happened with Duffy? He couldn't get out of the cage.'

She stared at him, willing him to register the desperation in her eyes.

Mr Tiffert leaned his back against the centre pole of the tent. 'He's had a touch of fever for a few days – that's why his timing was off – and a few broken ribs, I dare say from the blow from the tiger. The cage bolt's been a bit sticky of late, but he's gone off to have his scratches seen to.'

Lilly could feel the press of Royce's hand at her back and knew she must stall. If he forced her outside of the tent, she was as good as dead. 'What happened to the tigers? I heard a couple of shots.'

'We had to destroy them, but I hope the new King appreciates the drama we laid on for his coronation.'

Suddenly she thought of Noel, that he'd let nature take care of the tiger she shot. 'Will you take the remains into the bush?'

342

'Is there bush in Cawnpore?' He quirked an eyebrow at Royce.

Lilly gave the minutest shake of her head, hoping again that he had seen her alarm.

'Goodness me, I mustn't forget my manners. I don't know whether you've met my husband?'

Royce peeled off his white evening gloves folding the cuff of one around the other and held out his hand. 'I hear there was a last-minute reprieve with the insurance and permits. No one in Cawnpore thought the circus would go ahead. Congratulations though. You must have friends in high places, mustn't he, Plumpty?'

A master of deadpan, Mr Tiffert's face was expressionless. He considered Royce's outstretched hand but did not take it. 'There was never any question that the circus would be aborted, Mr Myerson, if that's what you mean? I accepted your sponsorship money in good faith and Margot is right now entertaining your guests in her tent.'

'Why don't you pop along and join them, old fellow,' Royce drawled. 'I'm taking Plumpty home.'

'Her name's Lilly,' Mr Tiffert said quietly.

'Sorry, old chap. Didn't quite hear you. Were you telling me how to address my own wife?'

'Oh Royce, let's not go straight back. John Robinson is throwing an after-show party and I promised to look in.' Lilly was certain Mr Tiffert would now pick up the emergency. Dodo had told her John Robinson was a signal to cut short or abort an act. It was rarely used so its urgency was never diluted. It had to be enough.

Mr Tiffert rolled his eyes to heaven. 'I'm sorry, Lilly, but you won't be able to get over to John's just yet. Belle's in front of the exit standing guard and no one can get her to budge. She won't let anyone else put her to bed

343

so you're going to have to move her yourself before you put on your glad rags.'

'She'll be frightened after the tigers because she had a bad experience when she was young,' Lilly invented. 'I'm not sure how long it will take me to calm her down and I think you might have to help me.'

Mr Tiffert picked up her cue and nodded. 'They're natural enemies, tigers and elephants, coming from the same habitat. What if' – he turned to Royce – 'you joined the rest of your party in the hospitality tent and Lilly can scoop you up when we're done?'

'I don't think that's such a peachy idea, old chap. Why don't you hop out of the way and get someone else to sort out the troublesome beast?'

Lilly saw Mr Tiffert take a deep breath as he put his whistle to his lips. 'Your wife is under contract to this circus, Mr Myerson. Breaking it mid-season will incur the severest of penalties.'

As he gave his summoning blast and brought Belle inside the ring, lifting clouds of dust with her slow, steady tread, Lilly wondered if he knew just how close to the truth his words had been.

When she saw Lilly, her ears flapping wildly, her trunk swinging from side to side, Belle threw back her head and trumpeted so loud the air seemed to shiver.

Royce cursed and took two steps to the side, clenching his fists as Belle emptied her bladder on the sawdust, splashing pints of urine on his polished leather shoes. In that brief space, while he registered his disgust, Lilly took advantage of the pause and gently stroked her trunk. 'Utha, Belle.'

The elephant squeezed her eyes shut and lifted her left leg. Lilly hopped up and grabbed hold of her harness, landing on her back, light as a feather.

Royce walked towards her in that way she loathed, elbows out, leaning slightly forward. It was then she saw the bulge of the gun inside his jacket.

With that look on his face – the disgusted, horribly disappointed one that generally ended with a punch to her stomach – he pulled the revolver from his coat and curled his finger around the trigger. 'Get off the elephant.'

Lilly held onto Belle's headdress, her fingers slippery from fear and hoped that she would not fall. 'Give me a divorce and my little boy.'

Her show of spirit did nothing to impress him. The hand holding the gun went up to still her. 'There is no way on God's earth that I will give you charge of my son. You may drag yourself into the sewer with the tiger trainer but you're not taking Teddy with you.'

'Are you going to shoot me, Royce? In front of a witness?'

In the tone he used for directing the servants, he shouted, 'Don't whine in that adolescent way of yours and you can't count on your precious witness to save you. He's had the good sense to go. No man's going to interfere with a husband disciplining his wife.'

Whether Mr Tiffert had gone or not, she didn't dare to check. 'You are making a mistake not taking me seriously,' she called down from Belle's neck.

He laughed, mocking, as if she had amused him. 'Well, that's the whole point about you, isn't it? There's absolutely nothing about you to take seriously. You're as thick as shit. Now get down off that elephant, before I lose my temper and put a bullet in your brain. I'm your husband and it's your duty to obey me.'

'Give me a divorce, Royce.'

'Not in your lifetime, old thing.' He raised the gun and aimed the barrel between her eyes.

'Baitho, Belle,' Lilly commanded, her voice sharp with need.

The elephant did as Lilly instructed; she went down on her knees as the gun went off. Lilly felt the burn as the bullet grazed her arm.

He stared, silent for a long moment and Lilly knew he was assessing how quickly he could try another shot.

She felt for Noel's pistol in the pocket in her cloak. She drew it out, the curved grip unfamiliar in her palm but the metallic click when she cocked the hammer was reassuring; this was something she had practised year in, year out in England.

She squinted her right eye and fixed his head down the barrel of the gun. 'Drop the gun, Royce.'

He had begun to move, raising his arm, taking aim. She knew that now was not the moment for hesitation.

She aimed the revolver at his forehead, between the right eye and ear; she exhaled slowly and pulled the trigger.

'Why did you make me do that?' she said, her voice a soft moan.

The sound of the gunshots brought people running.

Surprisingly it was Nattie who took charge. 'Get down off Belle, Lilly. We heard Royce say he brought his horse-less carriage. Where would he have parked it?'

Lilly was too panic-stricken to think straight. 'I don't know. There are only about three people in Cawnpore who have motorised carriages. Royce has a black and red Oldsmobile – a Curved Dash.'

'He said he'd left it by the entrance.' Dodo dropped a towel over the dead man's face.

Lilly slid to the ground and stared at the body, her last reserves of courage draining away. The power he had exerted over her all these years – the invisible gun he'd held to her head that controlled her life, the terror that she would lose Teddy – was over.

And yet she felt no triumph. No relief. She felt emotionally adrift, stripped of everything, numb. 'I've just shot a man. I've robbed my son of his father. How am I ever going to live with that? I have to turn myself in.'

Nattie put a hand to her lips. 'No one is calling the police, just yet.' There was reassurance in her words. 'Tiffy will do that later.'

Lilly swivelled her head, trying to take in the entire tent and fixed on Mr Tiffert. 'Where did you go to? I thought you were here the whole time. That's what gave me the courage to shoot.'

'It was self-defence, Lilly. I was behind the quarter pole all along and had just got him in my sights, but you saved me the job.'

'What will you do with him?' Sweat was running down Lilly's back.

Mr Tiffert stood for a while, then touched the body with the toe of his riding boot as if to check he really was dead. 'We'll take care of him. I don't think you need to know the exact details. That way you won't implicate yourself if anyone asks.'

'What's done is done but if it's any consolation, I do know how you feel.' Nattie turned away, pulling Lilly along behind her. 'Now we have to get you to the dressing room and out of your costume.'

'You can't possibly know how I feel.'

Nattie stopped and turned back. 'But I can, Lilly. I killed a man too because he was abusing my sister.' She spoke in the softest of voices.

Lilly was stunned. 'Are you just saying that?'

Despite the heat, Nattie shivered. 'Alfredo Costa molested her right from the very first night when we left in his wagon and almost daily after that. She would sob, beg him not to, but he would pin her up against the side of the wagon and latch the door from the inside. She was eleven years old. Now, come. We must get you out of those clothes.'

Lilly followed her back to the dressing tent. 'At least Royce didn't do that to me.'

'Didn't he? I don't see any difference between a physical and verbal assault; they are both violent and unacceptable. If he made you feel scared, lonely, unworthy of love and worthless, he may as well have pulled up your dress and thrust himself upon you.'

'And once you are in hell, there is no escape.'

'Unless you find a way.'

Lilly sat down on her chair. 'Go on.'

Nattie coughed and looked down. 'One day Dodo got up from dinner and Alfredo grabbed her from behind. He took hold of her dress, threw her across the back of a chair and began to push down his trousers. We both knew what was happening. When you are a twin – I don't know how to explain it properly – you feel the same sensations. Without her saying the words out loud, I knew she wanted him dead. I picked up the frying pan and smashed it against his skull and that was enough. We saw the blood trickle out of his ear, and I think he was dead even before he hit the ground, but I hit him twice more. Just to be sure.'

Lilly's tongue felt glued to the roof of her mouth. 'What did you do with him?'

'We dug a trench in the woods and put him in it, then hitched up the wagon and drove to the next town.'

'How do you bear the guilt?'

'We share that secret. There's no more certain way to bind us together. I'd do it again if I had to, without a moment's regret. That's why Dodo has been so hard on you for not standing up more to Royce. She didn't either because, exactly like you, she *couldn't*. She's borne the culpability of it for years, feeling that if she had done more to fight her corner, I'd never have had to whack him with a pan. She didn't want that for you.'

Duffy and Margot share a terrible secret too, Lilly thought. 'You are lucky to have each other.'

Nattie ploughed on. 'I can't imagine having to bear the sole weight of something I needed to keep hidden. I think I'd have buckled from the enormity of it, constantly looking over my shoulder and being terrified of discovery.'

Lilly nodded at that. 'People do go to great lengths to conceal the truth. Royce hated the fact that his father had taken up with an Indian woman. He felt the stain of the association in more ways than merely the hue of his skin and did everything he could to proclaim his "whiteness".'

Dodo returned to the dressing tent, her sense of urgency almost palpable. 'Come on, Lilly. You have to hurry up. Get changed and put on your froth and feathers. In five minutes, you have to join Margot and the bank managers in her tent.'

'They'll ask where I've been,' Lilly said, turning in her chair.

Dodo stood behind her and began to tease out her hair. 'Say you sat somewhere else so that Royce could have the box for business. Tell them about the performance. Then they'll know you were where you said you were.'

Nattie knelt down by Lilly's chair. 'Margot will have heard the shots. Dodo told her Royce was here in the sponsor's box and something like this will not shock her. She will have put two and two together and be telling them some sort of story.' She pulled Lilly's slippers from her feet.

'They'll know I've been away in the hills for the hot weather, like their own wives. They won't expect me to be here.'

Dodo laid a soothing hand on her arm. 'It's unlikely they'll have given you a thought. You told me Royce was always trying to invade their circle so I doubt, from what you've said, that they would have invited him to anything – and certainly not without you. He has Indian blood in his veins and the British won't ever forgive him that.'

Nattie pushed Dodo out of the way and began to dress Lilly's hair. 'Say you came back early as a surprise. Especially for the coronation performance, to support Royce. You haven't even had time to go home yet. Make it up, Lilly.'

Lilly dipped a cloth in her water bucket and scrubbed at her face. 'I have no idea what to say. My mind's a complete blank.'

Dodo pulled her evening dress from the bottom of her cabin trunk and held it up. 'It's too big for you now. We'll pad you out – there's no time to pin you. We've got to be quick to be plausible. Tell them Royce told you to meet him at the tent. You got lost and couldn't find it. Pretend you are confused that he's not there.'

Lilly didn't bother with the kimono as she pulled off her costume. 'He grazed me with a bullet. Can you find the disinfectant?'

Dodo hunted in her trunk and soaked a cotton pad. 'It looks like a carpet burn,' she said and dabbed at the wound. 'It hasn't broken the skin, thankfully.'

Lilly winced at the sting of the liquid. 'That's enough. I need to know what you have done with Royce.'

Dodo dropped the saturated pad by the trunk and draped the discarded clothes over a chair. 'He's in his motor, behind the wheel and ready to drive off. That way you can say there must have been a misunderstanding about where you were to meet. For you, though, it's show time. You'll need to give your most dazzling, convincing performance ever.'

'And then what?'

'We'll send you home to your son.'

Chapter 34

That night, the monsoon came.

Lilly sat in Teddy's room watching the rise and fall of his chest behind the mosquito net as rain rattled in a solid deluge on the iron roof. Fighting the urge to climb into bed with him and smother his face with kisses, she stared blankly at the shadows behind his head and tried to come to terms with what had happened.

The District Superintendent had been summoned to the circus ground but almost as soon as he arrived, she was on her way home, armed with a story that the others would tell.

Her mind was too full to sleep. She dozed off and on, crying from time to time, reliving the moment when she'd shot him. She reasoned that he'd given her no choice but in the hour before dawn, she didn't feel elated or free. She'd committed a murder and would be held to account.

Sitting down to a breakfast she didn't want, Lilly was buttering a rubbery triangle of toast when the summons came. She frowned at the letter by her plate signed, but undoubtedly not penned, by the District Superintendent himself.

Mrs Myerson was to be informed that an Anglo Indian (half native for clarification purposes) – and presumed to be her husband – had been found dead in his horseless carriage (known to be in his ownership), which was parked by the circus ground. He had suffered a suspicious injury to his head, which was the result of a bullet fired at close range by a person unknown and would she, as soon as was convenient, pop in for a bit of a chat.

She read the note several times. At first, she was glad of its unthreatening tone before her anger set in; the offhand message was almost flippant, and intentionally out of tune with the seriousness of the incident. She stuffed the flimsy sheet in its envelope.

Would the District Superintendent have been so casual, she wondered, had the victim been one of British India's very own?

The Collectorate was an imposing building in the centre of the European quarter. Lilly knew it well enough; it was built with a nod to both the English and the Indian, half British merchant bank, half Nawab palace, and like all Indian architecture, was plastered and daubed with white paint.

Legs stiff with dread, she shook out her umbrella and announced herself to the Indian clerk behind a desk at the entrance. He was attired as an Englishman, much as Royce would have dressed, and spoke perfect, but heavily accented, English. He directed her up a flight of stairs then a short distance down a corridor on one side of which, a row of office doors stood open to catch any breeze from the veranda. Along the tiles, cloths were strewn like stepping stones to ford the water that covered the floor.

Slitting envelopes and drinking his tea, the District Superintendent sat behind a wooden desk, a high, winged collar chafing the soft skin on his neck. Lilly could see the darkened edge where sweat had started to gather. Sir Penderel Rivett-Moon pushed his chair back and rose as

Lilly went in. As far as everyone was concerned, he was judge and jury, gaoler and chief executioner. It was vital she remembered the detail.

He clasped her hand, deliberately prolonging the pressure, and indicated a chair, inviting her to sit. 'May I comfort you in your loss?' He spoke the words, but there was no regret in his tone.

Lilly almost shrank from his touch but sniffed loudly and twisted the handkerchief she clutched in her fist. They had never been included in his official events when Royce was alive, and the pretence of concern for her now made her sick. 'It's hard to take in what happened. Royce was supposed to drive me home from the circus but when he disappeared, I took a rickshaw back to the house.'

His smile was friendly, but he kept his eyes fixed on a point somewhere above her head. 'Do you need help with the funeral arrangements?'

Lilly didn't know what it was about the District Superintendent that made her dislike him so much. She shook her head slowly. 'My mother-in-law will want to cremate him with full Hindu rites, but the servants told me this morning she's in Delhi with her daughter. Royce has a lychee farm there and his mother's side of the family live on the property.'

'Flowers, ghee and rice in the mouth. That sort of thing?'

'And coins in his fists. I'm sure she'll insist on a bed of reeds which my son will have to torch as he is now head of the family.'

'Isn't he rather young for that?'

'Only a male member of a Hindu family can perform the last rites, whether he's five years old or fifty.'

He wrinkled his nose in distaste. 'Whatever you decide, you must do it within the next day or so. I am happy to organise the affair, but I must know where to deliver the remains. Would you not prefer a—'

'What? Christian burial? I think that would be the ultimate in hypocrisy, don't you, Sir Rivett-Moon? Given that he was not accepted as white during the whole time he lived in Cawnpore? Would you have me lay him to rest in the European section of Christ Church's cemetery, next to his father Colonel Henry Myerson whose impeccable military background earned him a chestful of medals?'

She watched colour suffuse his cheeks.

'The best course of action will be to cremate the remains and, thereafter, I'm sure you will organise the most appropriate send-off for him, Mrs Myerson,' he blustered. 'In the meantime, I have some delicate questions to put to you in respect of his demise.'

Don't let your guard down. 'I'm not sure what more I can tell you. Your note told me he had been shot and found dead in his car. It was a very terse message.'

He looked at her properly then, taking in the hint of challenge in her tone, and drawled in his schooled British voice, 'I understood that you were in the hills for the hot weather.'

'I have been since May with my mother, that is true, but I came back as I was missing my son and I wanted to support Royce with his coronation events.'

'When did you return?'

Lilly glanced up in surprise. 'Am I a suspect? Do you think I shot Royce?'

He barely entertained the idea. 'I would stake my life on the fact that you would not know one end of a gun from the other and you were in the tent with witnesses at the time he must have been killed. Did your mother come back with you?'

355

'She had already left. I believe she has gone to Simla via Mussoorie where she was to meet a friend. She is between husbands and is travelling alone.'

Lilly thought he looked quite shocked.

'What did your husband think of this?'

She stalled for a moment. 'I wouldn't know. My mother is not accountable to Royce and as far as I'm aware didn't ask his permission to leave me on my own in Nainital. I didn't ask his permission to return early either.'

He looked at her reproachfully. 'A wife should trouble a little more about obedience and not do whatever she pleases.'

She looked at his jowly, perspiring face and decided that even if she owed Royce no loyalty, she would not give the man a reason to suspect there had been monumental fissures in the foundations of her marriage. 'Should she?' she asked innocently.

It seemed that this line of enquiry was proving a disappointment to him. Apparently sensing her reluctance to give him something more salacious, he turned the conversation back to the shooting of her husband. 'I have had so many differing reports of what happened last night, it is difficult to winkle out the truth.'

'Royce has – had – always loathed the circus. No one was more surprised than I to learn he had sponsored the coronation performance.'

'Did you hear the gunshot?' He ran an eye down his notes, worrying at the tip of his moustache. 'Some time after the end of the show?'

'There were two, in fact, and we all heard them. The circus proprietor put the tigers out of their misery. At least, that is what we understood.'

He nodded and Lilly knew her explanation would match what the others had said. He tapped the page with his pen, freckling the paper with ink. 'Was your husband unpopular to the point that anyone would shoot him?'

There it was, the question that they had prepared which demanded the full extent of her acting prowess. Although in essence it was true, the detail was somewhat embellished. *Tell the fewest lies possible but don't say what you did*. 'Royce always maintained that the pre-monsoon climate had an unfathomable effect on a man's temperament. Possibly one of his business associates became frenzied in the heat.'

'That's an interesting explanation.'

Lilly stared at the set of his thick lower lip, the pile of paper under his hand. She knew her voice must sound natural as she dragged in the tale by its heels. 'Even though Royce's father was white, European Cawnpore viewed him as a half-Indian tradesman and thus condemned him to the periphery of acceptable society. The Indians, on the other hand, saw him as a half-native champion, and looked to him to smooth things over with the white community when their masters pushed too hard.'

He shifted uncomfortably in his seat. 'What are you getting at?'

'The vast majority of the natives here are uneducated and find the three banks run by white bureaucrats so intimidating that Royce offered to keep their money safe. He kept proof of deposits and withdrawals and the balance of the money they had lodged with him, recorded in a ledger at his shop.'

'And so?'

Lilly nodded. 'Royce found that it was more convenient to use the money he held for his Indian depositors than to use the British bank himself. Most of the Indian money in town was in his hands just waiting to be spent. On things like sponsoring the circus and the expensive new feature act with the Italian cycling star.'

He gave her an indulgent smile. 'Even if he had made himself unpopular with the natives, I'm more inclined to think his death had something to do with that circus.'

'Why on earth would you think so? The circus has only been in town for five minutes. I'd hardly think there was time for anyone to do anything other than perform. I'd be more inclined to think that one of his so-called clients was after a refund of his money.'

He shrugged one shoulder. 'It is not my policy to intercede in Native offences.' He pushed a thick file towards her. 'Look at my paperwork. I have all these past cases to investigate. These will never lead to the conviction of an offender, which gives me an unacceptable crime to resolution rate.'

'It certainly seems a heavy workload.' She twisted her face into a mask of understanding.

He nodded with the confidence of someone who had just solved his mystery. 'Royce may have been spending money that was not legally his, but he had drawn to my attention the fact that the circus has been operating illegally. Insurance invalid and no performing licences, don't you see? Two days ago, we were going to shut the circus down but in the nick of time, the proprietor produced the money to cover the outstanding fees.'

Lilly picked a piece of fluff from her sleeve while she processed his remark. 'The men were all talking about that very thing last evening in the hospitality tent. Royce told them the coronation performance was not going ahead and that he would organise something better to celebrate the occasion than have them watch a third-rate show. He sent a note round apparently at the eleventh hour to say that the circus was back on.'

'Did anyone seem more or less relieved than anyone else?' He stared at her with his strange, light eyes.

'Not that I noticed. The tigers had nearly eaten their trainer, which led to the performance being cancelled. I doubt anyone in that tent would have been thinking beyond that unpalatable fact.'

He reflected a moment. 'Mr Myerson as well?'

She lifted her head, knowing that she must make this perfect. 'He wasn't there. It took me some time to find the tent when we all came out of the Big Top just after the ringmaster ordered the end of the show.'

The superintendent consulted his notes, shuffling papers, hunting for inspiration. Lilly knew she had tipped his enquiry off its flimsy base. 'The question is, where did he go and why and how did the accident happen?'

Lilly found the second handkerchief she'd stowed inside her sleeve and made sure he'd seen. 'I don't know.'

He leaned over the desk and pressed her hand. 'If you need to cry, my dear, don't feel you must hold back your tears in front of me. It's perfectly natural for a lady of gentle birth to have a good weep. Thanks awfully for sticking it all so well.'

He closed the folder on his desk and screwed the lid onto his fountain pen. 'If I were a betting man, I would say he was shot for the cash in his pockets. Regrettable as it is, I think the likelihood of finding the person responsible for your husband's death is slim to non-existent.'

Lilly got up, stunned at the lifeline she'd been given. The District Superintendent was drawing a line under the murder of a Eurasian, rather than pursuing an enquiry that might improve the success rate of his investigations.

She looked about the office. The walls were painted mud brown, the windows tall and undraped; it was a man's

359

room and smelled of leather and tobacco. A tall bookcase was well stocked with legal volumes but there were no ornaments on shelves, no rug on the floor or softening of the space other than an old yellowing photograph which hung on the wall.

She walked towards it and glanced at the portrait; next to a younger version of the man in the room was a face that was entirely familiar. In a handsome silver frame, it had looked out conspicuous and solitary from the top of Conti's grand piano in the drawing room of the bungalow in Nainital.

She stood stock-still for several seconds in front of the picture, as if seeing the face for the first time. 'This is a fine photograph of you, Sir Rivett-Moon. How do you come to know Noel Moore?'

A smile lit the District Superintendent's eyes. 'That's not Noel but his father, Matthew. A finer fellow you could not hope to meet.'

'How did you know him?'

He ran a finger inside his collar, apparently trying to release one of his chins from its celluloid prison. 'He stalked a man-eating tiger for us when I was stationed up country at Dalkarnia.'

Lilly was half afraid of what he might tell her, but was compelled to ask, 'Was he successful?'

He pulled his tobacco pouch from a pocket and started to fill his pipe. 'Yes, but not before it had taken over thirty human lives, one of whom was said to be his native "wife" and it completely undid him. He went a little mad after that.'

Lilly instantly thought of the *mangalsutar* necklace that once belonged to a very great friend of Noel's father. Why had she not been more curious and encouraged Noel to talk? She saw his face clearly, the shy and compassionate expression, the twinkling grey eyes and his thinning, sandy hair. The unexpected reminder of him, after all these weeks without hearing from him at all, really struck her hard.

For a second she reeled. She put out a hand to steady herself on the desk and as she swayed, the District Inspector shot from his seat and helped her into the nearest chair. She put a hand to her chest as she fought the tide of emotion. 'May I please have a glass of water? Suddenly everything seems too much.'

He moved to the door and pushed it shut. 'I think you need a private moment, old dear, while I fetch you some brandy. What with your husband, you've had the most awful shock and it's all just catching up with you.' He went over to a cupboard and mixed her a weak brandy 'peg' then sat in front of her, perched on the edge of the desk. He waited until her glass was half empty before he spoke.

'What will you do when the dust settles? Go back to England, or brazen it out in this beastly climate and find a new father for your boy?'

She sipped at the brandy, supporting her head in her hand, and shielded her eyes from his gaze. 'Marriage caught me early. I was barely eighteen, Sir Rivett-Moon. I have a fancy to follow in my mother's footsteps and be independent, at least for a while.'

Whatever he'd expected her to say, it was clearly not that. He looked at her as though the monsoon heat had addled her brain. 'Pastures new?'

She set her glass on the desk. 'More of a clean break.'

He leaned forward and took hold of her hand, clamping it between his two damp palms. He bent lower and lower until his lips brushed her knuckles. 'You don't have to be on your own, you know. Not now or ever.'

His transition from sleuth to suitor was deeply alarming. As gently as she could, Lilly extricated her hand and fingered the gold band on her finger. She looked out of the window at the grey curtain of rain and shook her head. 'I'm feeling steadier now,' she said and rose from her chair. 'Thank you for the brandy, Sir Rivett-Moon, and the offer of support but I'm going back to the bungalow. Somehow in the next day or two I must find a way to tell my son that his father is no longer alive.'

He stood aside to let her pass but did not shake her hand. 'I'll take the cremation off your shoulders. I think that's for the best, and you can decide what to do with the ashes.'

Picking up her umbrella, she took her time to cross the floor, then turning sharply away, walked as fast as she could down the passage, trying not to break into a run.

Chapter 35

Temples throbbing from the heat, Lilly wandered through the bungalow, aware that for the first time since she'd been married, she was in charge of the army of servants. Royce had always insisted she left everything to the head man – from domestic finances to the hiring and firing of staff. At Granny Wilkins's house, he would have been called the butler.

But was she really my granny?

Trailed by four different servants, she found him in his immaculate white robes, in conversation with the cook. He stood before her clutching his hands together and bowed so low his many-layered turban touched the floor.

'The *memsahib* is wanting something? Some tea perhaps?'

There was no point in sidestepping the fact. 'You can bring me some brandy. Mr Royce has passed away. He was shot in the head and so we have to decide how best to carry on.'

He hung his head. 'This is most sad news.'

Robinder Singh would be calculating what this would mean for him, personally. He struck his lined forehead with his fist. 'You are wanting to dismiss household?'

She looked at him levelly. 'No, but we must streamline our domestic staff by at least a half. We don't need all these people in the house doing nothing all day.' She looked pointedly at the three *punkah wallahs* squatting on the veranda, 'spares' for the man who was actually moving the fan via a rope through the wall. 'Make a list of the servants who work here and bring me the household accounts. I will decide who stays and who goes.'

He began to protest but Lilly held up a hand to silence him. 'In the hills we had a cook and his wife, a *mali* to oversee the garden and someone to wash our clothes. That will be quite sufficient for Teddy and me.'

'Miss Lilly, that is not suitable to a lady of your standing and Sahib Sir's mother. The smallest minimum we must be considering is ten.'

'How many servants work here?'

'Thirty-nine, I am thinking.'

'At what cost per month?'

He studied the ground, pretending to think. 'Three hundred rupees.'

'Are you sure?'

His smile was merely a movement of the lips. 'Maybe two hundred and fifty for you and Sir Sahib and some more for servants of Sahib's mother.'

'When is Mummy coming back?' She referred to her mother-in-law in the way Royce had insisted she be called.

'She is not telling me.'

'I want you to pack up her things and send them to the lychee farm in Delhi. Do you have the address?'

His head wobbled from side to side. 'I am helping you very much, *Memsahib*. Now that Sahib Sir is going, I am dismissing half our servant peoples and soon I am hoping you will be happy with myself.'

In her heart, she knew that she would not dismiss a soul. What would happen to them and their families? Where would they go? Too well she understood the prospect of destitution, of being forced to beg for help and would not wish that for anyone. But it wouldn't hurt to shake them all up, now she was in charge of the house – particularly Robinda Singh.

She also suspected that he had been stealing from them systematically for years. The goods that came into the house did not tally with the amount he said they cost and he must have been personally skimming off a very handsome profit. She spoke to him in his own language so that there would be no misunderstanding. 'I will decide who stays and who goes, not you, and I will write to Mummy and tell her what has happened. She will stay with her daughter from now on.'

'What shall I do with Sahib Sir's belongings?'

'I'll leave that up to you. Pack everything into boxes but don't throw out any papers or photographs. I want to keep them for Teddy for – later on – when he is older.'

She turned around and through a doorway saw her son – her precious little boy – propped up half asleep on his chair, a pencil in his hand. You hold my heart and soul in the palm of that hand, she thought as his face screwed up with concentration. The tutor sat by his side, leaning back in his chair, beating the desk with his fingers. Rap. Rap. Rap. *Rupees Annas Pice. Get that in your thick head, Plumpty.* Rap. Rap. Rap.

Children were resilient. When he'd woken that morning and found her in his room, she might never have been away. Did he have any notion of the passing of time? Were minutes and seconds the same as days and weeks or was his life so ordered and her participation in it so minimal that he scarcely registered her at all?

But as he sat up and smiled, her heart turned over with joy. She had been waiting for weeks, hardly daring to hope that she would hold him again in her arms.

She gathered him to her and buried her face and her thoughts in her little boy's neck. He was the reason she'd come back, the reason she'd robbed a man of his breath and she vowed, as she locked his body to hers, that she would never leave him again.

For now, she would go carefully and not change too much of Teddy's routine; he would find out soon enough that his father had gone from this life.

Lilly reverted to English, the language of command. 'Send the tutor home after lunch. Teddy is five years old. He needs to play with toys and run about in the garden.' *And get to know his mother.*

'He is for his examinations to school preparing. Sahib Sir says he must do very well. Be top of tree.'

'From now on, I will decide about his education. No more tutors. Tell the tutor now, then bring me the brandy and ask *Ayah* to have him wash his hands for tiffin. And bring me the accounts books so I can see what you've been spending.'

Lilly trailed her shoe along the edge of the rug, deliberately mussing the perfectly aligned tassels. A servant appeared at the door, followed by another, both armed with a measuring stick and comb. 'Leave them,' she said. 'I don't want them combed straight like hair. I prefer them this way.'

She stood still for a long time, thinking of another rug in another house in the Nainital hills, and the sun on the threadbare patch where a sandy moustached man would stand with his dog.

She felt giddy but there was no time to collect her spinning thoughts as Robinder Singh came back, the brandy and a heavy glass on a silver tray. He balanced it in the palm of his left hand, poured out a measure and ostentatiously ground the stopper back into the neck of the decanter.

If she had any intention of staying in this house, the man would be out on his ear.

'Here is your brandy, *Memsab*. That you are wanting.'

She held his gaze for a while, an uneasy silent challenge, before she said, 'I want you to find someone to tune the piano.'

From the look in his eyes, she could see he was not pleased, whether because it was she who'd asked him or whether he had no idea where to start. He rocked on his heels, clutching the tray with both hands as if she'd tried to wrest it from him.

'And two more things. Mr Royce's motor is outside the circus ground filling up with rain. Could you send the driver to fetch it and, on his way back, I want him to send a telegram.'

That afternoon, after a meal alone with Teddy attended by a half-dozen servants, Lilly's trunks arrived in a closed, horse-drawn carriage, accompanied by Dodo, Nattie and Margot.

They found her in the drawing room playing checkers with her son.

Margot was resplendent in an immaculate white blouse and navy silk skirt, the hem of which had darkened with the monsoon rain. As soon as she sat down, Teddy abandoned the board game and climbed onto her lap, fascinated with the feathers in her hat. She turned to Lilly. 'How are you managing?'

Lilly tried to stand but found she could not. She leaned forward in her chair and spoke to her son. 'Teddy, darling. Go and play with *Ayah* for a while. I need to chat to these ladies and you will get very bored if you stay here with us.'

Teddy slid off Margot's knee and as he trotted off in search of his nurse, Dodo remarked on the fit of Lilly's clothes. 'Have you had the tailor here already?'

Lilly gave the minutest shake of the head. 'These were what I wore before I was expecting Caroline. It was always my intention to lose the weight I'd gained when I was pregnant but, as part of his control, Royce made me eat food I didn't want. Those extra pounds I shed at the circus were all to do with the exercise and so on. I wasn't always the size of an elephant.' She sucked in her cheeks to illustrate the point.

Lilly could not see Dodo's face but heard the snort of laughter. 'How did it go with the pompous Britisher? Are you about to be hung for murder?'

Lilly flapped her hand, indicating that she should lower her voice. 'He put Royce's case in a huge file he keeps of unsolvable crimes because the investigation, he says, will turn up no culprit.'

'A good outcome then,' Margot said.

'On the shooting, yes.'

Dodo sat up at that. 'What else happened? You don't seem as relieved as you should.'

Lilly pushed up from her seat and went to the fireplace. She took hold of the gold-edged card that sat on the mantel-piece and proffered it to Dodo. 'I had barely been back from the interview five minutes before this arrived by messenger.'

She rolled her eyes. 'What is it the British say? Is he plighting his troth?'

Lilly thought of Sir Rivett-Moon's slobbering lips and shuddered. 'He all but pounced on me at the Inspectorate this morning, giving me brandy and kissing my hand. By inviting me to join his party at the Coronation Dinner and Dance in the assembly rooms tomorrow night, he's either wanting to drag me into society as an acceptable European or is suspicious I've not been telling the truth about Royce.'

'Don't go.' Margot put a hand on her arm.

'I don't intend to.'

'Has he been to the Emporium and spoken to Paramjit? When he came to Lucknow on Royce's behalf, I got the impression they were thick as thieves.'

Lilly began to muse. 'I don't know. I wouldn't have thought he'd have had time yet, but the money lending is true, and that money will have to be reunited with the depositors. Speaking of money, I owe quite a sum at the Commissary.'

Margot crossed her legs at the ankles. 'I think you owe nothing at the circus.'

Dodo gazed at the ceiling then looked across at Lilly. 'I brought your wash bucket along with both of the trunks. I thought you might appreciate the reminder if ever you doubt yourself again.'

'I don't know how you thought of that yesterday, on the spur of the moment.'

'Nattie told me to put the bucket in front of you when we heard him carrying on. She said you would understand the visual metaphor.'

Perched on the arm of the sofa, Nattie bent her head to light a cigarette but said nothing for a moment. Lilly thought she was going to make a quip about the lettering on the pail but when she'd blown out the match, she wafted the conversation in a different direction. 'Duffy got a bit of a mauling, but he'll pull through. I thought you'd want to know.'

Lilly glanced up, glad at the news. 'I wasn't really surprised the tiger went for him. He insisted on tormenting it in his cage even though it was plain to see the animal loathed him. It made me wonder if he really knew what he was doing, that his training methods were flawed in some way.'

'Don't go and see him.' Margot shook her head then smiled as Teddy came back from his nurse and repositioned

369

himself on her knee. 'All that's done with now. You have other responsibilities.'

Prickly sweat broke out on her body. She could feel the flush of it, the tingle as she relived the sweep of his hands on her skin. 'I know.'

Dodo glanced at the clock on the mantelpiece. 'I've enjoyed getting to know you, more than anyone else in a very long time.'

Lilly raised her eyebrows. 'Are you leaving? I haven't even offered you tea.'

Nattie jumped to her feet and sighed. 'We aren't good at goodbyes.'

Her stomach flipped over. Noel had written those same words on a rough scrap of paper and she hadn't seen or heard from him since. She leaned back against the chair, watching the pattern the rain made on the window and felt the last flicker of hope die inside her.

'I won't see you again?' Lilly suddenly felt very vulnerable.

'Unless you come to the circus.' Nattie mashed her cigarette in the ashtray.

'But I can't just leave like that. I have to say goodbye to everyone and especially Belle. I didn't think yesterday morning that it would be my last day at the circus.'

'I dare say we'll manage without you,' Dodo said wryly.

When she thought back, Mr Tiffert had warned that the sisters would not be prepared to risk drawing her close, knowing eventually she would leave.

But he'd been wrong. For weeks now, Dodo and Nattie had become her closest friends – the centre and meaning of her world. She had laughed with them and cried; they had given her courage, lied for her and yesterday, Dodo had saved her life by encouraging her to stand up to Royce.

What she felt for these two was beyond gratitude; it was a deep, unconditional love.

Dodo lifted the parcel she had placed by her chair. 'I brought a present for Teddy.'

Teddy slid off Margot's lap and accepted the gift. 'Thank you very much,' he said. 'I am a very lucky boy.'

Lilly had to give Royce some credit; his son's manners were flawless. Teddy sat on the floor, cross-legged, and untied the string. He wound it into a ball around his finger, then eased it off to maintain its shape. He held it out to Lilly. 'Tidy at all times, Plumpty,' he said and then pulled off the brown paper to reveal the box beneath. She forced out a smile as he mimicked his papa, horrified that Royce's behaviour was shaping their son. 'Thank you, darling. I'll be sure to put it away. Papa will be very impressed with how sensible you've been.'

On the lid there was a label – *Engineering for Boys* – a picture of a construction that looked like the Eiffel Tower and a circle within which was drawn the number one.

'What is it, Mama?'

Lilly shook her head. 'I don't know, Teddy. Open it up and explore what's inside.'

Teddy removed the lid and upended a book of instructions and several yellow tins on to the rug. 'I still don't know what it is.'

Dodo knelt down on the rug and opened the tins. 'It's a very clever toy. You can make models with the metal strips. You fix them together with nuts, bolts and screws. There should be a set of spanners and a screwdriver in the box as well. Do you want to see if you can find them?'

The thoughtfulness of the gift brought a lump the size of a croquet ball to Lilly's throat and tears welled up behind her eyes. She flapped her hand up and down, unable to speak.

Teddy giggled; it was a sound of pure delight as he found the spanner and handed it to Dodo. 'Here!'

'I bought one of these sets for my own little boy. He loves it and I hope you will too.'

Lilly glanced down at the rug, then looked up at Nattie. 'At least now I'll have money of my own to buy things for Teddy. I used to have to ask Royce's permission to spend anything.'

Nattie made a gesture that seemed to imply the problem was gone. 'You're your own person now.'

The clock over the mantelpiece chimed the hour, bonging five times like Big Ben. The afternoon had flown by too quickly.

Nattie edged towards the door. 'Come on, Dodo. We were only going to be five minutes. We have rehearsal at six o'clock remember, as some of the acts have had to be changed.'

Dodo got up from the floor and shook out her clothes; she was wearing what she referred to as street wear: skirt and blouse, married together by a wide leather belt. She set her chin, her expression thoughtful. 'He's a dear little thing, Lilly. Choose where you want your son to grow up and put down some roots, but not here. The air is tainted. You can almost smell the man. Don't taunt yourself with what you did, but it's inevitable you will for a while.'

Lilly nodded, biting her lip.

They didn't say goodbye as they whisked out of the room, closing the door on their friendship.

Terrified they'd slip away from her for ever, she hid her face behind her hands, trying to hold them in her memory. Through her tears she saw their sparkling costumes as they skipped into the ring. Sisters Dodo and Nattie, with their swings and trapeze; the snapping of Dodo's band at her wrist to give her courage against the height at the top of the Big Top.

Dodo's head twisted back; the only thing holding herself and her twin in the air being the strength of her jaw.

Nattie's utter trust in the sister for whose protection she had killed.

The door clicked and for one joyous moment she thought they'd come back. But it was the *khansama*, bringing their afternoon tea.

She felt her face fall. Waiting until the tea things had been laid out on the table, she said to Robinder Singh, 'Take Teddy for his tea, please. I'll call you when I want you to clear.'

Margot pulled up her chair. 'Are you all right, Lilly?' she whispered.

Lilly nodded towards the door, as the servant shut it behind him. 'Not really.'

'It's not up to them to save you, Lilly. Only you can do that, but they will miss you, even though you might not think it.'

Margot busied herself with the teapot. 'I gave Dodo my hatpin. The one with the especially sharp tip.'

'I thought you loved that pin.'

'Oh, I do but not as much as I love you. Dodo was worried, you see. Royce was in the audience and you were frightened for your life. She said if all else failed, she would stab him herself.'

Lilly accepted the cup but set it down untasted. 'When did you give it to her?'

'During the intermission while the tiger cage was being set up in the ring.'

'Why ever did she not say?'

'It's not her way. You know that. Tiffy was also on standby. That was why he was sweeping up the sawdust, lingering in the Big Top until you both came out. It was no coincidence that Belle was outside the tent flap and he had the gun in his pocket he'd used to shoot the tigers. He would have shot Royce too without a moment's hesitation if you hadn't done it first.'

Lilly almost laughed, almost cried. Margot had told her that if the circus accepted her, they would go into bat for her if ever the chips were down.

'Has it all been for nothing?'

'No, Lilly. You mustn't think like that. You must not look back with regret or it *will* all have been pointless. Think of all the positives that you've gained. You've become tough – both mentally and physically. You have learned to say no to a bully. You have regained the person you thought you'd lost so don't waste what you have achieved. Make it count.'

'Shake up the reins and ride the horse?'

Margot smiled. 'I might have used those very words myself. Don't become a martyr to what has happened. You are a people person. Don't hide yourself away. By the way . . .' She delved into her handbag. 'Tiffy sent you a present. He said you nagged him enough for it.'

Lilly took the proffered card and turned it over. It was her performer's licence made out in the name of Lilly Wilkins, Artiste. She closed her eyes, momentarily over-whelmed by the gesture.

'Tiffy said when you have your grandchildren on your knee and tell them that once, a long time ago, you ran away to the circus, you can show them this, to prove it.'

'He used my maiden name.'

'Duffy told him you might prefer it.'

'Is he really all right? Apart from the mauling, I mean.'

Margot shrugged. 'He has periodic flair ups of malaria. He's known since Lucknow, but he's been trying to hide it.'

'There's a sanitorium near Nainital. At Bareilly, I think.'

She shook her head. 'No, Lilly. I told you Duffy is not your future. He's shown you what passion can be, but he will never put down roots. Call it circus mania if you like, a marvellous madness that could never endure.'

'What's his real story, Margot? He told me once that he was hiding in the circus but not from a wife who doesn't exist. What is it that has made him change his name so many times?'

She sat back and lit a cigarette. 'Duffy is wanted by the authorities for non-payment of his taxes. Five years ago, he was deported from Madras and on the way to the United States of America, he jumped ship in Cape Town, changed his name and came straight back to India.'

'So South Africa wasn't a lie.'

'He was there for five minutes, Lilly. Forget him. You have to let him go.'

It was too much effort to hold onto the expanding bubble of despair that rose in her chest. Lilly began to cry, wracking painful sobs that she couldn't control.

Margot drew a startled breath and reached out to take her hand. 'There's more to this, isn't there?'

Lilly wiped at her face with her hand. 'When Royce came into the dressing room yesterday, he told me something I never knew about Binnie.'

'What did he say to distress you so much?' Margot persisted, her voice troubled.

'He said that my father was not my father, my links to England are bogus and my mother is a trollop. The shame

I feel for that is almost unbearable.'

'Dodo said that he had been firing cheap shots at you in the dressing tent, but I'm certain he had no more idea about Binnie's past than you do.'

'He must have had some evidence or he wouldn't have said all those things.'

'Are you sure, what with everything else going on under the canvas last night that you understood him properly?' Margot pulled on her cigarette.

'There can be no doubt. Both my parents were fair, and I am dark. My father found out that Binnie had been having an affair and she sent me off to England to hush it up and my father' – she gave another great sob – 'put a gun in his mouth and shot himself.'

Margot looked away from her; Lilly couldn't see the look on her face, but she heard the sigh. It was a short, exasperated sound. 'You are so accepting of what others tell you. You told me the policeman – or whatever he's called – decided that Royce had been shot by an opportunistic mugger. How did Royce know for certain that Binnie had an affair and tricked your father, who then took his own life?'

Lilly rubbed the heel of her hand across her forehead. 'I told him I didn't believe him but was he really telling the truth? I'm almost certain he wasn't but now I'll never find out for sure.'

'I'd be more inclined to ask why you should believe it. Your mother sent you to England to be raised by your father's people. I can't imagine why she would do that if he wasn't your father.' She made another noise, as if tired of the conversation. 'Your answers lie with Binnie. Seek her out, pin her down and don't let her off the hook until she tells you what went on.'

'I wouldn't know where to start to look.'

'Nainital. Call it a woman's intuition, your cards or something, but that's where you'll unearth the truth.'

Chapter 36

For nearly a month, the monsoon confined Lilly to the house.

Day after day, sheets of grey water fell from the heavy skies; an endless bombardment of rain assaulted the iron roof and the garden became a swamp. Frogs croaked, cicadas chirped in the long grass and fleas drove them mad.

The District Inspector brought Royce home in a clay pot. Lilly had no idea what to do with his cremated remains, so she put him at the back of his wardrobe and turned the key.

But even after weeks in the empty house, the bungalow was saturated with memories.

Royce haunted her dreams, hovering like a ghost, a reproachful finger wagging. Sometimes she would enter a room, convinced he was standing there – a silent shadow half hidden behind the curtains. In her head she heard the staccato clip of his shoes on the wooden floor, the approaching steps, felt the blood pounding in her ears and even saw red pressure marks on her wrists where he would restrain and hold her down.

She shut up his bedroom and avoided his study, practically living in one room; but however hard she pretended otherwise, as Dodo had said, the house was still full of him.

★

One morning in the last week of August, Lilly sat in the sitting room before the grand piano that stood in one corner, at right angles to the window.

She closed the lid and stood up, seized with a bitter sense of frustration. The *khansama* had rustled up a fellow from the bazaar who'd arrived brandishing a tuning fork but had less idea how to reclaim the piano's former voice than she had herself.

Some of the felts had disintegrated and several of the beautiful ivory keys had swollen and jammed with the damp. The playing was more about practising her fingering than producing a sound she was happy to hear.

A listless Teddy lolled on the rug, slapping at mosquitos. 'The noise is hurting my ears.'

'Is my playing that terrible?' she laughed.

'The insects are buzzing by my face. And I'm all itchy.'

'Try not to scratch, darling. You'll make the bites worse. Why not play with Dodo's game?'

'Don't want to.' He pushed himself up from the floor and set off towards the window putting one foot, toe to heel in front of the other, arms stretched out wide as if he were walking on a wire. The squeaking of his leather shoes seemed to echo up to the ceiling and she looked up expecting to see the roof of the Big Top tent. A faint tapping sound drew her eyes to the window where a beetle was butting its head against the glass, over and over, until that was all she could hear.

Lilly looked about her. Ice-blue curtains hung in rigid folds and were fettered behind restraining metal clamps. Her mother-in-law's mynah clawed at the bars of its cage and pecked at the rigid metal. She should set it free, but where would it go?

It's like one of Duffy's tigers — a victim of its surroundings, caged against its will.

Teddy drew a small peephole on the fogged glass. His hair was now cut shorter and slicked back with Yardley's Old English Lavender brilliantine. It was one of the first things she'd changed when she came home. Constantly hanging into his eyes, whatever Royce had instructed *Ayah* to oil it with, it smelled like the drains in the city.

'The rain has stopped, Mama. Can we go out like before?'

One day last week, when the rain let up briefly, they'd sloshed their way to where the circus ground had been. There was nothing to show it had ever been there; all that remained was an area of trampled mud and a few oily puddles.

As she'd turned her back and headed for home, she held onto Teddy's hand. He complained her grip was too tight, and she forced herself to stare straight ahead. But as they walked through the place where the entrance had been, Lilly turned to catch one last glimpse of the circus that had briefly been her home. 'Thank you,' she said as she waved her fingers goodbye.

Now Lilly stared beyond the window where her little boy stood. Teddy was wrong; it was still raining. *Pat, pat, pat,* drops tapped against the glass. *Bang, bang, bang,* her heart replied. *I don't know what to do.*

Despite having Teddy to herself, she was lonely to the point that she could barely get out of her seat. Isolation had become a new prison. She had become so afraid of human contact that she had dropped herself into that same dark hole through shame and self-loathing. Bizarrely, Royce's death left her feeling betrayed on some level. She had developed the quirks of the lonely. She mumbled to herself and made strange facial expressions; she only knew this because Teddy told her she did.

Wrapped in her thoughts, she didn't hear Robinder Singh come in. He never knocked on the door; none of the servants did.

'This has come.' He held out a silver tray on which lay the circus route card. Lilly felt excitement mounting and snatched it up, not certain what she would find.

Choose company not confinement.
Go to Nainital.
Margot.

Lilly turned her gaze, eyes pricking with tears, and focused on the mantelpiece where Pearl Pinkney's telegram had sat for weeks, propped up behind the clock. She had left it there unanswered, and allowed herself to drift. What's the point? she asked herself again and again. Will finding out end the pain?

But now, with the arrival of Margot's note, she was being told to draw back the veil.

Five days later, with Teddy, his *ayah* and a carriage full of luggage, she retraced her steps to Nainital.

Winding up her affairs had been straightforward. She poached a European manager with a Scottish wife from Packham & Co; he would run the Emporium with Paramjit and live in the bungalow with his family. Money from the business would be deposited monthly into a newly opened account and, along with what was left when Royce's depositors had been fully refunded, she would never be short of funds. And last of all, she dismissed the dishonest Robinder Singh and replaced him with a tall Muslim called Mustapha.

For three days they sat on the train on leather-covered benches, which converted to beds at night; with arms folded

381

on the window ledge, Lilly watched a rain-drenched India crawl past the carriage windows. When the train pulled into the stations, hawkers ran up and down the platforms, trays on their heads offering anything from spicy tea to the latest issue of the *Good Housekeeping* journal.

Delays were interminable, the halting incessant, but as the countryside changed from plain to hillier terrain, her heart began to lift.

From Kathgodam, the journey in the *dâk gharry* was a repeat of the one she'd made with her mother, with a damp, uncomfortable night spent at the mildewed Murray Hotel in Kaladhungi and the trek up the narrow well-worn path that snaked amongst the grassy slopes to Nainital.

In the pouring rain, Lilly laboured up the gravelly slope and when the road became too steep, she mounted a hill pony and rode legs astride like a man. She hired a horse-drawn carriage for Teddy and his *ayah*; it was a rudimentary affair, little more than a cart with two large wheels and a canopy overhead. The bearers were frightened of landslides and needed a great deal of persuasion to take them but at least, under the roof, the passengers gained relief from the rain.

At Jeolikote, a regular halt on the road to rest the ponies, they stopped by a lion-headed spout from which murky water gushed into a moss-covered trough. Giant lilies were in bloom, the scent from their flowers heady in the cool air; a carpet of violet-blue columbine fluttered like little butterflies in the breeze, and when she breathed in the tang of rain-soaked pine, she knew she was almost home.

At the rickshaw terminus at the Talital end of the lake, Lilly tried to negotiate transport for her son, his *ayah* and their luggage to Rohilla Lodge. They had only paid, it transpired, to be left by the side of the lake.

The first bearer to arrive beside the tonga folded his arms across his narrow chest and drew a line in the mud with his foot. 'No.'

A second walked around the luggage and eyed up their party and his empty rickshaw. He had beads of sweat on his upper lip. 'No.' He shook his head and spat.

'Can you take the tonga up the lane with two passengers and the luggage? I'm not expecting you to pull your rickshaw up the slope.' She opened her purse and held out a rupee.

At this, several more candidates appeared.

'Who is prepared to lead the horse up the slope?' She gazed up at the monsoon sky, distracted by the *piaw piaw* call of a Himalayan barbet. For a moment she watched it fly overhead; almost a foot long, it had a scarlet smudge under its tail and a bright blue patch in the middle of its breast. Showy, she thought, like a circus artiste.

A hillman dressed in a topi and white cotton pyjamas stepped forward. He wore a short-sleeved shirt and had an umbrella slung across his shoulders. He stretched out his hand and plucked the note from her fingers. 'I will lead the horse up the slope,' he said, and took hold of the halter.

Lilly set off down Mall Road, beckoning for the man to follow. The initial climb to Rohilla Lodge was gentle as she passed the tiny graveyard behind St Francis Church, but as it continued onwards past a white cottage on the right with its green iron roof and pots of geraniums on the porch, Lilly's calves began to burn. At the steepest pitch of the lane, she paused to catch her breath and let the tonga pass. All the way up, out of practice with the thin mountain air, she concentrated on her breathing and wondered what she was going to say. Eventually the path flattened out by the low, mud wall in front of the elderly guesthouse.

Lilly banged on the front door and waited.

Both Miss Pinkneys – white-faced with frightened eyes – answered her knock. A cloud passed over Miss Pearl's face. 'Is Royce with you?'

'No. May we come in?'

Pearl Pinkney exhaled slowly as if she'd been holding her breath. 'Of course, dear. It's been too long a time.'

She took them to her private sitting room without another word. She pushed the door open and went to the window, pulling the curtains closed.

Hovering on the threshold, Miss Opal seemed to sense that she was not wanted in this conversation. 'Teddy looks done in. Let's find him something to eat and then the *ayah* can sort out a bath.'

Teddy held up his arms and allowed himself to be lifted. He snuggled his head against *Ayah*'s shoulder and wound his legs around her waist. *Ayah* rained kisses on his head as they walked towards the door. Lilly was frightened by her feelings; that she was once again redundant, cast aside by her child for a much preferred toy. She closed her eyes and sought out the place where the new Lilly lived. 'I will put Teddy to bed when he's had something to eat. An egg and a piece of toast, *Ayah*, and however much he carries on, don't let him have any sweets.'

The nanny walked slowly to the door, eyes on the floor. If she was surprised at the instruction, she kept her thoughts out of view.

Pearl Pinkney went to the double-fronted sideboard where she kept her spirits. 'Have you come back to Nainital to escape again? Is that why you sent the telegram last month?'

'Is that what you think?'

'Well, have you?'

'I came back because there is no place else for me to go.'

'Have you given Royce the slip?'

Lilly stared at her hands. 'Royce is dead.'

The old lady carried on with what she was doing as though she hadn't heard her. 'I'm going to mix you a stiff peg and while it is coming, you can tell me what happened. Exactly.'

Lilly told her that Royce had come to the dressing tent while the tigers went for each other. Then, when he tried to drag her from the circus, he pulled a gun on her, fired and grazed her arm. If she hadn't had Noel's gun in her pocket, he would have murdered her, there was no doubt in her mind. 'The police think it was a robbery gone wrong as there was no money in his pockets when he was found slumped in his car.'

Pearl Pinkney picked up the glass and turned back to the room. She raised an eyebrow, the merest hint of enquiry flickering across her face.

Lilly licked her dry lips and accepted the drink. 'I had no choice. In the end it was me or him.'

'We didn't like him one bit – Opal and me. He was a nasty bastard.'

Lilly choked on a mouthful of gin. 'Miss Pinkney!'

A smile pushed at the corners of Pearl Pinkney's mouth and Lilly thought she was trying not to laugh. 'I have quite a vocabulary of language you might not expect me to know. Remember, I met Royce a couple of times and I would say that he was pitiless. He set out to break your spirit and you had about as much chance of long-term survival with that man as a chicken in a snake pit.'

Lilly sat down on the well-worn sofa in her favourite place by the armrest and listened to the rainwater as it plopped into a collection of old porcelain dishes. 'I'm going to have your roof repaired,' she said. 'I have money of my own now.'

Pearl Pinkney took the chair to the left of the sofa. 'How does independence make you feel?'

'Is it wrong to say I'm not sorry he's dead?'

'It is no crime to voice what is in your heart. Is the matter now closed with the police?'

Lilly nodded. 'They didn't try very hard to find the culprit. The District Superintendent showed me a folder full of unsolved mysteries he had on his desk. He seemed to pluck his explanation out of thin air – he said it was an armed robbery – to save himself the bother of an investigation.'

'He was probably running late for lunch at his Club.'

Lilly took a few deep breaths. 'But I shot Royce, Miss Pearl. I killed a man, and I am tormented with the guilt of it.'

Pearl Pinkney removed her *pince-nez* and let it dangle from its chain. 'When men were caught up in the Mutiny in 1857, it was a question of kill or be killed. I would have readily held a gun to a man's head if it might have saved Wilfrid. I'll let you read his letters. He wrote of crying, sobbing, shaking – a grief so terrible at times he felt himself drowning in it. He wasn't alone. Many men were overwhelmed by their guilt.'

For a few moments they sat in silence. Eventually, Lilly turned to face Miss Pearl and slowly shook her head. 'I can't read your personal letters. It's already enough that you gave me his jewellery, which I sold to save the circus. Royce was intent on destroying that too.'

There was a firmness in Pearl Pinkney's voice. 'He would have killed you, Lilly, or you would have killed yourself. I was very worried about you when you were here with your mother. You know he came back again?'

'When?'

'After you had left for the circus. That's why Conti sent you the telegram. He'd been up to Lake View and tried to bully her into telling him where you were. He wanted to know where Binnie was too. He was almost more furious that she had disappeared than you.'

The moment had come to confront the elusive elephant. 'I need to talk to you about her.'

Pearl Pinkney repositioned her *pince-nez* on her nose, a little spot of colour heightening her age-lined cheeks. 'I don't know where she is.'

Lilly was not going to be fobbed off. Not any more. 'Do you think when she sent me to England when I was a baby that she had any intention of ever seeing me again?'

Pearl Pinkney seemed resigned, as if she had been expecting this question. 'Only she would know that.'

Lilly knew she was hiding something. 'Unless she told you.'

For several seconds Pearl Pinkney sipped at her gin. 'It's not my story to tell.'

Lilly folded her hands in her lap, thinking if she shared her own information, it might encourage Miss Pearl to reveal what she knew. 'When Royce turned up in the dressing room at the circus to drag me off home, he told me that Binnie had had an affair with a native and my father took his own life.'

Pearl Pinkney continued to sip as she recounted the story Royce had told her and when she got to the end, Lilly looked straight at her to make sure she was listening. 'Did Binnie send me to his parents even though we were not related?'

Miss Pearl seemed to have overcome her reluctance to speak. Sincerity rang out in the old lady's voice. 'No.

Your father was your father. As for consorting with a native, I've never heard of anything so ridiculous. Binnie discovered she passed in the crowd and would never have done anything to jeopardise that.'

'That's an odd thing to say.'

'Binnie has mixed blood.' Miss Pearl's voice was determined. 'Her English socialite mother was something of a tearaway in her day and had taken up with the son of a family friend. Parental discipline and decisions prevailed on both sides. The boy was married off *tout de suite* and Binnie's mother was shipped out to the East with a decent allowance but her marriage prospects in tatters. I'm not so clear on what happened next but she set herself up in the fashion business selling clothes to the British out here. Her goings-on began again but this time she fished in the local pond and Binnie was the result. With fair colouring herself, and moving in wealthy European circles, your mother learned early on she could pass herself off as white.'

Lilly felt as if the breath had been syphoned from her lungs. She started to speak yet something in the set of Miss Pearl's face warned her not to interrupt.

'One of the least attractive features of British India is its preoccupation with colour. When I was young, good-quality Indians were acceptable as matches for good quality Europeans but that's all changed in the last fifty years. Binnie was fully integrated in her Bombay circle and there was no way that she would have upset that by having an extra-marital affair with a local.'

Lilly accepted more gin and was glad it was strong. 'She is a fraud and I will never forgive her for that.'

Pearl Pinkney seemed relieved that she was able to say something unflattering at last. 'She is indeed someone who has learned to deceive.'

Suddenly thinking, Lilly asked, 'Did Royce know that Binnie has mixed blood? At the séance, Margot spelled out the word "imposter" on a piece of paper and showed it to everyone there. I talked to her about that not so long ago and she was adamant that it was not a parlour trick.'

Lilly could tell Miss Pearl was struggling whether to answer the question. She looked away but then turned back. 'I don't think it was ever your mother's intention to spy on you at the start, but when she saw you getting close to the tiger trainer, she panicked. That's when she started to feed information to Royce. There's no doubt in my mind that she was the informant who gave him your whereabouts.'

'But she had left Nainital before I ran off to the circus. I have told myself over and over that it couldn't have been her because she didn't know where I'd gone.'

'I wondered about that too, but remember, Naini is a small place and however much you think your business is private, it never actually is. Royce on the rampage handing out groats for gossip would have found him what he wanted to know.'

Lilly paused for a moment, knowing this had to be true. 'Going back to my father, do you think he guessed that Binnie had strayed? Royce said he'd put a gun in his mouth as his wife had been unfaithful.'

Pearl Pinkney seemed surprised. 'I'd think that most unlikely. It was he who chose your name. Binnie wanted to call you Buttercup, but William said that he was not having a child of his named after an English weed. He said you would be Lilly, his beautiful flower. But when he died, your mother found herself in a huge house with a tiny child and no income. Keymer Cecil came along and almost immediately after meeting him, she sent you to England to your father's people.'

Lilly blinked. 'How do you know all this?'

'She was here in Nainital at the Lady Dufferin Hospital and that's how I met her. About five years ago.'

'What was wrong with her?'

Miss Pearl lowered her eyelids as if remembering the event. 'She miscarried a baby and she was very unwell for a time. I was helping out, visiting patients with no visitors, that sort of thing. "Doing good works," Opal called it. There were moments when Binnie felt she might die and that's when she told me all of this. Perhaps it was a confession of some sort.'

'I've never understood why she summoned me back.' Lilly rattled out the words.

Pearl Pinkney caught her hand and held it against her heart. 'I don't know how to say this without causing you the utmost distress.'

'There's more?' Lilly gasped.

'When your grandmother wrote to say you were about to be presented at court, Binnie knew her secret was in danger of coming out. She had to get you back to preserve her own fiction.'

Lilly disengaged her hand and pointed two fingers at her head. 'At least she stuck to her guns, fully loaded and aimed at me.'

'I can understand your bitterness, but your grandmother did fight for you at first, until Binnie dropped her *chee-chee* bombshell.'

Lilly felt herself falling into a memory; the echo she had struggled for so long to recall was suddenly loud in her ear. Granny was in the porch of her house, tight-lipped, white-faced as Grandfather brought around the car. 'Why am I going to India?' she asked. 'Your mother's a *chee-chee*,' she answered. 'What's that word, Granny?'

Lilly felt she was spinning, coming apart. *Chee-chee!* It was the pejorative label for a mixed-blood woman.

Pearl Pinkney rubbed her cheek. 'When you came back to India, Binnie knew that if you married someone of your choice – a European, say – the likelihood of your child being dark-skinned was too high to risk. To ensure that would not in any way raise the question of your heritage, she insisted on you marrying an Eurasian. That way, any colour inconsistency or a throw-back dark-skinned child could be rationally explained.'

'Betraying one's child is a terrible thing.'

Pearl Pinkney let out a sigh. 'Can you not find it in your heart to pity her? Imagine spending a whole lifetime holding onto a secret you can never share.'

Lilly understood all too well her mother's dilemma. She lived in fear of it all the time and it was only by the grace of God, a disinterested policeman and loyal friends, she had, so far, not been arrested for murder. 'Lies will always come out. However good an actor you are, or however good a memory you have, some tiny thing will eventually catch you, such as a confession to a stranger when you think you might die. Does Noel know?'

'Know what?'

'That I am – let me work it out – a quarter Indian, and my son is a quarter Indian from his father and an eighth from me so would make him three-eighths Indian.'

'That's an impressive calculation to make in your head. I thought you struggled with your accounting book.'

'I've always had a fondness for figures but if someone stands over you and beats you senseless if you make a mistake, everything flies out of your brain. You say the first thing that jumps into it in the hope that the beating will stop.'

Miss Pearl's concern was genuine now. 'Oh, my dear.'

Lilly asked again, 'Does Noel know?'

'Only because he saw Binnie for what she was. He spent his childhood amongst the native boys – he may have told you – and there are apparently certain signs such as blue marks in the fingernails and bluish gums.'

'Binnie always wears gloves and hardly ever opens her mouth. I thought that was because her teeth are poor. No wonder he never answered my letter.'

Miss Pearl reached for her glass. 'There is more substance to him than that, Lilly. Both he and Conti have known what you are from the outset and that has not diminished their feelings for you in any way whatsoever.' Miss Pinkney massaged the knuckles of her left hand. 'My arthritis always plays up in the wet.'

'What's wrong?' Lilly knew her well enough to know something else was brewing.

Pearl Pinkney bent forward and watched her closely. 'I want you to write to Binnie and forgive her.'

Lilly was stunned. 'For twenty-four years of neglect and spying on me for my husband?'

'Twenty-four years of living in fear, I would say. You are the only person in the world who can free her from the secret she has hidden for so long.' Her face was closed against refusal. 'Would you condemn her to an old age like mine? She has a child and a grandchild. Don't deny her that pleasure.'

Before Lilly could reply, Miss Pearl turned her attention to the other hand.

'There's more?'

'When you wired to say you were coming, I didn't think you would have an entourage in tow.'

Lilly stared at her blankly. 'There are three of us. That's hardly an entourage and you have the room. I told you I have money now so I can pay you properly.'

Miss Pearl shook her head. 'When Royce came that time, we said that we do not accommodate children at Rohilla Lodge, and we did not make that up. I had a child and gave him up and Opal was never blessed. Even though we are old now, it is difficult to admit that we still – for different reasons – suffer the anguish of childlessness. We avoid reminders. It is less painful.'

Lilly dropped her head. 'I am so sorry.'

'I don't think either of us imagined a life without children. Opal had miscarriages and it has taken her a very long time to get over them emotionally. I did hold my own tiny baby briefly but when I see others with children, the years of grief and sadness at having to give him away come welling up.' She reached into the pocket of her shapeless cardigan and, pulling out a handkerchief, she quietly began to sob.

Lilly felt a swell of pain and swallowed hard. 'I know what it's like to lose a child. My mother-in-law had a very poor opinion of me from the start and now I am beyond salvation in her eyes. She probably thought I should have made offerings to the god Shiva and that is why my daughter died. The pain almost broke me.'

'Grief makes people say things they don't mean.' The elderly head sank lower towards her chest. 'And yet you have Teddy. Opal and I will never know the love of a child. No one will ever call us Mama. And as we get older still, we are forced to realise that there will be no one to look after us when we are unable to do for ourselves. We are both hoping that we will be the first to pass, for being left by oneself, possibly going gaga, is too devastating a scenario to imagine.'

'But you both have me.'

Pearl Pinkney looked up, her eyes shining with tears. 'Do we?'

Lilly took hold of her hand. 'For ever and ever. Margot read it in my cards.'

Chapter 37

Conti blustered into the guesthouse a few days later, armed with Lilly's silver dressing table brushes, a toy for Teddy and a full set of questions.

'I heard you were back. Have you given Royce the slip again? How was the circus? What happened with Duffy and Margot? Have you heard from Binnie? Where's Teddy?'

Lilly held up her hand. '*Ayah*'s taken Teddy out for an airing. No news from Binnie. Duffy has malaria and Margot is looking after him. The circus was the best thing that has ever happened to me in my entire life and Royce is dead.'

Conti sank onto a stool, hands clasped round her knees. 'Golly! What happened to him?'

'I think one could call it death by misadventure.'

'What did he do that was stupidly dangerous?'

'He tried to shoot me.'

Conti's eyes were as round as saucers. 'That was foolish of him. Noel always said he wouldn't want to cross you if your dander was up.'

'How is he?' She hoped her mood seemed light. 'I was talking about him with Pearl Pinkney only the other day and thought I might pop up and say hello.'

Conti glanced at her, a shade of curiosity on her face. 'How did he come up in conversation?'

Lilly was ashamed of the untruth. 'I wanted to return the gun he loaned me.'

'You could have walked up to Lake View and left it with me. That's a very poor lie you just told.'

She hung her head. 'I know. Truthfully, I want to see him and yet I fear running into him. We didn't part on the best of terms in Bhimtal, but thank you for retrieving the brushes by the way.'

'The *dâk* keeper sent them to us, so we can't claim the glory.'

'At least I've got them back. They're irreplaceable.'

'Are you not going back to England?'

Lilly shook her head. 'Not just staying in India but here in Nainital. Already I've been to All Saints College up the road and put Teddy's name down on their list. He's too late for this year but he's down for next March.'

Conti tilted her head to the side. 'I'm surprised you came back here. We weren't convinced that you really embraced life in the hills.'

'I owe a great debt to the Miss Pinkneys and I want to take care of them when they are unable to look after themselves. They are scared that they have no one and if I can make them feel relevant and cared for, it's what I'm going to do.'

'Anyone without a child – or close familial ties – feels that sense of terror. I do if I allow myself to dwell.'

'You will get married one day and have your own family. You just have to find the right person.'

'Do you think Noel will too?' She said it with such feeling that Lilly flushed and turned away.

'The Miss Pinkneys have asked me to find somewhere else to stay. They find it difficult with a youngster in the house. I've been thinking about approaching your mother for one of her rentals, but now I'm wondering if you would like a houseguest to help out a little money-wise? I can pay my way now – not cadge off you like before.'

'Noel was more upset than I have ever seen him when he came back from Bhimtal. He'd found the tiger for Duffy quite by chance. It had been trapped in a pit and put in a cage with metal bars. I know he'd have bought it himself and set it free if he'd had the option. But as you know money is tight and he's trying to do the right thing by the people at his farm so every penny counts.'

Somewhere in the distance Lilly heard a dog bark and she found herself thinking of Goose. 'Did Noel ask you to clear out my room when he got back from Bhimtal?'

'What?' She didn't seem to understand. 'Why ever would he have done that? We both told you we'd keep a room for you with us, if ever you found your way back. That's one of the many reasons for me coming over today – to ask if you wanted to camp out with me for a bit. I know you've been here for a few days and frankly I thought it was a bit rude that you haven't sought me out before now, but I'd be glad of the company to be honest.'

Lilly heard the affront in Conti's voice. 'You're right. I should have come to see you both straight away, and if you will have me, I think it would be good for all of us.'

'All right.' Conti held up her index finger. 'But it will just be with me for the time being until Noel comes back.'

'Has he gone away?' It hadn't occurred to Lilly that Noel would not be at home. With a shock, right then and there, she knew that she loved him.

'He went to England a few days after you left for the circus.'

She groped about her for a chairback for support. 'He didn't get my letter?'

'Nor the telegram.'

She sank down on the seat and put her head in her hands, trying to make sense of this. 'Do you know when he's coming back?'

Conti got up from her stool and moved towards the piano. The lid was open. She picked up the book of Beethoven sonatas from the music rest. 'Have you been playing?'

'Yes. I'm trying to resurrect my music.'

'For you or for Noel?'

Lilly hesitated. Initially she had begun to play again to give herself something to do but as her technique returned, the music had been all for Noel. 'More the latter, I think.'

With a nod, Conti lifted her hands and placed them on the keyboard. She didn't turn as she played the opening bars of the Sonata 'Pathétique'. 'This is one of Noel's favourite pieces; I really miss him in the house, Lilly.' She stopped quite suddenly and threw over her shoulder, 'Will you play it for me?'

'Let's wait till Noel comes home. Then I'll play Beethoven for both of you.'

Conti shut the lid of the piano and Lilly waited for her to speak.

'I haven't heard from Noel in months and there's no certainty attached to him coming back at all. I wouldn't get up your hopes that you'll ever see him again.'

The days passed.

Lilly moved up to Lake View with Teddy and his *ayah* and instilled some order into her life. Every morning after breakfast, she sat at the roll top desk in Noel's study and set about her correspondence. She'd found pens, paper and ink in one of the drawers and made a list of letters she knew she must write. *Grit, Lilly.* She set the wash bucket on the desk, propped her performer's licence against it, and got down to business.

First, she wrote to Granny Wilkins in England, setting out everything that had happened in black and white. One last effort, she thought, to open up a line of communication. If she held to her guns and refused to write back, at least she could say she had tried.

She searched in her trunk for the name and address of the lighthouse keeper in Rangoon and wrote to Walter Barnes, introducing herself as the half-sister to his granddaughters they most likely didn't know they had.

Inside the striped lining in the lid, she retrieved Duffy's gold bangle and the *mangalsutar* Noel had given her. *The thread will tie you to us and bring you back to Nainital*. The bangle had been Duffy's apology for overstepping the mark. It seemed ridiculous now after all they had shared but she put it on her wrist and the necklace around her neck. Gifts from two very different men and she would never part with either.

Another day, Lilly wrote to Dodo and Nattie.

And then she wrote to Margot, who very quickly replied. She would come back to Nainital, next year she said, when the hot weather returned and would bring Belle to enjoy her time off.

Lilly fiercely missed her loyal, intelligent elephant. She recalled that final day with Belle as if it were yesterday. Gorging on Reggie's large doughy rotis for her breakfast, her eyes squeezed shut with happiness, then after, taking her bath. Running towards the river, gurgling in her throat because she was happy, she wallowed and played in the river while Lilly scrubbed her head and whispered encouragement into her ear. And later in the tent, after the coronation show, Belle had sensed danger and unwaveringly saved her life.

Akin to missing Teddy all over again, Belle's loss was as painful to bear. 'Go safely little one,' she breathed to herself. 'I'll be waiting when you come to Naini next year.'

On the matter of Lilly's mixed blood, Margot was phlegmatic; why make an issue of something she couldn't change? Lilly knew she was right. In fifty or a hundred years, the whole world would become the colour of coffee and she mustn't alienate Teddy from his roots. It was important he knew where he came from and she wouldn't cut him off from his family.

And Lilly did write to her mother. As with the letter she had written to Noel, the words did not come easily. She rejected draft after draft until she composed a version she felt able to send. She copied it out neatly and tracked down the Commodore through the Yacht Club; he had gone to Simla, they said, and was staying at the Cecil Hotel. It seemed likely that Binnie would be with him, so she sent her letter there. If it came back unanswered, she would cross that bridge later.

And the tiger trainer? She turned the slim band of gold on her wrist and smiled. For a brief spell, their passion had been intense but Margot had told her why it would never endure. And if she was honest, she'd known in her heart that her future would not be with him. As she stared at Margot's handwriting, it dawned on her then, like Dodo and Nattie, they were two siblings sharing a secret. They had each other and did not need anyone else.

Lilly knew she would get through the days, weeks and months ahead, but it would be a long time before she was at peace with what she had done.

At Lake View, Conti mourned the lack of company as, like migratory birds, the summer visitors packed up and returned to their lives on the plains. She still attended the Club and Lilly sometimes went with her, but it felt strangely empty and dull without the latest fashions and bonnets. They played cards, drank cocktails but they never talked of the circus.

Several times a week, Lilly visited the Miss Pinkneys and accompanied them on strolls along Mall Road or took them to tea at The Grand. For those outings, she left Teddy at home with Noel's dog. They had become such friends she didn't know which of the two was more devoted to the other.

Teddy hardly mentioned his father and her own relationship with her son remained distant. She supposed that this was how they had brought him up; arm's length parenting, she called it. Very British, very India; the way it was done.

Autumn wore away and by the time the first snow arrived in October, Lilly had begun to accept that India was where she'd call home. Confined more to the house, she spent long stretches of time in front of the fire with a book. Once a day she ventured outdoors but a few minutes were enough. The cold, dry air burned her lungs and the sun sparkling on the snow-white landscape was too bright and dazzled her eyes.

As the snows deepened and winter proper set in, over the door frames, Conti hung rugs from curtain poles which didn't quite reach the floor.

'Homemade draft excluders,' she announced proudly. 'Noel's invention.'

Lilly stuck out her hand to see if they worked. 'But they don't touch the ground and the wind whistles underneath.'

'The dog has to be able to get in and out. Goose doesn't understand confinement. He slithers underneath like a limbo dancer when he needs to escape. Noel thinks it's a hoot.'

'They're next to useless.'

Conti shook with laughter. 'I know. I think that's entirely the point.'

Within a fortnight of writing to her mother, Binnie appeared at Lake View just after teatime, blowing like a horse. She unpinned her hat, a deep vertical line between her lovely black brows.

'Well?' she wheezed. 'What on earth did you mean by saying I am in danger of condemning myself to a lonely old age and what was so urgent it couldn't wait till after Christmas? I shall be very angry indeed if I miss out on Lahore week.'

Lilly looked up to find her mother standing in the open doorway and held up a finger. 'That will rather be up to you. First, good afternoon. Now sit down, get your breath back and drink some tea. There's still some in the pot but the water's hot if it's too strong. You can doctor it with that and tell me when you came up to town.'

Binnie chose a seat by the fire and flung out her arm in a sweeping gesture. 'Yesterday. I'm staying with the old girls down the road, but you seem pretty well set up here. Snug as a bug. Perhaps I'll come and join you while I'm in the hills. It'll save me a few pennies if I camp out with you.'

Lilly's heart was beating in her throat. It was now or never for what had to be said. 'I know you gave me away to Royce.' The words fell crisp and clear like pebbles in a well.

For a second, shock held her silent. 'I would never do such a thing.'

'The day Royce died he said that he had given you

money to spy on me and that I have mixed blood.'

Binnie looked at her, for once, mute; then she smiled but it was as forced as her words were guarded. 'How could that be possible? Your father was English and I, too, am white.'

'Pearl Pinkney told me about your chats in the Lady Dufferin Hospital.'

Binnie rose and lit a cigarette, all vestige of colour gone from her face. 'So, I am as a dog would say to a rat, in a jolly tight corner.'

The unsteadiness of her mother's face cut her to the heart. 'Why couldn't you just have kept me?' She spoke so low, Lilly wondered if she had heard.

Binnie straightened her spine. 'India has such strong prejudices. I was so frightened for your future when William died, I sent you to his people, thinking that was for the best. I cried for weeks when I'd given you to the doctor's wife on the P&O.'

'Did my father know you had mixed blood?'

'Of course, and he didn't care. We were so in love, you see – that's all that mattered in the world to us and we wanted you so much. And when he died, I was utterly heartbroken and had no idea what to do.'

Lilly shuddered as the question formed on her lips. Had what Royce told her been the truth? She summoned her courage and asked, 'What did happen to my father?'

Binnie blinked at the ceiling as if reliving the scene. 'He was thrown from his horse and hit his head. He died straightaway and wouldn't have known anything about it.'

With a bitterness towards her husband she could hardly bear, Lilly framed her next question. 'Could you not have gone to your family?'

She shook her head. 'I'd been on my own since I was

fifteen and I never knew my father. You have always been my number one priority – like Teddy is to you – even though I know you don't think that.'

'India's a cruel country for separations.'

It seemed Binnie's self-control was shattered. She sank into a chair and hid her face, trying to conceal the tears that streamed down it.

Lilly sat by her side, her heart shredded with sorrow. She gently touched her mother's arm. 'My father didn't tell his people, did he? About you I mean, and that's why Granny sent me back.'

Binnie uncovered her face. 'He was frightened of what they would think. They had such deeply entrenched views, he thought keeping quiet was the better option. We both got so much wrong.'

Lilly drew her mother towards her and held her close. 'No one knows better than I what a mother will do for her child. I killed a man and you sent me away. Whether it was the right thing to do or not, we will both bear the guilt of that until the day we die. Thank you for telling me, Mama. It means a great deal.'

Binnie turned her head. Tears threatened again and her voice shook. 'Do you know how long I have waited to hear you say that word?'

'I do, Mama,' Lilly said with a smile. 'Almost twenty-four years.'

Chapter 38

Day after day, as October drew to a close, Lilly traipsed around the house, in and out of rooms, but mostly lived in Noel's study. She felt close to him in his room; a blend of russet and green, it was restful and lived in. She knew it intimately from the wide comfortable sofa and two threadbare chairs either side of the fireplace, to the books on his shelves and the dark landscape on the wall. She was even acquainted with the peel of plaster that started in the corner by the wooden rafter, where water had leaked in from the roof and turned it from yellow to brown.

Every day, when they sat over their tea, she asked Conti if there was news from Noel, in the hope that he might soon return. But Conti shook her head; she always shook her head, and said she'd not heard a thing.

Late one afternoon, a Saturday in early November, Lilly let herself into the drawing room and prodded the sleeping fire into life. This was the time of day she devoted to her practice, when the shadows lengthened, the light in the room was soft and the house was almost silent.

Turning up the lamp, she sat down at the piano and let her fingers rest on the keys. Conti had been playing earlier, so Lilly adjusted the piano stool, raising it up until her hands were comfortable over the keyboard. She straightened her back and sat perfectly still; she'd been taught to play without unnecessary movement. Her grandmother had given short shrift to performers who felt the need to sway backwards and forwards, contorting their face as they pressed down the keys as if writhing in pain.

Lilly missed Goose's presence in his usual spot on the rug, covering the bald patch by the hearth where his master might have stood. Muzzle up and ready, he loved Beethoven's sonatas; they always made him sing. But the dog was elsewhere in the house playing with Teddy and for that she could only be glad.

In the middle of the adagio, she felt the stir of air at her back and thought Conti had abandoned the novel she was reading and wandered into the room. She concentrated on her playing and at the end of the third movement – the Rondo she now found so easy with her fingers supple and strong from the circus – let her hands fall into her lap.

A voice, rich and familiar, brought her back to the room.

'Thank you,' he said. 'Your Pathétique was just gorgeous.'

Without a word, she swivelled on the piano stool to face him, her throat constricted with emotion. For a long moment they stared at each other until Lilly rose and held out her hands. In two long strides Noel reached her and grasped them between his own. There was so much to say to him and yet a sudden shyness rendered her unable to speak. She tried to withdraw her hands, but he held firm and tightened his grip. 'No,' he spoke under his breath. 'Unless I've come back for nothing.'

He stared at her with such intensity that she felt he was drawing her soul into his own.

'I killed Royce,' she blurted, not bothering to pick over her words.

'I know, Lilly.' He put his fingers against her lips and spoke so softly that she had to strain to hear him. 'You shot a man and he died in a tent at the circus. I gave you the gun to do it.' He dropped his fingers from her face and held her eyes with his.

'Did you know that I would kill him?'

'I saw you shoot a tiger to save a man's life and that gave you courage. I knew you could shoot a monster to save your own if there was no other way out.' There was no trace of censure in his voice. 'I'm sorry I've not been here to soothe your hurt.'

Lilly felt very calm. She put her hand on his chest and felt the beat of his heart through the thick cotton of his shirt. 'Since I've been in the house with Conti, I've learned to accept that it was my choice to shoot him. I feel dreadful for robbing my son of his father, but I can't regret what I did.'

He put his hand out and pulled her towards him.

Her heart pounded as she pressed her cheek against his chest, conscious of how warm his body felt, how his clothes smelled of soap and how badly she had misjudged her feelings.

She fixed her eyes on the rug. 'When I was at the circus, Margot did a reading for me and she told me . . .' She broke off and felt herself flounder.

'What did she tell you?' Noel put his hands on her shoulders and when she didn't look up, gently lifted her chin with one hand. 'What did she tell you?' he asked again.

'She said I had to come back because . . .' She breathed in deep and looked into his eyes. 'This was where I'd find happiness. Here in Nainital, with you.'

He stood for a moment, then slipped his arms around her and squeezed her close. 'She read mine too, when she was here.'

She relaxed and sighed, knowing this felt right. 'What did Madame Margot say?'

'If you only look at what's under your nose, it's extraordinary what treasure you'll find.'

Acknowledgements

An author is nothing without the team behind them and there were many people involved in bringing this book to life whose assistance was substantial.

Firstly, I am grateful beyond words to my friend Lynne Duncan for a chance insight into her family history over a glass of wine. In the 1930s, her grandmother – Marjorie Seale – ran away to Harmston's Circus in India and this provided the spark of inspiration for the book.

On researching this strand, I was fortunate to come across a direct descendant of this circus, Tony Harmston. I am indebted to him for freely providing much of the circus detail, in particular the intricacies of the high wire acts.

Thanks are also due to Joanna and Iris Hastings for their generous and sensitive assistance with my character Margot.

I continue to work with my editors Salome Jones and Tim Dedopulos and send them heartfelt, unending thanks for doing what they do so well.

To my marvellous agent, Hattie Grünewald and all the wonderful staff at The Blair Partnership, my deepest thanks and also to Rhea Kurian, my publisher at Orion Dash whose insightful and intelligent input greatly enhanced the text and the book is all the better for it.

Finally, to family and friends, I thank you all for your patience and support as this book grew wings and took off.

Printed in Great Britain
by Amazon